No Rest for the
Witches

No Rest for the
Witches

MARYJANICE DAVIDSON

LORI HANDELAND

CHEYENNE McCRAY

CHRISTINE WARREN

St. Martin's Paperbacks

This is a work of fiction. All of the characters, organizations, and events portrayed in this novel are either products of the author's imagination or are used fictitiously.

NO REST FOR THE WITCHES

"The Majicka" copyright © 2007 by MaryJanice Davidson.
"Voodoo Moon" copyright © 2007 by Lori Handeland.
"Breath of Magic" copyright © 2007 by Cheyenne McCray.
"Any Witch Way She Can" copyright © 2007 by Christine Warren.

Excerpt from *Swimming Without a Net* copyright © 2007 by MaryJanice Davidson.
Excerpt from *Thunder Moon* copyright © 2007 by Lori Handeland.
Excerpt from *Wicked Magic* copyright © 2007 by Cheyenne McCray.
Excerpt from *Howl at the Moon* copyright © 2007 by Christine Warren.

ISBN: 0-312-94921-9
EAN: 978-0-312-94921-1

Printed in the United States of America

St. Martin's Paperbacks edition / October 2007

St. Martin's Paperbacks are published by St. Martin's Press, 175 Fifth Avenue, New York, NY 10010.

10 9 8 7 6 5 4 3 2 1

Contents

The Majicka

by

MARYJANICE DAVIDSON

For my agent, Ethan Ellenberg, for always getting me fabbo deals, and for Monique Patterson, for offering same fabbo deals. And to me, for just generally being fabbo!

Yeah! Ha! Weren't expecting that, were ya? It takes a special kind of author to dedicate a story . . . to herself! Bet you didn't see that coming. In your wildest dreams you couldn't have guessed the deep dark hole my ego has carved out of my soul.

Anyway, thanks, Ethan and Monique.

Acknowledgments

Thanks to my family, especially my husband and my brilliant, gorgeous, self-entertaining children. Thanks also to my father-in-law, who had the bad taste to get cancer (these Along men!), but the good taste to get better. Dad A., these tiresome ploys for attention have just got to stop. You're not fooling anybody.

Alcohol is like love. The first kiss is magic, the second kiss is intimate, the third is routine. After that, you take the girl's clothes off. —RAYMOND CHANDLER, *THE LONG GOODBYE*

Zombie: a person believed to have been raised from the grave by a sorcerer for purposes of enslavement. The zombie is used by its master to perform heavy manual labor and to implement evil schemes. —THE COLUMBIA ENCYCLOPEDIA, SIXTH EDITION

To George F. Babbitt, as to most prosperous citizens of Zenith, his motor car was poetry and tragedy, love and heroism.
—SINCLAIR LEWIS, *BABBITT*

Take off my magician robes. —WILLIAM SHAKESPEARE

I am my father's daughter. I am not afraid of anything.
—QUEEN ELIZABETH I

Fate, it seems, is not without a sense of irony. —THE MATRIX

[Ireland] is a nation of contradictions, sir. Consider this: Ireland is an island nation that has never developed a navy; a music-loving people who have produced only those harmless lilting ditties as their musical legacy; a bellicose people who have never known the sweet savor of victory in a single war; a Catholic country that has never produced a single doctor of the Church; a magnificently beautiful country, a country to inspire artists, but a country not yet immortalized in art; a philosophic people yet to produce a single philosopher of note; a sensual people who have never mastered the art of preparing food. —PAT CONWAY, *THE LORD OF DISCIPLINE*

Prologue

Micah set the empty bottle of Jack on the corner table. If this was a story, he would have been so drunk he would have miscalculated and the bottle would have hit the hotel carpet with a shocking thud. In fact, he *was* drunk. But his marmosetlike reflexes saved him (again) and he simply caught it by the neck and righted it.

He stared up at the ceiling—all hotel ceilings looked the same—and tried not to glance at the germ-infested pile of bedspread huddled in the far corner. He'd face down a rabid werecricket before he'd lie on a hotel bedspread.

Micah was bored. It had been at least fifty years since he'd found and trained the last Majicka, and that guy had been in his prime. Terrified of his responsibility, too worried about making a mistake, but in his prime. Much too careful to do something stupid, for certain.

Likely there would be nothing to do for the next sixty or seventy years (their kind was certainly long-lived, which, unfortunately, meant so was he) except wander the world, seek out various Sheraton Suites (the only permissible choice for a neat freak, plus you couldn't beat the free

Continental breakfast), and try to pickle his liver in new and interesting ways.

Now if he could just get rid of the damned migraine.

(It's no migraine.)

It *was* a migraine.

(It *was* not.)

Here came the spots, slowly growing blobs in his right eye that he couldn't see through. Here came the nausea (most likely from the whiskey). Here came the crashing pain on the right side of his head. Definitely a migraine.

He sat up to vomit, and blood burst from his nose in a fine spray.

Okay. Not a migraine.

He flopped back onto the bed, ignoring the blood running down his cheeks like war paint.

So, time to find another one. Train him. Disappear. Wait. And wait.

Chapter 1

Cannon Falls, Minnesota
Pop: 6,660
7:28 P.M. CST
Wednesday, just before the Friends *marathon on TBS*

I reland Shea tripped over the zombie huddled next to the headstone, and flopped facedown into the mud. Sadly, this wasn't an unusual occurrence for her. It wasn't even unusual for the week.

She scrabbled to her knees and rubbed the wet dirt out of her eyelashes before it gummed them shut. At least she'd missed the thorny raspberry bushes, which ran wild along the south edge of the cemetery.

"Hi," she said, then spat out a glob of mud. "What are you doing here?"

The barefoot zombie—probably female from the tattered gray dress, and shredded black pantyhose (probably black . . . sunset was about five minutes away and they were on the downslope of the cemetery's south hill)—said nothing, just clutched more tightly to the headstone.

"Right," Ireland said, as if she (it?) had replied. "But you can't stay here. It's the full moon."

Nothing.

Ireland leaned forward, mindful of the zombie's doubtless

need for brains, and poked her (it?) in the shoulder. No response. It was like poking a beanbag.

"Seriously," she said. "You can't stay here. You really can't."

Zip.

"I assume you don't want to be a squeaky toy for a pack of werewolves?"

Nada.

"Seriously, miss—um, miss. Is there something I can help you with?"

The zombie curled further into herself and stared at the ground.

"Look, I don't know if you're guarding or lost or whatever, but you really can't stay here. Cannon Falls is a deceptively benign-seeming small town crawling with denizens of the undead. It even says so in the brochure—the head of the Chamber of Commerce is a warlock. So you better come home with me."

"Oh no you're *not*," a deep voice said from behind her.

Ireland smothered a sigh, and when she turned to face the newcomer it was with her prettiest smile.

"You have mud on your teeth," Ezra Chase informed her. Even if she had not known the moment they met that he was a vampire, he was right out of Central Casting. Tall—over six feet. Whip thin. Cadaverous complexion. Brown hair that looked black against his white skin. Eyes like onyx that glittered in the dim light. She had lived with him for five years and his creepy charisma still hit her like a fist. "And on your knees."

"Why, Ezra! What brings you—"

"Do not," he said, "embarrass yourself further."

"Sunset already?" she asked weakly. "I thought it was a few minutes away."

"With *this* overcast? And how many times must I tell you to toss your *Farmers' Almanac*? It's not the, ah, the be-all-end-all of nature's happenings."

She smirked at his inability to say "bible." "Look at this poor thing here. Leave her in the mud? And it's supposed to rain later. Give me a hand with her, will you?"

Ezra folded his extremely long, skinny, white arms across his chest and sniffed, a good trick as he did not have to breathe. "I certainly will not. There is no reason we need to take *that* into our home."

"My home," Ireland reminded him, hanging on to her smile. She'd known her roommates would be difficult, but had no idea it would begin so soon. She'd just spotted the poor girl! Zombie! "If you help me now, we can get her home before the others even notice."

"Judith will notice the instant this thing touches the car."

"I'll deal with Judith. Come on, be a pal."

Ezra blinked down at her. She was pretty sure he blinked. Man, it had gotten dark in a hurry! She could already hear scattered wolf howls beyond and to the north.

"Is your life not complicated enough?" her vampire pal wondered aloud, staring at the full moon with his hands on his bony hips. Normally Ireland would have answered, except she knew darn well he wasn't speaking to her. This was his way of talking to himself to arrive at a decision. "With all the complications in your life, you seek out yet another one? The others will not be pleased."

"We have lots of room at the farm."

"Do not interrupt, infant."

"M'mm not an infant," she mumbled. "M'mm twenty-six."

"Talk to me when you've hit your first century. No, I will not help you. I'm afraid you'll have to leave it here, and just as well. Think of the ruin to Judith's upholstery!"

"If we don't tell her, she won't—"

"This 'stray-animal adoption' quirk of yours was amusing at one time. Now it's merely tiresome."

"You didn't mind when I invited *you* to stay," Ireland pointed out.

"I remember things entirely differently," Ezra twanged in his annoying Medford drawl. "I seem to remember saving your ignorant ass on more than one—"

"Fine! I'll get her home myself."

"Ho, ho," he replied, the closest to laughing he ever came.

Muttering about the general uselessness of the undead in general and Ezra in particular, she knelt, grabbed (gently) the zombie's arm, flung it over her shoulders, shifted the zombie's weight, then slowly lifted.

Ah! The fireman's carry worked nicely in this instance, and it wasn't as bad as she'd feared. The zombie didn't smell like rotten meat or feel like squirming maggots. More like dust and mud and old dirt. Ireland had smelled plenty worse. Just last week, she'd forgotten to clean out the fridge and that had been—

"If you think I'm holding the door for you, you are out of your petite mind."

"Nnnnff," she replied, staggering toward the red Escape which was parked between Todd Petit, Faithful Friend, Husband, Father; and Janie Opitz, God Grant She Never Return.

A silvery howl split the air and she nearly flipped the poor zombie ass over teakettle back down the gentle slope. Ezra had no doubt scented, or heard, him coming but, being a typical stick in the ass, had not warned her.

"Is it the whole pack?" she gasped, scrambling up the slope to the car. "Or just him?"

"Just him," Ezra replied, brushing pieces of bark off the knees of his brown silk slacks. "You know they keep running him off. Poor sot cannot take a hint to save his silvery hide."

Speak of the devil (or the local rogue), Owen sprang over yet another tangle of raspberry bushes and plopped into the middle of their group.

He was the size of a golden retriever, with the coloring of an albino, blue eyes she could see gleaming even in the near-dark, wide white tail lashing a greeting, teeth flashing in the moonlight in what Ireland knew was a greeting.

"There's nothing really going on," she said, shifting her weight so as not to drop the (thankfully quiet and complacent) zombie.

"Oh, like *hell*," Ezra snapped in his fading (but not fast enough) Massachusetts accent. Ireland figured he'd need to live in the Midwest at least another forty years before he was rid of it completely. "Our beloved landlord has found a new project."

Owen barked.

"Thanks for the backup," Ezra said dryly.

"It'll be fine," she said, hobbling toward the car. "Owen, you better get lost in case an unfriendly pack member finds you. You—"

Ezra opened the rear passenger door, looking resigned, and Owen leaped in at once.

"Aw, Owen," she complained, then went around to the other side, waited for Ezra to open that door (he took his time, the bum; her knees were trembling by the time he swung the door all the way open), then plopped the living (unliving?) doll next to Owen. She started to fumble for the zombie's seat belt, then stopped. What was the point? The poor girl's head could come off and she'd still be walking around.

"The others," Ezra predicted, "will not be pleased."

"The others," she replied, "will get over it or hit the road."

"Fascist."

"Prig."

Ireland searched for her keys while Ezra hauled his bony limbs into the front passenger seat, refusing (as he always did) to share a seat with anything that had fleas or the potential to rot off body parts. Prig.

Just when she was resigned to hot-wiring the car (how hard could it be?) she felt the lump of her keys. Ah! They had slipped way down into her front pocket. She fished them out, climbed into the Escape, and started the engine. Too late, she remembered she hadn't shut off the radio when she'd parked, because the first thing she heard was an angry squeal of static that sounded like a woman's shriek of anger.

Followed by, "What the *hell* are all these *things* doing in my car? Ireland? You jerk, you've got some explaining to do! So talk! Right now!"

Ezra, in his one moment of kindness (must be a Wednesday), reached out with long white fingers and shut the radio off. She flashed him a look of gratitude, put the car in gear, and made for the Shea Family Farm.

Chapter 2

Shea Farm loomed around the corner and, as always, she grinned like an ape when she saw it. Old Man Willow stood guard in the field across the dirt road, and when she pulled past him (never it) and into the drive, the bright red barn rose up on her left, with the squat house on the right. Her earliest memory was of falling down in the dirt beside the gigantic willow tree, and gripping the bark to pull herself back up.

Unlike most traditional farmhouses, Shea Farm was a sprawling ranch, complete with hot tub, mother-in-law apartment (though she knew never to call it that in Ezra's presence), dog track in the back yard, ski lift in the beyond back yard, five bedrooms, three baths (not counting the extra bedrooms and bathrooms in Ezra's section), two parlors, and a full-sized dressing room between one of the baths and one of the bedrooms.

Despite the fine accessories, the house had a lived-in, haphazard look, as every generation someone would add on a wing or two.

Farming had treated her parents and grandparents, God rest them, very very well. Too bad about that awful threshing incident . . . if only her mother hadn't skipped her meds, and then lured her father . . . but it was pointless to think about that now. The important thing was, they had left her well taken care of, which was a relief as her roommates were more or less a full-time job.

"Where are you going to put it?" Ezra asked.

"Where else? One of the spare rooms."

"It's going to sleep in our house?" Ezra, to his credit, did not quite gag.

"I don't think *she* needs to sleep, but she should at least have her own room."

"Just let her run around with Owen on the dog track—yee—ouch!" Ezra whipped around in his seat and fixed the werewolf with a forbidding glare. "Don't bite my ear; you don't know where it's been."

"Can we argue about this once we get inside? It's been a long day, annoying roommates withstanding, I need a bath, you've got that creepy 'I haven't bitten anybody yet' whine in your voice, and I— Help!"

"I have told you and told you, first clutch, *then* brake!" Ezra shouted over her yowl.

"It's Judith!" Ireland wrestled the wheel for control, but it was like holding on to a live thing. Using all her strength, she barely managed to avoid the tractor. She stood on the brakes with both feet, only to feel the wheel wrenched to the left and the small SUV headed straight for the (closed) barn doors.

Ezra quickly turned on the radio. "All right, Judith. Your wrath has been duly noted."

The Escape shuddered to a stop about—as Ireland could best guess—three inches short of the barn door.

"What is the matter with you?" Judith blared instead of the dulcet soft rock tones of 102.9 Lite FM ("Your Station at Work!"). "Bad enough that furbound fuckface is shedding all over my back seat, bad enough you're getting mud all over the clutch and brake, but now there's a *corpse* in the car?"

"Two corpses, if you count Ezra."

He snorted. "That was not remotely amusing, foul infant."

"*What are you trying to do to me?* Like I don't have enough trouble trying to break the curse and—"

"Walk and talk like a *real* boy?" Ezra finished, clasping his long white hands over his bosom and fluttering his eyelashes.

There was the sound of grinding gears and the entire car shuddered. "And *you!* I saw you. I know you were the one who shut the radio off. I'm stuck in this stupid SUV until someone breaks the spell—"

"At least it's a hybrid," Ireland piped up helpfully. "You can save the environment while you're ensorcelled."

"—and the only chance I can talk is through the radio, which one of you is always shutting off—"

Possibly, Ireland thought, *because you're such a jerk on wheels all the time. Literally! A jerk on wheels!*

"—and now that—that *thing* is rotting all over my leather interior!"

"Not for long," she said. "I was just bringing her up to the house."

"Oh, *ugh.* Don't even tell me what Lent is going to say about that."

Ireland, in the act of tugging on the door handle (God only knew when Judith would let them go), swallowed a whimper. She'd forgotten all about her other roommate, the Violent Fairy.

While she was pondering those difficulties, the door swung open of its own volition and she was, for the second time in half an hour, facedown in the mud.

"Don't forget," Ezra called from his seat, "goodness is its own reward."

Chapter 3

I reland heard the roar of the Escape as Judith took off down the driveway. Great. Now, when she needed a car, Judith would probably be sulking ten counties over. Well, she'd be back. Eventually.

As if reading her mind, Ezra asked, "Why not buy another car? Your trust fund is healthy enough."

"You know why."

"That's true," Ezra replied, sounding morbidly cheerful. "I do."

"Then—other than to torture me—why ask?"

"Only to torture you," he admitted.

The fact was, while Judith was temperamental, vocal, determined, shrill, and had a martyr complex, she also prided herself on being Ireland's main mode of transportation. In fact, she'd saved Ireland's life more than once. The time Ireland had rented a Honda during Judith's fifty-thousand-mile tune-up, Judith hadn't moved—or spoken—in a month.

The two of them (three, counting the zombie Ezra had gingerly thrown over one shoulder . . . the poor woman's long, muddy hair was dragging on the tiles) made for the hot tub. The Violent Fairy's room was right next door and, this time of night, he could be found in one place or the other.

Not bothering to knock (two years of trying to teach the fairy manners—or natural modesty—had been a dismal failure), they opened the door and walked in.

"Hi!" Ireland shouted over the hot tub's grinding motor. As usual, Lent had it cranked so much, the windows were utterly fogged over. She instantly felt all the pores of her body open. Beside her, Ezra coughed and tried to wave away the steam. "What's up?"

"Avoiding human small talk is up." The Violent Fairy was lolling on the far side of the huge tub. He was so long, his toes touched the far edge. "What's that you got there?"

"Ireland's new project," Ezra snarked.

"Owen?" Lent yawned.

"Took off for the hills once Judith let us out."

"Supper?"

"You already had three suppers. Do you know anything about zombies?"

Lent yawned again. "Yeah."

"Well—"

"First things first, Ireland, *dear*. Let's get this thing cleaned up. She's ruined this suit jacket already."

"A little compassion, Ezra!"

"I'm holding it, aren't I? It's leaking nasty bodily fluids all over my second favorite jacket, isn't it?"

"Jesus wept," Lent grumped, which was curious as he wasn't a Christian, and stood. Gallons of water cascaded off his six-foot-seven, two-hundred-sixty-pound (fat-free) frame. Ireland tried frantically to look everywhere but at the large naked fairy climbing out of the hot tub and marching toward her.

With no further comment, the Violent Fairy pulled the zombie off Ezra's shoulder, carried her like a doll to the tub, then slung her in.

"Uh—you're not boiling her, are you?"

"Temp's just under forty Centigrade. Humans can handle higher. Especially dead ones." He stirred her around as if she were a zombie stew, and Ireland tried not to stare at the crack of his ass. Or the rest of him, for that matter. She wasn't especially attracted to him, preferring men who weren't as tall as small telephone poles, but it was hard *not* to look at a six-foot-seven-inch nude fairy. His wings looked like crumpled tissue in the humid room.

After a long moment, he fished the zombie out, looked her over critically, then dunked her again.

"And to think," Ezra sighed, "I didn't think we'd do anything fun tonight."

Out she came. Was examined by the fairy. Back in she went. "Where'd you find her?" he asked over one mammoth shoulder.

"The cemetery on the edge of town."

"She try to bite you?"

"No, she was just huddled there, all pathetic and grimy."

"And our Ireland naturally could not resist," Ezra added, also unable to resist.

She ignored him. "Remember, I was trying to do some of those gravestone rub—"

"Don't care. Zombie's done."

"That's odd," Ezra said. "I didn't *hear* the oven timer."

Lent, long used to ignoring his roommate's nasty comments, fished the zombie out and sat her on the bench nearest the door. When she sagged, he propped her upright, then matter-of-factly climbed back into the whirlpool. "Did you bring anything to eat? Besides her?"

"Very funny, tough guy, we all know you're a vegetarian. You said you knew something about zombies?"

"Yeah." The Violent Fairy yawned, then shook hot water out of his short-cropped, wheat-colored hair. His eyes, Elizabeth Taylor purple, were slitted with boredom.

Ireland waited. Ezra stared at the ceiling. The zombie

slumped four inches to her left. Finally, Ireland almost shouted, "Well?"

"Oh, she's supposed to be somebody's slave. Find out who rose her from the dead—"

"Raised," Ezra corrected.

Lent ignored him, as English was his ninth language and the occasional grammatical error didn't bother him. Nothing bothered him. "—stick a two-by-four into their heart or crotch or decapitate them or suffocate them or chop them into pieces or shoot them in the face, and poof. Bye-bye, dead girl."

"Oh," Ezra said.

"Yeeesh," was Ireland's comment. "My to-do list is already pretty full. And you made me throw away all the guns."

"It was a condition on his moving in," Ezra reminded her. "Fairies and iron never ever mix."

"So what are we going to do now?" Ireland asked.

"*We* should have left her in the cemetery," Ezra said, triumphantly flicking graveyard mud off his lapels.

"But how do we find out who she was? Or who the bad guy is? And when we find him—or her—do we just, you know, axe them? Can we reason with them first? Why am I the only one brainstorming?"

Lent, who had already submerged, didn't come up for nearly five minutes. They had no choice but to wait patiently; he could hold his breath longer than a seal. When he finally came up, it was to mumble, "Check the grave she was guarding."

"Guarding?"

"Protecting, shielding, defending."

"I know what it means," Ireland muttered.

"Probably hers."

"What?"

"The grave, dumbass human."

"I've asked you and asked you not to call me that," she whined. "Besides, nobody's died in town this weekend.

There's less than seven thousand of us; deaths make the news."

Lent snorted, then nearly choked on the bubbles. "In *this* town?"

"Point," Ireland muttered, and went to get some towels for the zombie.

Chapter 4

The next morning, Ireland entered the kitchen in time to see the zombie tip over until her head was resting on the table, Owen wolfing down the heel of a loaf of bread, Lent spearing an entire head of lettuce and forcing it into his mouth (it went, easily), and Ezra reading aloud from *Entertainment Weekly*.

"Halle Berry's getting divorced *again*," he greeted her. "Poor girl must have the self-esteem of a grubworm."

Ireland had no sympathy for a gorgeous, rich, talented woman with an Oscar on her mantel, having enough troubles of her own. "Anybody have any ideas in the night? Owen, that better not be the last of the bread."

"Of course it is," he said cheerfully. In a house of dour or taciturn roommates, the rogue werewolf was a breath of fresh air. She didn't understand why his pack wouldn't have him, and felt guilty for being glad they wouldn't.

It couldn't be something so dumb as his coloring. In wolf form he was gorgeous—snowy-white fur and gleaming sapphire-colored eyes.

In human form, he was a little on the small side for an American male—about five foot nine—but powerfully

muscled and charming besides. It was the rare moment
when he wasn't smiling or laughing. Even casually dressed
in cutoffs and a STOP ME WHEN I'M AS BORING AS YOU
T-shirt, he was devastatingly good-looking.

Owen was nearly as pale as Ezra, with shoulder-length,
white-blond hair and of course those amazing eyes. He
was almost as strong as Ezra, too, and a bit quicker. She'd
be proud to have him in her family—*was* proud—and
didn't understand why his pack had driven him away. Even
three years later, he had never given up the details. And she
valued his friendship—and privacy—too much to ask.
That had not stopped Ezra (Lent literally could not have
cared less), but the vampire hadn't gotten any more out of
Owen than she had.

"But there's lots of bacon and sourdough rolls," he continued. "And Cap'n Crunch."

"How can you *eat* that?" Ezra bitched good-naturedly,
turning the page. "Doesn't it shred the roof of your mouth?"

"The bacon or the cereal?" Owen teased.

"How'd she get out here?" Ireland asked, nodding at the
zombie.

Lent belched, rattling the coffee cups, and answered.
"Pulled her out of the spare bedroom and brought her here.
It's morning. Everybody gets up and has breakfast in the
morning."

"Your human studies are coming along well," Ezra approved.

"Yeah, that's great, Lent. Thanks. But, um, maybe next
time you could dress her first?"

"Human traditions," Lent said, forking another head of
lettuce, "are stupid. Figured that out right away."

"She looks about my size," Ireland guessed, staring at
the zombie's mottled gray back and mop of black hair.

"I think not," Ezra said. "She's three inches shorter and
twenty-two pounds lighter."

"Save your eerie vampire powers for when I've had some coffee. And she can wear my sweatpants and stuff."

"Lovely thought. As if I hadn't already despaired of you finding an appropriate style."

"You lay off my style," she ordered. "Can I help it if I like to be comfortable?"

"Really, Ireland. You're much too pretty to slop around in leggings and sweatshirts *ad nauseam*."

"What's *that* have to do with anything?"

"Don't bother," Lent said, masticating furiously. Tiny green shreds flew everywhere. "She's stupid that way."

"I've asked you repeatedly not to call me stupid."

"And I," he replied, "have asked for a bigger hot tub. But we're both screwed."

"You people are costing me a fortune!" she shouted, slamming her seat into the chair and nearly going sprawling. Ezra had waxed the floor—again. "Your hot tub is plenty big enough. Ezra, pour me a cup, will you? And somebody get that poor woman a robe."

Nobody moved. Ezra broke the silence with, "Can you believe they're casting for *another* Spider-Man movie? How much money does Columbia need? My God, Tobey Maguire is going *gray*. He's the oldest college student on the planet. This is worse than fifth-season *90210*!"

"You guys," Ireland whined, "we have a serious problem here. How are we going to help this poor girl?"

Lent shrugged. Ezra didn't comment. Owen slurped down the rest of the bacon. "What poor girl?"

"The naked dead girl with her head in the sugar bowl!"

"Oh." Owen licked grease off his upper lip. "Right. Isn't she going to move in and, you know, be one of your merry men?"

"I realize that's the way things usually go," Ireland admitted, "given the present company, but I don't think letting her shack up indefinitely is helping her."

"It certainly hasn't helped *me*," Ezra commented.

"Like Lent said, somebody did this to her. She doesn't want to be a zombie—who would? So it's up to us—"

"You," Ezra said.

"—to help her."

"How?" Owen asked.

"Well. We could go back to the cemetery. Check out the grave she was guarding. It's a start."

"Or," Ezra said cheerfully, "we could go to bed. Not all of us can run around like bugs at a picnic during daylight hours."

"Who," Lent demanded, ruffling his wings, "are you calling a bug?"

Ireland drummed her fingers on the tabletop, thinking. It was true, due to Ezra's great age (he never said, but based on casual conversation she put him between a hundred and a hundred and twenty), he could walk around during the day, provided the shades were drawn. And naturally, every room in the house had thick shades. She had installed them twelve hours after he turned up.

"I think—" she began, and that was when Judith began blaring her horn from the driveway in Morse code.

"A-U-N-uh-M?" Ireland guessed. Her Morse sucked.

"Aunt Key!" Ezra nearly screamed, and Lent dropped his third lettuce head, knocking over the creamer.

"Quick!" Ireland shouted. "Hide the zombie!"

Chapter 5

I reland ran down the foyer, lost her footing, and slid the rest of the way, fetching up against the front door with a teeth-rattling thud. Ezra had waxed the entryway . . . again.

She fumbled for the doorknob, cursing her fastidious roommate, and swung the heavy mahogany door wide. As Judith had warned, her maternal Aunt Jessiciah ("Key" was the best the three-year-old Ireland could do with a mouthful like "Jessiciah") was standing on the front step.

"Ireland!" the small woman shrilled. She was dressed in buttercup-yellow slacks and an eye-wateringly bright green blouse. With ruffles. All of which clashed with her dark red Lucille Ball wig. Everyone on her mother's side had red hair; only Aunt Key felt the need to pretend she was still a natural redhead. Not that her nutball mother had lived long enough to—"It's been too long!"

"Seventy-two hours," Ezra whispered from behind her.

"Hi, Aunt Key." Ireland extended her face for the ritual cheek-peck. "What brings you by? Again?"

"Oh . . . the usual. Places to go, you know, and people I want you to—oh!" She had spotted Ezra, with the usual reaction. It wasn't that he was the invisible man or anything; he just stood so uncannily still it took a few seconds for people to really see him. "Hello, Ezra."

Ezra inclined his head in a partial bow. "Jessiciah. What a . . . lovely blouse."

"You should have Ireland wear more cheerful colors, instead of those icky sweatshirts."

He sighed. "I try, madam. I try." Ezra courteously stepped back and did the butler-fade-thing, allowing her aunt Key to begin the harangue.

"Darling, I hate seeing you cooped up on this awful, awful farm," Aunt Key began, kicking off her green clogs. She massaged her left heel for a moment, then followed Ireland into the kitchen. "You should meet a nice boy and start a family."

"I have a family, Aunt Key."

"I don't mean just *me*," she went on, oblivious. "I promised your dear mother, God rest her crazy soul, that I'd look after you and I've failed. I've— Good God!"

"What?"

Aunt Key was staring wildly around the kitchen which, to be fair, looked as though a cyclone had whipped through. Her roomies were used to the drill, and had vacated accordingly.

"Oh, that," Ireland said. "I was . . . really hungry."

"The least those others can do to earn their keep is some light housekeeping," she sniffed. "It's bad enough they don't use their, um, special skills to help you, um, coordinate."

"Owen isn't gay, Aunt Key."

"The other one, then."

"Neither is Lent."

"I heard him refer to himself as a fairy with my own ears!"

She coughed. It had taken her a while to break the Violent Fairy out of his habit of referring to most people as "stupid humans" and himself as "superior fairy."

"It's just a game we play."

"A very odd game. And then there's . . . you know."

"Ezra isn't gay. He's just old-fashioned." *Very* old.

"Darling, you *never go out*. It's not natural for a beautiful young lady to surround herself with—ah—"

"The dregs of society?" she said cheerfully, handing her aunt a shred of lettuce.

Aunt Key stared at the small leaf, then let it flutter to the floor. "Honey, I really would like you to meet some people who—"

"Aunt Key."

"At least come with me tonight. My neighbor's nephew is in town and he's a wonderful boy, he used to be a dot-com millionaire—"

"And now he's a janitor?" she guessed.

"He's a Libra," Aunt Key retorted. "He—oh. Hello, dear."

Ireland looked—and nearly screamed. The zombie—clothed, thank you, Jesus—had wandered into the kitchen and was poking through the detritus on the table with a vacant look in her cloudy eyes.

"This is, um, Z-Zelda. She's—"

"Oh, don't even tell me." In a lower voice, she added, "That sweat suit does nothing for her. Makes her coloring look positively *ghastly*."

Zelda the zombie was, Ireland was swooningly grateful to notice, clean, dry, and combed out. Except for her grayish complexion and cloudy eyes, she looked almost normal. In fact, her hair was actually pretty, falling in a rippling dark wave to her waist. Fortunately Aunt Key was so self-centered that—

"So will you? Come to my place later?"

"I don't know," she hedged. "Some stuff has come up."

"What's more important than pleasing your last living blood relative?"

Ireland heard Ezra snort from the next room, and was grateful he didn't rattle off the long list. "It's just that there's a lot going on right now."

"This is what I'm saying! You need to do something nice for yourself. You never do anything nice for yourself. You've got this big farm to run, too much land to keep up, not to mention the buildings and house. Promise to come over."

"Aunt Key, I'll try. I really will," she lied. "I've just got so much, um, work."

"You work awfully hard," her aunt said suspiciously, "for someone who doesn't have a job."

"Tell me," Ireland sighed.

"Oh *here* you are!" Owen cried, bounding into the kitchen. He seized Zelda by the forearm and grinned at Aunt Key, who had her usual reaction to Owen's too many teeth.

"Ack!"

"Nice to see you, Aunt Key. Now if you'll excuse us, me and Tina—"

"Zelda," Ireland supplied.

"—have a hot date. Come on, honey pie," he crooned, leading Tina/Zelda toward the doorway. "The *Family Guy* marathon awaits."

"Really, Ireland," she said after the odd duo had departed. "You have to get out more. Spend some time with . . . you know . . ." She lowered her voice. "Normal people."

"I'll think about it," she replied. "Really."

Chapter 6

Sunset

Micah pulled into the long driveway, noting with disinterest the rustic barn and ranch-style house. There was a red Ford Escape parked a bare inch or two in front of the barn doors and, other than the far-off barking of a dog, no sign of life.

He climbed out of his rental and started up the path to the house, stifling a sigh. He'd been through this many, many times in his long life. He'd been doing it since before the Great War. The real one, not the follow-up fakes.

First, the Magicka would be in utter awe of his/her new-found position in society, of his/her responsibilities. An endless period of questions and answers would begin. Then, the teaching would begin. Decades of tutoring. Then, bye-bye, birdie, out of the nest. Then, he/she would die of extreme old age or in some eternal good/evil struggle, and Micah would be on the road again, ready to train the new one.

And so on.

And so on.

He heard gravel crunching and turned. To his mild surprise, the SUV was quite a bit closer than it first appeared.

He could have sworn it had been nearer the barn. Much nearer.

He shrugged and raised a hand to knock. Before his fist could land on the wood, the door was jerked open and he was nearly run down by a teeming horde. As it was, he had to jump into the bushes lining the walk to avoid being trampled.

"That's taken care of Aunt Key for the day," a ridiculously pretty redheaded woman with chocolate-brown eyes was saying. "God! I thought she'd never leave." She was shrugging into a light jacket, and thank goodness, because anything was an improvement over that shapeless sweatshirt.

"I could eat her, if you want," the blue-eyed werewolf said, hot on the woman's heels.

"Don't be ridiculous, Owen," a brunette vampire snapped, bringing up the rear. "Chewed bodies are always messy and invariably involve the authorities. Even here."

"So we squash the authorities," an inordinately large man rumbled—was that a *fairy*? In this day and age? He was dragging a washed-out, grayish brunette behind him, this one wearing a sweat suit identical to the other woman's. "Boom, squish, no more problems."

"Don't be silly, Lent," the first woman said. She glanced over at Micah and seemed not at all surprised to find a strange man lurking in her bushes. "Hello, we've already accepted Christ into our hearts, good-bye."

"The hell we have," the vampire almost shouted.

Micah stared at what was absolutely the oddest assortment of magical beings in three hundred years. He'd seen them all at one time or another, of course. *Separately.* Why, vampires and werewolves didn't even believe in each other, and fairies were notorious loners, even when they had been plentiful on this earth. As for the other one, what was she doing without her—

"Move your ass, Ireland," the fairy ordered. "I want to be back in time to try new bath salts."

Micah cleared his throat. "Ah, I am the Tutor, and I am here to tell you of a sacred duty, for you are the One, the newest Magicka, and it is your destiny to—"

He was talking to their backs. And the SUV was running, with all four doors open. It must have one of those automatic-start things.

"Wait!" he yelled.

"Can't," the werewolf said.

"Gotta go. Cemetery," the fairy said.

"But you can come with, if you promise not to sell us anything," the Magicka said.

Mystified, Micah trotted after them.

Chapter 7

O h now, what's this?" the radio squawked. Micah, who had beaten the vampire to the front seat by a bare half second, stared at the source of the noise. "Ireland, how many fucking people do you have to drag around?"

"It isn't *my* fault," the redhead said. "He just showed up. What'd you say your name was? Mr. Tudor?"

"No, I'm *the* Tu—"

"Don't drip anything on my upholstery," the car commanded.

"Excuse me," Micah said, trying to cover his shock. "Are you talking to me?"

"Who else, dingleberry? Mess up my interior and you'll find out your seat belt doesn't work at an important moment, get my drift? And what is *she* doing back in here?"

"We're going back to the cemetery," the redhead explained.

"To look for clues!" the werewolf piped up.

"And then get pie," the fairy finished. "Bakery's open until nine."

Micah craned his neck and saw the werewolf and vampire

sitting shoulder to shoulder, while the other woman was on the fairy's lap, staring dully at the scenery.

"You live with all these people, Magicka?"

"Actually, *they* live with *me*. And the name's Ireland."

"Ireland?"

"Don't start," she warned.

"We all know," the vampire said.

"It's a *stupid* name," the car and the werewolf chorused.

"But her mom was crazy and her dad was indifferent, so there you go," the car finished.

"Shut *up!*" the Magicka howled, knuckles whitening on the steering wheel. "Can we focus on one thing at a time?"

"A fine idea," Micah said, still completely flabbergasted by the events of the last five minutes. "I have come to tell you your duty, Magicka, to make you aware of your destiny, to—"

"—make you a turkey sandwich on rye, not too much mayo," the fairy finished.

Micah turned in his seat again, unable to resist. "I thought your kind were extinct."

"No, we just slept for a really long time." The fairy yawned, as if accentuating his point. Micah could see the male's tonsils.

"And aren't you supposed to be loners?"

"Hey, I only live with the stupid human, I don't interact with it."

"Snob," the vampire snarked. He looked miserable, squashed in the middle as he was.

"Do you often make evening journeys to the local cemetery?" Micah asked, fascinated in spite of himself.

"Oh, sure," the Magicka replied. "It's like, our weekly thing. Followed by eating cream puffs and playing bingo at the Veterans' Hall."

The gears ground just then. Or the car laughed. Micah couldn't be sure.

Chapter 8

"Well, here we are again!" Ireland said, forcing cheer. They all clambered out of Judith and stood around the car in a loose group. The stranger, Micah, had a look on his face she'd seen more than once. He looked like someone had whopped him on the forehead with a hammer made of putty. "Now what?"

Owen barked, then sniffed around the tombstone where they'd found Zelda. He had changed to wolf form in the car, to everyone's dismay and the stranger's near-panic, and now they were all covered in white fur. Judith had stalled twice in protest, but had finally brought them where they needed to go after Ireland promised to vacuum her out the next morning.

"May I?" Ezra asked politely. Without a word, Micah reached into one of the pockets of his tan trench coat and extracted a bottle. Ezra unscrewed the top, guzzled enthusiastically, capped it, then handed it back.

"How'd you know he brought booze?" she asked.

"Ireland, he practically clanks when he walks."

"Oh." The Magicka looked at him. She was, he had decided during the drive, more than pretty. Quite beautiful, actually, with the vivid hair and the piercing eyes, the freckles and the cream-colored skin, really very nice. Long, strong limbs. Ready smile. "Having that kind of week, huh?"

"That kind of century," he said truthfully. He glanced around the small cemetery, intrigued. It was hard to remember he'd been bored half an hour ago. And yesterday. And last year. And fifty years ago. And— "What are you going to do now?"

She was already kneeling in front of a tombstone and brushing mud away. "Marnie Trevor," she read aloud, "Nineteen sixty to two thousand six. Is this you, Marnie? Is this your grave?"

The zombie shook her head.

"Well, that's progress, anyway," Ezra said. "We know she understands, at least."

Ireland tried again. "What were you doing here, honey?"

"Help."

"Yeah, we're trying. Help how? Help you?"

"Help."

"I'm bored!" Judith called. They'd left her engine running and the doors open. Her headlights were the only lights in the cemetery; they needed her. " 'Help,' she says. Well, duh."

"Can you tell us who brought you back from the dead?" Ireland asked.

Nothing.

Owen, meanwhile, had been nosing through the raspberry bushes and through the small wood running along the southern border. He came back after a few minutes, obviously empty-handed (empty-pawed?), and sat beside Ireland, tail swishing in the mud.

"Well, this has been a rather large waste of time," Ezra muttered.

"What else could we do?" Ireland wondered. "This is where we found her. There should have been a clue or . . . or something."

"Why did you ask who brought her back from the dead?" Micah asked.

"It's obvious, isn't it?"

"I'm afraid not," he admitted. He was having trouble keeping all their names straight, never mind following their trains of thought.

Ireland rolled her eyes. New guy was cute, if slow. "Somebody had to bring her back from the dead, or she wouldn't be a zombie."

"A *zombie*?"

"Yeah. What the hell else could she be?"

Micah started to laugh. He couldn't help it, and didn't try. When he finally finished, his face was wet with tears. "You poor things, you don't know anything. She's not—"

Just then, Zelda cried out, held her middle, and slowly sank to her knees. This was startling, and no one knew what to do. So they did nothing as she rocked back and forth in the mud for a few seconds, whimpering quietly.

After a minute, Ireland knelt beside her, putting a steadying hand on the other woman's shoulder. "What's wrong, honey?"

"I am being killed."

"You—what?"

"I die."

This time, "What?" came from Ezra.

"It is the nature of Man to destroy. I am dying."

"Uh-huh. About that." Ireland cleared her throat. "Can you give us a little more detail?"

"Man kills. Thus, I die."

"Yeah, but we can help you if you, just, you know. Elaborate."

Zelda blinked painfully, big gray eyes luminous with tears. "The planet is yours, now. You kill as you like. I am dying."

"Can somebody change the record on this girl?" Judith bitched. "I'm still bored out of my mind."

"Shut *up*, Judith!" Ireland took a breath and forced "shrill" from her tone. "Zelda, we can't help you if you don't give us more information."

"My self is dying."

"Yeah, you—"

"I die. They are killing me even now."

"There's no one here but us, Zelda. Please talk to us. Enough with the riddles! Tell us how to help you. I know you don't want to be a zombie forever."

"I die."

"I *know*. Can't you come up with anything else?"

Zelda cried out again and huddled tighter into a smaller ball. Ireland had never seen someone in such pain outside an emergency room. "Help," she said softly. "Help."

"Wait," the Violent Fairy said. "You aren't asking us for help, right? You're telling us you came here to *find* help."

Zelda nodded. "Help."

"Who was going to help you here? There's nothing." Ireland took another glance around, just to be sure. "It's all trees and bushes and gravestones."

Zelda nodded again. The attack, or whatever it was, seemed to have worn off, and the Violent Fairy picked her up out of the mud and brushed her off as if she were a toddler. "Help."

"She's not a zombie, she's a dryad," Micah said. "Somewhere, right now, somebody is killing her tree. Once her tree is dead, so is she."

Dead silence, followed by Ezra's, "Well, hell."

Chapter 9

"Explain, New Guy," Judith ordered, headlights flickering.

"What else do you need? This is a dryad. Not a human being. Her life force is tied to her tree. If her tree is hurt or dies—is cut down, or what have you—she ceases to be. The end."

"But why would she come here?"

"For help, as she said. The oldest trees in any city can almost always be found in the local cemetery."

Ezra snapped his fingers. "Damn it all. I *knew* that one."

Micah continued: "Obviously she came looking for more of her kind. Poor creature; it was a long shot and it failed." He blinked, staring at Ireland. "Except it didn't, not really."

"I thought they were legend," Ezra said, looking Zelda up and down.

"Says the vampire," Micah retorted.

"Okay, okay," Ireland interrupted. "So, she's a dryad. That's an improvement over zombie, right? None of you were happy about a zombie joining our band of merry men."

"As long as she doesn't drip or dribble," Judith said, "I don't mind. Much."

"Okay, where's your tree, honey?"

At once, Zelda the non-zombie stood and began walking out of the cemetery. The small group watched her go, until Ezra finally said, "I guess we're to follow her?"

"She's not real verbal," Lent said. "It's not like she can sit in the car and say 'Turn left at McDonald's.'"

"She's a tree! It's a wonder she can talk at all."

"Her liveliness, for want of a better word, is tied to her tree. As her tree recovered, so did she. But then . . ." Ezra trailed off. "Then whatever happened . . . happened again."

"That was so vague," the car said, "you shouldn't have bothered to talk at all. Let's go."

Ezra beat Ireland to the passenger seat, and Lent folded his considerable bulk behind the wheel, so Ireland climbed in the back seat with Owen and New Guy, Lent put the car in gear, Judith corrected him, and off they went.

At a crawl, to keep pace with Zelda. Judith groaned as the scenery inched by. "I'm burning out all kinds of pistons and things doing this," she complained.

"What is her story?" New Guy whispered.

"What is *your* story?" she whispered back. She brushed Owen's tail out of her face and gave the werewolf a shove to get more room. Squashed in the back seat between the stranger and the werewolf, she had a moment to reflect and had the usual thought: *I must do something about my life.*

At least New Guy wasn't still walking around looking like someone had hit him. But she supposed anyone ridiculously tall, with a young, unlined face and snow-white hair, had a few stories to tell.

"You first," he replied.

"Judith was engaged to an archmage. That's a—"

"Leader of magicians."

"Right." Pause. "How d'you know that?"

"I'm the Tutor. At the very least, I know the names of things. If it's in a book somewhere, I'll find it. Once I find it, I remember it forever. It's my job to teach what I know to the person who can actually use the knowledge."

"All right. I'm not biting, you know. Not falling for it."

"That's nice. I don't know what you're talking about."

"I'm going to keep on pretending what you just said had nothing to do with me." Micah opened his mouth but she bulldozed right over him. "Anyway, Judith was engaged to an archmage and she cheated on him."

"Oh."

"Multiple times."

"Ah."

"With various parties."

"Bad idea."

"And got caught."

"Yikes."

"And cursed."

"Naturally."

"He bound her into— I'm not sure exactly how it works, because before she was in this Escape she was in my grandpa's old thresher . . . anyway, she's bound into engine-run machinery until . . ." Ireland raised her voice. "Hey, Judith, what do you have to do to break the curse again?"

"Shut up."

"Seriously."

"I am being serious," the SUV said crossly. "Shut up and stop babbling my business to New Guy."

"I'm not the new guy," Micah said. "I can assure you— all of you—I'm strictly a temp worker. As the Tutor, it's my duty to—"

"One project at a time, okay?" Ireland said.

"Is that what we are?" Ezra bitched. "Projects?"

Yes, Ireland thought. "No, of course not, don't be silly, that's just so silly."

"This is *so* bad for my engine," Judith commented as the downtown area crawled by. Fortunately there were only three other cars on the street, and they handily passed the SUV. And didn't notice the dryad leading it or, if they did, had no comment, or interest.

God, she loved the Midwest.

They were going so slowly, in fact, the Violent Fairy had time to hop out, buy half a dozen cream puffs from the Cannon Falls Bakery, and hop back in.

"You did tell me her story," Micah reminded Ireland. "So it's only fair I tell you mine."

"Not if it involves any actual work on my part."

"Lazy," he teased.

"No, just bitter and disillusioned," she retorted, "and there's a history of insanity in my family, so watch out!" She was startled that last had popped out, and decided to pretend she had been teasing, and forced a laugh.

Chapter 10

Later, when Micah looked back on that endless, lightning-quick drive back to the farm, he had no real idea how long he and Ireland huddled in the back seat, talking.

He found a reason to look at a county map some time later and observed the actual distance Judith had driven was 7.3 miles. Which she had taken at roughly three miles an hour.

So, not long at all. Not a terribly great distance.

Or, to look at it another way, just long enough to fall in love for the first and last time in his life.

Chapter 11

B ut this is Old Man Willow!" Ireland exclaimed nearly two hours later.

Zelda the former zombie had led them all back . . . to the Shea Family Farm. To the enormous willow tree arching into the sky directly across the road from her house and barn.

"This was your tree all along? But then you must be . . ." Ireland shut up and thought about it. Zelda was decades—maybe hundreds of years old! Had lived right across the road during Ireland's life, her father's, her grandfather's. "How come I've never seen you before?"

"You're human," the fairy said, "she's dryad. Unless something's wrong, you'd never see her. Even when something goes wrong, you'd probably never see her. Who *ever* sees them? I lived in a forest for sixty years and never saw one. It was just a coincidence that she was in the cemetery the exact time you were."

"No," Micah said. He'd climbed out of Judith after Ireland, and now they were all standing in the field beside Old Man Willow. Zelda had broken from their small group and leaned against the tree, resting her forehead against the bark. "No coincidence. She's the Magicka."

The group blinked at him for a moment, then dismissed his comment as one. "But there's nothing wrong with Old Man Willow. See?" Ireland rapped her knuckles on the trunk. "Ow."

"Nothing we can see," Ezra said. "You can't see cancer, either, until the very end. I'm sure Willow, here, has a slightly different opinion about the health of her tree."

"But her name is Zelda," Ireland whined.

"No," the fairy said.

"Nope," Judith said.

"Willow suits her much better," Ezra added, trying not to look smug. "And besides, she— What on earth has gotten into Owen?"

For the normally amiable werewolf was growling and stalking around Old Man Willow's trunk, actually digging up the soft turf with his paws. His growls were so low and continuous, he sounded like a well-kept motor.

"He's never done that before," the fairy commented, as if watching a new and previously undiscovered insect do something new and previously unsuspected.

"Toss him a Milk-Bone," Judith sneered.

Distressed, Ireland reached for Owen—only to find her wrist seized by Micah. "I wouldn't," he warned.

"Don't be silly," she said impatiently, "it's Owen. He'd never hurt me. He'd never hurt any of us."

"He's a werewolf."

"Yes, I know. A werewolf having some sort of nervous breakdown."

"Maybe he's going rabid," Judith suggested helpfully. "Anybody see *Old Yeller*? I think it's the kindest way to handle this."

Ireland ignored her. "Owen, you're freaking everybody out. What's the matter?" She caught herself. "And why am I asking you when you can't talk?"

Owen yipped in reply, a *yi-yi* sound that was halfway between a groan and a giggle.

"I die," Willow said, and followed it with a disconsolate sigh the exact moment an evening breeze ruffled the leaves of her tree.

"I don't think I've ever been so bored *and* mad at the same time," Judith commented. "If you guys need me, I'll be in the driveway trying not to burn out my engine with what's left of my oil." Without another word, the SUV put itself into gear and roared out of the field.

"That's good advice for all of us," Ezra pointed out.

"What? Why?" Ireland looked around at the small group. "We can't just quit. There's so much left to do." Even as she heard herself, she thought, *This is why you have multiple roommates but no real life.*

"I realize you've got the smell of a good mystery in your nostrils, Daphne, but there's nothing more to be learned until Owen changes back, which at best guess is . . ." Ezra glanced at the moon. "Six and a half hours away."

"So we just . . . what? Quit?"

"Regroup, if you like the sound of that better. Until Owen is once again verbal, I suggest we eat. Or get some rest," he added with a pointed look at Ireland, which she ignored. If Ezra had his way, she'd be tucked into bed every night at nine o'clock.

"Forget that. You guys go," she replied. "I'll stay here and guard Willow's . . . uh, willow."

Ezra actually slapped his forehead. "Of course. We can't leave her tree alone until we get to the bottom of this. In fact, posting a guard might be the way we *get* to the bottom of this. We'll go in shifts."

The Violent Fairy yawned. "We will? You're the nocturnal guy. You can stay up all night in the cold—"

"It's sixty-five degrees out," Ezra said mildly. "Practically room temperature."

"—and not even notice."

"I'll take a watch," Micah offered.

"As will Willow, presumably." They glanced at the now-silent woman, still leaning against her tree and looking as if she would fall, if not for the trunk. "Poor thing."

"I'll watch, too," Ireland said, "seeing as how it was my idea and all. Rock, paper, scissors for first watch?"

"Ah . . . no," Ezra said, glancing at her extended, grubby fist with thinly concealed distaste. "I will take the first watch. As the fairy pointed out, I am uniquely suited to the detail. Relieve me in three hours, please, Micah."

"Hey!"

"No, it's fine," Micah said quickly. He smiled at her, and for a moment, he looked younger than all of them. "I should earn my keep, right?"

"Bossy," Ireland muttered to Micah, but started for the house.

Micah, hot on her heels, said, "I hope you don't mind if I spend the night."

"And if I did?" she teased. "Cannon Falls doesn't have a Marriott."

"I'd camp out in your field. It wouldn't be the first time I'd slept on the ground. It wouldn't even be the hundredth."

"Mm-hmm, that's not mysterious or creepy or anything. But never mind."

"Yes." He sighed. "It's always never mind, isn't it?"

She ignored him. "We've got plenty of room."

"So!" they heard Ezra say to Willow. "Have you read this week's *Entertainment Weekly*? Can you believe David Hasselhoff is making a *fourth* comeback?"

Chapter 12

Ireland rolled over and looked at the clock.

Nope. Still far too early to relieve Micah.

She rolled back, stared at the far wall, and tried to count in her head. She hadn't been to sleep; she hadn't even wanted to climb into bed. But the fairy, who was horrifyingly practical in addition to being infernally smart, pointed out that there was no point in remaining up when people were deliberately staying awake in the middle of a darkened field so everyone else could rest.

So to bed she had gone. And waited to fall asleep. And waited. And waited. She was tempted to pop an Ambien, except that would knock her out for a good seven hours and leave her groggy all morning. And she wouldn't get to see Micah all night.

Wouldn't get to relieve him, and watch out for Willow's willow, is what she meant.

Honestly.

Wouldn't get to see Micah . . . where had *that* come from?

She decided it had been at least half an hour and rolled

back over to peer at the red, glowing numbers of her alarm. How she hated the thing.

Exactly two more minutes had passed.

She hated the clock, but she was a deep sleeper, and only its strident *"NEHHH! NEHHH! NEHHH!"* would wake her. Just knowing it was there, ticking like a time bomb, was enough to rob her of sleep some nights, and—

She looked again.

One more minute.

She thrashed around in her lonely bed like a rolling log with red hair. Poor Micah.

Poor Micah? Why poor Micah?

Because, she answered herself, she had never met anyone with pure white hair and a young face to go with it. Because he seemed so sad, even when he smiled. Because he had allowed himself to get swept up in her

(madness)

crazy life.

And for what? Now he was all alone in the field in a strange place, alone except for Willow and her willow, and no doubt the two of them (three of them?) weren't exactly having a scintillating conversation, the poor guy, and he'd be lonely and hungry and *thirsty*. So far today she hadn't seen him eat or drink a thing.

She sat up.

She flung the covers back.

She would . . . she would feed her guest! Yes, that was it. After all, it wasn't wasting their efforts at keeping watch if she was devoted to keeping their strength up while they kept watch. Er, right?

It had nothing to do with Micah-with-the-white-hair. Why, if it was still Ezra's watch, she'd trot right out into the field and offer him her wrist. He could have all the O-negative blood he—

Well, no.

No, she wouldn't do that. Had never done that. Would never do that.

She had never even *seen* Ezra eat, for that matter, although she knew he did, every single night. Judith had hinted that he had worked out an "arrangement" at the Cannon Falls Nursing Home with a few of the ladies, but since she knew he never killed to feed, she decided the rest was none of her business.

Besides, she'd volunteered at that nursing home all through high school. She'd never seen a building filled with angrier, pluckier people. Victims, they were not.

Anyway, the point was, Micah also needed to eat. And drink.

How unfortunate that she couldn't cook.

Maybe she could bring him a salad in a Ziploc.

And a thermos full of dressing.

If only Lent hadn't gobbled down all the lettuce heads!

She tossed the blankets back and fairly bounded toward the doorway. No matter! She'd find something, even if she only brought him some sugar packets and a bottle of ketchup.

She paused, her hand on the knob, and contemplated her sleepwear: a pair of the Violent Fairy's lavender shorts, which had shrunk in the wash and were now too small for him, and a sleeveless yellow T-shirt with the logo SOME DAYS IT'S NOT EVEN WORTH CHEWING THROUGH THE LEATHER RESTRAINTS.

Prob'ly should change, she thought. But into what, she had no idea. Her wardrobe wasn't exactly, ah, current.

For the first time in her admittedly exciting life, she wished she had more in her closet than a tasteful array of sweatshirts and leggings.

$\mathcal{C}$hapter 13

Ireland tiptoed out of the house, the snores of the Violent Fairy still ringing in her ears. Even better, she hadn't run into Ezra, so she assumed he'd run into town for a bite. Heh. So nobody was——

Too late, she heard the crunch of gravel as Judith pulled up beside her. "Whatcha doing?" the SUV asked brightly.

"Shhhh!"

"But it's not your watch yet."

"I'm bringing Micah something to eat," she said, waving the Ziploc in the direction of Judith's windshield.

"You don't have to walk all the way over there. Just toss it on my front seat and I'll run it over to him."

"That's okay."

"No, really. Toss it in there and go back to bed."

"No, Judith, *really.* It won't take long to walk over there."

"It's no problem."

"I'll do it."

Her engine raced, the SUV equivalent of an exasperated sigh. "Come *on,* Ireland. You know I almost never have the impulse to do something nice and, on the rare occasion I do, I almost never obey it." She added, in an even rarer moment of self-introspection, "Maybe that's why the curse is taking forever to break . . ."

"It's fine," Ireland almost groaned. Of all the times for Judith to be pleasant and helpful! "I'll take care of it."

"But—"

"I said *I'll take care of it!*"

"Take care of what?" Ezra asked, materializing out of the shadows. Ireland screamed and Judith stalled.

"Sorry," he added, smiling with too many teeth. "Did I startle you?"

With a click, Judith restarted her hybrid engine. "No, you just scared all the oil right out of me! Seriously, there's going to be an embarrassing puddle right here."

"Jesus!" Ireland gasped, trying not to fall down. Ezra flinched away from her, but she couldn't say she was sorry. Her heart had nearly leaped out of her rib cage in protest at his out-of-nowhere question, and she was still recovering from the adrenaline surge. "Ezra, how many times do we have to tell you? Either stop doing that or wear a cat collar!"

"But what are you doing out here?"

"She's going to try and jump New Guy's bones," Judith sneered.

"I am not! I'm bringing him something to eat, is that so damn awful?"

"Not at all," Ezra soothed, "but there's no need to trouble yourself. I'm wide awake and happy to—"

She clutched the Ziploc protectively and backed away from both of them. "I'll do it! I just want to do this one thing and you people can't leave me alone! Now *back off!*"

"But you don't cook," Ezra said.

"*And* you don't fuck," Judith added.

"Wrong on both counts," she said triumphantly, waving the thermos at them. "Now leave me alone, both of you. Judith, go park and die. Ezra, go hop in your coffin and do the same."

"You know very well I would never, ever rest in one of those tacky things."

"And I'm not parking anywhere until somebody gives me a pint of oil."

"Since I was the one who startled you," Ezra (thank goodness!) said, "I suppose I should tend to you."

"I totally agree," Ireland said fervently.

"Me, too! How about a tune-up while you're at it?"

"How about, never? Do I look mechanically minded?"

"You look like a big pouf to me."

"Well, this pouf does not wish to soil his suit. Allow me a few moments to change."

"See, in the time you said all that? You could've dunked some 10W-30 into me. Takes maybe ten seconds."

Ezra, who had started toward the house, turned back. He folded his long skinny arms across his chest and sneered down at Judith. "The last time I opened your hood, you spit radiator fluid all over me."

"It was a *joke*."

"I had third-degree burns."

"For about five minutes. Then you healed. Jeez, what a crybaby."

"I did not cry. But if I had, it would have been a perfectly acceptable reaction to a psychopath's idea of harmless chicanery!"

"Off my ass, Lazarus! Is it my fault you lost your sense of humor about the same time you gave up breathing for Lent?"

"How dare you! This, this is why you were cursed, young lady! Your cavalier attitude about anyone's feelings save your own. It's no wonder . . ."

As Ireland crept toward the field, their voices faded away. They weren't following her. Oh, thank goodness.

Micah, she thought, *sustenance is on the way!*

Chapter 14

Micah heard what was definitely sinister rustling. His eyes had adjusted to the dark, and he could make out a solitary figure coming toward him.

"Pardon me, Willow," he called to the dryad. "Is that anybody you recognize?"

"Yes," Willow answered from far above him. At one point she had ceased hugging her trunk and scaled the tree like a ring-tailed lemur, quickly and gracefully. Now she was seated in the fork of a branch some twenty feet over his head. "It is."

It occurred to Micah that a centuries-old dryad probably recognized just about everyone. Especially one who wasn't afraid to leave her tree, as this one was. Therefore, it had been a stupid question to ask. He tried again: "Is that somebody you can—"

"Micah?"

He leaped to his feet. "Ireland!" The distracted, messy, gorgeous, clumsy, redheaded Magicka was here! In the field! With him! Alone! (Except for the dryad.)

"Here!" He waved idiotically. *She knows where you are, chump.* "I'm right here!"

"Yeah, I know." She jogged the last few feet in order to reach him more quickly.

As soon as he had that thought, he instantly banished it. *More quickly? Oh, the ego on you!*

"It's not your watch."

"Why is everyone so damned concerned about when my watch starts?" she practically shouted at him. *Whoa.* "It's like living with a bunch of clock-obsessed nuns!"

"All right, all right, don't pull your gun."

"I don't have any guns," she sulked. "The fairy made me get rid of them."

"I imagine. Fairies plus iron equals bad, bad, bad."

"Right." She stood, her hands behind her back, and looked at him. He stared back, happy to gaze into her—her—well, it was awfully dark out here so he couldn't exactly see the color of her eyes (though he remembered their vivid brown quite well, thank you), though he could make out her face.

"Right."

"Uh-huh."

"So. And don't get angry—but if your watch hasn't started, what are you doing out here?"

"Oh." She appeared to mull that one over. Then, "I brought you supper."

"Oh, gosh, you . . ." She held up a plastic bag full of . . . were those . . . ?

"Lucky Charms," she clarified. She handed him a small thermos. "And milk. I hope you like skim. And also, please please *please* don't tell Lent I gave you some of his cereal."

"That's so—" Weird, he had been about to say, but quickly reconsidered. "Thoughtful. Ah . . . how am I supposed to . . . ?"

"I figured you could pour the milk into the bag. Here, I've got . . ." She dug into her pockets and at last produced a spoon of questionable cleanliness, which he accepted gratefully.

It occurred to him that he was starving. Usually he had

alcohol for dinner, followed by alcohol. Sometimes a sand-wich, followed by alcohol. Not that he had a problem, exactly—he had gone for weeks, sometimes months, with-out a drink (and don't start with that "the first step is admit-ting you have a problem" stuff, because his *problem* was training Magickas since time out of mind, his *problem* was spending the time between Magickas not trying to slit his wrists from sheer boredom). But when he was in between Magickas, drinking was something to do. It certainly beat staying up all night and staring at hotel wallpaper.

His long silence must have made her uneasy, because she hesitantly added, "Is it all right?"

"Thank you," he said, and promptly sat down, cross-legged in the dirt, and did as she suggested. "It's deli-cious," he said with his mouth full.

She laughed and leaned forward, wiping his chin with her sleeve. He nearly flinched—not at her touch, but at how close she was to him when she leaned nearer. It took most of his willpower not to toss the bag o' Charms into the dirt and grab her.

"I was lying in bed and couldn't sleep, and got to think-ing about you out here, hungry and cold   "

"It's sixty-some degrees out here," he reminded her. "Barely sweater weather, now that the rain has stopped."

"Even so, you're still going to get mud everywhere. I mean . . . we're in a field. Of mud."

"So we are. So, you were lying in your bed." Hastily, he shoveled in more Charms, lest he say something really boneheaded.

"Yup. I was indeed." She peered up at the tree and spot-ted Willow. "How's it going up there?" At the predictable lack of answer, she shrugged. "She seems better. She climbed twenty feet, for God's sake."

"Yes, whatever's wrong seems to come and go, like waves of pain." He shrugged. He had never, in his long life, met a dryad. "Or something."

"I can't believe there's been a dryad across the road my entire life and I never knew it."

"I can't, either," he said bluntly, "and it's one of the things we need to talk about once we solve Willow's problem."

"What is a Magicka?"

"Ah, finally! A question. Some interest in what I have to say."

"Now, be fair, Mr. Tutor."

"Just Tu—"

"You showed up out of the blue and started babbling about my sacred destiny or whatever, and you can't get mad because I didn't drop everything and get all 'Please, Obi Wan, tell me more.'"

"All the others did," he grumped, and gulped down another spoonful of sugar-fortified cereal. "And from the looks of things, people drop in out of the blue all the time."

She laughed. "There's a bit of truth in that! I didn't go looking for any one of them, they all found me."

"Out of nowhere," he said. It wasn't a question.

"Well, yeah."

"And you just took them in, without question."

She looked a little hurt. "It's the way I was raised. I've got the room, and plenty of money. Who am I to begrudge—"

"Multiple freeloading roommates?"

"Now, quit. They earn their keep. Heck, two years ago Ezra nailed a dirty cop from a few towns over, and last spring Lent figured out why all the kids at the high school were getting so sick. And Owen—" She cut herself off and, even in the dark, Micah could tell she was troubled. "Owen needs me," she continued, and he tried to ignore the vicious swipe of jealousy across his heart.

"He . . . needs you?"

"It's hard for a pack animal to be on his own," she began, "and especially— You know what? I really shouldn't be talking about this. This is Owen's business and he'll tell you if he likes. Or not, if he likes."

"Don't ask, don't tell, is that your policy?"

"Me and the Army's," she said gloomily. "It makes things easier."

"And it's important to make everything easier for everyone, isn't it?"

"Stop psychoanalyzing me. I heard enough shrink talk growing up."

"All right. Your point was that they all earn their keep."

"Right! Even Judith—well, okay, Judith is a gigantic pain in my ass, but she's had a run of bad luck. It's not her fault. Not really."

"Just an innocent victim, oh definitely," he agreed. "But the point is that these magical beings showed up one day? Over and over again?"

"Yeah, they pretty much fell out of the sky. In the Violent Fairy's case, literally." She rubbed the back of her neck, remembering. "Landed right on top of me. I thought Ezra was going to have a heart attack. I'd always thought fairies were teeny and dim. Not huge and smart. Who'd have thought those gossamer wings would support all that weight?"

He laughed, picturing the scene. He was dying to know *all* their backstories, but right now it was none of his business. He understood perfectly why they had all been drawn to her; what he didn't understand was why, once she solved their problems, they remained.

"So that's what you do."

"I'm a landlord for supernatural beings, yup."

"More: that's what you are."

"Right. Didn't we just say so?"

"No. You're a Magicka the way Lent is a fairy. He's not human, and neither are you."

"All right," she said kindly, and he was momentarily taken off guard. She got it! She understood! Why, this was going to be— "No more Lucky Charms for you," she finished, and snatched the dripping bag away.

Chapter 15

Micah, who was really very handsome for a crazy person, was still babbling about the Sacred Duty of the Magicka. And she had quit listening. Not because the very idea of being something so fundamentally different and—and *weird* was scary. Because it wasn't.

It was just, he was wrong. That's all. He was completely utterly totally wrong. So she watched his mouth move and waited for her turn to talk.

After a minute, it was. "You're wrong," she said as nicely as she could. "You've got the wrong girl."

He snorted.

"What an awful noise you just made. And you really do. I'm not the magic one. My friends—*they're* the magic ones, the weird ones. Yeah, that's right, I said it: *they're weird*. But I'm normal! I'm totally, totally ordinary."

"The lady protests overmuch."

"Yeah? This lady hasn't even started protesting, big boy. I'd be laughing if this weren't obviously such a big deal to you."

"But it's not a big deal to you at all."

"It's nothing to me, Micah, because you're wrong."

"You can say that after the day you've had? Which as I understand it is a very typical day for you? You can say that while sitting in your field with a stranger and a dryad?"

"Like I said," she repeated patiently, "it's not me. It's them. It's them all the time. It's one hundred percent all them."

"But, honey, why do you think they find you?" The "honey" had slipped out and he could feel himself blush in the darkness. Thank God she couldn't see him. "You, out of any other person on the planet?"

"Because I live on a secluded farm in the quiet Midwest and have plenty of room and an open-fridge policy?" He could hear the rising irritation in her tone. Interesting. She certainly tightened up whenever he started nosing around the truth. After all this time he had fallen in love with a Magicka, and after all this time, he had found a Magicka who had completely deluded herself about her true nature.

With a little help from her friends, of course.

The others had known. On some level, they had known. But Ireland . . . she not only seemed determined not to know, she seemed invested in it.

"Ireland, to answer your question, a Magicka *is*. Just like a dryad is, or a werewolf. You're the guardian of the Magick."

"Is 'the Magick' like 'the Donald'?"

"Your friends were drawn to you," he continued patiently, "because they sensed what you've managed to keep from yourself: you keep them safe."

"No, I don't! I don't keep anybody safe; cripes, the PTA almost burned Lent at the stake last year! They didn't know fairies are fireproof. My friends look out for themselves; they have to. *I* don't have to do anything."

"Ireland—"

She steamrolled over him. "Look at Ezra: ten times as strong as me, and quick as a cat on crack. Look at Lent! As smart as he is big; fireproof *and* waterproof. Heck, look at Judith! Nobody can hurt her unless they're driving a semi, and even then she'd just jump into another vehicle and come back twice as bitchy."

"I'm not saying they know what you are and are keeping it from you. I'm saying they sense it, the way you sensed your friends were all special, one way or the other. I'll bet you weren't surprised at all when Owen changed during the full moon that first time."

"Actually, I found him in the back field, badly hurt, in his wolf form," she admitted. "I got Lent to carry him back and we fixed him up. Of course, when he turned back he was all better, but at the time we didn't—"

"If *anyone* else had tried that, Owen would have bitten their face off. Any werewolf would have. But he trusted you. He knew you'd keep him safe. Even if he didn't know that on the top of his brain."

"Listen: in this group, I can't be the weird one. Hear me? I can *not* be the weird one!"

"Who said anything about weird? *I* never used the word 'weird.' And even if I did, what's wrong with being special?"

"My mother was special," she said bitterly. "And so was her mother. Really super-special. It's not for me. It *isn't me.*"

"Ireland, your family history doesn't matter in the least."

She shook her head. Showed what he knew. Some Tutor. "Micah, you are the nicest crazy man I have ever met. And I have known a lot of crazy people, so that's not just a backhanded compliment."

"Thank you. But let's get back to you. Picture it like this: you walk around in a perpetual force field of protection. And you can throw that force field around any supernatural creature, like a net or a web. And lo, they're safe."

" 'Lo'?" She shook her head. "That is the dumbest description of a superpower I've ever heard."

"Yes, but as I've said, it's not what you can do, it's what you are."

"Micah, I'm not the special one. I'm really not. It's them. It's always been them."

He reached out and gently pushed a red wave off her forehead. "And why, Ireland Shea, is it so difficult for you to believe you're the special one?" And he leaned forward, not quite sure what he was going to do until he did it, and kissed her.

Chapter 16

Ireland had been hoping something would break this awful train of chat they were trapped on, and lo! (as Micah would say) he had kissed her. This saved her the trouble of kissing him. It was either kiss him, or punch him. Because she couldn't be expected to listen to his craziness for one moment longer.

She'd had enough craziness growing up, thanks.

But the kissing was working. Yes, it had nicely distracted him from all that

(why do you think they find you)

utter nonsense. It was pure insanity, not to mention nutball intense! And to suggest that her friends were somehow

(they sense it)

in on the whole thing on some sort of unconscious level, like they all had some kind of paranormal Bat Sense was just

(you're the guardian)

beyond silly. Ever since her parents had died, it had been all she could do to keep from tearing her hair out from sheer loneliness, but to suggest she pulled people to her like she was made of Magicka Sticky Tape was

(you're the guardian of the Magick)
untrue and almost unkind.

Nobody with her family background could be responsible for any one person, never mind an entire subset of creatures who were—ech!—dependent on her like she was the sheriff of Crazytown

(you walk around in a perpetual force field of protection)
just looking for a fabulously dangerous job.

The last thing she needed was a shovelful of "You're the Magicka, you have to protect not only your roommates but any other Tom, Dick, or Werewolf"

(like a net)
who happened to come

(or a web)
knocking on her door.

And even if they *didn't* knock! Did he expect her to ride the range of the world, looking for people to save? He didn't even know her! How could he expect so much of someone

(why is it so difficult)
he didn't even know?

Didn't he understand? Didn't he *realize* she couldn't be responsible, it was too much, it was too big, too frightening, too bizarre, and too damned strange? Didn't he know that she was perfectly happy living

(hiding)
on the Shea Family Farm? Didn't he realize he was messing with the very fabric of her life? Worse than Aunt Key ever did, or could do? Didn't he know that everything fell through her fingers if she tried to hold on to it?

(why is it so difficult for you to believe you're the special one)

Well? *Didn't* he?

"Well?" she demanded, grabbing fistfuls of his shirt until they were nose to nose, kneeling across from each other in the mud. "Don't you?"

"Wha?" he managed. She saw he was rumpled and mussed, as if *he'd* been thoroughly enjoying their kissing while, inside, a big rat of doubt had run around in *her* brain until she couldn't take it anymore. Well! That was nice.

Actually, that *was* nice. She yanked on his shirt until they were mouth to mouth and kissed him back. Anything to get that damned rat out of her brain. And where it went, she did not care.

"It's muddy," he groaned against her mouth.

"I know, I know, it *is* lovely."

"No, it's M-U-D-D-Y."

"So? The others will be out here after my watch and then we can change our clothes. Or Judith can come out here and take part of my watch while we go on and shower."

"Right," he agreed. Then, "Wait!"

Quick as thought, he unbuttoned his (formerly) spotless blue oxford, whipped it off, spread it on the mud, and eased her onto it. She decided not to mention all the cold mud squishing all over the backs of her legs. Who knew what he might whip off next?

She pulled him down to her and ran her fingers through his white hair. "When did your hair start—"

"Sixteen."

"Wow. But you don't look any older than me; I swear you don't have so much as a laugh line. So how old—"

"Three hundred nineteen."

She sat up so fast, they bonked foreheads. "Ow!" her incredibly decrepit, ancient, crumbling lover-to-be howled.

"You're older than *America*? I'm about to make it with a guy who was old when Martin Van Buren was young?"

"Yes," he groaned, rubbing his forehead. "And what an odd comparison."

"Aren't you just a little skeeved out to be jumping someone my age? Next to you, I'm a fetus!"

"Well," he said, reasonably enough, "I never found anybody my age I wanted to jump."

"Men," she grumbled. "God help me when you go through your midlife crisis."

"I don't like vampires for sex partners because you have to share blood to guarantee monogamy," he explained, "and I've never met a female fairy, and I didn't know there were dryads until yesterday. And you're the first Magicka I . . . you know." He paused and cleared his throat. "You're the first Magicka I liked enough to—anyway, that's about it for the paranormal. To the best of my knowledge. Which I feel obliged to remind you is considerable. And a human with a seventy-year life span is absolutely out of the question."

"What about me?" she asked, chills running up and down her arms as the new, unwelcome thought struck her. (Well, the chills could have been from the fact that they were wriggling around in the muck like a couple of mudfish.) "How long will I—how long do my kind live?"

"Every Magicka I've known has died of old age, even if, at the end, they were in some sort of epic good/evil thing," he soothed. "To be blunt, you're too damned powerful to be killed off. Your energy has to be—"

"On second thought, don't tell me." She chewed on that one while he chewed on the collar of her shirt. Too powerful to be killed off? People were drawn to her? Well, shit! That made her a . . . a . . . "A damned Mary Sue!"

"What?"

"Oh, it's this silly thing Ezra told me about. He reads about nine books a day, you know, and don't even ask me how many magazines. He said a Mary Sue is a heroine who is the bestest prettiest coolest powerfulest awesomest heroine in the history of fiction. So nauseatingly sweet you could just as easily barf on her as fall in love with her. He says they're running rampant in historical romances."

"Oh. Well, that's not you," he said, and she perked up. "You're not sweet at all," he went on with heartless cheer, which was less fun. "You yell a lot, and you stammer, and

you fall over everything that isn't nailed down, and sometimes you've got kind of a dirty mouth. You're a great big
bundle of flaws."

"Thanks," she mumbled.

"What is your shirt made of? Titanium? These buttons . . ."—he struggled with them—"will not . . . budge!"

"That's because they're snaps." She demonstrated, sliding her hand down the vent. Her blouse obligingly sprang
open. "How old did you say you were?"

"Be quiet." He glanced up in the branches. "Do you
think Willow can see us?"

"You've never done it in front of a tree before?"

"Good point. Kiss me back."

She obliged. And obliged. And obliged.

Chapter 17

This is like dying. I am dying.

The clothes had finally come off (most of them . . . it was damned chilly in the wee hours of the morning) and they moved and strained against each other. Her hair was the brightest thing in the field, the world. Her soft, ripe mouth opened for his, bloomed like a black orchid, her limbs twined with his, her pelvis met his, her eyes met his.

He could see everything, feel everything: the sweat beading in the hollow of her throat, her temples. The way her eyes were slitted, the way her body tightened in an all-over spasm as she came and came and came again. The way her nipples were hard points against his bare chest, the way her nails dug into his ass. And still they rocked together in the mud and he had a dim thought

(where'd the dryad get to?)

which he couldn't quite catch hold of. Then his orgasm started at the base of his spine and roared up and out of his central nervous system, leaving him shaking, leaving him exhausted, leaving him in the mud with the woman he loved, would always love, no matter how long he lived and no matter how long she did.

So this is what it's . . . he had time to think, before drifting off.

Chapter 18

"U ck," Ireland said, and stretched. Tried to; Micah was sprawled on top of her, snoring with an odd "*whee . . . wee—wee—wee!*" sound. Good thing he hadn't done that before she'd taken off her pants. At least she was warm, if slightly squashed. She couldn't believe they had both dozed off after their muddy humpy sex, long day or no. "Micah?"

"Um?" he said, and raised his head. He looked around the field with total incomprehension, and then the light dawned. Literally: the sun had come up, best guess, ten minutes ago. Then: "We fell asleep? Ack, God, I'm freezing. And I've got mud everywhere."

She giggled. "I'll bet. I—"

"Hey, monkeys."

They both looked up at the totally unfamiliar voice.

There was a circle of four faces around them, all unfamiliar, all male, all scowling. Except for one.

"Aunt Key?" she gasped, thinking: three visits in one week? And she caught me in postcoital slumber after a four-year dry spell? *What are the odds? Dear God, WHAT ARE THE ODDS?*

"This lifestyle you lead," the older woman tsked, shaking her head. "Really, Ireland."

"What are you doing here? What are all of you doing here?" She thought of an even better, more relevant question. "Who are you?"

"Don't you remember? I told you." Key shrugged out of her coat and dropped it down onto them. Micah sat up, eased Ireland up, and while she struggled back into her jeans he pulled his shirt out of the mud and handed it to her.

Ireland contemplated the muddy rag for a moment, then pulled on Key's red windbreaker. "Told me what?" she almost snapped.

"The *buyers*."

"Don't *you* remember? I already told you, Aunt Key, I'm not selling this field. I'm not selling any of my land. And can we have this discussion *any place and time but here*?"

"I thought if you met them you might change your mind," the older woman said brightly.

"So you brought them over at the crack of—" At "crack," Micah started to laugh. She silenced him with a glare and finished. "Dawn?"

"Well, they wanted to—"

"Shut up," one of the strange men said.

"—visit the field like they've been doing—"

"Shut the fuck up, monkey."

"—since I showed it to them last week." Aunt Key gasped and turned to the men. "What did you just say?"

"They said shut up," Micah said.

"Then they said shut the fuck up," Ireland added, getting a very bad feeling.

Where the hell was Willow?

"Aunt Key, what have you done?"

"What I've always done," the older woman replied. "Looked out for you. Tried to make your life easier. Tried to stop you from making things too hard on yourself. These men—they have lots of money."

"But I have money, t—"

"If you only had the house and barn to worry about, maybe you'd go out more! And maybe those roommates . . ." Her shrill, accusatory voice trailed off and Micah jumped into the gap.

"Maybe those roommates would leave if they didn't have all this land to, um, romp around in?"

"As you can see," Aunt Key sniffed, clutching her purse to her (ample) chest, "I'm not here a moment too soon."

"All right, that's enough monkey chit-chat."

"Why," Ireland began, "do you—"

"'Monkey' is very unpleasant werewolf slang for 'human,'" Micah explained. He was getting to his feet very slowly. He did not, she noticed, give her a hand out of the mud. "A dirty, filthy, lice-picking, descended-from-primates human."

Ireland gaped. Two of the others gaped back in a perfect imitation of her expression, then gleefully elbowed each other. "You're werewolves?" she nearly squeaked.

"Yeah. This is Brian, I'm Doug, that's Ian."

"And you wanted to buy my land? Which isn't," she added, glaring at Key, "for sale?"

"Yeah, well, we're always looking for more territory. If we can't get it one way, we'll get it another," Ian, a blond man with a porn-star moustache and the build of a fire hydrant, explained. "We figured you'd want to sell if your pet tree died."

"Well, you were wrong!" Ireland snapped.

"How were you doing it?" Micah asked, which was annoying. He was catching on much, much faster than she was. *Mary Sue, my big pink ass! Everyone else is ten times quicker than I am!* "Is werewolf piss caustic? Is that how you were making the tree sick?"

"Jeez, no," Ian said, and Ireland wondered if the other two could talk. They seemed perfectly happy to let the tallest one do all the verbalizing. "Every time we came over to 'look at the property' we brought a picnic. Insecticide in the thermos bottles."

"Oh, that's *very* nice," she snapped, leaping to her feet and nearly skidding back and falling down. She steadied herself on Micah's arm and added, "What'd Willow ever do to you?"

At once, it all made sense. Poor Willow! Helpless against werewolves who came back . . . and came back . . . and came back! Right under her very nose; that was the part that really hurt. If she'd ever spotted strangers strolling around in her field, she wouldn't have thought a thing about it: this was the country. You didn't automatically distrust strange faces.

And each time they showed up with cups full of what the casual observer thought was Kool-Aid, but was really—

"You pieces of *shit*!"

"Yeah, yeah," Ian said, almost yawning. "So, sell. All right?"

"I—you—we—" She could feel herself sputter with rage as ten insults fought for dominance. "Douchebags! That's really nasty human slang for 'werewolves,' you know. I'm not going to sell my land or her to *you,* you scumbag . . . scumbags!"

"Who is 'her'?" Ian asked, puzzled.

"I didn't want to sell before you were up to this shit, and I'm sure as shit not going to sell *now,* you pieces of shitty . . . shit!"

"Ireland!" Key gasped.

"And you!" she shouted, rounding on her last living relative. "My mother didn't ask you to run my life for me! She sure as hell didn't ask you to play Realtor behind my back. And even if she did, hello? She was crazy! Regardless, just because you don't approve of my roommates is no good reason for you to stick your nose into my business."

"They're unnatural," Key hissed, "and you know it!"

The hilarious thing was, Key had no idea how true her words were. She thought the others were gay.

"They're unnatural," Ireland agreed, "and I *love* it. Hear me? Love. It. So take your fuzzy friends and get the hell off my land before I remember where I hid the guns after I told Lent I got rid of them."

"Well, there's going to be a small problem with that," Micah said, "although I'm incredibly proud of you right now. And that's—"

"Sign on the dotted line," Ian said, bored, "or we'll kill and eat your aunt."

Ireland snorted. "So?"

Micah, warningly: "They mean it, Ireland. Werewolves are not inclined to bluff."

"Again: so?"

"You know you don't mean it."

"No, but you have to admit: talk about poetic justice."

"What are you fool young people talking about?" Aunt Key demanded.

"Pay attention, monkey, we're threatening you. Now: sell us the land or— Stop that."

Micah had lunged forward and slugged the large blonde with what appeared to be all his strength. And now he was hobbling in a circle, clutching his ruined fist and groaning in pain.

Ian, who hadn't rocked backward with the blow, rubbed his chin. "I've had harder punches from my cubs. What are you?"

"I'm a teacher," Micah groaned, cradling his hand with the other hand. "Ahhh, God! I think I broke most of my knuckles."

"Don't worry," Ireland soothed. "I'll throw my, uh, incredibly lame net of protection around you. Isn't that how it works? Hey, that's right, I'm invulnerable!" She stepped up to Ian and thrust out her chin. "Hit me with your best shot, you big stupid blond—"

Chapter 19

Three minutes and eighteen seconds later . . .

Ireland opened her eyes and looked up at a now-familiar circle of faces, including Ian's and Key's. "I thought you said I was invulnerable," she moaned, massaging her jaw and deciding it wasn't broken, just bruised.

"I never said that. I *never* said that!" Micah cried, leaning down to pull her to her feet. "I said your kind lived to old age. I never said you couldn't be hurt!"

"Well, shit." She swayed, then steadied herself, then swayed some more. It sounded just right for the situation, so she said it again: "Well, shit."

"As you can see," Ian said, staring at them as if they were crazy people, which meant, if nothing else, he was a good judge of character, "we don't mind hurting you to get what we want. So why don'—"

"Ian!" A baritone bellow split the morning air. "You monkey-fucking sly sneaking rogue son of a bitch! Get away from them *now*. Yeah, that's right, it's me. Didn't expect me to come over upwind, did you, you pretending bastard?"

"Who is that, now?" Ireland cried, and turned. To her complete amazement, Owen was stomping toward them, his normally pale complexion flushed to the eyebrows. She had *never* heard him talk like that, not even when she had cooked his raw hamburger on Judith's hot engine and eaten it without a qualm. "Owen, wh—"

"I knew it was you assholes, I smelled you all over the place last night. At least you saved me the trouble of tracking you this morning. Get off our land."

"Her land," Aunt Key corrected. Then she corrected herself: "I mean, not for long."

"Did you really think you could turn us down and not ever pay the consequences? Did you think anybody who gave you shelter wouldn't get bit?" Ian smiled, a good trick since he looked so furious. The frightening thing was, it was a genuine smile.

Ireland decided: *He likes being mad. That's why he's smiling.*

"Oh ho," Micah said quietly. "Trying to form your own pack? Thrown out for whatever dull reason, stricken from the group—which can be like death for your kind. But you couldn't stand the thought of a true rogue turning you down?"

"True rogue?" Ireland asked.

"A rogue who asks the Leader's permission to leave," Owen explained absently. "A legitimate rogue, I guess you could say. Are you guys hurt? You don't smell hurt."

"We're fine. I cast my web of protection over Micah, so he only broke *half* the bones in his hand. Then I cast my net of suckitude over myself, and got knocked cold. Owen, I didn't know you were—" "Hiding" seemed like the wrong word, but what was the right one?

"It's not your problem, Ireland, it's mine. It's always been mine. One of these days I'll see about mending fences, but I'd eat salads for a decade before I'd join up with these idiots. Ian, it's not that you guys are mean. It's that you're dumb. I mean, even a rogue has standards, you know?"

For reply, Ian's fist came whistling through the air toward Owen's face. Ireland didn't even have time to gasp a

warning—not that Owen needed it; he ducked with time to
spare.

"You sure you want to get into this?" Owen asked, his
bangs actually ruffling from the wind of Ian's blow. "There's
no walking away from this one."

"Why do you think there are three of us? We'll take you,
we'll take the land, we'll have more territory and we'll be
rid of you and the monkey you're shacked up with. It's
what the monkeys call a 'win/win.' "

"I'll show you monkeys," Ireland began furiously, at
which point a couple hundred pounds (and then some)
dropped straight down onto Ian.

"Lent!"

"Stupid werewolves," the Violent Fairy snickered,
stomping Ian's head into the mud for good measure. From
the werewolf's complete immobility, the landing had
knocked him unconscious. At the very least. "Never look
up. Just follow their nose. Harder to track a vegetarian; we
don't smell like crap."

"Lent!" Ireland screamed, strongly resisting the urge to
fling herself into his arms and sob like a toddler denied a
cookie. "I've never been so glad to see anybody in my—"

There was a roar, a squeal, and then Judith was parked.

On the second werewolf.

"Oh gross!" Now Lent was screaming. "Not the head,
Judith, *not the head*! You didn't listen to the plan."

"Sure I did," Judith said, setting her parking brake with
a satisfying creak. "I just decided it was a dumb one. Ireland, are you guys okay? We saw you go down and, as they
say, sprang into action."

A solitary creature, the third werewolf, a skinny brunette
with skin the color of recycled paper, shifted nervously on
the balls of his feet. "Okay, I guess I'm in charge now," he
began, and it was a pity his voice cracked on "guess." Otherwise it might almost have been worrisome.

Almost.

They ignored him. "But how did you guys even know—"

"Willow," Judith explained, just as her hatch opened and the willowy (hee!) brunette climbed out. "She came to get Ezra, who was just turning in. Ezra told us. We came out, Lent told us the plan, we swooped like the avengers we apparently are."

"Judith," Ireland said reproachfully. "You made Willow ride in the trunk?"

"Hey, she's still a little funny-smelling. You have no idea how tough it is to get odors out once they—"

"Shut up," most of them said in unison.

Willow, meanwhile, had gracefully walked up to the last werewolf. She stood very close to him, arms at her side. She was very still; if Ireland hadn't known she was a dryad, she would have known something was off. Willow didn't move, stand, talk, or react at all like a human. She had planted herself in front of the third werewolf like the tree she was, and Ireland had a feeling nothing could move her unless she wished it.

"I die," she informed the werewolf. "You made me I die."

"Not anymore, Willow," Micah said. "We figured out what they've been doing. They won't do it again."

"Get away from me," the werewolf—was it Brian or Greg?—said nervously. "I mean it. You think a vegetarian scares me?"

"She's not a—" Micah began, then cut himself off. "Actually, I suppose technically she *is* a vegetarian, but—"

Impatient and spooked, Brian-or-Greg swung a fist into Willow's left cheek. They all heard the sickening crunch and Ireland almost screamed, thinking Willow had been badly hurt.

"Do not I die ever again," Willow said. The blow hadn't moved her, ruffled her, harmed her, or moved her face so much as half an inch. "Do *not*."

"It's tough to hear her," Lent commented, "over the screaming. Did she basically tell him to shove off?"

"Yeah," Micah said, also shouting to be heard over the werewolf's howls of pain as he ran in small circles, blood running down his wrist and forearm in lengthening streams. "Basically!"

"Huh."

"What, huh?" Judith shouted. "Just a minute, you guys. *Hey, werewolf! Cut the shit or I'll park on your face!*"

Still shrieking, the last werewolf ran off.

"That's better," Judith sighed. "I guess you can't knock a dryad on her ass unless she wants you to."

"Not when they root themselves like that," Lent said. He was looking at Willow, Ireland noticed, in a whole new way. And . . . was that a smile? On *Lent's* face? "Huh."

"He doesn't date," she whispered to Micah. "He's afraid of hurting the girl. And he told us last year he hadn't seen a female of his kind in over twenty years."

"Don't tell me," he groaned. "I don't want to even think about the unstoppable offspring of a dryad/fairy union."

"I'm just saying." Then, louder, "Well, thanks for coming to our rescue, you guys. Although I must say, Micah here had it all under control."

"We could tell," Judith said with poisonous sweetness, "from the way he got his ass kicked."

"And as for you." Ireland rounded on her last living relative, who smiled sickly.

"Ireland, dear, you know I only had your best interests at heart."

"No, you only had yours. You're a bigot, Aunt Key, a contemptible nasty-minded bigot who has always hated the fact that not only did I never need you, I never even liked you. You get off my—*our*—land and never, ever come back."

"But Ireland—"

"Or my faggot friends will take turns kissing you on the mouth."

"Good-bye and good riddance," Aunt Key proclaimed, then spun (clumsily; it was still awfully muddy) and started marching away.

"Ah," Micah said.

"Yep. So goes the last living relative of the Shea family."

"Well—"

"Oh, Micah! Tell me you weren't going to say something mushy and awful like 'But you have a family, a family you made, and we'll be together forever.' "

"I was going to say, 'Well, I think it's time we went up to the house and got some breakfast.' "

"I don't believe this!" Micah cried, squatting beside the smashed, parked werewolf. The first one was still unconscious.

"Ugh, I know. I'd like to go one month without a secret moonlight burial," Ireland complained.

"No, I mean he's alive. I knew werewolves were tough, but Jesus!"

"That's fine," Owen said, staring down at the blond muddy mess. "I'll bring him around and explain the facts of life. Not that it'll take much explaining. And thanks, Ireland."

"Huh? What? All I did was get my ass kicked."

"You never asked any questions. In three years, you never asked. I just wanted to tell you I appreciated it. And like I said, I'll go back one day and settle this unfinished pack business." He grinned, looking like the sunny, cheery Owen of old. "But not today."

"So, how about some green tea?" Lent asked Willow, who replied, "I drink," and followed him up to the house.

"That's just great," Ireland said, following them. Beside her, Micah took her hand. "Everybody's got their happy ending but me. And Aunt Key. And her henchwolves."

"That's what you think. If you think I'm sticking around for the next twenty years to teach you but not marry you, fight with you, piss you off, and get laid regularly, you're crazier than your whole nutty family."

Ireland stopped short. "What? How'd you know?"

"You mean besides careful observation of current events?"

"Point," she admitted.

"I told you. If it can be found in a book, I can look it up. You think you're the only one with a bunch of crackers in the family tree?"

"Noooo," she replied, so relieved that her knees kept wanting to buckle. "But you have to admit, it's certainly colored my judgment over the years."

"Yeah, well. I can understand not wanting to be 'the weird one' after growing up the way you did, but that's years behind you now."

"Just like that, eh?"

"No, of course not," he said gently. "What do I know about families? I've never had one. I never even knew my parents—Tutors are given up at birth and trained, also from birth. I'm just saying, your family shaped you into the woman you are now, right?"

"No."

"Now you're just being stubborn."

"Nuh-uh."

"No more hiding behind your family. No more hiding, period. We'd have been in deep shit if your friends hadn't come helped. And that's fine. But the time will come when they'll be in deep shit without you. And you've got to be ready. I'll make sure you're ready."

"Slavedriver," she grumbled.

"Well, that's not to say we can't shower, eat, and then have another roll in the mud, so to speak. Then I'll take up my slave-driving ways."

"Pervert."

"Your pervert."

"I suppose." She smirked. "Just what I always wanted. My own pervert. Now if I can just catch the measles again my life will be utterly, utterly perfect."

The Tutor chased the Magicka up to their home.

Epilogue

I reland discovered that mud did not come out of silk panties, and threw that pair away. After that, she stuck to cotton.

Micah decided that drinking after dinner didn't agree with him, and gave the whiskey to Ezra.

Ezra renewed all his magazine subscriptions for the next three years, and fell in love with the newest resident of the Cannon Falls Nursing Home: Ida Harris, aged seventy-two. They are currently dating. Jack Daniel's agrees with both of them very well after dinner.

Lent discovered that Willow had unbreakable bones. She is expecting their first child in the summer.

Owen, at the time of this writing, hadn't bothered to fix things up with his pack . . .

. . . and Judith is still cursed, and overdue for her ninety-thousand-mile tune-up.

Voodoo Moon

by

LORI HANDELAND

Chapter 1

D EVIL'S FORK—2 MILES

"Yee-ha," I muttered.

I couldn't believe I was headed to a town called Devil's Fork. But they appeared to have a serial killer, and that's where I came in.

Special Agent Dana Duran, FBI. Do *not* call me Scully.

I wasn't an *X-Files* fan even before the nickname. I'd never understood why anyone would waste an hour watching something so utterly far-fetched. I preferred just the facts.

That's right; Joe Friday was my hero.

I'd touched down at Louis Armstrong International Airport in New Orleans at eight PM, nabbed a rental car, and headed northeast, per my MapQuest directions.

Being near the end of October, the sun had disappeared, though the air remained warm and a bit sticky. I skirted the city proper and headed over the Lake Pontchartrain Causeway toward St. Tammany Parish. On this side of the lake sat several upscale suburbs that drew young urban professionals who worked in either New Orleans or Mississippi. The school systems were better, the traffic less dense, and the crime on the low end.

Except in Devil's Fork over the past three months.

The road I traveled had never seen a streetlight. The mammoth pine forest bordered by the Honey Island Swamp shrouded the area in darkness. I began to wonder if I'd taken a wrong turn. I'd left the suburbs several miles back.

Then I blinked, and I was driving down a city street. One minute trees, brush, unknown wildlife; the next Devil's Fork National Bank.

The town was pretty large, which was a shock out here in the middle of diddlysquat. Devil's Fork wasn't a suburb. No cul-de-sacs, fast-food joints, or supermarkets. Instead the buildings were old and weathered, though still well maintained. From the Internet propaganda I'd read before getting on the plane, Devil's Fork catered to the fishing crowd.

They had all the essentials—small grocery store, gas station, the aforementioned bank, plus several specialty shops and cafés where I assumed the wives or significant others spent their time while the fishermen fished. Farther down, near the end of Lafayette Street, sat the police station.

Oddly, there was no one out. Sure, it was dark, but it wasn't late. Usually at least one or two people took a stroll, walked their dog. If it weren't for the occasional light in a window, the smattering here and there of pumpkin, witch, or bat in deference to the upcoming holiday, I'd have thought I'd come across a ghost town.

I parked in front of the police station, which still had an old-fashioned hitching post. Hadn't seen one of those in . . . forever. Opening the door, I walked in.

Hello, Mayberry RFD.

One desk. A file cabinet. A door leading to a back room next to two empty jail cells.

"Andy?" I called.

"Who the hell are you?"

Guess the cells weren't empty after all. I'd missed the man taking a nap on one of the cots.

He sat up, rubbing a palm over his shaved head. He

didn't look anything like Andy Taylor. He really didn't look like Otis.

As the guy unfolded himself from the cot, my gaze traveled up, up, up. He had to be six-six, about 350. His hands were as big as ten-pound canned hams. He had tattoos running up both arms and another winding up the side of his neck. I wondered momentarily what he was in for.

The thought flew right out of my head when he walked to the cell door and pulled it open.

Where *was* that sheriff?

I hadn't realized I was backing away until my shoulders smacked into the door. My fingers crept toward my gun.

"Where you going?"

Instead of coming after me, hands outstretched for my throat, the convict moved to the desk, lifted a long-sleeved tan shirt from the chair, and shrugged it over his wife-beater T-shirt, effectively covering the tattoos.

Once they were out of sight, I registered the insignia on the pocket. DEVIL'S FORK PD. I let my arm fall back to my side.

"*You're* the sheriff?"

His dark eyes narrowed. I suppose he got that a lot. As much as I got called Scully. Maybe more.

"I am," he said slowly, the pace and his accent revealing he'd lived here, or near enough, all his life. "Marcus Brody. And you are?"

I straightened away from the door. "You requested an on-site consult from Behavioral Analysis at Quantico."

"English, honey."

Oh, boy. I loved it when guys called me honey before they even bought me a drink.

"Special Agent Duran. FBI."

He looked me over, from the top of my blond head to the tips of my clunky dark shoes—a distance of about sixty-four inches. "I think we're gonna need a bigger agent."

I might be short but I'm solid muscle. While the FBI no

longer enforced a height requirement for their agents, it did have a body fat requirement. Considering the rigorous course I'd been put through to become a special agent, body fat had never been an issue.

Regardless, I trained harder than anyone else to make up for my petite stature. I ran, lifted weights, studied karate. On top of all that, I was scrappy. Everyone said so.

"I can assure you, Sheriff, I'm well qualified." I'd been dreaming of the FBI most of my life. While other kids imagined careers as rock stars, fashion models, or professional athletes, I pretended to be Clarice Starling. I never said I wasn't a strange child.

I was thirteen when I first saw *Silence of the Lambs*. You'd think that would have given me nightmares. Instead I found a calling.

My father had died a few years before—cancer, the stuff of which true nightmares were made. My mother worked two jobs after that. She wasn't around a lot; she couldn't help it.

What I learned from Clarice was control. If you were in the FBI, you had it. I wanted it. 'Nuff said.

I'd gotten a degree in criminal psychology, spent several years in the field, then done whatever I had to do to become what I'd always wanted to be. Special Agent Duran. So why wasn't I happier about it?

"You wanna show me some ID?" Brody asked.

I complied; he barely glanced at it before motioning me to a chair on the opposite side of his desk. "What do you need to know?"

"Everything."

"I sent a report to the field office in New Orleans."

Proper FBI procedure called for local law enforcement to request help through the closest field office. The case then wound its way up the food chain until it reached the appropriate department head, who would decide if an agent or agents, maybe even a task force, would be dispatched to the area. In the case of Devil's Fork, they sent me.

"I saw the report, but it didn't say much."

"There isn't much to say. I got nothin'."

"When you say nothing—"

"I mean absolutely freaking zilch." Brody's big hand swung up and he rubbed his head again, making me think he was new to the Bruce Willis look. He behaved as if he was used to running his fingers through his hair in agitation. Considering the whole serial-killer problem, maybe he'd rubbed his hair right off.

"No suspects?" I pressed.

Brody's answer was a snort.

I was beginning to get frustrated. He'd called for help, and now he was acting as if the facts of the case were a state secret.

"We have six dead," Brody continued. "And every one of the MOs is different."

Which was why I'd been sent here alone. Serial killers were a bit obsessive about their modi operandi. Just a little quirk of being totally crazy. That the MOs differed in Devil's Fork made the powers that be skeptical about a killer of the serial variety. However, there were enough dead bodies to worry them.

"Let me see your file."

Brody's eyes met mine. In them I saw wariness and a trace of fear. What on earth did a guy like him have to be afraid of?

He opened a drawer, withdrew a thick folder, and slid it across the desk. I reached forward, but he slapped his huge paw on top. "I have to say something before you open this."

My eyebrows lifted. "Say it."

"You aren't going to believe what you read."

"And why is that?"

"There's something strange going on in Devil's Fork. Something I can't explain, and I don't think you'll be able to, either."

"Everything can be explained, Sheriff, if you keep trying long enough."

He shook his head. "Not this."

"Let me be the judge of that." I tugged on the file, and at last he let go.

I shuffled through, glancing at photos, skimming over details, my frown deepening with each turn of the page.

According to the data, verified by both officers and the ME, there wasn't a single clue at any of the murder scenes. No sign of forced entry. Not a fingerprint or footprint. Not a hair. No bloody glove. Not one damn thing.

Unless you counted the voodoo dolls—and a bit of dirt.

"Why didn't you mention this in your initial report?" I asked.

"You think the FBI would have sent anyone to help me if I'd told them everything? They'd have tossed my report into the X-file."

I winced. He was right.

"You expect me to believe people are being murdered by voodoo doll?"

"The manner of death in each case matched the manner of mutilation on the voodoo doll."

"It's a signature, that's all." I sat up straighter. "And a connection. The killer believes the dolls are killing the victims. Therefore the MO is the same."

I loved it when things made sense.

"How did the killer get into the victims' homes and then out again, leaving every door and window locked?" Brody asked. "How do you explain the lack of evidence? What's up with the particles of dirt on the doll?"

I frowned. I hated it when things didn't.

"I'll need to see the crime scenes," I said. "And the dolls. Who have you questioned?"

"The whole damn town."

"Anyone give you a tingle?"

He turned his perpetual scowl in my direction. "What?"

"Someone you think might know more than they're saying? Or maybe saying less than they know?"

Brody gave a sharp nod. "Julian Portier. Local shopkeeper."

"What gives you the wiggies about him?"

"His voodoo shop."

I blinked. "Yeah, that'd do it. A voodoo shop seems a strange choice for a town that makes its living on fishing excursions and tourism."

"We're only a hop, skip, and a jump from the voodoo capital of America."

"Then why isn't the shop there?"

"New Orleans is mostly for the tourists. Outsiders aren't interested in anything but the Hollywood version of voodoo. Portier's shop deals in the real thing."

"Sure it does."

"Guy's got skills." Brody lifted one massive shoulder, then lowered it. "He's kind of spooky."

"And you didn't arrest him?"

"Being spooky isn't a crime. In this part of Louisiana it's more of a business. Besides, he had an alibi."

"For every murder?"

"Yep."

That set *me* tingling. The only way to be alibied for half a dozen random nights was to know that they weren't random.

"Convenient," I murmured.

"Airtight. He was either teaching a class in his shop, in plain sight of ten-plus people, or in New Orleans meeting with the local voodoo priestess. Still"—he spread his big hands—"strange things happen around him, although less so since his sister died."

"She one of the victims?"

"No. She had cancer."

I must have made an involuntary movement—something I no doubt did whenever the big C was mentioned—because Brody cast a curious glance in my direction. When I didn't comment, he continued. "Jill died about four months ago. Before everything went to hell."

"When you say strange things happen around Portier, what are you talking about?"

"Storms coming up from nowhere. Lightning striking in his backyard."

"That happens."

"Three times?"

Maybe not.

"What else?" I asked.

"Sightings of strange animals on his property."

"What kind of strange animals?"

"Wolves, owls, snakes."

"What's so strange about that?"

"There aren't any wolves in Louisiana. Haven't been for centuries. And some of the snakes people have seen . . ." He shook his head. "We don't have any pythons or cobras in these parts, either."

I went silent for several seconds, thinking about what Brody had told me. In my opinion the murders had unhinged the populace. They were running scared, seeing things that weren't there. Happened all the time.

"Can I take the file?"

"Just make sure I get it back."

"And the dolls?"

He pulled out a wad of keys, used one on a desk drawer, and pulled out a brown grocery sack, which he shoved in my direction.

"That's your evidence locker?"

He shrugged. "We never had much evidence before."

I stuck my hand in the opening and pulled out six gallon-size plastic bags, each containing a crude rendition of a human being. If stick men were the bare bones of portraits, then these figurines had to be the bare bones of dolls.

They reminded me of lightly stuffed gingerbread people, differentiated from one another by the color of the hair—or rather, thread—that had been sewn onto the lump of a head. Crude genitalia had been fashioned with more thread, either stitched on or left . . . hanging.

The faces had been sewn on as well, eye color indicated by green, blue, or brown embroidery floss.

The only other distinguishing features were the implied manners of death. One doll had a needle stuck in the region of its heart, another had been pierced in the back, and yet another in the eye.

"Knives?" I glanced at Brody.

"No murder weapons." He lifted, then lowered his hands. "But the ME said the wounds are consistent with a stiletto."

I continued to take inventory. The next doll contained a bullet hole in the chest, complete with powder burns, as if the gun had been pressed right to the cloth. A fifth had a crude noose pulled tight around its nearly nonexistent neck, and the sixth showed a distinct watermark at the same juncture, as if the doll's head had been dipped into a lake—for a few weeks.

Brody tapped the plastic covering the last doll. "This victim had water in the lungs."

My forehead creased. "And he was found . . . ?"

"In bed. Not a drop of water anywhere in his house, not even on his clothes."

There had to be a logical explanation. Because if it wasn't logical, it wasn't an explanation. Not in my book.

"The dirt?" I asked.

"From the area, near as we can tell. The weird part is, if someone had carried the doll in with them, there'd be a dirt trail."

"But there isn't."

"No." He paused. "There is one more thing." From the expression on his face, he didn't want to tell me this, either. "The murders always take place on the same two nights every month."

"Which ones?"

"The full moon and the night that follows."

I glanced out the window. "Hell."

The full moon was tonight.

Chapter 2

"You don't seem particularly surprised by that," Brody commented.

"A lot of serial killers do their dirty deeds at the same time each month."

"Why?"

"They like the shade of blood beneath a full moon."

He flinched. I didn't blame him. It had taken me a while to get used to the peculiarities of the psychopathic brain. Not that I ever really got used to it, but I had stopped being shocked. Much.

"You can lock those up again." I indicated the creepy dolls. "Is there somewhere I can get a room?"

"Bed-and-breakfast right next door. Genevieve Henson, a former professor of literature from Tulane, runs the place." Brody picked up the file and handed it to me. "Will it bother you if the place is haunted?"

"Not one bit." I didn't believe in ghosts—or anything else I couldn't see, hear, touch, or investigate.

I meant to go next door, get settled into my room, look over the file more thoroughly. With the moon all shiny and full, I had no time to waste. But when I went outside, a sign on the other side of the street caught my eye.

VOODOO.

That was all. One word painted onto the front window in blood-red letters.

I stepped off the curb. Like I said, I had no time to waste.

I didn't expect the shop to be open, wasn't sure what I'd planned to do beyond peer through the glass. Except when I got there, I saw light, sensed movement. And when I reached for the door, it swung open before my fingers so much as brushed the surface.

The low beat of drums drifted out along with the scent of dried grass and something musty, old, though not unpleasant. The kind of scent that permeated your grandmother's spice cabinet. Familiar but subdued—vanilla and sage, cinnamon and bats' wings.

Laughter tickled the back of my throat. I forced it down and stepped inside.

Candles danced everywhere—talk about a fire hazard—though shadows still lurked in the corners.

Nothing moved now except me. I opened my mouth to call out, then decided to take a tour first. I hadn't walked into someone's home uninvited. I'd come into a retail establishment. It was the proprietor's job to find me.

The place wasn't large, but it was packed with stuff, most of which I'd never seen before. We didn't have any voodoo shops where I grew up. In Fargo we mostly had snow.

Besides the stacks and stacks of books with odd titles—like *Know Your Met Tet* and *Dictionary of the Loa*—I wandered past shelves stocked with dried herbs and grasses heaped in bowls and liquids of every shade swirling in clear jars. They'd have been pretty if I weren't afraid they were poisonous.

A glass display case, backed by a floor-to-ceiling wall of mirrors, drew me across the room. Inside lay jewelry—good stuff, silver mostly—crosses, fleurs-de-lis, several set with a gem of blood red, which I took to be garnet.

On top sat baskets of smooth stones in every imaginable color. I reached for one, rubbed my thumb across the cool blue surface, and in a rare display of femininity lifted it to my cheek to see if the rock was the same shade as my eyes.

A man stood right behind me.

I dropped the stone to the floor, where it rolled beneath the countertop. I spun around, tensed for an attack.

He merely stood unblinking, so near I should have felt the vibration of his steps when he approached. I wanted to back up, but I was already pressed to the glass of the display case.

His dark brows lifted toward a shock of blue-black hair that tumbled over his forehead and brushed the shoulders of his black turtleneck sweater. Everything about him was dark—his trousers, his eyes, his lashes. Even his skin held a dusky hue.

"May I help you?" His voice was so deep it sounded almost unearthly.

"I'm—a—"

I couldn't think with him so close. He was tall and I was short, so I had to tilt my neck sharply to see his face. By my estimation the man stood about six-one and could have used a good twenty pounds, although he wasn't exactly skinny—more wiry with muscle.

He smelled like rain. His hair seemed to glitter with it. I glanced at the window, but the moon still shone in a cloudless night sky, reminding me of why I was here. Shaking off the strange inertia, I pushed away from the counter.

He didn't move back. I resisted the urge to make him.

"Are you Julian Portier?"

"Who wants to know?"

I reached for my ID, and he grabbed my wrist quick as

a rattlesnake. The next instant my gun stared him in the face. I could be quick, too, besides being ambidextrous.

"You want to let me go," I said softly. "Now."

He didn't appear frightened, but he did let me go.

"Hands up. Back away."

"No."

"What do you mean, no?"

"Where's the doll?"

My eyes widened. "You think I'm the killer?"

"You're the one with the gun, *oui*?"

The French surprised me. He had no accent to speak of, not even a Southern twang. Just that soul-deep cadence that made my skin tingle at the thought of hearing him speak in the darkness of the night.

Jesus. Where had that come from?

"I'm the one with the badge." Keeping the gun on him, I used my free hand to remove my ID. "If you hadn't grabbed me, I'd have shown you."

"FBI?" He lifted his gaze. "About time."

I bristled. "We came as soon as we were asked. Contrary to popular belief, we can't just waltz into any old place and take over."

"No?" His lips curved. "Well, shame on Hollywood."

He had that right.

"If I put away my gun, will you refrain from grabbing me?"

"I'll manage." I holstered the weapon. "You can hardly blame me, Agent Duran. We do have a murderer on the loose."

"I look like a killer to you?"

"No. But then killers so rarely have horns or hooves or spiky satanic tails to clue us in."

If he'd been smiling, I would have laughed, but he appeared quite serious. Well, he was a voodoo . . . whatever.

"Can I ask you a few questions?"

"I didn't think you'd come in for a love charm."

I snorted. I hadn't had a date in—hell, I couldn't remember. Everything in me had been focused on becoming a special agent. And now that I was one, I wasn't satisfied. There was something missing, and it kind of pissed me off.

"You don't believe in love?" Portier asked.

"I don't believe in charms."

"I could change your mind."

I wasn't sure if he meant about love or about charms. I didn't care. Sure he was hot, in a deep, dark, exotic kind of way. The kind of way blond white girls from Fargo weren't supposed to notice. The down-and-dirty, make-me-come-screaming kind of way—a way I'd never had it before.

I rubbed my hand over my face. What in hell was wrong with me?

"What can you tell me about voodoo dolls?"

"Same thing I told Sheriff Brody. Voodoo dolls aren't voodoo."

I dropped my hand. "Excuse me?"

"Voodoo dolls are a European tradition, not Haitian."

"What does Haiti have to do with anything?"

"You obviously don't know much about voodoo, Agent Duran."

"Should I?"

"I suppose not. Allow me to enlighten you a bit?" I nodded. "Voodoo began in Haiti—or at least came into its own there. It's an amalgamation of all the religions of Africa. When the slaves were taken from their homes and dragged across the sea, they had nothing to bond them together until—"

"Voodoo."

"Exactly. Hundreds of thousands of slaves came to what was then Saint-Domingue. While they were there, they learned the secrets of our religion."

"You're a priest?" My voice sounded eager. If he was a priest, maybe I could stop secretly watching the play of his long, lean body beneath the black slacks and snug sweater.

"No. Priests and priestesses are more the Haitian voodoo variety. In the United States we're called kings and queens."

"You're a king."

"It's nothing more than a title of respect. You can call me Julian."

That'd be the day.

"I was told one of your alibis was a priestess in New Orleans."

His perfectly arched eyebrows lifted. I wished mine were shaped that nicely. "Cassandra is different. She studied for years, went to Haiti to be initiated. She's a true priestess of the old ways."

"And you're not?"

"I give advice, with a bit of herbalism thrown in." At my blank expression, he continued, "Natural cures, Agent Duran. Holistic medicine. Vitamins. Yoga. Prayers to the loa—the spirits of the earth."

"You believe in those things?"

"I have faith in some of it."

"Brody said you were spooky."

"Not anymore."

What was that was supposed to mean?

"How did you get involved in voodoo?"

"Years ago I began to research my family tree. I wanted to know where I'd come from, and why—" He broke off, shrugged, and went silent.

"You came from Haiti?"

"Not me personally, but one of my ancestors arrived here in chains." At my involuntary start, he turned a bland face in my direction. "Is that a problem?"

"If one of my ancestors was put in chains, I'd consider it a serious problem."

His expression lightened. "Yes, well, there isn't much to be done about it now except honor her memory. I followed her trail back to Haiti and discovered she was a skilled and magical priestess."

"Magical. Right."

"There are more things on this earth than we know, Agent Duran."

"Exactly, and none of them are magic." I needed to steer the conversation back to the problem at hand. "So what can you tell me about voodoo dolls?"

"As I said, they're a European tradition. Witchcraft. Called poppets. A human figure—clay or cloth—created to bring harm to another. The witch would personalize it by using hair or nail clippings or the blood of the one being cursed."

"If that's the case, then where did the whole voodoo doll thing come from?"

"A reporter in the nineteen twenties did a story on poppets. He knew witches used them and he'd heard voodoo was witchcraft, so he coined his own phrase: *voodoo doll.* We've been haunted by it ever since."

"You're telling me there's no Haitian tradition that uses dolls?"

"Actually there are two. The fetish is from West Africa. In that case the doll is said to hold the very spirit of the one it represents."

"And that person?"

"Loses their soul. Becomes a living zombie. Until the fetish is destroyed."

"People believe this?"

"In the old days any slave found with a fetish could be punished by death."

That I could believe. Breathing had been punished by death in those days.

"What's the other tradition from Haiti?"

"Messengers. They're small cloth dolls without features. They carry a message to the loa."

"On angel's wings?"

He ignored my sarcasm. "The message is written and tied to the figure with a ribbon, then it's left at the threshold to the world of the spirits, or in some cases the threshold to the world of the dead."

I remained silent, processing. "So you're saying that what's being left at the scenes of the murders are not voodoo dolls but poppets, and we're dealing with a witch?"

"I'm not sure what they are, who's leaving them, or why they're being left. The whole purpose of a poppet is to cause harm from afar."

"You don't really believe someone can kill just by sticking a sharp implement into cloth and cotton, do you?"

"What do *you* think is happening, Agent Duran?"

"The doll is some nut cake's signature. A psychopathic ha-ha to the world."

"And how, then, do you explain the lack of evidence? The lack of forced entry? In truth the complete impossibility of anyone entering or exiting the murder scenes at all?"

"How do you know that?"

He threw up his hands. "Everyone knows that. This is a small town, and people are nervous. Brody most of all. He told us to be on the alert, to watch out for one another."

"He shouldn't have shared the particulars of the case."

"Well, he did. Now what are you going to do?"

"I'm not sure," I admitted. "But I'll figure out something."

Chapter 3

Portier crossed the room with a dancer's grace. I couldn't help but watch him move. I couldn't help but ogle his ass when he bent and blew out the candles.

When was the last time I'd been attracted to anyone? Had I ever been this attracted, this fast? That's what I got for being all work and no play: I was not only a dull girl, but a horny one, too. I had to get out. I headed for the door.

Portier was there ahead of me to open it. "Let me know if you need anything else."

"I'm staying at the bed-and-breakfast." *Jeez.* That had sounded like a come-on.

"I thought you might." I looked up, and he shrugged; the play of sleek muscles beneath the smooth dark fabric made my mouth dry. "It's the only decent place in town."

Stepping outside, I glanced at my watch. After ten PM. "How late are you open?"

"Closing now." He flipped the sign in the window. "I live upstairs." Slowly he shut the door. Right before the latch clicked I heard him say, "*That* sounded like a come-on."

I stared at the locked door. I hadn't said anything out loud. Had I?

I lifted my hand to knock, then let it fall back to my side. Obviously I'd allowed my thoughts to appear on my face—an old habit I thought I'd kicked. I wouldn't be a decent investigator if I couldn't keep what I was thinking locked behind a stoic façade.

The lights went off inside, and I turned away. I had work to do. Maybe, if I was lucky, I'd see a pattern to these killings immediately, and I'd be able to stop the next one before it happened.

I lifted my gaze to the moon, which was creeping higher and higher in the night sky. Time was ticking away.

I'd expected Genevieve Henson to be a bony, white-haired little old lady. Instead she was a tall, strapping redhead who ran the bed-and-breakfast from the front desk while she typed a history of Louisiana ghost stories into her laptop.

"I'm so glad you've come," she said as she ran my credit card through her machine. "This has been horrible. People are actually leaving town after they've lived here all their lives. It's a shame."

"How long have you lived here?"

"I was born in Devil's Fork."

"Weird name."

"Oh, that's a wonderful story. I'm putting it in my book." She handed me a key. "You probably didn't notice since you came in at night, but the town sits smack-dab at a fork in the road—a crossroads, if you will."

"Okay, I get the fork, but where does the Devil come in?"

"You young people." She shook her head. "Don't know anything about history, myth, legend. It's a disgrace."

She was probably right, but since I could only fit so much info in my head, I tried to leave enough room for modern science, forensics, and investigative techniques.

"Crossroads are where black magic is performed," Miss Henson continued. "And the most common being invoked in such rituals is . . ."

"The Devil."

She beamed at me as if I were a prize student. "They say he manifested once, centuries ago, at the request of a woman. A witch. He granted her request; the price was her soul."

Even though I believed none of this, I got a little shiver at the thought of the Devil walking the earth so freely gathering souls. I guess that might explain the lack of one in so many of the people I ran into. Nothing else ever had.

"What was her request?" I asked.

"Beauty, youth, riches. The foolish things people ask for when they have no idea of what's truly important. She had twenty years to enjoy the benefits, and in that time she founded this town. We've been blessed with prosperity ever since. Until recently anyway."

"Odd that being founded by a witch who'd conjured the Devil would cause prosperity."

"I find it apropos. Isn't the love of money the root of all evil?"

She had a point.

Somewhere in the house, something shattered.

"That's just Mama." Miss Henson waved a hand. "She isn't ever going to leave. Woman nagged me all my life. She won't stop just because she's in the grave. You knock that off, Mama!" Miss Henson shouted.

I jumped, dropping the key.

"Sorry. She just makes me so darn mad sometimes."

"Uh, yeah. I can see where she might." I didn't think it prudent to inform Miss Henson she was nuts. She might kick me out. Now that she'd told me the history of Devil's Fork, I was hoping she'd tell me the history of some of the residents. It would save time.

"Not everyone in town's been here all their lives, have they?" I asked.

"Oh, no. The young couple who owns the gas station inherited it from her uncle. Came in from the North. Arkansas," she whispered.

I'd never considered Arkansas the North, but then, I wasn't from the South.

"And the girl who opened the bookstore—not that we need a bookstore, but it sure is nice—moved in, oh, 'bout a year ago."

"From the North, too?"

"New Orleans. Got washed out in Katrina and didn't have the heart to put it all together again. Figured if she was going to start over, might as well do it on higher ground."

"Probably a good idea. Anyone else new?"

"Julian, of course."

"Of course. And where is he from?"

Miss Henson's brow creased. "I don't think he ever said. He and his sister showed up 'bout a year and a half ago. Started the voodoo shop."

"And people didn't think that was strange?"

"That he lived with his sister? Nah. Twins stick together."

"I mean, didn't people think a voodoo shop was strange?"

Miss Henson looked at me as if I were crazy. "In a town called Devil's Fork?"

Oh, yeah.

"Of course voodoo doesn't actually have a Devil, per se," she continued, "just evil spirits, and crossroads are a big deal for them. Probably why Julian bought the shop that's right at the end of the street." At my blank expression, she rolled her eyes. "Where the road forks? The crossroads sits directly in front of his store."

Interesting. Just because Portier said the dolls weren't voodoo didn't make that true. It also didn't preclude folks coming up with their own brand of lunacy and labeling it whatever they liked. People who believed in the supernatural often did horrible things in their attempts to make the impossible come true.

"Do a lot of voodoo practitioners frequent Portier's shop?" I asked.

"From what I hear, he has the best selection in five counties."

Swell. That meant any one of his customers could be the culprit. They'd know voodoo, and no one in town would blink at them wandering around after a shopping spree.

I'd need a list of Portier's clients. Hopefully he'd give it to me without a court order.

"What about his sister?" I asked. "Was she into voodoo, too?"

"She might have been at one time. But when they came here, she was already sick. Didn't see much of her."

"What did she have?"

"Breast cancer." Miss Henson clucked and shook her head. "You get it that young, it's touch and go. She shouldn't have lasted as long as she did. Heard tell she was only given six months but she lasted two years."

"Experimental treatment?"

"In a way. Julian called on the loa to save her."

Loa. He'd called them spirits of the earth.

"You think that worked?"

"Something helped her, and it wasn't modern medicine. By the time Jill went to the doctor, the cancer had spread to all her organs, including the brain. You don't live long with those kinds of tumors unless there's magic involved."

"Maybe it was a miracle."

"Miracle. Magic." Miss Henson shrugged. "Potato. Pot-a-toe."

"If he was really capable of magic, then why is she dead?"

"There's only so much a body can do. Even one as powerful as Julian."

I opened my mouth, then shut it again. I could argue until I was breathless, but I wasn't going to change Miss Henson's mind, and I didn't have the time or inclination to try. After thanking her, I went to my room.

The place was clean, spacious, with a comfy bed, desk

and decent desk chair, love seat, recliner, and pristine bathroom with a huge claw-footed tub. In truth, it was nicer than my apartment in Virginia—a place I kept only to rest my head and store my clothes.

I should check in with my boss. I glanced at my watch and winced. Eleven PM. I'd check in tomorrow.

I crossed to the window and pulled back the frilly white drapes. My room overlooked Lafayette Street. Someone stood in the road.

Frowning, I leaned forward and bonked my head against the glass.

"Ouch." Rubbing the bump, I watched the man digging a hole at the end of the street, right where the road forked. That couldn't be good.

Dressed in black, he blended into the night. I wouldn't have seen him at all except the moon shone directly above, a beam of silver light cascading down like a waterfall, almost as if it were drawn by him.

He leaned over and tossed something into the hole, then covered it with dirt.

I held my breath, waiting to see where he went, what he did, straining forward until my nose crushed against the cool pane as I struggled to see his face.

He glanced up, right at me, and the sheen of the moon washed his features white, almost as if he wore a mask.

I reared back, shocked, and in that instant he vanished.

"What the—?"

I ran down the stairs, through the lobby, and out the door without a word to Miss Henson.

I'd blinked and he'd slid into the trees. That was all. He hadn't really disappeared. Such a thing was impossible.

Tell it to my brain—which continued to insist he'd gone *poof*.

The street was empty—the only sound the thud of my footsteps as I sped down the sidewalk toward the fork in the road.

The moon no longer shone like a beacon on the cross-roads. Once there, I could barely make out my own hands in front of my face. How could the orb have moved behind the cover of the trees so quickly?

I pulled a penlight from my pocket and shone the beam onto the ground. The earth had been dug up. I hadn't imagined it.

With the silent town at my back and the clutter of brush, pine, and low-hanging Spanish moss dripping from the cypress to my front, I felt utterly alone. Nothing moved in the trees but the wind.

After another useless squint into the dark surrounding woods, I dropped to my knees and began to dig. Since the ground had already been broken, it wasn't too difficult. Luckily I wasn't one for manicures, didn't care that I ended up with dirt beneath my short nails and scratches from the small rocks across my knuckles.

A few moments later, I uncovered a small soft . . . something. Lifting the penlight, I shined it into the hole.

"Shit," I muttered. Another voodoo doll.

I guess this explained how the dirt got on the dolls, although how the dolls got to the murder scenes without trailing particles like Hansel and Gretel's bread crumbs was beyond me.

I didn't want to touch the doll any more than I had already. Maybe we could find some clues on this one—a fingerprint, some DNA. Anything would be better than the nothing we had.

Moving the light closer, I frowned. The doll was larger than the others, in both height and . . . stuffing. It had no thread on its head, though there was an obscenely large bullet hole, which sadly obscured the shade of the embroidery floss eyes. The most telling features, however, were the ink marks on its arms. They resembled tattoos.

"Oh, hell." I lifted my gaze to the sheriff's office, which at first appeared dark and deserted.

Then a muted silver glow became visible beyond the windows, one that reminded me of the moon shining down on that black-clad figure, and the eerie sheen of his un-face.

I reached for my phone, and a gunshot split the night. Inside the sheriff's office, something flashed.

My gasp of shock sounded almost as loud as the report. My gaze zipped back to the hole.

The voodoo doll was gone.

$\mathcal{C}$hapter 4

B rody was dead when I got there.

Of course it took me a while to find my way in. The office was locked up for the night, the silver glow I'd seen earlier gone—if it had ever been there at all—the inside lit now by dim security lights that cast a sickly yellowish pall everywhere.

I rattled the front door, jogged around to the back and did the same, peeked in the window and saw him on the floor. I could tell I didn't need to hurry.

I was debating the merits of picking the lock over just shooting the damn thing off when Portier showed up.

"What are you doing here?" I demanded.

"I saw you running down the street as if the hounds of hell were on your heels."

Every time I heard his voice it startled me, the register far deeper than I expected.

"Where were you?"

"My apartment."

Above the voodoo shop, which was above the cross-roads. He could easily have seen me from his window. Or seen me as he lurked in the woods after burying the doll.

I scowled. I hadn't glimpsed the face of whoever had done that deed, hadn't been able to determine a body shape because of the angle and the night. Which only meant Portier wasn't off the hook this time.

"Why are you standing out here, Agent Duran?"

"Door's locked."

"That's odd." He frowned and, before I could stop him, opened the door.

"How did you do that?"

He lifted his hand, palm up, his fingers piano-man long, and wiggled them.

"Stay outside," I ordered, then pulled my jacket sleeve over my hand and flicked on the interior lights.

Sheriff Brody looked just like the voodoo doll. Spread-eagled with a bullet in his head. The reality was a lot messier than the tableau at the crossroads had been.

The figurine lay right next to him, particles of dirt scattered beneath but nowhere else that I could see, as if the icon had been transported from the hole at the crossroads to this room.

"Impossible," I muttered. Things didn't just disappear from one place, then reappear in another.

So what had happened here?

I had no answer, so I put away the question. I had more important things to do right now.

A soft footfall brought my head up. Portier had come inside. "I told you to stay out."

"You already knew what you'd find," he said softly.

Despite the head trauma, I checked Brody's pulse. He didn't have one.

"You were running here," Portier continued, "obviously distressed—"

"Who's second in command?"

"No one."

"Brody can't be the only cop in town."

"He is since one wound up voodoo-doll dead and the other took off to avoid more of the same."

I rubbed my forehead. "What about an ME?"

"Devil's Fork is too small to have an ME of our own. We don't even have a doctor."

"So what do you do when something like this"—I indicated what was left of Brody—"happens?"

"Until recently nothing like this had happened in a long, long time."

"How do you know? You only moved here a year and a half ago."

His brow lifted. "Been checking up on me?"

"That's my job," I said, but my cheeks burned.

"One of the reasons I came was the low crime rate."

"Where did you come from?"

"Miami."

If that was true, I could understand why a low crime rate had been appealing.

"After all this," he continued, "I'll have to rethink my options."

"Not until the case is solved, pal. You stay in town."

"Of course. Our ME is Dr. Sylvester. She's in Balfour, about five miles away. I'm sure you'll find her number on Sheriff Brody's desk."

He waved his hand in that direction. Papers fluttered across the surface as if a breeze had blown in.

Dr. Sylvester's card lay right on top. I supposed Brody *had* been using it a lot lately.

I called the doctor, got her out of bed. She sounded tired, resigned, but she told me she'd arrive in ten. I took the time to call my superior. Waiting for a decent hour was no longer an option.

"You're in charge," he said.

"Is that legal?"

"We were asked to come. They wanted our help. Until

they find a new sheriff—and with the way things are going I don't think there'll be a big line for the job—you're it."

"Wonderful."

"You've been looking for some excitement, Duran."

I frowned. How had he known? I certainly hadn't made my dissatisfaction public. I hadn't *really* been dissatisfied. I'd just thought there would be more to this job, that I'd feel like I was making a difference every day instead of fighting a tide that could never be turned.

"Be careful what you wish for," he continued. "I'll expect a complete report faxed tomorrow."

I'd only told him that there was another victim and it was the sheriff. What else could I say? What *would* I say? If I wrote in my report that I'd seen a disappearing man bury a disappearing doll, my career in the FBI would be over. I might be bored, but I didn't want that.

I ended the call. Portier leaned against the wall as if he hadn't a care in the world, although he did pointedly avoid gazing at the body.

"Did you see anything out there besides me?"

His perfect eyebrows lowered. "Like what?"

I hesitated, wondering how much information was too much to tell, but I had to know. "Like a man at the crossroads burying something?" Again I left out the disappearing act.

"Burying what?"

I pointed at the doll.

He straightened away from the wall so abruptly I jumped. "What did he look like?"

"Tall. Wore black. I didn't see his face. He . . . took off before I got there."

Portier stared at me for several beats, then turned to look out the back window at the surrounding tree line, his shoulders tense, his hands clenching and unclenching.

"What do you know about this guy?" I asked.

"I didn't see him."

Great. I was the only one who'd seen the murderer, and I hadn't really seen him. I kept getting flashes of his creepy white-moon face. How would I describe that to a police artist?

A car door slammed, and Dr. Sylvester blew in. At the sight of Brody, she stopped.

"Oh, Marcus," she whispered. I thought she might cry.

In her midforties, Sylvester was a handsome, athletic woman, with short, wash-and-wear brown hair and sharp blue eyes. She'd thrown on DUKE UNIVERSITY sweatpants and a ratty long-sleeved T-shirt.

She pulled herself together with a visible effort. "You're Special Agent Duran?"

"Yes." I crossed the room and we shook. "This is—"

I turned to introduce Portier, but he was gone.

The doctor had already moved to the body and begun to work. I'd been at a few crime scenes. I knew the drill. So did Dr. Sylvester. For a small-town ME, she was very good. Of course, lately she'd had a lot of practice.

While she did her job, I did mine. I'd been trained in crime scene investigation, though usually I came in after the techs had done their thing. In the case of Devil's Fork, there were no techs. Luckily I'd located all the gadgetry needed to do the deed myself behind Brody's desk.

I didn't find one damn thing—not a fingerprint, not a hair.

"Just like the other ones." Dr. Sylvester removed her plastic gloves. "You?"

"Same," I agreed.

"Different manner of death. Haven't had a head shot yet." She bit her lip. "That sounded so callous. To do this job I have to treat them like strangers. But Marcus—"

"You were friends?" She nodded, and her mouth trembled. "I'm sorry. He seemed like a good guy."

"He was. We went to high school together. He was wild then, caused his parents no end of trouble. But he straightened out nicely, and he was a good cop."

"I'll find out who did this," I said. "But I'll need some help. What can you tell me?"

"Not much. The wound on the doll is consistent with the wound on the victim."

"Same gun?"

"Most likely. But we won't be able to prove it."

"Why?"

"No bullet."

I blinked. "What?"

"You didn't see that on the other reports?"

"I didn't get the chance to go over them very closely."

"There's no bullet—at least not in the body. There's one in the doll, but without another to match it to I'd have a hard time stating anything conclusive."

I recalled the voodoo dolls I'd examined. There'd been a needle in the dolls, but no knives at the murder scenes. I guess it would follow that there was no bullet and no gun. Still . . .

"How can there be no bullet?"

"Your guess is as good as mine. There are powder burns on his skin, as if someone pushed the gun right up to his head." She stopped and took several deep breaths with her eyes closed. When she opened them again, she seemed determined to do what had to be done. "But no bullet."

"You got any theories, Doctor?"

She lifted a brow. "Voodoo?"

"According to the local voodoo king, voodoo dolls aren't voodoo."

"So I hear. I was being facetious. It's a bad habit of mine. I'm afraid I don't have any theories, Special Agent Duran. These people are being murdered, and there isn't a clue to be had beyond those dolls. I don't envy you your job."

I didn't envy me, either.

"I'll call the funeral home," the doctor said. "Have the body transported."

"Funeral home?" I asked. "Where?"

"In town. We don't have a hospital, so there isn't a morgue." She glanced at her watch. "I'll do the autopsy right away. You'll have my report by noon."

She pulled out her cell phone and made arrangements for the body. I waited until Brody was bagged and removed and the doctor on her way before I locked up using Brody's keys, then went looking for Portier.

Three AM and I should be dragging. Instead I was hopped up on adrenaline and curiosity. I'd never had a case like this.

Most murders are cut-and-dried. If it isn't the husband or the boyfriend, the culprit is someone the victim knows. Even with serial killers there's a pattern, and that's how we catch them.

Sure, sometimes it's just dumb luck, like Dahmer. No one even knew they had a serial killer operating in Milwaukee. The only reason Jeff got caught was because one of his victims escaped and ran down the street naked, dangling a pair of handcuffs from his wrist as he flagged down the cops.

That case was a complete and forever embarrassment to the hallowed halls of law enforcement.

The problem in Devil's Fork lay in the lack of a pattern beyond the voodoo dolls, not to mention the lack of evidence, beyond said voodoo dolls. I had no case.

Then again, if this job were easy everyone would do it.

For the first time in a long time I was interested in something; I wanted to find this guy bad. It felt personal, though I knew I couldn't let it be. Still, I'd liked Brody, and it pissed me off to see a good man in a body bag. Hell, it pissed me off to see anyone in a body bag who hadn't died in bed at the age of 106.

I left the sheriff's office and crossed the street to the voodoo shop. A quick glance at the crossroads revealed only the empty hole I'd uncovered.

I spent a few minutes going over the crime scene and

found nothing. Though even if there'd been something, it would have been suspect. Anything could have blown into the area while I'd been gone.

I should have secured the place, but I'd been a little distracted with Brody, and I hadn't had anyone to back me up. Alone, I could only do what I could do.

The streets were empty. Sure it was the middle of the night, but I was beginning to wonder if there was anyone in town besides me, Portier, and Miss Henson. I wouldn't blame people for leaving, and it did make crowd control easier. Not one gawker had arrived at the sheriff's office. I wasn't used to that.

The CLOSED sign hung in the front window of the shop. I went around the side, searching for a door that led to Portier's apartment. The backyard was protected by a six-foot-high plank fence. I would have thought Portier was hiding something, except the gate swung right open.

I found myself in a garden of trees. Many were species I'd never seen before, though I recognized a palm, a weeping willow, an elm. Each was decorated with ribbons of different shades and had candles, unlit at present, around their base. This guy had a thing for candles.

In the center stood a fountain, the faint trickle of water peaceful in the fading light of the rapidly descending moon. Nearby there appeared to be a fire pit with an iron bar stuck in the middle.

A kind of lean-to—it was tin-roofed, with a single open side—had been built against the opposite wall. The floor was dirt, the center post a tree trunk set in concrete and painted all the colors of the rainbow. A rawhide whip hung from the top.

"Seen enough?"

Crap. Busted.

Chapter 5

Portier leaned in the doorway of the store—shirtless, barefoot, with the top button of his black pants undone. I nearly swallowed my tongue.

The moon shone over the tops of the trees just enough to wash the planes of his chest in silver. I wouldn't think working as a shopkeeper would hone the biceps and belly quite like that.

He lifted his arm, and I had to fight not to gape as muscles rippled and flexed when he lifted a glass to his lips and sipped.

"I suppose you need to ask me all sorts of questions." The slight slur of his *s*'s told me he was well on his way to being smashed. I had to wonder why. Did he know something? Had he done something? Or did he merely drink every night since his sister died?

Sympathy welled—I understood how far a person would go to forget the pain of loss—and I fought to get myself under control. I'd come here to question this man, and question him I would. It didn't matter if I wanted to lick him from stomach to sternum. I couldn't. I wouldn't.

"What is this?" I indicated the lean-to. My voice came out hoarse, as if I'd been shouting for hours.

He pushed away from the door and moved toward me with that smooth gait I'd marked before. He looked as if he were skating along the top of the grass.

"A temple," he said.

"And the whip?"

"A symbol. To remind followers of their origins as slaves."

As if anyone could forget.

"What do you do here?"

"Sacrifice goats."

I tilted my head, watching as he took another sip of what appeared to be whiskey. "Seriously?"

"When you ask the loa for a favor, an offering is required. The bigger the favor, the bigger the offering."

I narrowed my eyes, and he rolled his. "You think I'm killing people as an offering to the loa?"

I hadn't, but I kept quiet and let him continue. Never knew what you might find out that way.

"Contrary to most horror movies," Portier said, "voodoo practitioners do not perform human sacrifice."

"But if you did," I murmured, "imagine what kind of a favor you could ask."

His eyebrows arched; he took another sip from his glass before coming closer—a lot closer. He was trying to intimidate me with his size, his nearness, his lack of clothes. I wasn't going to let him. I refused to move even when he crowded so near, I felt the heat pouring off his bare skin like a bonfire.

He smelled like spruce needles—an oddity here, much more common to my childhood home—most likely from the candles he seemed to burn everywhere, or perhaps incense, even cologne. But why spruce?

I found myself taking a deep whiff, drawn to the scent, caught unaware by a wave of nostalgia that left me a little dizzy. My father had dragged a spruce tree home every Christmas.

I stared into Portier's eyes—dark, endless—I couldn't look away even when I began to get a crick in my neck. A little dazed by his heat, if not his body, his face, the mere fact that he was a man and I hadn't had one in a very long time, I swayed.

"What could I possibly want," he whispered, "that would be worth someone's life?"

"Your sister back?"

I'd expected him to laugh. Instead, he kissed me.

He tasted of whiskey and fury. I wasn't sure what to do. I'd had suspects try to punch me. One had even tried to shoot me. None had ever kissed me. Of course, I'd never let anyone get this close.

Why on earth had I let him?

I was attracted. Who wouldn't be? But I knew better. I should not have questioned Portier here. I should never have questioned him alone—though in Devil's Fork I didn't have much choice. I definitely should not have needled him until he kissed me, and I absolutely *should not* have kissed him back.

At the first touch of his lips I gasped, but that only gave him access to my mouth. His tongue plunged within, met mine, and began to stroke.

A soft thud at my feet made me start, but his hands grasped my elbows, pulling me onto my toes, crushing my chest to his.

In the small sane corner that was left of my mind I understood that his having both hands free meant he'd dropped the whiskey. The glass had thudded to the ground, probably splashing alcohol all over my ugly black shoes.

The next second that last little corner of sanity was obliterated as the heat from his bare skin seeped through both my jacket and my blouse. I hadn't even realized I was cold. I wanted to burrow in and absorb everything—the warmth, the scent, the taste of him.

My hands were in his hair, tugging him closer, the soft dark strands cascading over my wrists, sliding along my palms as I cupped his head and tilted him just right so I could suck on his tongue.

He groaned, the hum vibrating against my mouth; my breasts, crushed against his chest, tingled from the rumbling sensation. I wished I were as naked as he so I could rub myself all over him.

His fingers left my arms and skated down my rib cage, pausing momentarily for his thumbs to slide between us, making one pass over my hardened nipples before moving to my waist and yanking me tightly against him. I gave in to the madness and flexed my hips, pressing us together intimately.

I saw stars behind my closed eyelids. It had been ages since I'd had anything pressed against that part of me except me.

As suddenly as Portier had grabbed me, he let go. We'd been plastered so tightly together the loss of his support left me flailing. I nearly fell on my ass, and wouldn't that have been special?

Portier stared at me as if seeing me for the first time. He seemed almost shocked, and I wasn't sure why. *He* had kissed *me*. I should be the one who was shocked, but I couldn't work up any emotion beyond a desire for more of the same.

"What the hell was that?" I demanded.

The sound of my voice seemed to bring him out of whatever state he was in. The shocked expression vanished, and his usual slightly disdainful demeanor returned. "Don't tell me you've never been kissed."

I scowled. "That was a lot more than a kiss."

He shrugged in a manner I could only call French, which—after that kiss—wasn't surprising.

"Why did you do it?"

I hadn't meant to ask. I wasn't sure what I wanted him to say. That he'd been overcome with lust? That he'd been unable to exist another minute without touching me? That the taste of my lips had ruined him for anyone else? I was an idiot. Of course being kissed as if she were the last living woman on a nuked-out planet could turn any girl's head to mush.

"I wanted you to shut up," he muttered.

"You kissed me to make me shut up," I repeated. "A simple *shut up* would have sufficed."

"Would it?" He spread those gorgeous hands, and I became distracted by how very much I wanted to feel them all over my body. "I doubt that."

He was right. I'd come here—to Devil's Fork as well as his walled garden—for a reason. I had a job to do, and questioning him was a part of it.

I tried to remember what I'd asked him right before he'd kissed me, but my brain was still fuzzy. *Damn him.*

"You asked if I was committing human sacrifice to bring my sister back."

"You read minds?" I asked.

"I read people, faces. It's a gift."

One I wished I had. It would come in handy during interrogations—like now.

He bent to retrieve the fallen glass, his face so close to my thigh that his breath warmed me. I inched away as he glanced up.

"Bringing the dead back to life," I said, and my voice cracked. "Wouldn't that be a zombie?"

"Theoretically."

"And aren't zombies a voodoo thing?"

"Yes." He straightened, towering over me again. "But I prefer a dead sister to an undead one."

"You say that as if it could happen."

"There is more to this earth than you know," he repeated. And we were right back where we'd started earlier.

Portier no longer seemed drunk. Had he been faking his inebriation in an attempt to get me to leave without questioning him? He'd have to try a lot harder.

"You admit sacrifices are a part of the voodoo experience," I pressed.

"Coffee. Rum. Tobacco. The loa are peaceful." He frowned and stared into his empty glass. "For the most part."

"Couldn't someone who isn't quite right in the head"—in my opinion almost everyone—"twist voodoo into something sinister?"

"It's always a possibility."

"I'll need your client list."

Portier shrugged. "Sure."

"You aren't going to give me crap about privacy?"

"I'm not running a hospital or even a library."

True, though I'd found that most people got pissy about turning over records.

"Follow me."

I glanced up; Portier was already heading into the building. Just inside the back door a staircase led upward, presumably to his living quarters. A shadow of movement made me jerk to the right, only to confront my own image in a mirror.

Mouth swollen, my pale skin scraped by his dark beard, and my shoulder-length hair mussed from his fingers, I looked as if I'd just climbed out of bed and thrown on my clothes after a long, luscious afternoon's delight.

Before I could think too long about my inappropriate behavior, I headed down the short hallway that led into the shop.

Candles blazed everywhere. I hadn't noticed any light in here before, but Portier hadn't had time to run around with a match.

On the counter sat an open bottle of whiskey next to a framed photograph. I didn't have to ask to know the woman in the picture was Jill, his twin sister.

Despite being fraternal twins, the resemblance was marked. The same silky black hair, fine blade of a nose, and dark, heavily lashed eyes. Even their lips were the same, though she smiled with genuine joy, and I couldn't recall his ever smiling with anything other than sardonic amusement.

Portier set his glass next to the bottle, reached for it, then hesitated, hand hovering open, thumb and forefinger framing the neck.

I froze, half in the hall, half in the shop, as he lowered his hand and brushed one fingertip over the photograph. The muscles rippled across his shoulders as his whole body seemed to tense. He took a deep breath, letting it out slowly as if coming to a decision.

"This is all my fault," he said.

Chapter 6

"How you figure?" I inched closer, my hand creeping toward my shoulder holster. I hadn't expected a confession, but if he wanted to give one . . .

"I brought him over."

I paused. Brought whom? From where? For what?

"I didn't mean to."

Suddenly Portier turned, and the speed of the movement had me drawing my gun, pointing it at him. Extreme déjà vu.

He didn't even look at the weapon. "I was trying to help her, to save her."

His sister. "What did you do?"

"I—" His voice broke. He turned away.

"Keep your hands where I can see them," I said.

"You think I care if you kill me? I'm dead anyway." He poured a shot into his glass and downed it in a single swallow. "Or at least damned."

"You're going to have to be more specific."

He faced me again. "Just the facts?"

Sometimes I swore he could read my mind as well as my face.

"Tell me what happened, Julian."

His eyebrows lifted at my use of his first name, but after the tongue tango, why bother with Mr. and Ms.?

"I can do things," he said.

"Everyone can do things."

"Not like this. I—" He spread his hands in front of him, staring at them as if they were brand new and fascinating. "I have powers."

I'd heard this already from Miss Henson. I hadn't believed it any more then than I did now. Either Portier didn't recognize my skepticism or he didn't care, because he kept right on talking.

"That's why I went searching for our past. I could always do what defied logic. I knew what I couldn't possibly know. Once I found out about our roots, it made more sense, and I began to study, to refine my power and increase it. I tried to save Jill with what I had, but it wasn't enough."

I had a bad feeling I was going to hear some bad things. Like human sacrifice, despite his earlier denials. I had to face the possibility that Julian Portier was crazy. Which was a sad damn waste of a beautiful man.

"First I appealed to Papa Legba; he's my met tet—like a guardian angel. He's the gatekeeper to the spirit world, so it would make sense that he would be mine."

"Why's that?"

"*Portier* means 'gatekeeper.' I've always been able to speak with him and gain his blessing on all that I ask. Until . . ."

"You asked him to save Jill."

Head down, he nodded. "Papa Legba is a rada spirit, one of light and life. He couldn't help me. Or maybe he wouldn't."

"Some things aren't meant to be changed."

"Fate," he spat, his head coming up, his eyes blazing. "I couldn't accept that. So I did what I'd sworn I wouldn't. I called on Kalfou."

He poured another whiskey, but instead of drinking it he merely swirled the liquid around in the glass. "Kalfou is a petro spirit, the dark side of Legba. He brings chaos. He's the way through which fate can be thwarted."

"How did you call him?"

"Black magic."

At my skeptical expression, Portier released a sharp breath—both exhaustion and annoyance. "Voodoo is about balance. Life–death. Good–evil. White–black. The rada spirits are essentially good. They're protective and passive, while the petro spirits are dark, dangerous, and violent. But they aren't evil."

"Dark, dangerous, and violent sounds evil to me."

"Petro spirits make things happen. They're most often consulted in times of great need, and they specialize in magic."

"I still don't see how any of this is your fault."

"I asked Papa Legba to heal Jill. She only got worse, and I got desperate. I'd learned black magic when I'd learned white, although I swore never to use it."

"Then why learn it?"

"Only someone who knows the dark side can have any hope of resisting it."

"You truly believed that magic could save your sister?"

"Nothing else could." He studied me for a minute. "Don't you believe in magic, Dana?"

"No."

"Really?" He flicked his hand at the ceiling, and a chill wind whistled through the back door. Every candle went out.

I clutched the gun two-handed, waiting for him to take it away. I should have cuffed him when I had the chance.

A sharp click and the electric lights flared. Portier still stood in front of me. A quick glance revealed that no one stood anywhere near the switch.

"How do you explain that?" he asked.

"I can't, though I wouldn't call it magic."

"And this?" He waved his hand in a sweeping semicircle; every candle flared to life.

I still wasn't convinced. "You can buy candles that won't blow out."

He shook his head, then closed his eyes, stretching out his arms, palms up. I couldn't help but admire his bare chest. Just because I might have to arrest him didn't mean I didn't want to touch him. I wasn't dead or stupid.

However, as he began to chant in several languages—I caught French, some Latin, and another I didn't recognize—I forgot about his body, his face, that mouth as thunder rumbled overhead and rain began to tumble down, making quite a racket outside in the garden as it struck the tin-roofed temple.

He brought his hands together in a sharp clap and lightning flashed—so close I felt its sizzle—and in the distance something howled. I could have sworn I heard the heavy *thwap* of a large bird's wings.

He clapped again, and the ground shook as the electric bolt struck the metal pole in his garden. My hair seemed to stand on end, and the scent of ozone hung in the air.

"Stop it!"

He opened one eye. "How can I stop what I can't possibly be doing?"

"Fine," I admitted sullenly. "You have some skills."

"Put away the gun, Dana."

"And if I don't?"

His palms came together once, and lightning struck right outside the still-open back door. In that millisecond of illumination I caught sight of something long with a thick triangular head slithering through the grass.

I put away the gun, my palms so sweaty I doubted I'd have been able to fire anyway, let alone hit anything.

Portier muttered several more unidentifiable words, brought his hands to his chest, then spread them out, palms down. The sky stilled, and the rain stopped.

"Brody said strange things happen around you."

He lifted a brow.

"I saw . . ." My gaze went past him to the garden, which appeared empty now.

"Representatives of the loa."

"What's that mean?"

"Each spirit has a symbol. When I call on them, the symbol manifests to help me"—he waved his hand in a vague gesture—"connect."

"Like a familiar?"

"In a way, though a familiar is in the realm of witchcraft—more a partner than a path, which is how I see the manifestations."

"There was a snake." I wrinkled my nose.

"The symbol of Danbala. The loa of wisdom and ancestral knowledge."

"The big bird?"

"A screech owl, which symbolizes Marinette." He paused as if he didn't want to say what he was going to next, but he did. "She's a sorceress, an aide for black magic. Marinette is very dangerous."

"Then why 'connect' with her?"

"She's also extremely powerful. To achieve great things, great risk is sometimes needed." He indicated the sky with one long finger. "The thunder is brought by Ogou Shango, the lightning by Ogou Tonnerre."

"And the howl?"

His gaze flicked to mine. "What howl?"

"Sounded like a wolf, though Brody said there aren't any here."

"Marinette."

"She has two symbols?"

"No. She's the patron loa of werewolves. They call on her for help."

"Werewolves," I repeated. "No way."

He didn't even bother to argue.

Since I had all I could deal with here and now without worrying about a werewolf, I pushed that concern aside and returned to the one right in front of me.

"You said you brought Kalfou out." He nodded. "Of where?"

"The land of the spirits."

"How?"

"I didn't mean to. I didn't even realize I had until you told me you saw him."

"The guy at the crossroads?"

"Yes. The word *kalfou* means 'crossroads.' They're a place of black magic."

"How do you know he was Kalfou? I couldn't see his face."

"Exactly."

Portier moved past me to a bookshelf. He yanked out a volume, rifled through, then laid it on the counter and stabbed a long finger at the page. The being I'd seen at the crossroads peered back at me. Or he would have, if he'd had any eyes.

Kalfou was a dark-clad figure, tall and slim, like any cartoon depiction of Death. However, a cowl didn't hide his face; he didn't have a face. Where it should have been was a silvery white circle of nothingness.

"His symbols are the darkness of night and the pale light of the moon."

I continued to stare at the picture. "Why is he here?"

"He's killing people."

"You said he wasn't evil."

"I know." Portier rubbed his forehead. "Voodoo isn't about human sacrifice, but black magic is something else. It feeds on death." He dropped his hand. "In fact, Jill's death may have opened the gate. Then, in order to stay, Kalfou would need more death to feed the magic."

"What's with the voodoo dolls?"

"Kalfou's a trickster spirit. He likes to create chaos and

confusion. I'm sure he wanted to make as much trouble for me as he could."

"Why?"

"I brought him out; I can put him back."

"How?"

Portier's eyes met mine. "I have no idea."

Swell.

"If black magic released him," I said slowly, "can't black magic return him?"

"I swore never to practice black magic again."

"Because it's evil?"

"Because it didn't work!" he shouted. "She died anyway."

"Something worked, pal. You brought a serial-killing spirit out of the gate, and you're damn well putting him back. What, exactly, did you do?"

Portier drained the whiskey in one swallow, setting his glass back on the counter with a click. "A simple spell, but most of them are. I went to the crossroads beneath the moon, chanted the chant—"

"That's it?"

"And poured the blood into the earth."

My neck prickled. "What blood?"

"Jill's."

"You took enough blood to pour from a dying woman?"

"No. I didn't want to do any of this, but I went to her room and she'd—" He broke off, rubbing a hand over his mouth. "She'd taken the blood herself. Jill was a nurse; she knew she didn't have much time. She begged me . . ." His anguished eyes met mine. "I had to try."

I swallowed, my throat clicking audibly. I understood desperation. "Then what happened?"

"Nothing. Or at least I thought nothing. I did the spell. When I came back, she was gone."

"And people started to die."

"Yes. But I was preoccupied with Jill—the arrangements,

the funeral. By the time I knew what was going on, there'd been two deaths, and the sheriff was questioning me."

"Except you had an alibi for all the murders."

He shrugged. "I've worked every night since she died. I had bills to pay, and I didn't want to be alone."

The way he said it tugged at something in my chest. Once my dad died, my mother worked nonstop. Sure, we'd needed the money, but I didn't think she'd wanted to spend time in the house where he'd died any more than I had.

"If the murders are being committed magically," I said, "then an alibi doesn't mean squat."

"I suppose not." His gaze flicked to mine. "You going to pull your gun again?"

"Maybe later."

What good would a gun do me when the man could call down a thunderstorm or turn on lights and set candles ablaze with a mere flick of his hand? He could no doubt take my gun away without even coming near me. I wondered what else he could do.

"Do you think you can figure out how to put him back?"

"I can try."

"What if you can't?"

"Kalfou will keep killing." Portier's face paled as his lips tightened. "He controls the evil forces of the spirit world. If the gate remains open, they could start to spill out. If they haven't already."

My eyes widened. "You mean there might be more than one out there?"

"If there aren't now, I think there will be."

I crossed the room until I stood in front of the biggest window, then lifted the blinds to reveal the crossroads.

And Kalfou, burying something else.

"Julian!"

He was at my side in an instant. The specter must have sensed us watching, or maybe it merely sensed him, because

Kalfou lifted his head, and the bright silver light of his face was too terrible to behold. I recoiled, and in that instant he disappeared again.

Julian grabbed my arm. "Come on."

Even though I'd seen him disappear, I wasn't taking any chances. I dug in, shaking my head. "He might be out there still."

Julian pointed to the eastern horizon, which glowed pink and red and orange with approaching dawn. "Kalfou is a spirit of darkness. He can't walk beneath the sun."

I certainly hoped he was right. Regardless, we had to go and see whom he'd buried this time, so I followed Julian into the sunrise.

At the crossroads, he dug his beautiful hands into the earth, scooping and dragging until the buried object was revealed.

"No doubt about it," I murmured.

The doll looked just like me.

Chapter 7

Yellow thread for hair, blue embroidery floss for the eyes—I guess the doll could have been anyone, except for the tiny FBI stitched into its chest and the itty-bitty gun holster.

"Wh-why didn't it disappear like the last one?" I left out the part where it reappeared next to me and I died. Or maybe I died and then it appeared. I wasn't quite clear on the order, and right now I didn't much care.

Julian picked up the doll. "Nothing can happen until the moon rises."

"Oh, well that's a relief. I get to live another day."

His hand clenched on the doll. My ribs protested as if I'd been the recipient of a particularly painful bear hug.

"Hey!" I clutched my middle and Portier released it. The thing fell to the ground—on her head. I suddenly needed an aspirin in the worst way.

"Give me that!" I snatched the figure up, cradling it carefully.

"I guess we'd better not destroy it," he murmured.

"Guess not."

Julian glanced at the sky. "We've got about eleven hours.

I'll figure this out." He brushed a knuckle across my cheek. "Trust me?"

What choice did I have?

"I don't see a cause of death." I turned the doll over carefully, swallowing against the sudden pitch and dip of the world.

"We can't worry about that now."

He was right, and I wasn't sure I wanted to know how I was going to die anyway. It was bad enough knowing when.

We returned to the voodoo shop, pulled all the blinds, and locked the place up tight. Not that any lock would stop Kalfou, but we didn't want any interruptions. No clients, no browsers; I even turned off my phone. Nothing from the outside was going to help us. For the rest of today, there'd be only Julian and me.

Until sundown, and Kalfou, came.

I set the voodoo doll on a bare shelf in the storeroom, far enough away from everything that I hoped it wouldn't get bumped or knocked to the floor. When I returned to the main room, Julian was on the phone.

At my curious expression, he held up a hand. "Yes, Cassandra, Kalfou. Uh-huh. Okay. I'll try." He hung up.

"Cassandra, the New Orleans voodoo priestess?"

"She's had some experience with black magic."

"Then why doesn't she come and put him back where he belongs?"

"Only the one who released him can return him."

"Figures."

"She said I need to find balance. The opposite of what brought him out should put him back."

Julian went to his bookshelves and began to yank volumes free. Moments later he set a stack of books on the counter. "Go through those."

"And look for what?"

"A reversal spell. Any mention at all of black magic, crossroads, or Kalfou."

"Okay." Seemed simple enough.

It wasn't. The hours clicked away as if the day were on fast forward. Every time I looked at the clock, expecting that ten minutes had passed, I'd lost an hour.

Julian divided his time between notebooks filled with page after page of sprawling handwriting and phone calls to other voodoo masters.

With dusk only an hour away he slammed the phone into the cradle. "What's the opposite of blood? Water? Dust? Earth?"

"I don't know."

"No one else does, either." He ran a hand over his face. "I don't know what to do."

His voice was so dejected, I moved across the floor and touched his shoulder. "We'll keep searching. We'll find something, and when we do, you'll stop him."

"Sounds like you really believe that."

"I have to."

He leaned down and brushed our lips together. One touch brought back the mad, passionate embrace we'd shared in the garden. I wanted to explore all that he made me feel, but there wasn't time.

Our breath mingled; softly he kissed me, then rested his forehead against mine. His hair sifted across my cheek, and I shivered. "You don't even seem scared," he whispered.

"What good would it do?"

"I want to spend weeks getting to know you." He pressed his mouth to my cheek. "In every way there is to know."

I wanted to sink into him and forget everything, but I couldn't. I inched back, and for a second he clung. "If I'm still alive tomorrow," I said, "I just might let you."

He smiled, though the expression didn't reach his eyes. "Give me a book."

We continued to search, but we didn't find. We had only half an hour until sunset, and we were no farther along than we'd been that morning.

"I could do the spell backward," he muttered.

"How do you get the blood out of the earth?"

"Hell."

I walked around the shop, needing to move after sitting so long. When I reached the shelf that held the voodoo doll, I stared at the figure for several seconds. An idea began to form.

"What if"—I faced Julian—"we make a doll like him and destroy it?"

"Voodoo dolls aren't voodoo."

"According to you they're witchcraft, but so what? Kalfou's using them, and if Kalfou can kill people using those dolls, why can't you kill him the same way?"

"Why can't I?" he repeated.

"Oh, hell!" I exclaimed.

"What?" Julian put himself between me and the door. "Did you see him?"

"The sun's still up. I was just thinking about the technicalities—we don't have time to run around buying cloth and thread to make a doll." My exuberance died.

Julian grabbed my hand. "Come with me."

On the second floor lay several doors. He passed the first two and opened the third, then ushered me in.

I stood in the center and turned a slow circle, my smile widening at the piles of cloth, the spools of thread. "Your sister liked to sew."

"It was the one thing she could do when she was sick," Julian said. "Can you sew?"

"No, but I doubt I'm going to be graded for the evenness of my stitches. Let's just throw this thing together."

Julian cut the body out of black cotton. We stuffed it with scraps, and I slashed the ends together as quickly as I could. When I was done, the doll resembled a puffy gingerbread man that had been left in the oven too long.

"Here." Julian held out a tiny round piece of shiny silver cloth, which I attached where the face should be.

"Good enough?" I asked.

Beyond the glass, the sun slipped below the horizon with a near-audible pop. Shadows spread like bony fingers across the streets of Devil's Fork.

"It'll have to be," Julian murmured.

He led me from Jill's sewing room into a bedroom farther down the hall. I could tell from the decor it wasn't his sister's.

We had a perfect bird's-eye view of the crossroads. Kalfou stared into the empty hole, then his head tilted upward, an empty silver glow where his face should have been.

Julian moved, drawing my attention from the window. A single wave of his hand, and the foot of the Kalfou doll caught fire. The flame sputtered and went out.

Cursing, he grabbed a book of matches off his nightstand—I was surprised he had any in the building—then tried to light the other foot. Nothing happened.

"Here." I handed him the needle I'd used to make the doll.

He stabbed the thing repeatedly. One look out the window revealed that Kalfou hadn't felt a thing.

I took my gun out of the holster. Five bullets later, the doll was toast; Kalfou wasn't.

A giggle trilled around the room—eerie, disembodied—I wanted to slap my hands over my ears but had a feeling it wouldn't help.

The laughter stopped and words whispered through my head: "You can't kill what isn't alive."

"Son of a bitch," Julian growled, and threw the doll into the trash.

I peered out the window, wondering what Kalfou would do next. I didn't have long to wait. The specter of death made a single slashing movement with one bony arm, and a silver glow permeated the room. When it faded, the doll that had been on the shelf downstairs lay on Julian's bed.

"Dana." Julian took my shoulders, turning me away from the sight, but I was transfixed, my head swiveling so that I could see the doll—waiting for the means of death to be revealed.

Then Julian kissed me. At first my eyes stayed wide open, but he put some effort into it, nibbling the tense line, licking the tight seam, then sweeping his tongue inside when my eyes drifted closed as my body began to respond. The adrenaline from the fear seemed to be morphing into a burning case of lust.

What the hell? I thought. *Might as well die happy.*

I wrapped my arms around him, rubbed my breasts against his chest, and pressed my stomach to his growing erection. His palms cupped my hips, urging me on.

The horrific scream had us stumbling apart, staring at each other wide-eyed, before we dived for the window. Outside Kalfou seemed to be melting, weaving like a snake as he shrank toward the ground.

"What's happening?" I whispered.

"I don't know. We kissed and touched and he—" Julian frowned. "Wait. Let me think." He turned away and began to pace. "Black magic feeds on death. Death brought him to life. So if we reverse that, life would bring him death."

"I don't understand."

"Sex is life."

"Maybe for you."

He shot me an exasperated look. "Think about it, Dana. When people believe they're going to die"—he motioned between us—"they have sex to reaffirm their life. Sex is meant to *create* life."

He made an excellent argument.

Julian glanced out the window. "He's getting back up."

I shoved in next to him. Kalfou rose like an inflatable evil spirit.

I grabbed Julian's face and planted one right on his mouth as I slid my hand into his pants and stroked him. Kalfou started screaming again.

I became distracted by the way Julian swelled and

hardened in my palm. By the time I pulled my mouth from his and checked the window, Kalfou was a puddle. At least he'd stopped shrieking.

"Let me get this straight," I said, leaving my hand right where it was as I continued to stroke him. "Having sex will put the evil serial-killing bastard back where he came from?"

"That's the theory." Julian's teeth clenched and un-clenched, making the line of his jaw so taut I wanted to lick it.

"Works for me," I said, and yanked him onto the bed.

Chapter 8

I landed on the doll and without thought shoved it over the edge and onto the floor. She hit her head; I didn't get a headache. Seemed like we were on the right track.

Desperate for both each other and an end to this madness, we tore at our clothes, tossing them every which way until we were both naked. Then I indulged my fantasy, running my tongue not only along the sharp line of his jaw but down the cords of his neck, over the spike of his collarbone, then lower still.

His skin was perfect, smooth and tan everywhere. I became fascinated with the pale line of my fingers drifting over him.

"We should—" he began, reaching for me.

I evaded his grasp. I didn't plan to rush. As long as we were having sex, Kalfou wasn't going anywhere. I might never have another chance, dead or alive, and I meant to make the most of it.

I ran my tongue across his belly, dipping it into his navel, then scoring his hip with my teeth. He stopped talking on a moan and tangled his fingers in my hair.

His penis brushed my cheek and I turned, licking the tip. His hand tightened; the world seemed to pause, breathless, as I took him in my mouth.

He was already hard, throbbing. From his response I figured he hadn't had sex in nearly as long as I had. With his sister ill and then dying, that was understandable. I wanted very badly to give him some joy.

His long fingers stroked my scalp; his thumb caressed my chin and cheek. I increased the rhythm until his hands fell away.

My lips curved against him. I'd never felt such power. Suddenly I could understand the pull of magic, however black.

"Dana," he managed. "Wait."

I didn't want to; I wanted him to lose control just once, but he had other ideas.

He flipped me onto my back, pinning my arms above my head as his body covered mine. "I have to remember the spell," he muttered. "You aren't letting me think."

The spell. Right. This was magic. I moaned as his lips found my nipple. In more ways than one.

He wouldn't let me touch him, though I tugged on my wrists and begged. Instead he touched me with his mouth, his tongue and teeth, his body. By the time he released my hands so he could move lower, I couldn't have lifted them from the mattress even if I'd wanted to.

He performed clever machinations that had me gasping, perched on the edge of orgasm, then falling away.

"Julian." I yanked on his hair and he lifted his head, gazing lazily up my body before turning to press his open mouth to my thigh.

"Relax."

"Relax?" I laughed. "I don't think so."

He laughed, too, the first laughter I'd heard from him. That we could do so in the middle of such horror—although the horror outside seemed far away—amazed me.

Julian fell onto his back next to me. "Time to get down to business."

I leaned my head on my hand. "You remember the spell?"

He nodded and opened his arms. I went into them gladly, and after a long, deep kiss he rolled so that I straddled him. "I'm afraid you'll have to do the work," he murmured.

"I don't mind." I lowered myself onto him and began to ride.

He chanted the spell—backward? Forward? I had no idea—in that odd combination I'd heard once before, French, Latin, and a language I didn't recognize but assumed was something out of Haiti. A kind of guttural French that, when spoken in his deep, mythical voice, made my toes tingle.

Or maybe the tingle was just him. With Julian inside me I felt complete for the first time in years, perhaps for the first time ever. Foolish, really; I barely knew the man. Certainly I'd felt a kinship because we'd both lost people we loved to tragedy. I could understand why he'd done what he'd done. We all do crazy things for love.

The moon peeked through the window, turning his black hair to sparkling silver. He continued to chant the mysterious words, eyes closed as he focused, body, mind, and soul.

His hands on my waist seemed to grow warmer; when he moved them, static electricity sparked with a muted pop. I started, moving harder against him, taking him deeper than I'd ever taken anyone. In the distance thunder rumbled, and the earth seemed to shake.

His gaze met mine and my chest lurched. He was staring at me as if he meant this, and suddenly I felt as if I meant it, too.

He sat up, folding me into his arms and flexing his hips. Pulling me close, he continued to murmur the spell against my hair like an endearment.

Lightning crackled right over the shop, or maybe the crossroads. An inhuman shriek had us both freezing, then falling silent as we scrambled out of bed and ran to the window.

Kalfou was a puddle of darkness in the silvery light. But as we watched, the puddle shimmered and began to take form.

"We have to finish this," Julian said.

He kissed me, hard, and I responded in kind, my body vibrating with the need for release. He broke the kiss, leaned his forehead against mine, and took several deep breaths. "I need to say the words."

"Okay." I began to move back to the bed, but he grabbed my hand, spun me around until I faced the window, then shoved my hair away from my neck and licked my nape.

I shivered, and he began to chant once more, even as he urged me to lean against the windowsill so he could slip into me from behind.

My sexual experience was adequate, though sparse of late, but I'd never been taken like this. What I'd always thought would feel submissive instead felt empowering. I wasn't on my back but on my feet and, if the break in his words was any indication, he was nearly undone. I could feel him shudder, on the brink of orgasm, so tense, so ready and ripe, all because of me.

His hands at my hips, he withdrew to the tip, then plunged inside. I arched, taking more of him, the slap of skin against skin an enticement, an encouragement, an epiphany. There was something here that went beyond sex, something I wanted to explore.

If I lived.

"Look," he whispered, and I lifted my head, watching the shadowy specter of the two of us reflected in the glass—his dark hair tumbling over my pale shoulder, my blond locks next to his black eyes. We resembled a sepia painting that began to run as rain tumbled down the windowpane.

He draped himself over me, his chest to my shoulders as he gathered me close. I turned my head, rubbing my face against his rough cheek as, shuddering, he came. One long finger stroked me, and that was all I needed to come, too.

My legs wobbled. He held me up, held me close. "Look," he said again, and this time I knew he didn't mean at us.

Lightning stuck the crossroads, and a fissure opened in the ground. Bright white light spilled out. What was left of Kalfou, a puddle of dark goo, was sucked into the earth so fast it seemed the whole world played on fast forward. The crack sealed up as if it had never even been.

"Whoa," I said.

Julian released me, and I had to grab at the windowsill for support. "Let's go."

I turned, and he tossed my clothes at me even as he shoved his feet into his pants and shrugged a shirt over his shoulders. Barefoot, hand in hand, we ran down the stairs and into the rain.

The violent storm had passed; the wind gone gentle now, and warm. We were soaked to the skin in seconds but it felt good, like a new beginning.

Together we stood at the crossroads. The ground wasn't marked in any way. No dark burn from the lightning. Not a ghost of a crack. Most amazing of all, there wasn't even an indentation where the hole had been. The earth had healed itself as if nothing had ever happened.

Except it had. There were seven people dead. How was I going to explain that?

"We did it," Julian said.

I almost laughed at the dual meaning to the words. We'd definitely done it.

Then he kissed me and any desire to laugh fled. I tasted rain and Julian. I wanted him all over again. This time just for us.

Our clothes were plastered to our skin. When I wrapped my palms around his biceps, all I felt was heat and the slick slide of fabric against flesh. From the way he deepened the kiss, his hands running over me, too, I knew he wanted the same thing.

I lifted my lips from his. "Anyone could—"

"No one's out here but us, Dana." He turned his face to the sky and opened his mouth, letting the rain tumble in.

He was right. The storm would keep people indoors, although the residents of Devil's Fork didn't seem to wander the streets much at night. Considering what had been happening lately, I couldn't blame them.

I didn't want to go inside. The rain felt so fresh. The night seemed so . . . ours. I tugged Julian into the cover of the trees and sank to the ground.

He stared at me, considering. I tilted my head, wondering at the sheen of silver that surrounded him. I leaned to the side, pondering the cloudy sky and the nearly full orb.

"Why can I see the moon during a rainstorm?"

He joined me on the ground. "Magic." He touched my lips to his. "I call it a voodoo moon."

"Because?"

"I brightened it just for you."

I found that both sweet and sexy. No one had brightened a moon for me before.

We were already soaked; soon we were muddy, too. Rolling around, kissing, touching, laughing like kids. I couldn't ever remember being this free.

He rose above me, the moon at his back, water dripping from his hair, his face, onto me. He filled his hands with my breasts, the slick slide of wet skin on wet skin glorious in the heat of the night.

This time when we came, we came together, face-to-face, staring into each other's eyes, and something happened. A connection. The kind that could last forever.

Huh. Hadn't expected that. I guess facing supernatural

death and saving each other with sex just might forge a bond. At least for me.

When the last tremors died, he kissed me once more and stared into my face with a solemn expression. "I swore I'd never use black magic again. Opening yourself to it changes a person."

I touched his face. "I'm sorry."

"No." He shook his head, and droplets fell upon me like rain. "Don't be. I'd do anything to save you."

I got all warm and fuzzy. "Thanks. But there's something I don't understand." I ran my hand over his hip, and his eyebrows shot up. "No blood, no death, no sacrifice—how is this black magic?"

His eyebrows shot back down. "You've got a point. This was more magic of the white variety. Which I guess would be the opposite of black."

Julian's expression lightened. "Whatever we did, we put Kalfou back where he belongs, and I don't ever plan to let him, or anything like him, out again."

"Amen," I muttered.

We dressed, then headed for the voodoo shop and hopefully a shower. As I stepped out of the cover of the trees, my gaze fell on the undisturbed ground. Suddenly I remembered what I'd come here for in the first place.

"What am I going to tell my boss?" I asked.

A shadow fell over the crossroads, seeming to blot out the moonlight. "I believe I may be able to help you with that."

Chapter 9

I gasped and reached for my weapon, but I wasn't wearing a bra, let alone a shoulder holster.

Julian moved in front of me, blotting out the light. "Who are you?" he demanded.

"My name is Edward Mandenauer. I must say your magic is quite impressive, Portier."

I scowled and moved to Julian's side. "How long have you been here?"

The tall, skeletal old man—he had to be at least eighty—lifted faded blond brows toward his thinning white hair. "Long enough." He sniffed, eyeing my muddy attire and tangled hair.

I crossed my arms over my chest as my cheeks burned. My soaked white blouse left little to the imagination.

"You aren't from here," Julian said.

That would have been obvious even without the heavy German accent that slowed the man's speech and made him seem as if he were from not only another place but another time as well. After what had happened in Devil's Fork, that observation wasn't as odd as it sounded.

"I am not," the old man agreed.

"Why are you spying on us?" I demanded.

"Ah, spying." His face took on an expression of fond nostalgia. "I haven't done that in years. I didn't think I'd miss it so."

"Listen, Mr.—" I couldn't remember what he'd called himself. I'd been a little distracted by his mere existence.

"Mandenauer." He gave a short, sharp bow. I half expected him to click his heels.

"Mandenauer," I repeated. "What are you doing here?"

"Observing you. This has been a test."

I opened my mouth, shut it again. I wasn't sure what to say to that.

"I needed to discover if you had the gifts you would need to join my secret society."

The guy was whacked. Why did I have all the luck?

"Okay." I reached for Julian's hand. "Well, nice meeting you. We've got to go now."

"You think I'm insane." The words weren't a question, so I didn't answer. "You wouldn't be the first. However, I'm not the one who saw an evil spirit and then put him into the earth."

My eyes narrowed. "If you've been here that long, why didn't you do something?"

"It was for you to do or not to do."

"This wasn't real?" I glanced at Julian, but he appeared as confused as I was.

"Oh, it was real," Mandenauer said. "We just sent you instead of one of my trained operatives."

"Who's we?"

"Your boss and I."

"My boss knows about this?"

"Well, not everything. He knows I want you for my group, which is top secret and elite."

"What kind of group are we talking about?"

"We are called the *Jäger-Suchers*."

"Hunter-Searchers," Julian murmured.

The old man's eyes narrowed. "You know of us?"

"I know German."

"Mmm," Mandenauer said, though he didn't appear convinced. "We hunt monsters."

"A serial-killing unit?" I asked. Why hadn't I heard of it?

"Not those kind of monsters. Real ones."

"Real monsters. Isn't that an oxymoron?"

"Not in my world."

I snorted.

"You've just seen an evil spirit take form and commit mass murder, yet you scoff at the existence of monsters. Your lover can call down a storm, speak to the spirits, and command the moon; he can give form to a being that had none, yet you don't believe in the supernatural."

"I didn't say that."

"Haven't you been feeling confined, Dana—a bit bored? Haven't you been wondering if there isn't more you can do to make a difference? Join me and you can."

I remained silent. I didn't know what to make of all this. In the past few hours so much had changed, including me.

"So I passed your test, and I'm not getting fired for sleeping with a suspect?" That alone seemed too good to be true.

"*Jäger-Suchers* are expected to do anything to get the job done." Mandenauer glanced at Julian with a twist of his thin lips. "Or anyone."

Julian's hand jerked in mine, and I tightened my grip. "I didn't know any of this five minutes ago," I said softly. "We did what we did together to put Kalfou back . . . wherever it was that he went."

"And the second time?" Mandenauer asked.

I lifted my chin. "That was just for us."

Julian pulled away. "I'll leave you two to talk."

"Wait," I said. But he was already gone.

The rain had stopped; the clouds blew away. The moon shone brightly across Lafayette Street. Julian went into the voodoo shop and shut the door. I wanted to run after him, and I would, as soon as I figured out what was going on.

"You showed more courage, more initiative, than any candidate I've observed in years," Mandenauer said.

"What if I'd cut and run? Or degenerated into a gibbering idiot after seeing Kalfou?"

"Then you would never survive as a *Jäger-Sucher*."

"Obviously. But what about the people here? *They. Were. Dying.*" I enunciated the last three words between clenched teeth. "What if I didn't measure up? Who was going to save them?"

His eyes, bright blue and colder than a Dakota midnight, hardened. "I would have dealt with the problem if you could not."

Looking into his face, I had no doubt he would have.

"Now that you've seen the evil that can walk this earth, Dana, don't you want to help?"

I did. I couldn't deny it. I hadn't felt this useful, this alive, in my entire life. I didn't think I could go back to the plain old FBI now that I knew there was something more.

"What will we tell the people of Devil's Fork?" I asked.

"I have an entire division that deals with such explanations."

"They lie."

"But of course. Part of the *Jäger-Sucher* job description. People don't want to know the truth; they can't handle the truth."

I waited for him to give me a Jack Nicholson grin, but he didn't. I had to wonder if Edward Mandenauer even bothered to watch movies. Probably not.

"You will report for training in Montana." He handed me a folder with directions and forms, assuming, rightly, that I was going to accept his offer.

One glance and my eyes widened. "You're part of the federal government?"

"Where do you think I'd get the money for such an operation?"

I hadn't thought of that at all. But a Special Forces monster-hunting unit funded by the US government? Talk about supernatural.

"Be at the compound . . ." Mandenauer glanced at the voodoo shop. "In three days."

"Thank you, sir."

"Tell Portier I will call him." At my curious glance he shrugged. "I also have a division of witches."

"He isn't a witch." I didn't think, though I wasn't exactly certain what a witch was.

"Sorcerer, magician." Mandenauer waved a pale, bony hand. "Whatever. As you've discovered, sometimes only magic can fight magic."

I shook hands with Mandenauer to seal the deal. I couldn't believe I was going to end up in the X-file sector after all. How's that for irony?

Mandenauer strolled off toward Miss Henson's bed-and-breakfast, presumably to begin damage control. I headed for the voodoo shop. I had a little damage to control myself.

I half figured the door would be locked, was pleasantly surprised when it wasn't.

But Julian wasn't in the shop; he wasn't in the garden. I stood at the bottom of the steps and really hoped he was upstairs.

The second floor felt empty. My throat tightened. What would I do if he was gone? I doubted I'd be able to find him if he didn't want to be found.

When I reached his room, the sight of him standing in front of the window made me dizzy with relief. "Julian?"

He didn't turn around.

"Talk to me."

"Are you going to join Mandenauer's group?"

I hesitated, unsure what he wanted me to say. But I had to tell the truth. "Yes. He wants you to join them, too."

He faced me, but I couldn't see his expression. The moon had risen past the height of the window, and everything lay in shadow.

"What do you want, Dana?"

"You'd be a lot of help. You could save lives like you did tonight."

"I don't think I want to travel around saving lives in the same way that I did tonight."

"Uh, no." My cheeks flared, remembering what we'd done and why—at least the first time. "I hope not."

"Why's that?"

I hesitated. I could gloss over what had happened, let him think that it had meant nothing. Go on my way, find a new life. Or I could take a chance. I'd rather have my heart broken than never know I had a heart at all.

Until I'd come to Devil's Fork and met Julian Portier, I hadn't really been living; I'd been existing, waiting for someone or something to make me come alive. I'd found the someone in Julian and the something in the *Jäger-Suchers*.

"I know this was an extreme situation. Life and death, all sorts of weird happenings, but for me—" I broke off; he remained silent. He wasn't making this very easy.

"For you?" he prompted.

"There was more," I blurted. "I felt something when we were together. More than I've ever felt before. I don't want to leave here and never see you again."

"Then don't."

"Leave?" I wasn't sure I could do that. I really, really wanted this new job.

"I know you have to leave. People need you. In truth, I'll be leaving. This place reminds me too much of her."

"You'll talk to Mandenauer?"

He turned his face toward the window. "I think I will."

"So when you said don't—"

"I meant—don't never see me again."

I wasn't sure what he was getting at. Double negatives were confusing.

Julian flicked his wrist, and candles sprang to life all over the room. He had to have been setting them up the entire time I was talking to Mandenauer. He'd known I would come. That kind of understanding was as rare as he was, as remarkable as what lay between us.

"I felt it, too," he said. "What we shared was more than just sex, more than just the spell, more than saving lives, it was—" He paused. "I'm not sure. But I want to find out."

I crossed the room until our toes touched. "I don't have to be in Montana for three days."

His lips curved. "That's a start."

He waved a hand toward the window, and the voodoo moon slid lower in the sky, bathing the room with cool silver light as he took me in his arms.

I couldn't wait to see where we finished.

Breath of Magic

by

CHEYENNE McCRAY

Acknowledgments

Thank you to Kia Dupree and the other wonderful ladies who did a stand-alone read and gave me the A-Okay. Annie Windsor, Tara Donn, and Patrice Michelle, batter up. Monique Patterson and Nancy Yost, thanks for fielding this one.

Chapter 1

I f only she could fly like Conlan, she could get herself out of this mess.

Sydney Aline gritted her teeth and clutched the ledge over her head as tightly as she could. The toes of her jogging shoes barely reached a much narrower ledge on the outside wall of the abandoned hotel.

Her and her damned divining.

She sure hadn't seen *this* coming. What good was a D'Anu witch who couldn't divine her *own* future? Especially when it involved dangling from a friggin' ledge.

The adrenaline pumping through her body helped keep her moving and glued to the side of the hotel. Sydney took a deep breath and started to inch her way toward one of the hotel's second-floor windows. Now that she was up close and personal with the building's wall, she could smell the age of the bricks and the pollution coating them.

Once she reached the window, if she held on to the ledge with one hand, she could use her other to release her magic and open the window. End of problem.

Please let it be that easy.

She'd scraped her fingers raw catching herself when

she'd slipped from the third-story ledge that was now *above* her head instead of *under* her feet. She'd been creeping along, doing just fine, until a part of the footpath crumbled. She'd slipped and barely grabbed an intact part of the ledge. She could have fallen three stories instead of one. Even though she was a witch, she wasn't likely to bounce and recover from that kind of fall.

Now she just had to get to that window.

And Conlan. Where was that Tuatha D'Danann warrior, anyway? The one who could sprout a pair of wings whenever he wanted to. The one who, sure as the goddess, could help her out, right about now.

That gorgeous hunk of a man who makes me hot with just one look.

Sydney groaned and moved another inch closer toward the window. Her arms ached and trembled. The only reason she should be thinking about Conlan at this moment was to save her butt. Dear Anu, how she hated being in a position where she needed his help.

Okay, skip that thought. Her pride would remain intact if he would return from scouting for demons, swoop down, and get her out of this mess. When she had climbed up the corner of the building, she'd been so sure she could just ease herself toward the window because that ledge was fairly wide. She wasn't afraid of heights. Well, maybe right now she was.

She hadn't been crazy about the idea of him flying her up there, so they had planned to meet at the third-floor window. No biggie. She'd just started without him.

Another inch. She bit her lower lip, putting all her focus into making it to the second-floor window instead.

When she'd divined that they would possibly find a dark warlock here—a bastard named Darkwolf who happened to be in possession of an evil god's stone eye—she'd certainly not seen herself outside in the foggy, dreary, San Francisco afternoon, clinging to the side of a hotel.

Too bad her Doberman familiar, Chaos, wasn't here to alert Conlan to her situation. She could use Chaos's magic to bolster her own. But his barking might draw Darkwolf's attention—if she had divined correctly and he really was here.

Her skin felt sticky against her body armor, which was covered by her T-shirt. Her jeans stuck to her legs, and her arms were coated in the fine mist. At least she'd spelled her glasses to resist fog so that she could see on these kinds of days. Which were frequent in San Francisco.

The body armor had been supplied by Jake Macgregor, captain of the San Francisco Paranormal Special Forces. Right now it was weighing her down, making it harder for her to move.

Slowly she worked her way toward the window. She did her best to ignore the pain in her arms and legs from clinging so tightly to the ledge, and from the tenseness in her body.

The wind whipped up, causing her dark hair to fly into her face and get caught in her glasses. Now she could see only out of one eye.

Sydney wanted to scream. But she couldn't let Darkwolf know she'd figured out his hiding place if he was here. Then he'd likely change locations and none of her sister D'Anu witches would be able to find him.

Not to mention the D'Danann warriors. The warriors were winged Fae fighters from Otherworld who had been helping the witches repel an invasion of demons.

Four of the warriors and witches had paired up—a witch with a warrior—and had been tracking Darkwolf for the past few days, each searching one quadrant of the city. Now Sydney was sure she had finally figured out where Darkwolf was and she was going to fall to her death before she caught the S.O.B. If Darkwolf was here, she'd contact the other witches and D'Danann before making contact with the warlock.

Darkwolf had started the whole invasion. The warlock

bastard had summoned powers too great for him to control—Fomorii demons who worshiped the ancient, wicked god Balor and his murdering bitch of a wife. Sydney ground her teeth. They'd been dealing with the totally evil goddess for weeks now.

Because Darkwolf had brought her to San Francisco, the she-goddess from hell had been able to slaughter thousands of humans and call her husband up from the depths of Underworld.

Balor was here. Now.

Thank Anu, Balor hadn't found his eye yet. And he wouldn't, if Sydney could keep herself alive and snag Darkwolf before he forked it over.

By the Goddess, when I get my hands around that warlock's throat . . .

Taking a deep breath, she moved another inch. Closer to her destination now. Maybe two feet away.

Her hair was driving her crazy the way it was stuck in her glasses.

I don't know enough swear words to express how I feel right now.

On the other side of the window she was headed toward was a balcony with sliding glass doors. Why couldn't she be closer to *that*?

Whose bright idea was it, anyway, to walk along a ledge to get in through the window on the third floor?

Mine, stupid.

Before Conlan left to scout out the rest of the hotel by flying around it, she'd told him she planned to climb up to the third floor and walk along that wide ledge to the first window.

Conlan had raised an eyebrow and given her a look that said, *"Yeah, right,"* only probably in Gaelic, and likely not that charitable. More like, *"You should know better than this, but you're a big girl. If you want to break your neck, who am I to stop you?"*

His teasing winks and sexy looks had made Sydney wonder what it would be like to kiss him. To *more* than kiss him. Only she didn't get involved with the playboy type. She didn't do casual sexual relationships, and Conlan had *one-night stand* written all over him.

Sydney grunted as she worked her way along the ledge. She *was* going to get herself out of this. The window was closer now. Her arms were nearly numb and her fingers felt like she was shredding them with every movement she made along the ledge.

One would think that as a descendent of the Ancient Druids and as a witch who practiced gray magic, she'd be able to use her powers to get along this ledge a little faster. But like other D'Anu witches, she had to have her hands free to use her powers.

Friggin' inconvenient.

Almost there.

When Sydney finally reached the window, she almost cried with relief. She was going to do this. She was going to make it.

Carefully, she pried the fingers of her left hand from the ledge. All her weight was now on her right hand and the toes of her jogging shoes.

Trying not to make any sudden moves, she lowered her left hand and blue sparkles of magic flowed from her palm to the window. She heard the click of the window unlocking. She tensed her jaw and moved her hand from the left to the right, opening the window with her magic. It made a screech like nails across a chalkboard that grated along her spine and sounded loud in the foggy afternoon.

What if Darkwolf heard it?

Sydney reached her left hand up to grasp the ledge again so she could climb in through the window.

The fingers of her right hand slipped.

She fell.

A scream tore from her throat.

At the same time she let loose a magic rope from her palm. It shot straight at the balcony on the other side of the window.

The rope wrapped around the top railing.

Heart beating like it was going to explode, Sydney clung to the blue magical rope with one hand. With a burst of effort, she swung her other hand up and grabbed the rope.

She almost sobbed with relief—and from the pain in her arms and hands as her own weight almost jerked her shoulders out of their sockets.

Idiot, idiot, idiot!

Thank the Ancestors she'd kept fit at the gym. She'd never been good at climbing the rope in gym class, but she had the willpower to do it now.

It seemed like it took forever, but fraction by fraction Sydney worked her way up the rope and to the balcony railing. Blood pounded in her ears and sweat covered her body.

When she grasped the railing, she pulled herself up so that her toes were on the edge of the balcony. She swung her left foot over the railing, then tumbled into an ungraceful heap as her other leg followed.

For a long moment Sydney lay on her back, staring up at the gray, foggy sky and the third-story ledge where she'd been minutes—or was it hours?—ago.

She was so sore she didn't think she'd be able to walk for a week. She barely had the strength to yank her hair out of her glasses so that she could see out of both eyes again.

After she'd caught her breath, she pushed herself to her feet. She wobbled a bit and grasped the railing to steady herself.

Sydney glanced down.

Conlan stood on the ground two stories below, a glint in his eyes and his mouth quirked into a smile.

If you want to break your neck . . .

She was going to kill him.

There was no doubt in her mind that he'd just watched what was now the most embarrassing moment of her life. He could have helped her at any time. She was sure he'd been waiting for her to fall before he'd swoop up and catch her. But she'd saved her own butt.

Conlan was a huge D'Danann warrior with a broad chest, a very fit, muscled body, long blond hair that dusted his shoulders, grass-green eyes, and a dimple in his chin. He wore black leather, from his sleeveless tunic to the pants tucked into his boots. He'd just arrived from Otherworld for the first time, so they hadn't had a chance to outfit him in human clothing.

Ooh, he'd look good in a pair of jeans and a tight-fitting T-shirt. Almost as yummy as in all that leather.

Conlan's features usually showed a hint of a smile and a teasing glint in his eyes. She'd known him for only a few days, but the man had already gotten under her skin. It irked her to no end because he wasn't her type. So why did she fantasize so much about him? With her. In bed.

After giving Mr. Wings-and-smile a glare that should have melted steel, Sydney whirled around—

And found herself face-to-face with Darkwolf and the evil god's eye.

*C*hapter 2

Before Sydney had a chance to throw up a spellshield, Darkwolf snaked his magic ropes around her, pinning her arms to her sides. The warlock jerked her in through the open sliding glass door into the shadows where he'd been hiding in the hotel room.

She screamed in surprise and fear as she stumbled and pitched forward, almost hitting her head on a bureau. With no way to catch herself, she twisted her body in mid-fall so that she wouldn't hit the bureau or end up on her face, not to mention crunch her glasses. She landed on the carpeted floor on her side, hard, knocking the breath from her.

When she rolled onto her back, she looked up to see Darkwolf standing beside her but not looking at her. Blood rushed in her ears. Darkwolf had her. What would he do now?

The stone eye hanging from a chain around his neck wasn't blazing crimson like she'd seen it before. No . . . it was quiet and covered in a thick, purple, magic shield.

Why was it shrouded like that?

Incredibly handsome, Darkwolf had black hair that curled at his collar, sensual dark eyes, and high cheekbones.

He wore a royal blue T-shirt tucked into snug, faded Levi's and a pair of pricey jogging shoes.

None of the gray-magic D'Anu witches let the warlock's good looks fool them. He was the biggest traitor and criminal the witches had ever known. And right now he held the key to a god's power.

A key they desperately needed to retrieve and keep safe.

The eye.

Sydney's heart pounded like mad, and she followed Darkwolf's gaze and saw Conlan standing on the balcony. The blond warrior had already drawn his sword and had folded his wings so that they vanished beneath his black tunic. Gone was the playful expression of just moments ago.

In its place was the fierce expression of a Tuatha D'Danann warrior.

Conlan's blood boiled. He knew by the stone eye hanging from a chain around the man's neck that this must be Darkwolf, the Balorite warlock the witches and D'Danann had been searching for. And Darkwolf had the witch helpless. The bastard was touching her with his filthy magic.

Conlan barely held back a snarl. He tightened his jaw and raised his sword high, his biceps taut and ready for battle. His thigh muscles bunched beneath his black leather pants as he stood on the balls of his feet.

He would behead the warlock and be done with it, and Sydney would be free. Conlan was a good ten feet from the pair. He started to charge Darkwolf.

Darkwolf made a small movement with his hand, and a glittering purple wall appeared between them.

Conlan slammed into the shield. The force of hitting something with such magical power propelled him backward to the railing, but he retained his footing with the grace of the Fae. Ramming his body against the surface of the shield hadn't hurt him, only infuriated him.

Veins coursing with fire, Conlan commanded, "Release the witch."

Conlan saw Sydney struggle against her bonds, but apparently the warlock's magic was too powerful. His gut churned. He had known Sydney for only a few days, but those days had been enough to give him a taste of her power and brilliance. He hated seeing her rendered helpless by this—this piece of filth.

Darkwolf's magic ropes wrapped her from her shoulders all the way to her hands. Conlan had learned that D'Anu witches had to have use of their hands to practice most of their magic. If only he could free her hands, she would fight like a tigress.

"It's not likely I'll be letting *either* of you go." Darkwolf gave an almost friendly grin that caused Conlan to narrow his eyes. "Since you've found us, Elizabeth and I need to find a new place to live. Without your help."

"Not Elizabeth," Sydney said with a snarl. "You mean that sickening demon Junga, who stole Elizabeth's body."

The warlock's grin faded to a scowl as he looked down at Sydney. "As I was saying, Elizabeth and I will search for a new place to stay. For now, I'll have to make sure you two are out of my way."

Damnation. He plans to kill her!

Conlan growled and swung his sword at the magic barrier. He hacked at it again and again, hoping to find some kind of weakness. Each time his sword bounced against the magic shield, the power of his strokes reverberated through him.

Darkwolf simply crossed his arms over his chest and watched.

Godsdamn! Conlan's rage doubled. *I must save the witch!*

When he could find no weaknesses in the shield, Conlan took a step back.

Sydney's heart had chilled when Darkwolf said he needed to make sure they were out of the way, and she swallowed hard. With Darkwolf's magic ropes binding her, from shoulders to the tips of her fingers, she wasn't exactly in the best position to defend herself. And Conlan would never be able to get through Darkwolf's shield.

But her legs were free.

When Darkwolf turned to face Conlan, Sydney rolled onto her side. She pulled her left knee to her chest. With everything she had, she slammed her foot into the warlock's ankle.

Darkwolf dropped. He grunted and had a look of surprise on his face as his feet flew out from beneath him and he landed on his ass.

His focus on the barrier wavered and the shield fell.

No doubt his hold on her didn't weaken because she was closer to him. She lashed out again with a hard kick to his thigh.

Admiration for Sydney surged through Conlan as he charged the warlock, crossing the ten feet between them.

Darkwolf flung a fireball at Conlan.

Conlan blocked the spell with his sword, and the fireball ricocheted across the room. The headboard burst into flame before the magical fire died. The smell of burned wood was strong, and smoke floated from the hole.

Darkwolf slung another fireball at Conlan. Again, he deflected the magic with his blade. The fireball hit a bedside lamp and shattered it, the shards scattering onto the bed.

Conlan was aware of Sydney trying to get into position to kick Darkwolf again, but the warlock had moved out of her range.

When Conlan reached Darkwolf, he cut his sword through the air. The warlock crouched, dodging the blow. He raised the palms of both hands, and a purple bubble shielded him and Sydney. Conlan's sword bounced against the warlock's shield, and he cursed in the old language of his people as he regained his footing.

After dodging another kick from Sydney, the warlock shook his head, sighed, and pointed his finger at her. More of his purple ropes of magic wrapped around her so that she was now bound all the way to her ankles.

A combination of anger and fear raged through Sydney, powerful enough to make her tremble.

Conlan swore again in Gaelic, and it sounded like he was making some dire threat.

Sydney growled in frustration. A fat lot of good she'd just done. But she had the satisfaction of having caused the warlock some pain.

Darkwolf sat casually on the carpet with one knee bent, his forearm draped over his knee, his injured leg stretched out. He observed Sydney. He didn't look mad or annoyed, just . . . amused.

What the heck?

His gaze cut to Conlan, who appeared so furious his face was red, his green eyes blazed, and his muscles trembled with obvious desire to cut the warlock down.

Darkwolf shook his head again and eased to his feet, the bubble shield rising with him. "I should have known better than to allow a D'Anu witch any freedom."

Sydney wondered if it would do any good to roll straight into his legs. Maybe that would knock his feet out again—

The warlock bent and grasped Sydney around the waist. As he rose, he threw her over his shoulder. She cried out in surprise as her head hit his strong back. Her stomach churned with fear as he turned and headed out the door of the hotel room.

Chapter 3

Sydney's heart beat faster. What was Darkwolf going to do with her?

From her position over Darkwolf's shoulder she saw Conlan through the shield that was moving with Darkwolf, and the warrior looked beyond pissed.

With his sword clenched in one of his fists, Conlan followed as Darkwolf went down a stairwell, from the second floor to the street level. The door slammed behind them as they exited.

Where was he taking her?

Darkwolf went around a corner into a hallway, instead of into the abandoned hotel's lobby.

They entered a kitchen that smelled of age and rotting food, and all the chrome surfaces were dulled with dust.

Elizabeth—no, the demon Junga—was there. In the shell she had stolen, she was a beautiful woman with black hair and startling blue eyes. But inside she was a demon. When she transformed into Junga, she was a hulking apelike creature with a tough blue hide, arms that dragged on the floor, and sharp needlelike teeth. She was queen of the Fomorii demons.

Right now, in her human form, she wore a blood-red tailored skirt and jacket, and had her arms folded across her chest. "What are you going to do with them?" Elizabeth-Junga asked. "You should have killed them already."

Ice filled Sydney's veins as Darkwolf withdrew a butcher's knife from a block with his free hand.

"I'm merely going to keep them out of the way," Darkwolf replied.

"Has the eye caused you to lose your mind?" Elizabeth-Junga clenched her fists at her sides.

Darkwolf ignored her and tossed a look over his shoulder at Conlan. "Don't bother trying to hurt Elizabeth." He held up the knife. "I know you don't want the witch harmed."

Such fury coiled inside Conlan that he nearly shook from it. Gods, how he wanted to rid them of Darkwolf and take the eye. They had to have the eye to keep it from Balor.

The evil god would come for it. He would find Darkwolf, and then all as they knew it would end. In one of the great battles with the Fomorii, Conlan had witnessed the complete destruction of many peoples when Balor looked at them with one sweep of his eye before the sun god Lugh shot out the eye.

Darkwolf continued walking until he came to a big chrome door. It had a bar across it, the only door lock Conlan could see. The warlock raised his hand holding the knife. Power flowed from his palm and he moved his hand from left to right. The scrape of metal against metal met Conlan's ears before Darkwolf used his magic to open the metal door.

Conlan thought about going after the demon-woman who stood across the room, but his concern for the witch's safety was too great.

The warlock's purple shield continued to blaze around him and Sydney, even brighter than it had before. He entered a room that appeared to be a pantry of sorts.

Conlan waited at the door, his sword in his hand, fury coursing through him. He had to get the witch and himself out of this situation. But how could he take out the warlock who had surrounded himself and Sydney with a shield of magic?

Darkwolf pulled Sydney from his shoulder and plopped her down next to a wall. She struck her head against the hard surface and groaned, making Conlan grind his teeth in anger.

"What are you waiting for, D'Danann?" Darkwolf asked as he straightened and looked at Conlan. The warlock raised the butcher knife. "I could kill her by choking her with my magic, but this would be swifter. Put away your sword and sit beside the witch."

Adrenaline surged through Conlan. If he just had a window of opportunity, he could ensure Darkwolf would never walk this world again. His concern for Sydney rose, driving any other possibility from his mind.

Conlan had no choice but to obey the warlock and go to her. He expected the warlock to demand that he relinquish his sword, but strangely the warlock did not.

Sydney's heart raced and she sucked in her breath at the sight of the knife's gleaming blade.

Crap, crap, crap!

Getting the eye. That's what they needed more than anything.

"Don't listen to him, Conlan!" She gritted her teeth before adding, "The eye is more important than me."

Conlan ignored her and glared at Darkwolf. "This is not over, warlock," he said in his thick Gaelic accent.

Darkwolf ran his free hand through his dark hair and sighed. "I don't have any doubt we're facing a whole lot of shit. I just need time to keep myself and Elizabeth safe long enough to prepare."

"So you're leaving us here to die?" Sydney couldn't keep the tremble from her voice.

Surprisingly, the warlock shook his head. "Your sister witches will find you. I'll make sure they do."

Sydney blinked.

What in the name of Anu?

Why would this evil bastard want them to be found?

She looked at the shrouded eye that rested against his chest. Had he turned against the one-eyed god? Was he keeping Balor's eye for himself for some reason? Perhaps to perform more evil acts?

"I don't want to kill her." Darkwolf held the knife beneath Sydney's chin. "But I'll do what I have to. Put away the sword and sit, D'Danann."

Conlan looked from the warlock to Sydney and back. With narrowed eyes, he sheathed his sword and walked toward her. Darkwolf stepped away, keeping his shield around him but leaving the magical ropes around Sydney.

When Conlan sat beside her, Darkwolf strode to the door, obviously not concerned with anyone attacking while he still had his shield protecting him. It no longer shrouded Sydney, but that didn't matter anymore. Darkwolf held all the cards.

He cast a glance over his shoulder at Sydney. "As soon as I'm gone, the bindings will disappear and you'll be released. Don't bother using your magic against the door. I'll leave it spelled . . . long enough."

Long enough for what? Our deaths?

Then he smiled. "Thanks for screaming. That and my divination told me exactly where you were."

With that, he slipped out the door and slammed it behind him. The sound of the bar sliding into place was muffled, but there was no doubt about it. They were locked in.

Conlan turned to look at her, and the ropes vanished as he watched. With the ropes no longer binding her, Sydney sucked in a deep breath and wriggled her legs and arms.

She waited for Conlan to yell at her, to tell her this was all her fault—which it was—but he merely shook his head and stood with the grace and ease of his people.

A gamut of emotions rolled through Conlan. Anger at

the warlock, frustration, concern. He strode toward the
door and began searching for a way to open it.

Fear for Sydney had slammed into him when he had returned and seen her clinging to the outside wall. Apparently, she had fallen from the ledge she had been walking
on. Certainly, he had not expected her to make her way
along the ledge alone while she waited for him to return.
He had left her at the corner of the hotel while he searched
for signs of the Fomorii. Unfortunately, he had not caught
their scent.

When he had returned, Sydney had reached the first
window and was opening it. He had prepared to catch her
when she fell, but she had done a fine job of saving herself.

She was a true warrior.

One of the many things he admired about her.

With his fingers, Conlan traced the outline of the door,
searching for weakness. Nothing.

Damnation! They had to get out of here and retrieve the
eye! Conlan used the tip of his sword, but there wasn't
space enough for even it to slide through.

In the few days he had known Sydney, he had learned it
was her way to insist upon her independence.

It was his way to not interfere.

But he would be there when she needed him. He admired her desire to accomplish tasks on her own.

Only, she could have fallen to her death if she had not
caught herself. Twice. Perhaps it was best to not leave her
alone with her apparent tendency to walk into danger.

He tossed a look over his shoulder to see Sydney's gaze
traveling around the room, as if looking for some way of
escape as well.

She was beautiful. Gentle curves, long dark hair, and
unusual lavender eyes. He had wanted her from the moment he'd met her. Something about the witch caused a
stirring not only in his loins but in his gut every time he
looked at her.

He clenched his fist around his sword. What was he thinking at a time like this?

Conlan turned his attention back to the door and shoved his sword back into its sheath. Somehow they were going to get out of here.

Sydney's body ached from her head to her toes. With a groan, Sydney pushed herself to her feet, then swayed.

"Any way out?" Sydney asked, then immediately felt stupid for asking the question.

But Conlan didn't make her feel like an idiot. Instead, he said, "Perhaps. Perhaps not." He gripped his sword hilt with one hand as he studied the door.

She watched as he held his ear to the metal and knocked. "Solid," he grumbled.

"Let me try." She pushed past him and rubbed her sore palms on her jeans before raising them to face the door. "Even though Darkwolf said he spelled the lock, maybe my magic is strong enough to break through it."

Too bad Chaos wasn't here. Her Doberman familiar could have helped Conlan before they were trapped. Maybe by taking on the demon-woman. Right now, she could use Chaos's magic to aid hers. It would have been satisfying to see him take a chunk out of the warlock's ass, too.

She closed her eyes for a moment, letting her magic build within her until it grew so strong she almost shook.

When she opened her eyes, she let loose with her blue magic. The power of it radiated from her palms. She pictured the sliding lock and moved her hands from her right to left, in the direction the bar could be opened from the outside.

Not a sound. She'd heard Darkwolf bar the door, certainly she would hear it unlock.

There was no handle on the inside of the pantry, so she used her magic to pull at the door, trying to draw it open.

Nothing. It made no movement whatsoever.

She tried again and again with her magic, attempting to

unlock the door and open it. When a fine sheen of sweat coated her skin and her breathing had quickened, she finally gave up and looked at Conlan.

"I'm sorry." She adjusted her glasses and stepped away from the door. "It's not working."

Conlan said nothing but with his hand motioned her out of his way. He took several steps back. With a running start he rammed his shoulder into the door.

Sydney winced.

When he backed away there was nothing but a small indentation.

Repeatedly he slammed himself into the door, with the same results.

In the short time she'd known him, Sydney hadn't been able to get enough of looking at the big warrior. All those muscles, blond hair that reached his shoulders, and eyes the color of spring grass. The way he looked at her sometimes sent butterflies straight to her belly.

She shook her head. Trapped and turned on. What a combination.

While Conlan did his macho thing, Sydney searched the enormous pantry. No hidden doors, just lots of canned food. The hotel hadn't been closed too long and obviously hadn't been cleaned out yet. Huge cans of soup, tomato juice, salsa, mustard, mayo, and ketchup lined one wall, along with lots of other things.

There were bags of flour and sugar and, to her delight, packages of tortilla chips that were still well within their freshness date. Chips and salsa sounded good about now. Despite the situation, she was hungry and her stomach rumbled to prove it. Not to mention that with the kind of appetite D'Danann warriors had, it was a good thing they were stuck someplace with food.

She rolled her eyes up to the ceiling. Darkwolf still had the eye. Demons were crawling through the sewers of San Francisco. Not one but *two* evil gods were on the loose.

None of the races in Otherworld had agreed to help but the D'Danann—who only allowed a handful of warriors to aid them, including Conlan. And she and Conlan were locked away, possibly to die despite what Darkwolf had said—and she was thinking about food.

Sydney sighed as she looked up at another shelf.

"Chocolate!" She couldn't help feeling a little excitement at spotting giant bars of her favorite, San Francisco's Ghirardelli chocolate. When things got rough, a good dose of chocolate was in order.

Conlan looked at her and raised an eyebrow.

Sydney had to stand on a small stepstool to reach it, but was able to snag one of the enormous bars. When she stepped back onto the floor, she unwrapped a portion and handed a piece to Conlan. He gave her a quick nod of thanks before eating the big chunk in one bite, then ramming his shoulder into the door again.

While Conlan played he-man, Sydney pacified herself by consuming more chocolate than she normally ate in a week. After Conlan'd spent at least an hour trying to get them out of the big pantry, he backed up and stared at the door.

"I'll try another tactic." Sydney wiped her sticky fingers on her black jeans, and he stepped aside so that she was in front of the door.

She studied it, trying to think of something she could do. A spellfire ball would only hit it, then ricochet around the pantry, and they definitely didn't need *that*. Magic ropes wouldn't work because there was nothing for the ropes to latch onto. No, she'd have to try to cast a spell. She should have thought of that earlier.

Blue magic sparked at Sydney's fingertips. She closed her eyes and imagined she was the wind. A tiny zephyr that grew into a strong breeze. She saw stars spinning in her mind as she envisioned a strong wind that quickly morphed into the force of a hurricane. Her body shook from the strength of her magic, and she felt power radiating through her. Power of those who could assist her in a time like this.

She chanted.

"I call upon the great goddess Anu,
The Elements and the Ancestors, too.
Please aid us as we face this task,
To free us from this prison is what we ask.
We plead that you will help open this door
So we shall be trapped here no more."

In her mind she saw lightning, heard thunder, and felt the wind around her body. It caressed her, rather than battering her, despite its powerful force.

With her mind, Sydney tried to open the door and rip it off its hinges using her mental hurricane.

She fought the door. Struggled with it. Mentally screamed at it.

But the storm in her mind began to die until even the rushing in her ears faded away.

Sydney didn't want to open her eyes. When she finally did, it was just as she'd expected—the door was still closed. A deeper indentation was at the center of the door, but everything else about it was the same.

She turned and faced Conlan, to see him studying her. She tapped the toe of her right shoe against the concrete floor. Despite his normally easygoing nature, this was where he was likely to curse and yell at her for getting them into this mess.

"I'm sorry." She ran her hand through her hair. "What are we going to do? We've got to get out of here. We've got to get to the eye."

He looked at his boots, then back up at her. "For now, we have done what we can. We will try again after we both have rested."

With an intense look on his face that Sydney had never seen on him before, he approached, reached for her, and captured her by her shoulders. She caught her breath in surprise and took a step back.

Conlan took a step with her, still gripping her shoulders. She went completely still. He began to knead the knots in her neck and shoulders where they were not covered by her body armor. His touch was magic, and the tension in her body was slipping away. Instantly she wanted to melt against him. All her aches and pains seemed to vanish.

While he continued to massage her arms, shoulders, and neck, he gave her his sexy playboy smile. It was the kind of smile that sent a thrill straight from her belly to that place between her thighs. Her nipples grew taut and her breasts ached with the swift and sudden desire that swept through her.

Uh, Sydney? Remember your rule on no Casanova types?

"What do we do now?" she whispered as she looked up at him, banishing the thought almost immediately.

His gaze settled on her lips. "For the time being, we may as well find a distraction."

She swallowed, hard. "How about some more chocolate?"

In his rich Irish brogue he murmured, "I can think of something much better than chocolate."

Chapter 4

Sydney blinked, unable to compute what he'd just said and what she thought he meant.

Conlan moved closer, the heat of him warming her even though the only place he touched her was her shoulders.

She opened her mouth, but nothing came out. She closed it, then tried again, but couldn't say a word.

Conlan's eyes turned a dark green. He slowly slid both of his palms from her shoulders, up her neck, and into her dark hair. He brought a lock of her hair to his nose, and his chest rose as he inhaled. "Raspberries," he murmured. "You always smell of raspberries on a summer day."

Sydney's belly twisted at his words. He released her hair, and she shivered as his look became more intense and definitely filled with desire.

He lowered his head, bringing his mouth close to hers. Sydney swallowed. What was she doing?

Heck, who cares?

She was trapped with a gorgeous man and she didn't know if she'd ever escape.

So why not?

What was that again about not doing casual relation-ships, Sydney Aline?

Screw that.

Heart racing, she brought her hands up to his chest, feeling the steel of his muscles beneath her palms. He moved a fraction closer, bringing their bodies flush. His erection pressed against her belly, sending new heat to the juncture of her thighs.

Conlan's scent washed over her, filling her senses. She caught the hint of a forest breeze and sun-warmed skin.

He massaged her scalp as he kept his lips so close to hers it was driving her crazy. She clutched his leather tunic in her fists and shuddered with desire.

Another smile tipped the corners of his mouth. "Your eyes. I have seen nothing like them. Lavender blooms beneath a moonlit sky."

Whoa. Sydney swallowed. *Does this guy know how to seduce or what?*

He slipped her glasses off and set them on a nearby shelf. "Why do you hide your eyes behind pieces of sand-glass and metal?"

His lips came closer to hers again as she murmured, "I need them to see far away, and I can't wear contacts."

"You are beautiful with them. You are beautiful with-out," he said.

God, he's good.

When his lips finally met hers, she sighed and closed her eyes. He barely brushed his mouth over hers, but it was enough to send tingles throughout her body. He pressed a little harder, drew back, then pressed his lips to hers again.

A soft moan rose up within her, and he caught her lower lip between his teeth. She gripped his tunic tighter and re-sponded to his kiss. She darted out her tongue, tasting his lips and then inside his mouth. A hint of chocolate and a masculine flavor that she found even better than chocolate.

Conlan cupped her head and brought her tighter to him, his kiss becoming more urgent. A low groan rumbled in his chest, and Sydney's body flamed—she was on fire.

Another moan rose from her throat, but he stole it from her as he kissed her. She melted against him, feeling his muscular body against her softer one. He slipped his fingers from her hair, slowly moving his palms from her shoulders, over the swell of her breasts and the indentation of her waist. When he reached her hips, he cupped her ass and ground his hard cock against her belly.

Sydney gasped and opened her eyes as he raised his head. "I want you, sweet little witch."

What was a girl to say to that when she was locked away, possibly trapped forever?

With a man who was making her head spin with lust.

He gripped her ass tight as he moved her so that her back was up against a wall. Sydney wrapped her arms around his neck and moved her lips along the late-afternoon stubble on his cheek.

"I don't know about this, Conlan." She flicked her tongue out, tasting the salty flavor of his skin. "We've only known each other for a few days."

He drew away, a look of genuine surprise on his features. "Why would that matter?"

She cocked an eyebrow. "In Otherworld it doesn't?"

He shrugged. "Of course not."

"Far be it for me to challenge you on that one." Sydney smiled as she moved in closer and nuzzled his neck, drinking in his male scent. He smelled good enough to eat. Good enough that she nipped at the spot between his neck and shoulder, and he gave a deep groan.

Conlan tugged her T-shirt out of her jeans and pulled it over her head. He immediately unfastened her body armor and threw it aside.

When she was bare of everything but her bra, he moved his callused palms up the flat plane of her belly. She shivered

as he neared her breasts. He paused, his thumbs just below
her bra, his big hands gripping her sides.

He took her mouth again. This time his kiss was rough
and his palms found her breasts. He kneaded them while
he stole her breath away with his kiss.

When he pinched her sensitive nipples through her bra,
she sagged against him. He pulled at the material of her
bra and raised his head when it wouldn't give.

With one finger, he traced the satin of her bra. "Remove
it." His voice was husky, his gaze never leaving her breasts.

Sydney's hands shook as she released her hold on his
neck. She pushed against him so that she could reach behind herself and unclasp the bra. Her hands shook so badly
it took her a couple of tries before she finally got it right.

He sucked in his breath as she let the straps of the bra
slide down her arms. She let it fall away to the floor.

Conlan looked enraptured as he stared at her chest. He
trailed one of his fingers up the swell of her breast. "I have
wanted you from the time I first saw you."

Sydney caught her breath as he traced his finger around
her nipple. It tightened even more. "You're just saying that
because you want to get into my pants."

And he was doing a good job of coming very close to
doing exactly that.

He raised his head and his mesmerizing eyes studied hers.
"I speak only the truth." He pinched her nipple and brushed
his lips over hers. "I knew it would be but a matter of time."

No time like the present.

Sydney gave a soft moan as he brought his other hand
up so that he was pinching both her nipples. "You're a little presumptuous," she said just before she groaned again.

His lips brushed hers again and he murmured, "I think
not."

Sydney thought about pushing him away, but that
thought didn't last long. He dipped his head and circled her
nipple with his warm tongue, and this time she whimpered.

She shivered as his long blond hair trailed over her skin while he began sucking her nipple.

"You taste so sweet," he murmured as he moved his mouth to her other nipple.

She sagged and braced her hands on his shoulders, lost in the sensations. As he sucked her nipples, he hooked his fingers in the waistband of her jeans and tugged.

He made a frustrated sound. "How do you remove these?"

Sydney would have smiled if she wasn't experiencing the hottest foreplay of her life. She couldn't even talk.

First, she kicked off her jogging shoes and vaguely heard something crash when the second one went flying. Then she brought her hands from his shoulders, unfastened the button on her jeans, and unzipped them.

"That is better." He pulled her panties and her jeans to her feet. She stepped out of them, and he pushed them aside. He peeled off each of her socks, then rose up to face her.

Sydney trembled as she stood completely naked before this gorgeous D'Danann warrior.

"A goddess." Starting with her face, his gaze slowly traveled down her body. He lingered on her breasts and her mound, where she kept the soft dark hair trimmed. "I have known many goddesses in my lifetime, and none have been as lovely as you."

As he said the last words, his gaze met hers and warmth flushed her body. There was such sincerity in his eyes mixed with heat and passion.

He grabbed her ass and crushed her naked body against him at the same time he took her mouth in a rough kiss.

Sydney's senses went wild. Her folds dampened even more, her breasts ached. As he kissed her, his leather tunic abraded her nipples, and his weapons belt scraped her waist while his cock pressed against her belly.

Oh, how she wanted to see what he looked like without his clothes. He sure looked good in them.

Before she had a chance to help him undress, he knelt on the floor and grabbed her ass cheeks. Her stomach pitched and her body trembled as he brought his face to her mound. She heard his deep inhale, and caught the scent of her own musk as well. He swiped his tongue on the lips of her sex, teasing her. She wanted to feel his touch on her folds and her clit. He licked her flesh again.

"*Now,* Conlan." She didn't know whether she sounded like she was commanding him or begging him. But she really didn't care. She couldn't wait any longer.

A soft laugh rose from him and he buried his mouth against her folds.

Sydney gave a shout of pleasure as he licked her with quick, short swipes of his tongue. He moved his attention to her clit, and she gave another cry.

She slipped her fingers into his hair to keep her balance and to keep from falling, because her legs didn't want to hold her up. Her entire body tensed as she came closer to climax, and her legs wobbled some more. A spinning sensation started in her head, like the world was tilting. She grew dizzy with the power of the orgasm rushing toward her.

Conlan licked harder and growled against her clit.

It was as if everything exploded around them. An honest-to-goddess bunch of fireworks soared through her mind. A cry tore from Sydney that was somewhere between a shout and a sob. Tears filled her eyes from the power of her climax.

Her body shook and bucked, and he drew out her orgasm by continuing to lick and suck her clit. This time it was a sob when she said, "Conlan, stop." He licked her a few more times, causing her to cry out and her hips to jerk against his face.

When he finally let up, he rose, and she collapsed against him, pressing her cheek to his chest and wrapping her arms around his neck. Her breathing was hard, but her mind finally stopped spinning and the contractions in her core began to subside.

"I don't know what to say but wow," she murmured against his chest.

"And that means . . ."

"It means that orgasm was out of this world. Unbelievable. Incredible. All of the above."

Conlan chuckled and nuzzled the top of her head.

Sydney drew away enough to tilt her chin and look up at him. She couldn't think of anything else to say as she saw more desire than ever in his eyes.

He brought his mouth hard to hers. Delving his tongue inside her, licking, sucking. She tasted herself on his tongue and smelled her own musk mingling with his masculine scent.

Her kiss was just as demanding as his. What would it feel like to have his cock deep inside her? She felt the hardness and length of his erection against her belly and she knew he would fill her.

At this point she could care less about this being a one-night stand. All that mattered was the moment, and, dear goddess, how she'd wanted him from the first time she'd met him.

She drew back and saw the rise and fall of his chest, the flex of his muscles, and the intensity of his gaze that told her he was doing all he could to restrain himself. She reached for him and he groaned when she cupped his cock through his pants. She moved her hand from balls to tip and back.

Conlan had felt this way with none of the many women he had bedded over the centuries of his life. What was this witch doing to him? Since the moment he had met Sydney, she had made him want her with such intensity it nearly made him shout to the gods.

Lust. That was all it could be. He simply desired her. Perhaps more than the many women he had fucked, but the feeling she stirred within him was simply lust nonetheless.

He had never been one to be tied to any woman. He enjoyed all women far too much.

She knelt so that her mouth was level with his erection, then brought her hands to the ties of his leather breeches. He sucked in his breath as she released his cock and balls. She made a low purring sound and circled the head of his erection with her tongue.

He couldn't hold back his loud groan of pleasure as she licked the length of his cock in slow, deliberate swipes. He fisted his hands in her dark, silky hair and pumped his hips against her face.

When his gaze met her lavender eyes and he watched her flick her tongue along his erection, even more desire spiked through him.

Sydney gave him a wicked smile. When she slid her lips over his erection, it nearly drove him to his knees. He clenched her hair tighter in his hands and pumped his hips as she took him as deep as she could. He was too big for her to take too much of him, but, gods, did it feel incredible.

She used one hand to fondle his balls, while her other hand worked his cock in tandem with her mouth. He ground his teeth as he felt the oncoming storm of his climax. She matched him by increasing her speed as he moved his hips a little faster.

"I am close to filling your mouth with my seed," he said in a low rumble.

Her beautiful eyes gazed up at him as she continued to take him. He watched his cock move in and out through her soft lips.

The storm of his climax hit hard enough that he couldn't hold back a shout. It felt like the room was tilting, and he could barely retain his footing. Sydney continued to suck him, extending the sensations of his climax.

Just as he was about to withdraw his cock from her mouth, he heard the sound of the door's bar scraping, and then the door swung open.

Chapter 5

S he was going to die from embarrassment.

Heat flooded Sydney's entire body as her friends rushed into the room—to see her naked, on her knees, with Conlan's cock in her mouth.

Conlan slipped himself from between her lips and stepped in front of her, hiding her with his big body. Sydney rushed to get to her feet and pressed herself to his back. She felt him adjust himself, and assumed he was lacing up his leather pants.

"Uh . . ." Mackenzie was the first to have some kind of semiverbal reaction.

Sydney kept her face and body against Conlan's back and gripped his leather tunic in her fists as more waves of heat burned through her.

"Sorry," Silver said. "We'll give you both some time to—to . . . well, whatever you need time to do."

Hawk chuckled, and Silver hissed, "Shut up!" before Sydney heard the heavy pantry door shut.

Sydney's grip on the back of Conlan's tunic failed when he turned around to face her. She pressed her cheek against his chest. "I'm so mortified. I'll never be able to face them."

Conlan hooked his finger beneath her chin and forced her to tilt her head up and look into his eyes. "You have nothing to be embarrassed about. Do you think they have not done the same?"

She bit her lower lip before saying, "Yeah, but not in front of an audience."

He gave her a gentle smile and released her chin. "Dress, and we will leave this place."

Sydney glanced at the door, then back to him. "I don't know if I want to."

Conlan kissed her forehead. "We will finish our business later, my sweet witch."

"Maybe." Sydney pushed away from him and reached for her underwear. "I can't even believe we did *this* when we barely know each other."

He stopped her from stepping into her panties by catching one of her breasts in his palm and circling her nipple with his thumb. "We know each other well enough now."

A groan rose up within Sydney. It felt so good when he touched her. So good she could almost forget she had to face her friends.

But not quite.

Sydney took a deep breath, pushed his hand away, and pulled on her panties. She dragged out getting dressed as long as she could, putting off the moment when she would have to walk outside the pantry.

Conlan folded his arms across his chest and watched her. Not the slightest bit of embarrassment showed on his strong features. No . . . he looked gentle and concerned. Not his usual teasing look.

Sydney almost sighed. This was a man she could fall for. And hard.

She put on her bra, slipped into her body armor, and pulled on the rest of her clothing.

When she couldn't put it off any longer, Sydney slid on

her glasses, took a deep breath, and let it out slowly as she walked toward the pantry door. "Okay. I can do this."

Conlan caught her arm before she could pull open the door. He brought her to him and took her mouth in a fierce but sweet kiss.

After he had thoroughly kissed her, Sydney sighed as she looked up at him. His green eyes were dark again. "We will finish this," he repeated before taking her hand, opening the door that had been left ajar, and leading her out.

She raised her chin and walked through the doorway, all the while wanting to turn and run back into the pantry. Heat prickled her skin. Her face burned so hot she had no doubt her cheeks were stained red as she faced the six people who had just witnessed the *now* most embarrassing moment of her life.

Mackenzie grinned. "Well, we don't have to ask if you're all right," the petite blond said.

Ian, the D'Danann warrior standing beside the entrance to the kitchen snorted. Alyssa cleared her throat and looked like she was trying to keep a straight face. Cael, the warrior at the back exit of the kitchen, grinned and winked at Sydney.

Hawk laughed, and Silver elbowed her husband before approaching Sydney. Silver had long, beautiful, silvery-blond hair, and her gray eyes were filled with concern.

"You're okay, aren't you?" Silver took Sydney's hands in hers, then frowned as she turned them so that they were palms up. She examined Sydney's fingers before looking at her. "What in the world did you do to your hands?"

Sydney tried to look casual and shrugged. "It's a long story."

"Hold still," Silver said as she released Sydney's fingers.

Sydney complied, and Silver raised one of her hands.

Blue light radiated from her palm as sparkles of magic began healing the cuts and scrapes. The pain in Sydney's fingers faded. The aches weren't entirely gone and the scrapes would need a little more magical attention when the bunch of them returned to their current headquarters. But for now it was a huge relief.

"Much better." Sydney tried to make her expression bright and pretend nothing out of the ordinary had occurred. "So, how did you find us so fast?"

"That's the weird thing." Silver looked like something disturbed her, and she darted a glance at Hawk, who narrowed his eyes. "Hawk and I were searching our section of the city for Darkwolf when the warlock's voice came into my mind. He said he wanted to make sure you and Conlan were found."

A near growl came from Hawk, and Silver took his hand. She continued, "There's always been some kind of mental communication between Darkwolf and me that I can't seem to break. But this time he was doing something to help us. I don't get it."

"A trap." Conlan's gaze searched the kitchen. "The bastard probably planned to have us ambushed here."

Hawk gave a nod to Ian and Cael, the warriors guarding the entrance and the back exit. "We thought as much. It is unfortunate that we do not have more warriors in San Francisco at this time to call upon."

"Or witches," Sydney added.

"Time to get out of here." Mackenzie's jogging shoes squeaked on the floor as she started making her way down one of the aisles in the chrome kitchen.

"Shhh!" Silver hissed and held up her hand.

Everyone went still and completely quiet.

Voices.

Distant at first but growing stronger.

The D'Danann warriors drew their swords. Conlan and Hawk went to the entrance, and each stood on one side of the thick doorframe. Hawk was next to Ian. They pressed themselves against the walls and held their swords up.

Conlan motioned with his hand for the witches to get down.

All the D'Anu witches prepared to do magic at the same time they hid at strategic points around the kitchen. When it came to fighting Fomorii demons, gray magic was in order. The gray magic Coven of witches used powers the white magic witches scorned and forbade.

Even though it had saved their butts a few times, thanks to Sydney and her Coven.

Sydney's heart pounded as she ducked and hid behind the chrome counter from which Darkwolf had taken the butcher knife. She peered around the corner at the entrance.

Even though they sounded like they were trying to keep their voices low, they became close enough that Sydney could hear a few of the people speak.

"This hotel is enormous." A woman's murmur. "How will we find them?"

A man, obviously trying to keep his voice down, too, said "Ceithlenn visioned that they would be in the kitchen."

"Shush!" came a third voice.

For a moment there was silence.

Sydney held completely still as she continued to peer around the corner, just far enough to see a group of men and women stride up to the kitchen entrance, but she could only make out the first three: a man dressed in a business suit; one beautiful blond woman in a T-shirt and jeans; and a redhead in a sassy, short skirt.

"No one's here and it's far too quiet," businessman whispered as he eased through the doorway.

"The pair might be hiding," short and sassy skirt said. "Darkwolf and Junga could already know we're here."

Sydney frowned. It sounded like these people were looking for the warlock and the demon-woman, not for her and her teammates. Something didn't compute.

"You two were fucking loud enough," growled T-shirt and jeans.

Stealth was definitely not a Fomorii forte.

The first three intruders passed the D'Danann guarding the entrance so quickly that they didn't notice the warriors. More men and women appeared in the doorway.

The woman in the T-shirt and jeans glanced over her shoulder. She whirled and shouted, "D'Danann!"

At the same time she shouted, the woman began to shift—

Into a Fomorii demon.

In seconds her features morphed from the beautiful blond into a hideous demon. This one had a huge mottled head with three eyes, and four arms hung from its thick body.

Just as fast, the man and other woman changed into their demon forms. One was deep blue with two arms and ears that looked like a bat's. The other demon was multi-legged and bright orange.

Other Fomorii poured into the room at the sound of the first demon's cry.

Roars and snarls echoed in the kitchen, and the sickening Fomorii odor of rotting fish made Sydney gag.

Despite the stench, Sydney took a deep breath to try to calm her pounding heart before she shot from her hiding place straight for the first demon.

Sydney flung magic from both hands and wrapped the ropes around the demon, immobilizing its arms. In spite of its bonds, the demon snarled and came at Sydney with its gaping maw.

She whirled out of its reach just in time for Ian to behead the demon. Its body instantly crumbled into silt.

Around them, a small war waged. Witches' spellfire balls flew, demons clawed, D'Danann hacked away with swords. Spellfire crackled and exploded into fireworks whenever it struck any of the chrome surfaces in the kitchen.

Sydney's ears rang from the screeches and shouts, the crashes of bodies being flung against the counters, and swords striking Fomorii iron-tipped claws. Utensils scattered over the floor, frying pans sailed across the room. And Fomorii—they were everywhere.

Dear Anu, here are so many demons!

Another Fomorii turned its attention to her. Sydney flung her magical ropes at the creature, but it still charged forward. Sydney backpedaled. She ducked and barely missed being gutted as a demon at her side slashed at her with its claws.

Now two demons were charging her.

Using one hand, Sydney threw a spellfire ball into the mouth of the first demon. Its head erupted into flames, and it screeched so loud her ears rang. The spellfire wouldn't kill it, as the demon would heal almost at once. Only be-heading it or taking its heart would eliminate the beast.

Sydney whipped out a magic rope and tied it around the massive legs of the second demon, causing it to trip—and almost fall on *her*.

Sydney dropped and rolled under one of the counters, almost losing her glasses. The demon hooked its claws into her arm and sliced a path from her shoulder to her elbow.

She couldn't hold back the scream of pain that ripped through her. Goddess, it was like fire! If she were Fae or Elvin, those iron-tipped claws could potentially be deadly to her just by entering her flesh.

The snarling creature swiped at her again. Sydney grit-ted her teeth and held her injured arm to her chest as she scrambled out of its way. Blood from her wound smeared the floor as she made it into the next aisle in the kitchen.

She got to her feet just in time to face yet another demon.

With a shout almost as loud as a D'Danann warrior's cry, she launched a spellfire ball straight into the demon's eyes. It roared and staggered backward. Into the path of Conlan's sword.

The warrior lopped the demon's head off, and it rolled onto one of the counters, trailing blood across the surface until the head turned into a small pile of silt.

As the rest of the demon's body crumbled at their feet, Conlan and Sydney gave one another a quick look. His gaze took in the gash on her arm and the blood dripping down to her fingers.

His jaw tightened. "Are you all right?"

She nodded. "Fine."

Battle lust mixed with concern was in his eyes before she turned away and ran toward a demon that Alyssa was fighting off.

Sydney had no time to think. She nearly blew the head from another demon's shoulders with a spellfire ball.

She might need to rein it in a tad.

Gray magic witches would do what it took to save their people from evil—almost anything. They would incapacitate, slow down, fight off, and bind demons. But they couldn't and wouldn't kill—they left that up to the D'Danann. Silver had killed a demon once—by accident—and it had nearly torn her apart.

Adrenaline pumped through Conlan, and he growled as he beheaded the closest demon. Before that demon turned to silt, Conlan had already taken out another Fomorii.

The entire time he fought, he never completely took his attention off Sydney. Whenever she battled a demon, his chest tightened and blood pounded in his ears.

And her arm. Gods, how bad was it?

The thought of her dying sent a black rage through him.

He beheaded the beast that had clawed her so badly, then jumped over the counter to take on the next demon she was fighting. The fact that she had been hurt ripped at his insides. He should have been there to stop the demon.

With his centuries of training, fighting was as natural as breathing. He was keenly aware of all that went on around him and still kept Sydney in his thoughts.

The witches' spellfire balls seared paths straight toward the oncoming demons. His brethren battled with swords and dodged Fomorii claws. The demons knew one weakness of Fae and Elves, and had purposefully tipped their claws with deadly iron.

It seemed as if the battle lasted forever, hacking, slicing, clawing, magic burning. But it was over within what was but a breath of time to the D'Danann.

A quick glance around the kitchen told him the witches and D'Danann had fared well enough with the exception of Sydney's arm.

That was until he saw the young warrior Ian drop his sword. It clattered to the floor as Ian grabbed his belly with both his hands.

"Ian!" Conlan's gut churned as he jumped over the two counters between himself and Ian. Just as he made it to Ian's side, the warrior started to pitch forward.

Conlan caught Ian to him and cursed in Gaelic. "Where are you hurt?" Conlan said.

Ian's face was growing white. He opened his mouth and blood dribbled from its corners.

"Godsdamnit!" Hawk swept everything off one of the counters and it all went crashing to the floor.

Conlan lifted Ian and laid him flat on the counter. Blood coated both of them, but most of it was Ian's. When Conlan moved Ian's arms from where he'd been grasping his stomach, Conlan's body went cold.

Ian's belly was ripped open and blood poured from the gaping wound. Iron from Fomorii claws was already eating away at his vital organs. If it had been a surface wound, he probably could have been saved . . .

But not this.

"It is beyond any of our healers' skills." Conlan looked at Sydney. "Or your healers'."

Ian groaned, and more blood bubbled up from his mouth to slide down the side of his face. His words were difficult to discern as he spoke. "I go to join my brethren in

Summerland." He grasped Conlan's hand. "Rest easy, brothers," Ian said as he looked at all three men. "And D'Anu sisters," he added before he began to fade away.

Conlan held Ian's hand until there was nothing left to hold. Ian's form wavered and vanished, leaving only a few sparkles where his body had been. They winked themselves out, and he was gone.

The shock of his death and the screaming pain in her arm made Sydney's head spin. Her knees gave out and she hit the floor.

And fell into darkness.

Chapter 6

Balor sniffed the stifling air in the sewer passage and grasped with his senses, reaching out for his eye. Even though it was somehow shrouded, the eye Darkwolf kept from him still drew Balor like a lodestone.

He ground his teeth, and fury caused such an intense heat that the sewage at his feet boiled. Filth coated his body and his loincloth, and the stench clogged his nose. But it was no worse than the place he had been used to before he had been drawn from Underworld by his goddess wife.

Where was she? He missed Ceithlenn's fire, her body, her love.

With his hands pressed to either side of the rough brick sewer passage, he moved blindly onward toward his eye. The eye that should have been returned to the center of his forehead the moment he was brought to this Otherworld.

The eye he could use to slay thousands by merely focusing on them.

Balor's magical powers were great even without the eye, but he needed it to make this world his. He would return to Ireland, where he had ruled among the other gods two millennia ago. The old gods had retreated to Otherworld.

Now only Balor and his wife would own this Earth Other-world.

But Darkwolf and that bitch of a Fomorii demon had betrayed him. Somewhere the warlock was hiding.

Balor would find him. And kill him.

He came to an abrupt stop. All his senses burned with the knowledge. Darkwolf and the eye were leaving whatever sanctuary had shielded them so well.

The god clenched his fists and turned in the direction his eye was moving.

*C*hapter 7

When the seven remaining D'Danann and D'Anu arrived at Sydney's house, she thought she was going to collapse. Exhaustion hit her as her adrenaline rush faded. Hanging from the ledge, using the spells to get out of the pantry, fighting the Fomorii, and the wound on her arm—

Oh, and let's not forget getting caught buck naked with Conlan's cock in my mouth.

Just the memory sent a rush of heat throughout her entire body.

Chaos greeted them at the door with a whine and bark. Sydney could tell right away the Doberman familiar sensed her pain and her injury. Normally he jumped up and planted his paws right on her chest in greeting. This time he trotted at her feet, making whimpering sounds of concern as her friends helped her toward the kitchen.

The pain in her arm from the Fomorii claws was so great that her eyes watered and she had to grit her teeth.

When Sydney had passed out at the hotel, Silver had used magic to help stem the blood flow and begin the healing process. Conlan had taken off his leather tunic and wrapped it around her arm to further protect it until they reached Sydney's home.

Silver immediately sat Sydney down at the kitchen table to work on her arm, Mackenzie and Alyssa joining them. Hawk and Cael headed off to take showers, Hawk in the downstairs bathroom and Cael upstairs. Conlan followed the witches into the small kitchen.

Unlike the six other gray magic D'Anu witches who had lived in an apartment building in the Haight-Ashbury district, both Sydney and Hannah owned houses. Hannah was wealthy enough to have bought her own, whereas Sydney had inherited hers. Due to a great battle with the goddess Ceithlenn, the other witches and Hannah had lost their homes. Fortunately, Sydney hadn't been identified as one of the witches who'd fought in that battle, and her house had not been seized.

Since returning from Otherworld, the four D'Anu and four D'Danann had been using Sydney's house as their base while they searched San Francisco for Darkwolf and Junga.

Seven now. There were only seven of them remaining. Sydney's head swam and her heart ached at losing Ian.

Rage bubbled inside Sydney, pushing aside the pain. "Damn the Fomorii, damn Darkwolf and Junga!" she shouted and clenched her fists. Witches didn't believe in hell or damnation, but Sydney could think of no other words to describe her fury at them at this moment. "I can't believe Ian's gone." She choked over her words as she looked at the faces of her friends in her kitchen. "And what will we do without him?"

From behind her, Conlan settled his hands on her shoulders. Her anger made her want to shrug out of his grasp, but she let him massage her neck and shoulders instead.

"We will send word to Otherworld of Ian's passing on to Summerland." Conlan's hands worked magic with her tense muscles. "Another warrior will come to aid Alyssa."

Ian had been Alyssa's teammate. The witch looked

shell-shocked as she sat in the kitchen next to Mackenzie, across the table from Sydney.

Mac had come out unscathed, but Alyssa had a gouge on her neck, and she was holding a bloodied cloth to it. Her T-shirt was shredded across her chest, exposing the body armor beneath—armor that no doubt had saved her life.

"Where are your healing supplies?" Silver asked Sydney as she went to the oak cabinets.

"To the left of the sink." Sydney winced as a fresh wave of pain washed through her arm. Chaos laid his head on her lap, and she felt the power of his magic in the comfort he gave her.

The kitchen was one of Sydney's favorite places in her home. It had oak cabinets, marble countertops, and a rack hanging from the ceiling above the kitchen island with gleaming copper-bottomed pots and pans. The kitchen floor was oak, too, and Silver's jogging shoes made soft sounds as she returned with several bottles and jars.

Conlan stayed behind Sydney's chair and continued to work his own magic by massaging places he could reach without the interference of her body armor. She focused on taking deep breaths and relaxing, pushing thoughts of the cyc, thc battlc, and dcath from hcr mind.

As Conlan pressed his thumbs along her neck up to her scalp, she wished she had the body armor off so she could get the full effects of his massage.

Wished she and Conlan had everything off and were naked. In her bed.

Sydney groaned at the mental image, and he paused. "Am I hurting you?"

Her face heated as she snapped back to the moment. "No. I'm enjoying it."

Mackenzie winked at her, and Sydney's face grew hotter. *How can I even think of sex at a time like this? And with a guy like Conlan who has a reputation for playing the field?* Perhaps it was her mind's way of dealing with the horrors they had experienced.

Silver handed Alyssa and Sydney each a lodestone. She wrapped her hand around hers and immediately the pain in her arm lessened. Mac started attending to the gouge on Alyssa's neck while Silver unwound Conlan's tunic from Sydney's arm. She grimaced from pain when the leather stuck to her torn flesh as it was pulled away.

"Ouch." Silver grimaced, too, as if the wound were her own. "All three slashes are going to need stitches. They're too deep to close up any other way."

"Great," Sydney grumbled. "We should be out looking for Darkwolf, not having to mess with my arm."

The need to find the warlock and the eye was so intense she felt it in every muscle of her body. If Balor reached Darkwolf before they did . . .

In past battles, they'd had several more D'Danann to aid them in the search and in the battle with Ceithlenn, the evil goddess wife of Balor. But after losing their headquarters, they hadn't yet found a location to house a larger contingent of warriors.

Only eight people would fit into Sydney's small house, and that was pushing it. So for a few days, just the group of them would be in on the hunt until they could get backup.

The kitchen's normal scents of the dried herbs hanging over her stainless steel sink combined with the smells of healing powders, creams, antiseptics, and blood. The tea tree antiseptic was the most intense of all the scents. Marigold cream and comfrey ointments were also used on her wounds, along with a good dose of Silver's magic.

Silver then grabbed another jar out of the cabinet and held it up for Sydney to see, when the three claw marks had been cleaned and were ready to be stitched up.

"Yup." Sydney nodded and added, "I think I'd rather be asleep for this one."

Just a single breath of the sleeping potion and Sydney entered darkness again.

Chapter 8

When Sydney woke, she blinked away the blurriness of her vision. Silver was rubbing something that felt soothing on her stitches. They crawled up Sydney's arm in three long rows like marching spiders.

She was still in the kitchen, only now she was in Conlan's lap. He had wrapped his strong arms around her waist, and her back was against his bare chest. His scent surrounded her, mixing with all the other smells.

Only now there was one more. She sniffed. "Chicken noodle soup." Her words came out a little slurred, but her stomach growled quite clearly.

"Nice to see you awake." Silver started gathering the supplies and taking them back to the cabinet. "Soup will be ready after you take a bath. You'll feel better. Stronger."

"I think you're right." Sydney's head spun a little as she eased to her feet, placing one palm on the tabletop to brace herself. Conlan stood with her, steadying her.

She leaned into him as he took her to the large downstairs bathroom that adjoined her bedroom. He shut and locked the door behind them, then turned on the water in the whirlpool tub.

For some reason it felt totally natural for him to be undressing her. After he removed her glasses and set them on the marble countertop, he tugged her T-shirt over her head, taking care with her injured arm.

"I worried for you, sweet witch," Conlan murmured as he unfastened her body armor and dropped it to the tile floor. "But you are a strong warrior."

Sydney smiled. She still felt a little groggy and woozy from the knockout potion, but the man was turning her on. Her arm didn't hurt right now, although her body ached from the day's events. Yet he still caused butterflies to flutter in her belly.

"Hold on to that bar," Conlan told her when she was naked. She wrapped her fingers around the towel rack and he released her. She listed a little to one side but was too fascinated by watching him strip out of his clothing to really pay any attention to it.

His finely carved chest was already bare. Her mouth watered as he removed his boots and she watched the play of muscles across his shoulders. It still amazed her that there were no signs on his back of where his wings appeared when he wanted them to. Just smooth, golden skin.

When he pushed down his leather pants, she sighed with pleasure. He was so gorgeous. Every hard, sinewy, inch of him.

Yummy.

Conlan helped her into the whirlpool tub. Her stitches were magically waterproof, so she didn't have to worry about them.

It was heaven as she sank into the warmth. With a big splash and swell of water, Conlan slid in behind her so that her back was to his chest, his very hard cock against her ass. Using one of her loofah sponges and her favorite raspberry-scented body gel, he began to wash her body, and she sighed.

She'd never done anything like this in her life. In past relationships she'd always dated the man for a while before she would allow the relationship to progress to a sexual stage. If the man was truly interested in a relationship with her, then he'd be willing to wait.

Two times she'd had her heart broken, and she'd broken a heart once herself. But none of the relationships had been serious. All three relationships had been enjoyable, romantic, special in their own ways, and it had hurt to end them. But to this day she remained friends with each of the three men—they were all good guys, just not *right* for her.

Conlan was so different. He made her crazy. Made her thoughts twist and turn until she was willing to do anything with him. She'd known the man, what, a few days, and she'd already gone down on him and was now naked in a bathtub with him? Was she out of her mind?

Yup. Certifiable.

Sydney threw herself into the moment, putting aside her misgivings to enjoy what he had to offer. Right here. Right now.

"Tell me about yourself," she said as he massaged her at the same time he washed her.

He paused in his movements before continuing. "There is not much to tell."

Sydney snorted. "Oh, yeah. You're probably like the other D'Danann, around two thousand years old. After living forever and a day, how could you not have anything to say about yourself?"

Conlan kissed the curve of her neck, and she shivered. "I have been a warrior since I was a youngling. It is all I have ever known." He kissed the other side of her neck, and she shivered again. "My parents were both warriors who died in battle against the Milesians, the time when the

D'Danann fell and left to form our Sidhe in Otherworld. That was long ago."

"I'm sorry." Sydney was quiet for a moment. "My parents live in Seattle. They're both D'Anu witches, but not gray magic like I am. I'm so glad they don't live here. I wouldn't want them in this kind of danger." She had to thank Anu that so far the war was contained in San Francisco. If it spread beyond the city—she didn't even want to think what that could mean.

He began washing her again. "While you slept, Silver said you are what is called a CEO of an advertising agency."

She found it hard to talk with the way his hands soaped her body. It felt soooo good. "I took a leave of absence when things started getting really rough with the demons. I've taken so much time off, I'm not sure I'll have a job when all this is over."

The thought of the probable coming battles made her stomach twist. *Please let it all end with sending Balor, his bitch of a goddess wife, and all the Fomorii back to Underworld. And soon.*

Conlan continued to wash her. It was the most sensual bath she'd ever had. His fingers and hands were so skilled.

Well, he *had* lived around two millennia, after all. He was bound to have *loads* of talents.

They talked while he gently and slowly brushed every part of her with the loofah and bath gel. He told her a few stories from when he was growing up and asked her questions about her own childhood.

The whirlpool tub was large enough that he was able to turn her sideways in his lap so that he could even reach her toes. It was one of the most erotic things she'd felt—to have each of her toes and the bottoms of her feet washed by a man. Absolutely delicious.

When he washed her breasts, the loofah was rough against her nipples. He skimmed his lips over hers at the same time, and she released a long, low moan against his mouth.

He teased her between her thighs, barely brushing the loofah over her mound and the outside lips. His eyes held hers as he slipped the slightly abrasive sponge inside her folds, and she gasped when he stroked it over her clit.

She was so close to climaxing, but he just smiled and set the loofah aside when he finished cleansing her.

After arranging himself close to the water faucet, he forced her to turn her back to him and began washing her hair. He used a cup that had been on the side of the bathtub, filling it with water from the faucet and pouring it over her dark hair until it was completely wet. Then he began to work shampoo into it, massaging her scalp in a way that had her sighing with pleasure.

Because of her injured arm, Conlan wouldn't let her bathe him. She turned in the whirlpool tub so that she could watch him run the soapy loofah over his gorgeous body.

By the time they finished bathing, Sydney felt like she knew him almost as well as any man she had dated. They had shared so much in one sensual bath.

Rather than feeling sleepy from the knockout potion, she was wide awake now and so turned on she was vibrating with desire. Conlan helped her out of the tub and grabbed one of her thick towels and dried her off, her body tingling everywhere the cloth touched. He paid close attention to her breasts, his hands rubbing her nipples as he swiped the towel over them, making the nubs so hard they ached. She groaned and grew damp between her thighs.

He was more than careful around her injured arm, but right now it didn't hurt and she probably wouldn't have noticed it anyway.

She wanted him inside her. And she wanted him now.

Sydney trembled with need as she helped dry him. When she reached his groin with the towel, she wrapped her fingers around his cock.

It was his turn to groan. He murmured something in Gaelic, then cupped her face in his palms. The slightest brush of his lips across hers made that place between her thighs ache so bad she could hardly stand it. He slipped his tongue into her mouth, and she moaned with pleasure at the taste of him. So male. So good.

She skimmed her hand up and down his cock, and he moved his hips in rhythm to her strokes. Their kiss intensified and grew so wild that Sydney felt like she could climax just from his kiss. He drew away, and his eyes were a stormy green that told her how turned on he was. With a shiver of anticipation, she released his cock to take one of his hands in hers. She unlocked the bathroom door, opened it, and led him into her bedroom.

They eased onto the bedspread, lay down face-to-face, and studied each other.

He trailed his fingers over the swell of her breast and down to the curve of her waist. "I told you we would finish this, sweet witch."

Sydney shivered at the contact of his callused fingers on her soft skin. "I want you, Conlan." She reached up and stroked her thumb over his stubbled cheek. "I want to feel all of you. And so you don't worry, I'm a witch, so I will conjure a magical shield inside me."

A low rumble rose up in him, and his eyes darkened. "I will be inside you. Soon." He grasped her ass and jerked her close so that his erection pressed against her belly and her nipples brushed his chest. She reached between them, grasped his cock, and squeezed.

Conlan slid his hand from her ass up and into her wet hair. He brought her to him and caught her lower lip between his teeth. The feel of him sucking on her lower lip made her sigh, and when he released it to slip his tongue between her lips, she moaned.

All her senses were on fire. The way his muscled form pressed up against her made her whole body burn. His earthy male scent filled her, surrounded her. The soft groans coming from him created an excitement within her—to know he wanted her as much as she wanted him. She didn't want to stop kissing him, his taste was so addictive. Whenever she looked at him, his beautiful green eyes drew her in, and she wanted to lick every inch of his glorious golden skin.

She almost felt a sixth sense with him, too. As if she could communicate with him in her mind and feel what he was feeling.

"We can mind-speak," came his voice in her head.

She jerked away from his kiss and stared at him. "Did—did you just talk in my mind?"

"Yes, sweet witch." He was smiling and he wasn't moving his lips.

Embarrassment and irritation rose up within her. "You were reading my thoughts?"

"No. You merely projected your desire to speak with me on this level." He ran his thumb across her moist, kiss-swollen lips. *"You can mind-speak with me, as well. Project what it is you wish to say."*

Her anger died a quick death. She sensed no dishonesty in him. Only the intense desire to fulfill her fantasies.

And he was a fantasy man if she ever saw one.

"Kiss me again," she said forcefully in her thoughts. *"And hold me tight."*

He smiled as he brought their mouths together and hooked his thigh over her hip so that they were pressed even closer to each other. *"My pleasure, sweet witch."*

Sydney's head spun from the kiss. He spoke soft words in Gaelic in her mind as his mouth mated with hers. She'd never been so aroused in her life—having him speak to her while kissing her—it was amazing.

He slipped his hand from her hair and moved it down her side, then grasped her ass and clenched his hand in the soft flesh.

A moan rose up in Sydney. *"I want you so badly,"* she said to him in her mind. *"I don't think I can wait much longer to have you inside me."*

This time a low growl rolled through her thoughts. *"Be careful, or I will fuck you so hard and so deep you will scream my name."*

"Do it." His words sent a rolling thrill through her belly and she pumped her hips. She couldn't wait much longer for the real thing. *"I've never screamed before. Make me scream."*

In a slow movement, taking obvious care not to hurt her injured arm, he rolled her onto her back. His eyes focused on hers as he slid between her thighs. He rocked his hips, brushing her folds with his cock and rubbing her clit with its hardness.

Sydney lifted her hips to meet him, wanting him so badly she could taste it. *"Take me,"* she almost screamed in her mind. *"Take me, now!"*

Conlan's jaw tightened. He grasped his erection and placed it at the entrance to her channel. She tensed. He made her wait only a fraction of a second more, and then thrust his cock deep inside her.

She cried out loud. It felt more wonderful than she'd ever imagined. He was thick and long, stretching her and filling her. He held himself motionless inside her, his hips pressed tight between her thighs.

When he began pumping in and out in long, sure strokes, Sydney thought she was going to lose it. If her body had been on fire before, now it had gone supernova. Her orgasm started to twist inside her like a fire serpent.

"Scream my name out loud," he said in her thoughts. *"I want to hear my name on your lips."*

Sydney was incapable of thought at that moment. All she could do was feel.

She closed her eyes, but the moment she did, Conlan

commanded, *"Look at me. I want to see those beautiful lavender eyes when you climax."*

An unintelligible sound rose in Sydney's throat as her gaze locked with his. His thrusts became harder. Deeper. Faster. His jaw was tense and his forehead covered with beads of perspiration.

All her senses whirled around her at once, and when he said in her mind, *"Come for me, sweet witch,"* she lost it.

"Conlan!" she shouted, letting his name tear from her throat loud and long.

Sydney's body vibrated as if she might fly apart. She felt like sparks prickled every spot on her skin and wouldn't have been surprised to see her body glowing.

Conlan grunted as he continued his thrusts. Her core contracted around his cock, and she desired more, more, more. She never wanted this moment to end.

She climaxed again when he shouted, "Gods, Sydney!" He pumped a few more times before collapsing on top of her.

For a moment she could barely catch her breath because of his weight. But she loved the feel of his sweat-slicked skin against hers so much that she didn't care if he moved or not.

When he finally rose, he braced his hands to either side of her chest and looked down at her. His cock was still inside her, and he pressed his groin tight to hers. They smelled of soap, sweat, and sex and she'd never felt so good in her life.

"Beautiful witch." He smiled. "I think you have cast a spell upon me."

Chapter 9

Sydney snuggled closer to Conlan, feeling more sated and happy than she had in a long time. Maybe forever.

Which was a crazy idea since she barely knew the man.

Her stomach rumbled.

Conlan nuzzled her neck and chuckled. "We had best get something into your belly."

Sydney sighed. She'd rather stay in bed with Conlan.

They showered together—and it was a wonder they made it out of the bathroom as hot as their shower turned out to be.

When they finished, Sydney slipped into one of her lavender satin robes. It brushed her toes and caressed her body. With her magic, she dried her hair and smoothed it so that it lay straight, curving only slightly at her shoulders. She put on her glasses, which she had always been told looked elegant on her.

One of the benefits of being D'Danann, was that Conlan had clothing spelled by the Fae to clean itself. All he had to do was murmur a few words in Gaelic, and his clothing was no longer covered in Fomorii blood—or sweat for that matter—and was mended as well. It was as if the clothing were new again. Maybe it was something about the magic that made him smell like he'd been flying in fresh forest breezes.

She really had to get herself some of that clothing.

He had left his tunic in her kitchen, so when they walked out of her bedroom, he was bare from the waist up. Mackenzie, Alyssa, and Cael were in her living room.

"Didn't realize you had such thin walls in this house," Mackenzie said with a grin. Cael chuckled, and Alyssa hid her smile behind her hand.

Dear Anu. They heard me scream Conlan's name.

Sydney was certain she turned five shades of red. "Where are Hawk and Silver?" she asked, doing her best to change the subject.

Mackenzie replied, "Otherworld." The pert blond leaned back on Sydney's cranberry-colored couch. Alyssa perched on the end of the love seat, and Cael relaxed in the recliner.

"To bring back another warrior, I assume." A heavy weight settled in Sydney's belly at the thought of Ian's death.

Mackenzie's smile faded. "Yeah. I imagine they won't be gone long—probably back by morning. Silver took your car to Golden Gate Park to get to the gate to Otherworld. That way they can return faster once they cross worlds."

Sydney nodded. San Francisco's famed park covered over one thousand acres with more than a million trees. Hidden deep in a meadow that only the D'Anu and Elementals knew, was a bridge, a gate to Otherworld.

Only those of Elvin blood could pass through the gate, or escort someone across the worlds, and Silver was one quarter Elvin.

A loud rumble rose from Sydney's stomach, and Mackenzie grinned again. "I guess all that hard work . . ."

Sydney knew exactly what Mackenzie was talking about, and she was tempted to put cayenne in the witch's dinner.

Conlan stood silent beside Sydney, and when she glanced up at him, he looked down at her and he smiled that sexy playboy smile.

She was such a goner.

Throbbing in her arm woke Sydney the next morning and she groaned. Her head pounded, too. She hoped Silver was back and could brew up a pain remedy. The only witch who could outdo Silver was Cassia who was half-Elvin, and Cassia was in Otherworld right now. They were all descendents of the Ancient Druids and healed faster than normal humans. But it would still take some time.

Sydney stumbled out of bed, naked, and looked back at the rumpled sheets. A smile tugged at the corners of her mouth. Conlan had spent the night with her and they had made love twice more.

It had been so long since she had sex that she ached between her thighs, and her nipples were sensitive from his sucking on them.

Sydney rubbed her eyes and staggered to the chair where she'd tossed her robe. She was worthless without her morning dose of caffeine, and the rich smell of coffee brewing in the kitchen called to her.

She didn't bother looking in the mirror. In the morning, before she had her coffee, she didn't care what she looked like.

Yawning, Sydney opened the door and padded out of her room and into the hallway. She came to a dead stop.

A beautiful blond woman wearing royal blue robes had her arms wrapped around Conlan's neck.

Her lips on his.

"Come back," the blond said as she drew away. She trailed one of her fingers down his chest to the waistband of his pants, close to his cock. Emeralds glittered on every one of her fingers. "I cannot bear to be parted from you any longer. I need you in my arms again."

Ice coated Sydney's skin and her heart. She could barely breathe. A strangled sound came from her throat, jerking Conlan's and the woman's attention to her. Sydney whirled and ducked back into her room.

She shut the door, locked it, and sank to the floor with her back against the hard wood. She wrapped her arms around her knees and tilted her head so that her skull met the door. Her eyes were dry as she stared up at the ceiling, but her heart hurt.

Conlan belonged to another woman, and he had fucked around on that woman.

And, worst of all, Sydney had started to fall in love with him.

Conlan gave a low growl as he reached up and grasped Chaela's wrists and pushed her away from him. His blood burned, knowing what Sydney must think of him at this moment.

And what she thought of him mattered more than he wanted to admit.

Chaela, the D'Danann High Chieftain, scowled and looked at the closed door behind which Sydney had vanished. "So. As soon as you leave my bed, you fuck a common witch?"

"Return to your chair in the court, High Chieftain." Conlan met her emerald eyes, which matched her rings. "You do not belong here. Nor do you belong in *my* bed."

"You will return." Chaela straightened and lifted her chin. "Or you will be banished."

Conlan crossed his arms over his chest. "You would tell the other Chieftains to banish me because I will not fuck you any longer?"

Chaela's cheeks tinged pink. "You will not be allowed

to return as you are disobeying a direct order from the High Chieftain. None would believe that I would bed a common warrior such as you. And you are far too honorable to bring it before the Council."

He studied her for a long moment. "You are angry for the moment, but I do not believe you to be petty."

Chaela clenched her fists, but then she relaxed her hands at her sides. Her chest rose and fell as she took a deep breath and her expression softened. She raised one hand and cupped his cheek. "I was wrong to send you away because we were seen by that warrior and witch. I miss you."

Conlan caught her hand and drew it away from his face. "I respect you, Chaela, and I care for you. But we can remain only friends. A friend you will not even acknowledge, as you did not when I bedded you."

"You know I could not and cannot." She let her hand fall to her side. "I am the High Chieftain. I can consort only with the court and with Pleasure Partners. Not with a warrior."

"I know." His voice softened. He took one of her hands in his. "Farewell, Chaela."

She blinked rapidly as if fighting tears. But her expression immediately tightened and she bowed from her shoulders. "May you have fortune in your quest to find the eye."

"I thank you." He returned her bow.

Chaela gave him one last look, and with a swish of her robes walked from the hallway and to the living room.

Conlan raked his fingers through his hair and stared at the door to Sydney's room. What she had heard and seen—she must think him the worst of bastards in all the Otherworlds.

He moved to the door, pressed his forehead to it, closed his eyes, and projected his words in mind-speak. *"Please let me in, Sydney. I would like to explain."*

A moment and then he heard the click of the lock. He raised his head as Sydney opened the door. She looked rumpled from sleep and tired and absolutely beautiful. But something more was in her lavender eyes.

Before he could speak a word, she said, "I heard everything, Conlan." She took a deep breath. "I didn't mean to listen at first, but I was sitting by the door. Now I understand that woman was your sex partner, but she's not anymore."

He smiled and pushed the door open wider so he could take her in his arms. "Thank you."

She backed away, avoiding him. When she looked up, her eyes were misty. "I can't do this."

Conlan went still and his smile faded. He was afraid to breathe. "What do you mean?"

"You. Me. Sex." She raised her arms and let them drop to her sides. "The world is wrong. My life is wrong. And I can't run to sex to heal that."

He firmed his expression and gave a low nod, his muscles aching from being so tense. Apparently he meant nothing more to her than sex. "As you wish," he said in a tight voice. He turned and walked out the door, shutting it behind him. Perhaps harder than he should have.

Sydney stared at the closed door, her eyes aching to cry. But that wasn't going to happen. His easy acceptance of what she'd told him made it clear that he was what she had expected. A playboy. She meant no more to him than that woman, Chaela, had. A good fuck for the warrior.

She sucked in a deep breath. There was no time for this kind of crap. They had a warlock and a god's eye to find.

After plenty of caffeine and a shower to wake up, Sydney settled herself at the large oak table in her dining room with Silver, Mackenzie, and Alyssa. The three other witches seemed just as jumpy and unsettled as Sydney felt.

The High Chieftain had been escorted back to Otherworld, along with the warrior she had brought with the intention of substituting him for Conlan. Another D'Danann, Darian, had been left behind to take Ian's place.

Sydney held her coffee cup in both hands. Its warmth did nothing to thaw the ice in her veins that formed just by thinking about the task ahead. Chaos stirred at her feet as he tried to give her some comfort with his magic.

The four witches had their divining tools before them, and were going to attempt to locate Darkwolf again. This time they would stay together, rather than breaking the city up into quadrants like they had before.

All four D'Danann were in the living room, working out strategies while they waited. The witches had chased them out of the dining room so they'd have fewer distractions when they performed their divinations.

"Why did I find him so easily?" Sydney stared into her mug, the lighting reflecting off the coffee in its depths. She looked up. "Every other time, when all eight of us have been together, we've never been able to find him. Why now?"

Silver's heavy fall of hair slid across her shoulders as she shook her head. "I don't get it either. Unless your power has grown that strong."

Sydney thumped her cup onto the table. "I'm a powerful witch—we all are. But I don't think I'm *that* powerful."

"Don't sell yourself short," Mac said as Sydney turned to stare outside.

Late morning sunshine spilled into the dining room through the bay window that overlooked Sydney's garden. Unfortunately, she hadn't been able to tend it since the battle against the Underworld demons had begun before Samhain. If the war didn't end soon, she was probably going to miss planting season.

A smile almost creased her face at the thought of gardening, but instantly her mind clouded again. Too many people had already died because of the demons and the evil goddess from Underworld.

She had to focus and remain focused.

And that included keeping her mind off a certain warrior.

Sydney clenched her hands around her coffee cup, and clenched her teeth just as hard.

"Everything's wrong," she muttered as her thoughts grew darker. "All wrong."

"This will end." Alyssa's soft voice drew Sydney's attention to her. "And I believe we will win this war."

Sydney sighed. The only other sound was Mackenzie shuffling her tarot cards. Chaos moved and settled himself on Sydney's feet.

"I pray to Anu and the Ancestors you're right." Sydney reached for the dragon incense burner. She lit the cone of patchouli incense that would help serve as protection during their divinations.

Against all their lives, against everything they knew to be, the clock was ticking. Sydney could feel it in her mind and heart. They had to find Darkwolf *now*.

Mackenzie started divining by placing tarot cards in a circle spread in front of her. As she turned the cards she frowned. "Why is the news always leaning against us?"

A tightening sensation gripped Sydney's belly.

After studying the cards a little longer, Mackenzie looked up. "If anything about Darkwolf can be called good news, we *are* going to find him. Bad news is there's going to be a whole lot of trouble along with him."

Okay, good. They were going to find Darkwolf. The eight of them could take him and the demon-woman. Sydney's shoulders remained tense, though. What about that other trouble Mackenzie was talking about?

When it was her turn, Alyssa took a deep breath. Using a wooden matchstick, she lit her candle, which was purple for psychic work and lilac scented for clairvoyance. She blew out the match, leaving behind a hint of sulfur. For a long time Alyssa stared into the dancing flame.

"I can see Darkwolf . . . and the eye." She shuddered. "Somewhere near water. Maybe on water. Underwater?"

"Anything else?" Silver rubbed Alyssa's back with her palm. Alyssa had always been the most sensitive of the eight witches in the gray magic Coven.

"The eye—it's shrouded." Alyssa tilted her head. "As if covered with lilac silk."

Sydney nodded. "It was very strange when we met with Darkwolf and saw the eye. It was surrounded by what appeared to be his purple magic." She looked at all the others. "I think he's hiding from Balor."

"I wonder why?" Silver had a thoughtful look on her face as she tapped her fingernails on the table. "Is there some other plan he has for it?"

Something Sydney remembered the Fomorii saying before they walked into the hotel kitchen came to mind, and she put her palms flat on the table as she looked at the other witches. "The demons—they were looking for Junga and Darkwolf." She shook her head. "Not for us."

Mackenzie frowned. "How do you know that?"

"One of the demons said something about Darkwolf and Junga possibly already knowing the Fomorii were there," Sydney said, the memory coming to her more clearly now.

"That's right." Silver looked at Sydney. "Maybe Darkwolf didn't set us up. Maybe we were just at the wrong place at the wrong time."

"I don't know." Mackenzie wore a skeptical expression. "I don't trust him for any reason."

"I'd better go next." Sydney struck a match on the small matchbox and held her palm close to the flame as she lit the candles in front of her. The heat was warm against her skin. After she blew the match out, the sulfur smell was replaced by the scents of blueberry from the blue candle for protection. She also took Alyssa's purple, lilac-scented candle and a black, patchouli-scented candle for protection and removing bad luck.

Chaos stirred. He stood and put his head on Sydney's lap, and she felt the power of his magic join hers.

Sydney drew in a deep breath before she picked up the black candle. Her injured arm ached as she tilted the candle over her silver bowl of consecrated water and dripped the wax into it. She frowned at the cloud that formed from the black wax. She set the candle down, then dripped wax from the purple candle. It developed into the shape of a lion. Also not good. Last she dribbled wax from the blue candle and a snake formed.

Just great.

She set the candle down and continued to stare at the shapes. Her eyes unfocused and the shapes began to move.

In the patterns in the water she saw Balor.

The god's heartbeat began to pound inside her head and she wanted to scream.

When she could tear her gaze from the vision, she fought to thrust the pounding sound from her head. She looked at her Coven sisters and she cleared her throat. "The usual as far as trouble brewing and to be on guard against an enemy. That enemy is definitely Balor." Her stomach churned. "The one-eyed god is close. Very close to the eye."

Everyone was quiet until Silver said, "Let's finish up so we can figure out what to do now." Silver brushed her hands on her jeans.

Silver usually wore short skirts and heels, but the time for that had passed now that they were at war. Sydney herself used to wear only fitted jackets and skirts or nice dress slacks. But for the time being they'd pretty much all gone to wearing black from head to toe, like the D'Danann, but in jeans, T-shirts, and jogging shoes.

Silver gripped the edge of her pewter cauldron and peered inside. The cauldron was filled with consecrated water. Sometimes Silver would see visions in the placid surface, and other times three-dimensional images would rise from the water.

This time the water remained silent to those around the

table. Silver's mouth twisted into a frown as she gazed into the cauldron.

When she raised her head, she looked a little pale. "I saw Darkwolf and the Dark Elves. Something is up with him and the Drow." Silver's throat worked as she swallowed. "Sydney is correct. Balor is close to Darkwolf and the eye."

Silver looked directly at Alyssa. "You're right about him being close to water. And I think I know exactly where he is."

Chapter 10

The eye was close now. He could sense it.

Balor felt his way along the sewer. In some places the bricks of the walls crumbled beneath his palms. After living in Underworld centuries without his eye, he was used to feeling his way around, always in the dark.

But he was sick of it. He had manipulated Darkwolf all these years through the essence in the stone eye to escape that detestable existence. Balor and his wife had drawn the once-white witch to the eye where it had surfaced on the shores of Ireland. The moment the witch touched the eye he had transformed into Darkwolf, the most powerful warlock who served Balor.

At Balor's bidding, Darkwolf had worn the stone eye on a chain around his neck. Through the essence of the eye, Balor had twisted Darkwolf's mind, brought the darkness to him. The warlock had performed blood sacrifices, had murdered, had used all forms of black magic at Balor's commands.

Why was Darkwolf now fighting him? Balor ground his teeth. Why had Darkwolf kept the eye and attempted to hide it from him?

How was Darkwolf able to block his mind from Balor's intrusion? How had Darkwolf grown so strong?

Balor growled and the tips of his fingers crackled with his magic. None of this would matter. Darkwolf would be the first being he murdered once he had retrieved his eye.

Even over the stench of raw sewage, Balor smelled salt water.

He was nearing Darkwolf.

Chapter 11

S ydney took a deep breath and shivered. It was so dark around the warehouse it made her skin crawl. An electrical pole stood off to the side of the dock, the light shining from it quickly devoured by the darkness.

Conlan and the other three D'Danann had flown to their posts at the top of the warehouse. Mackenzie, Silver, and Alyssa stood behind Sydney, and Chaos was at her side—another shadow in the night. All were prepared for whatever happened next—at least Sydney hoped they were.

They faced the pier and the mostly calm bay. Gentle swells rolled in, making soft slapping sounds against the rocky shore. A low mist hovered above the water, and the chill air caused Sydney to shiver again. The smell of fish and brine was strong, mixed with the smell of pitch from the pilings that held up the pier. At first the fishy odor caused her heart to pound—what if the smell was from the Fomorii? But their rotten-fish stench was far worse and enough to clog a person's senses.

The last of the evening's sunlight had vanished not long before they arrived. Since they were all wearing black, they easily melted into the darkness. The witches could have pulled glamours, making them disappear from sight, but glamours worked only on humans. Otherworldly beings could easily see through the magic.

Sydney's feet began to ache from standing so long. Her injured arm throbbed, so she reached into her jacket pocket to wrap her hand around the lodestone. Instantly the pain lessened, and she relaxed a bit.

The city's nighttime clamor was far enough away that the dock was fairly quiet. Around the dock were stacks of old boxes and a shipping truck.

The sudden appearance of two people startled Sydney into taking a step back.

Her foot landed on Mackenzie's, causing the witch to hiss through her teeth, probably from pain.

Chaos gave a soft growl.

Darkwolf and the demon-woman had arrived via Darkwolf's ability to transfer himself and others to various places. Sydney wondered if it was the eye that gave him that talent.

The pair stood just outside the light so that Sydney could barely make out their faces.

Sydney almost crawled out of her skin when four men strode from the darkness, as if they had just crept out from beneath the pier. She squinted as they walked into the light. The tall, imposing figures were dressed like warriors of old, with shoulder- and breastplates. Quivers of arrows were slung over their shoulders, and swords hung from their belts.

Then Sydney realized what truly made them different. The four men had bluish-gray skin.

They were Drow. Dark Elves.

Slowly Darkwolf and Elizabeth-Junga walked toward the Drow, who met them halfway.

The shrouded eye against Darkwolf's chest glowed from the purple magic wrapped around it.

Low voices carried from the six people—beings—standing on the pier.

"Where is your king?" Darkwolf said in a voice filled with anger. "Only he can take it from me."

"We were ordered to bring the eye to him," one of the Dark Elves said.

Darkwolf stood still for a moment, his face appearing both angry and indecisive.

"The eye must go with you," Darkwolf said at last with a heavy sigh. "It can't remain in this world. Somehow, the eye must be destroyed, and the only place I can think of is Otherworld."

Sydney's heart beat faster. If what she was hearing could be believed, Darkwolf was attempting to keep the eye from Balor—and trying to destroy it.

But were the Dark Elves to be trusted? They were neutral beings who chose whatever cause was most beneficial to them. Who was to say they wouldn't turn the eye over to Balor in exchange for something they wanted? Or was there some way for them to use it to their advantage?

Darkwolf brought his hands to his neck and picked up the chain. He started to bring the chain over his head, then stopped.

Sydney frowned and glanced over her shoulder at her teammates. She gave a nod, the signal to get ready to charge Darkwolf and the Drow.

With narrowed eyes, Sydney paused to watch Darkwolf.

His hands trembled. His jaw tensed, and it looked like he was breaking into a sweat as his whole body began to shake. His muscles strained against his T-shirt.

Darkwolf dropped to one knee, releasing the chain and bracing one palm on the ground. "Fuck!" he shouted. "I can't get the goddamn thing off!"

"Then come with us to Otherworld," one of the Dark Elves said in a commanding voice.

Darkwolf looked up at the demon-woman, who took a step back. "I cannot go," Elizabeth-Junga said with her head raised, her voice clear and strong. "My kind has been banished from Otherworld."

Darkwolf hung his head and closed his eyes, his hand on the ground clenched into a fist.

That's when she saw it. The tiniest bit of crimson leaked through the magic-shrouded eye Darkwolf wore.

Balor was near!

Her witch's senses told her that it was true.

"Now!" she cried in mind-speak to Conlan. *"Balor is close. We've got to get the eye now!"*

It took only moments, then in the faint light, four figures came to land quietly, surrounding Darkwolf and the Drow. The witches charged forward, their footsteps loud in the night.

The warlock jerked his head up. Before he had the chance to throw up a shield, Sydney flung a rope of magic around him, pinning his arms to his sides, as he had so recently done to her.

Only she had Chaos, too. The Doberman slammed into Darkwolf with his front paws, forcing him to the ground. He growled at the warlock, his face close to Darkwolf's neck.

The D'Danann had drawn their swords and advanced on the Drow and the demon-woman.

"We have no quarrel with you, D'Danann," one of the Drow said.

"Over the eye, we do." Conlan raised his sword, ready to behead Darkwolf.

Sydney's gut churned. This was no demon that would turn into silt when his head was taken off. This was a man, warlock or no.

"Stop!" Sydney raised her hand. "You can't kill him. The Paranormal Special Forces have enough on him to put him in prison for a long time."

Conlan made a low growling sound and didn't change his stance. When Sydney pushed down on his arm, he finally lowered his sword.

"Shit!" Darkwolf's face twisted as if he was in excruciating pain. He looked down at the eye, which was growing brighter red beneath the purple shroud. "Balor is here. You have to free me or he's going to get his fucking eye."

A burst of flames came from out of the darkness.

It slammed into one of the Dark Elves.

He cried out—

Then vanished into sparkles of obsidian.

Sydney whipped her head in the direction the flames had come from. "Duck!" she cried as another blast of fire shot toward them. Sydney flattened herself to the ground.

The fire seared a path straight over her head. It hit the old shipping truck and consumed it in flames. The smell of burning paint, plastic, and upholstery caused Sydney to choke.

As Sydney maintained a tight hold on Darkwolf with her magic, and Chaos kept him pinned to the ground, Silver threw up a spellshield around the D'Danann, Drow, witches, and Darkwolf. Sydney saw Alyssa and Mackenzie add their powers to Silver's, making the spellshield glitter in a rainbow of colors.

More fire shot through the night. Only this time it slammed into the shield. Sydney felt the power and the heat of the blast and almost fell when she rose from her prone position to her knees.

"Our shield!" Silver cried. "I don't know if we can hold him."

The D'Danann stood with swords at the ready. The remaining three Dark Elves had drawn their bows and nocked their arrows. Elizabeth, the demon-woman, narrowed her eyes as she flexed and unflexed her hands, her fingers shifting to blue claws and back.

Sydney's whole body trembled, but she maintained her

magical hold on Darkwolf. She stared into the darkness in the direction the blasts of fire were coming from.

An imposing figure appeared in the pale glow of the dock's only light.

A being she had seen only once before.

Balor.

The Underworld god's muscles bunched and flexed as he strode toward them. He wore only a loincloth, showing his powerful swimmer's physique. If he'd been a man, he might have been considered handsome—if it weren't for the single eye at the middle of his forehead. Or rather the eye socket.

The god raised his hand, and more fire blasted from his palm and slammed against the shield. Alyssa dropped to her knees and cried out even as she kept her hands raised, trying to support the shield with her magic.

"Hold!" Silver shouted. "Dear Anu, I don't know if we can take another hit."

Conlan started to charge forward, but Sydney shouted to him. "Don't try to leave. It will compromise the integrity of the shield."

"Release me, witch," Darkwolf shouted at Sydney. "Can't you see he'll get the eye if you don't let me go? Your shields won't hold him. You need my powers to help you."

Sydney paused.

Chaos growled.

Dear Ancestors, did she dare?

"We're running out of time," Darkwolf said as another blast of fire slammed into the shield.

Sydney took a deep breath. Something inside her told her it was the right thing to do. Maybe it was Anu, the Ancestors, or the Elementals. Whatever—whoever—it was, she knew it was right.

"Get off him, Chaos," she said to her familiar.

The Doberman gave her a look that said, *What—are you crazy?*

But Sydney withdrew her magical ropes and set Dark-wolf free.

In one lunge he pushed himself to his feet. He flung his own shield of purple magic into the air and it melded with the witches' magic.

"My eye," came a dark and terrible voice. "Give me my eye and I will let you live."

"Like that would ever happen," Mackenzie said as she gritted her teeth and focused her magic on the shield.

Now that she had freed Darkwolf, Sydney was able to lend her power to the spellshield.

Another blast of fire slammed into the shield and then another. The witches cried out and Darkwolf staggered. The eye at his throat grew a brighter shade of red, and the purple that had shrouded it vanished.

"Do away with your magic and let us fight him," Conlan shouted.

The witches looked at one another. This time Macken-zie dropped to her knees and cried out when the next blast hit the shield.

Sydney's eyes met Conlan's, but she said, loud enough for everyone, "On the count of three."

"One." Their magic took another hit from Balor's flames. "Two." The following burst almost obliterated the shield. "Three!"

Everyone dived out of the path of the next bolt of fire, and Chaos yelped. It hit hard enough that it looked like a small meteorite had blasted a hole in the ground.

Blood churning, Conlan growled and clenched his sword as he spread his wings. The other D'Danann took to the air the same time he did. They circled Balor, dodging the bursts of fire he shot into the air at them.

At the same time, with his other hand, Balor blasted fire at the Dark Elves. The Drow were quick and lithe as they dodged the magic while shooting their arrows at the blind god. It was obvious Balor's senses were keen. Even though he didn't have sight, his hearing was apparently acute, his reactions swift.

The arrows bounced off Balor as if his skin were made of body armor like that the witches wore. Even though the arrows did not pierce his skin, they seemed to anger Balor more. He roared and hit one of the Dark Elves in the shoulder with his magic, causing the Drow warrior to shout. He stumbled back, his arm loosely hanging from his shoulder. He lost his grip on his bow.

The witches surrounded Balor and at the same moment spun their magic ropes around the god.

He flung them off as if they were made of water.

"No, Chaos!" Sydney shouted as the Doberman charged Balor.

The god was so consumed with fighting the Drow and the D'Danann that he didn't notice Sydney's familiar until the dog's jaws sank into his thigh.

Balor shouted and swung his fist at Chaos. The Doberman dodged the blow. Snarling, the familiar attacked again.

Heat burned in Conlan's body. He took the opportunity to dive, his sword pointed directly where the god's heart should be. A fraction of a moment before Conlan's sword would have pierced Balor's flesh, the god batted Conlan aside with his hand as if he were a mere bird rather than a D'Danann warrior.

The power of Balor's strike drove Conlan backward and sent pain searing through his shoulder. He ground his teeth against the pain and dove for Balor again.

If Balor took possession of his eye, they would all be dead the moment he inserted it into its socket and looked at them. Such was the power of his eye: he could slay with a single glance.

Memories of fighting Balor and the Fomorii centuries ago churned through Conlan's mind. When the sun god Lugh had shot Balor's eye out, it had incapacitated him long enough for all the gods to combine forces and send Balor and his bitch of a wife away.

Even without his eye, Balor had apparently grown in strength in many ways during the two millennia he had been relegated to the farthest reaches of Underworld.

Conlan and the other three D'Danann dove at Balor again. As they drove their swords at him from four different directions, Balor formed a shield over his head. The moment Conlan's blade hit the shield, an electrical shock jolted his body and the power of the rebound flung him at least twenty feet from the god.

Hawk, Cael, and Darian each fared much the same. The next time they came closer to Balor, their swords ready, but they hovered just above his shield. The god took one slow step after another, getting closer and closer to Darkwolf.

The Drow continued to fire their arrows at Balor, but his shield deflected them. The witches attempted to use spellfire, but the shield absorbed their magic. Chaos lunged again, but he gave a loud yelp when he came in contact with the god's magic.

Even though they couldn't touch Balor, he was able to use his flames. Mackenzie's shirt smoked from where fire grazed her back, fortunately over the body armor. Cael's arm was burned, and Conlan felt as if his arm had been dislocated from Balor's blow.

Nothing they did was working against Balor. And with every step he was getting closer to Darkwolf.

Conlan narrowed his gaze. Darkwolf stood calmly behind the fray, his attention focused completely on Balor. The demon-woman stood at his side, still in her human form but not appearing as calm as the warlock. Her jaw tensed, and he saw glimpses of the demon beneath the woman's skin. Her form wavered in and out, and he could tell she wanted to fight—but, like the rest of them, her attack would no doubt be just as ineffective.

The eye at Darkwolf's throat became a deeper crimson, and Conlan's gut tightened. The warlock was going to turn over the eye!

Just as Conlan started toward Darkwolf, the warlock held up one of his hands. Red light shot from the eye at the same time purple exploded from the warlock's palm. The two magics twisted together.

Then arrowed through Balor's shield and slammed into the god.

Balor shouted as he was driven backward by the power of his own eye and Darkwolf's magic. Before Balor could regain his footing, more magic blasted the god.

A third stream of red and purple magic shot toward Balor, but this time it was met by the god's magic.

The two magics slammed together with enough force to cause the ground to rock. Mackenzie fell on her ass and Alyssa dropped to her knees.

When the magics met, Darkwolf stumbled backward. But determination shone on his face. His stream of magic continued to battle Balor's.

Darkwolf wrapped his free hand around the eye.

A crimson glow encased his entire body.

Red magic exploded from Darkwolf toward Balor.

The power of it obliterated the stream of magic coming from the god.

Darkwolf's magic slammed into Balor. He stumbled back and roared.

The god vanished.

For a moment everyone on the ground went completely still. The D'Danann hovered in the air with slow beats of their wings.

All that could be heard was the crackle of the flames burning the truck and the lap of water against the shore. The stench of the fire overcame every other smell.

"Is he gone?" Sydney broke the silence and looked at Darkwolf. "Are we really rid of him?"

Darkwolf had not let go of the eye, which continued to bleed crimson light between his fingers, but his body was no longer glowing. "For now Balor is gone, yes." His voice was hoarse. "Permanently? I don't think so."

"Turn over the eye." Sydney held out her hand. "It has to be destroyed."

One of the Drow warriors stepped forward and frowned. "He was unable to remove it earlier."

"As if I would turn it over to you, witch," Darkwolf growled at Sydney.

"Allow me." Hawk scowled, raised his sword, and approached the warlock. "It will be easy enough to take it once we remove your head."

"No!" This time it was Silver holding her husband back. "The Paranormal Special Forces can take care of him."

Chaos bared his teeth at Darkwolf and growled. Apparently he agreed with Hawk.

Hawk kept his sword raised. "How could you feel any pity for this—this piece of dragon shit after all he has done to you and your Coven sisters and to all the innocents he has slaughtered?"

Silver gave a loud sigh. "I know. It's crazy." She looked at the warlock. "You're going to have to answer for your crimes, Darkwolf."

The warlock moved his hand to the arm of the demon-woman.

The corners of Darkwolf's mouth quirked. In a mere wink, the warlock, Elizabeth, and the eye were gone.

Chapter 12

"G odsdamn." Conlan stared at the spot where Darkwolf and the demon-woman had been standing.
He ground his teeth. The eye had nearly been within
their grasp, and again it was gone.

Sydney wiped the back of her hand over her cheek. Her
eyeglasses were slightly tilted, her face smudged, and with
her fierce expression, she looked as though she wanted to
slay a demon with her bare hands. Instead, she rubbed behind Chaos's ears as she gazed into empty space where
Darkwolf had been.

Emotions so strong welled up in Conlan's chest that
he could barely rein them in. His heart felt like it was on
fire—and not from the battle. He wanted to go to Sydney, to wrap his arms around her and keep her close to
him. To protect her and make sure nothing bad ever happened to her.

By the gods, he wanted her. The thought shocked him to
his core. He had never wanted any woman for more than a
night's pleasure, or maybe several. He enjoyed women.
Their silky soft skin, the taste of them, the feel of their bodies pressed to his, sliding inside their welcoming depths.

But Sydney . . . Suddenly thoughts of other women faded so completely that he could think only of her. Could imagine having only her in his arms, could imagine being inside only her body . . . her mind . . . her soul . . . her heart.

Conlan pushed his fingers through his hair, battling with the enormity of what raced through his mind.

He wanted Sydney as his own. As his mate.

Forever.

As if she could hear his thoughts, her gaze met his, and for a moment he could not breathe. She stood several feet away, but he could close that distance, sweep her into his arms, and take her to Otherworld with him. The look in her eyes—did she feel the same?

"The Drow." Mackenzie interrupted his thoughts, and he looked at the D'Anu witch. She stood on tiptoe and looked around those standing in front of her. "The Dark Elves are gone."

Silver braced her hands on her hips. "They probably returned to Otherworld."

With frustration, Sydney pushed her dark hair from her face. "How did you know they'd be here?"

Silver stared off into the distance. "Below the pier, in the rock wall, there is a door to Underworld. I was certain that if the Drow were involved, and it was near water, that it had to be here."

"Do we really know if they wanted to destroy the eye?" Sydney's jaw muscles tightened. "Or did they want to use it for other purposes?"

"If our envoy is successful, we'll know soon," Alyssa said, referring to another group of D'Danann and D'Anu witches who were currently in Otherworld seeking aid from other races in the fight against Balor and his wife.

"Like we talked about before, it was too easy locating Darkwolf these last two times." As Silver spoke, she drew Conlan's attention. "I wonder if he wanted us to find him, wanted us to know he's fighting Balor, just as we are."

Hawk scowled. "Darkwolf should be shown no mercy . . . as he gave none to the people he has slain."

"Hawk's right." Mackenzie came up beside the warrior and folded her arms across her chest. "Darkwolf is one of the vilest criminals we have ever known. He could be toying with us."

Conlan's gaze settled on Sydney when she spoke. "I agree with Silver. The only answer is that he *wanted* us to find him. In the past, every other time we've tried, it's been impossible." She glanced again to where the warlock had been standing. "He could have left at any time. But he chose to stay with us and fight Balor."

Hawk looked like he wanted to interrupt her, but Sydney continued, "Yeah, he's done some pretty screwed-up things—to put it kindly—but if he's fighting Balor and his bitch of a wife, we can use all the help we can get. And then we'll deal with Darkwolf and Junga."

Everyone was quiet for a moment, then Alyssa said with exhaustion in her voice, "Let's get back to Sydney's house. It's time to regroup."

After scratches and wounds were attended to, everyone took turns bathing or showering to remove the stench of battle. Conlan wanted to be with Sydney, but she had slipped away into her bedroom and locked the door.

By the time she emerged, Conlan had taken a shower in the upstairs bathroom and was waiting in the downstairs hallway for her. He stood with his arms crossing his chest, facing her door, and contemplated breaking it down.

The door jerked open. Sydney stumbled into him the moment she came out of her room. She put her palms against his chest to steady herself, and he unfolded his arms to grasp her hands in his. He held them over his beating heart.

For a long moment she looked up at him. Her eyes were

filled with desire, but her brows were drawn downward as if in concern. Was she afraid to care for him?

When she spoke, she tried to pull her hands from his, but he refused to let go. "I told you I can't do this."

"Yes." He brought her hands up to his mouth, brushed his lips across her knuckles, and he felt her shiver. "You can."

"Conlan." She clasped her fingers around his, and he raised his head to look into her eyes. "Everything's so wrong now. This war. My life."

"But we . . . *we are right*." His heart thrummed. "The two of us make a whole. Side by side we will work together."

"I could fall for you." Sydney stared up at him and her lips trembled. "I think I already have. A relationship that's purely sex without commitment—I can't do that. Not at this time in my life. It's better that we end this now."

He released her hands and slid his fingers into her hair. "I am speaking of a lifetime together. Many lifetimes. You are meant to be my mate, and I am meant to be yours. Even though we have known each other for a short time, I know in my heart and soul that this is true."

Sydney frowned—not the reaction he wanted to see. He brought his free hand up and brushed her lower lip with his thumb.

"Are you serious?" she finally said. "You're not talking about just a bunch of sex when we're together?"

"The sex is good." He smiled as he moved his hand over her cheek. "But having you for my own, to bond with you . . . that would be my life's greatest joy. In all my years of existence, I have never been so sure about something as I am about you and me."

The hint of a smile tugged at the corner of her mouth, and warmth began to wrap its way around his heart. "The sex *is* good." She slid her hands up his chest and clasped her arms around his neck. "But having you all for my own is better."

"Ah, gods." He clenched one fist in her hair, slid his free arm around her waist, and pulled her tight against him. "I will never let you go, Sydney Aline."

She smiled, the worries of the world seeming to slide away from her face. "And you'd better not plan on going anywhere without me."

Conlan crushed his mouth to hers so hard and fierce he was afraid he might bruise her lips. But the moan rising from her throat told him that she desired this kiss as much as he did. She tasted of fire and passion, of sweet nectar and spice. Her lips meshed with his, and their tongues met and met again.

The heat in his body expanded and his cock grew hard and fierce against her belly. He moved his hand over the satin of her robe and slipped it inside. A gasp rose from her throat when he pinched her nipple. Gods, but he had to claim her in every way, and he had to claim her now.

Sydney's mind, body, and heart were on fire. His kiss made her head spin, and she could barely remember where they were.

She knew this was right. Their relationship had happened so fast, but, in a way, war had a way of making things sharper, clearer. It made one realize just how important it was to hold on to loved ones and to take a chance on new love when it felt so right.

When Conlan pushed aside her robe and captured one of her nipples with his mouth, she couldn't think anymore. She could only feel.

"I love how soft you are in my hands," he said in her mind as he pushed her robe open wide, baring all of her to him. *"I love the beauty of your eyes. I love the way you taste. I love your spirit, your fire. I love everything about you."*

"Conlan." She gasped out loud as he pushed her up against the wall of the hallway and started trailing a path with his tongue down her belly. In her mind she told him, *"I love your acceptance of who I am and what I must do.*

That you don't hold me back. I love the way you care about those around you."

When he reached her mound with his tongue, she was incapable of speech in any form. He teased her by licking a path through her trimmed hair. Whimpers spilled from her lips as he slipped his tongue into her slit. She tilted her head back against the wall and clutched his hair, holding his face tight against her folds.

Sydney closed her eyes and totally gave in to the sensations of his tongue licking her in long strokes and his mouth sucking on her clit. Cool air brushed her breasts and tightened her nipples.

The climax building inside her was growing and growing in intensity until tears leaked from her eyes.

Her orgasm slammed into her, and she cried out as her entire body trembled with its force. Only the wall kept her from falling as her body shook against Conlan's face. When she looked down at him, his eyes met hers. He gave her clit one more lick, sending a spasm through her.

"Well, I'd say she's more than okay," came Mackenzie's voice.

Sydney gave a small cry and jerked her robe around her at the same time Conlan rose. He brought her tight against him.

Mackenzie had laughter in her eyes. "You sound like a wounded animal when you climax."

Hawk snorted and Silver slugged him.

For the second time Sydney thought she'd die from embarrassment. She had completely lost her mind from the moment Conlan started kissing her.

"Come on." Alyssa tugged at Mackenzie's arm. The witches turned away, but this time Mackenzie laughed out loud.

Sydney looked so beautiful when she was embarrassed, Conlan thought. He did his best not to smile as he scooped her up into his embrace and carried her into her bedroom. He shut the door with a kick, then took her to the bed.

Apparently they had both lost their minds in the hallway.

"I am sorry," he said as he lowered her on to the white sheets. He sat next to her and brushed his knuckles over her cheek. "You make me forget everything but you."

Her breasts rose and fell as she sucked in a deep breath and let it out. "Let's not do that again, okay? Um—the getting-caught part." Her face was still flushed as she added, "The other part—you can keep on doing that."

"Forever." He bent to kiss her softly on her mouth.

"Mmmmm . . . forever," she murmured against his lips.

Conlan pushed aside her satin robe, baring her beautiful body again. He caught the scent of her woman's musk mixed with raspberries.

As he stared at her body, he rose and began stripping off his clothing, starting with his boots. Sydney watched him, her eyes half shuttered.

"If we weren't caught, that would have been the best orgasm ever," she said as he moved onto the bed beside her.

"We will make up for it." He trailed his fingers from between her breasts all the way to her mound. Goose bumps rose on her flesh. "Soon I will bury myself deep inside you."

Sydney squirmed at the image of him doing just that. But then a thought came to her that caused her cheeks to heat. "Do I really sound like a wounded animal when I climax?"

Conlan's face took on a serious expression. "You sound beautiful. I want you to cry out like that every time we make love."

Make love. She felt jittery and shivery all at once. *We're making love. It's not just sex anymore.*

Conlan moved his hard body closer to hers as he continued to trail his fingers from her breasts to her mound and back.

If he was going to tease her, she could one-up him.

She slid her fingers down his muscled abdomen to his erection but didn't take it in her hand. Instead, she traced around his balls and the base of his cock.

Conlan groaned. He grasped her ass and pulled her to him, hard, and his erection pressed against her belly.

"You wish to tease me?" he said as he took his cock in his hand and slipped it between her thighs, against the lips of her sex. With slow, deliberate motions, he began sliding his erection against her folds.

Sydney dug her fingernails into his biceps and moaned. "No, I won't tease you anymore. Please just be inside me."

Conlan rolled her onto her back and slid his body between her thighs. He pumped his hips against her, not entering her. She looked up into his eyes that had turned from grass green to as dark as an oak leaf. Her belly flipped at the sight of this big, muscular man spreading her thighs apart with his hips. She shivered as his long, blond hair trailed her skin when he nuzzled her neck and breasts. He laved each of her nipples with his tongue until she was squirming beneath him.

"Please," she begged him in her mind. *"Please be inside me."*

Conlan raised his head, and his look was intense and almost fierce. He took his erection in hand and guided it to the entrance of her core. For a long moment his eyes held hers as he braced his hands on the bed to either side of her breasts.

"Now I will make love to you, my sweet witch." His sudden thrust was deep and filling. Sydney gave something between a moan and a cry as he began pumping his hips and driving his cock in and out of her channel.

Sydney squirmed even more as he kept his pace slow. She dug her fingernails into his ass and brought her hips up to meet his. Gradually their pace increased until he was driving into her so hard her head was rocking against the headboard.

Every orgasm she'd had with Conlan had been a different experience. This time, jolts of electricity fired through her body as one big ball of energy built in her abdomen.

The stinging sensation on her skin grew greater and greater until she was vibrating from the force of it.

When she climaxed, it was like the ball of electricity exploded inside her. Every nerve ending in her body tingled with sensation, and her core throbbed and throbbed around his cock.

With her orgasm came a cry rising from her throat she couldn't hold back. That she didn't want to hold back.

"That is what I love," he said in her mind as he thrust harder and harder. *"Always scream for me, just like that."*

A few more strokes and Conlan shouted her name. His cock pulsed inside her channel, and she spasmed around him, clenching down hard.

They both groaned with satisfaction when Conlan rolled onto his side, taking her with him. Their skin felt warm and sweaty against each other and their chests rose and fell with the same rhythm. The smell of sex was strong and it mingled with Conlan's male scent that she loved so much.

"It's been so fast, but it's so right." Sydney cuddled closer to him. "I'm totally in love with you, Conlan."

He pressed his lips to her hair. "And I love you, my sweet witch."

Any Witch Way
She Can

by

CHRISTINE WARREN

For JoJo. This time it is so *all about you.*

Chapter 1

Ａnd he stood me up! *Stood me UP!* Can you believe
that?!"

"No."

"I went home and I checked my voice mail *and* the voice
mail on my cell *and* my e-mail. I even looked out the
bloody window for a carrier pigeon. Not a thing. The slimeball didn't even have the courtesy to offer a lame excuse!"

"He's a slimeball."

Randy Berry glared at her cousin. "I'm detecting a certain lack of sympathy in your voice, Cass."

Cassidy Poe Quinn rolled her eyes and continued to
shove onesies into a voluminous diaper bag. "Miranda, it's
four forty-five in the afternoon. I had two hours of sleep
last night because the twins were up with colic starting at
midnight, and Sullivan and I have a plane to catch in just
over three hours. I'm sympathetic, but I'm also half-
comatose. Take what you can get."

Randy held up a hand. "Okay, rewind. Can we bring it
back to me here? I'm having a crisis."

Her cousin snorted. "Of course, Ran. How could I have
forgotten that it's all about you?"

"You're saying that like I'm some sort of selfish git. Believe me, I'm sorry you're exhausted, but you've got a husband who's so sexy there ought to be a law against it, two gorgeous little babies who could star in Gerber commercials, and you're packing to go spend six months at a sixteenth-century castle in Ireland that happens to be your family's second home. Me? I'm withering up like an unused piece of parsley no one wants garnishing their plate."

"Bitter, party of one, your table is ready."

"Hell, yeah, I'm bitter," Randy said. "I think I've got good reason. I'm thirty-two years old. If the term 'spinster' were still in use in today's vocabulary, I'd be the poster child."

Cassidy shut the top drawer of the nursery dresser and made a loud sound of disgust. "Oh my gods, Ran, you need a Valium or something. What the hell has gotten into you? This aging, man-crazy desperation thing is so not you."

"Maybe I'm turning over a new leaf," Randy shrugged, shifting in the enormous rocking chair she'd commandeered while her cousin packed baby gear in preparation for her trip. "I've been nursing this mad-on all day, but then I realized maybe the problem here isn't the guys I date. Maybe it's me. Maybe I drive men away, and I need to start resigning myself to a lifetime of loneliness and pet cats."

"Okay, now I *know* you need a Valium."

"No, what I need is a man."

Cassidy laughed and grabbed a handful of tiny white socks. "Trust me, you've had your share of men, Ran."

It was hard for Randy to take offense over something so true, especially since she didn't see any reason to think of it as a bad thing, but she gave it a try. "Gee, thanks, Cass. Here I am, baring my soul to you in my time of need, and you're calling me a whore."

"What I *meant* was that you've never had trouble finding men, and you know it. I think what has you all tied up in knots right now is that you don't just want a man; you want a mate."

Randy flinched. "You're forgetting that I'm from the black sheep side of the family, Cass. 'Mating' is for Others. I'm as human as heartburn."

"Stop splitting hairs. You're just bent out of shape because you've finally realized you want someone to settle down with instead of someone to take you to the newest nightclub."

"Oh, great. So now I'm a *vapid* whore."

"Miranda Louisa, you could try the patience of a saint—"

"Which is something I'm very pleased to report you're a far cry from, Cassie love."

Both women turned to the door of the nursery at the sound of that deep, masculine voice. Even after more than a year of marriage, the sight of Sullivan Quinn could still make Cassidy visibly melt, and Randy had to admit that the sight of the six-foot-two-inch werewolf standing there with his arms full of drowsy little babies would make any woman's stomach give a flip. His son snoozed away on Quinn's left shoulder while his daughter rubbed the sleep from her eyes with a chubby pink fist.

Cassidy rushed forward immediately. "I'm sorry, honey. I was just finishing up their bag while they were napping. Have they started fussing again?"

"They're fine. I told you a drop of whiskey would settle them down." Quinn dropped a kiss on his wife's forehead and turned to raise an eyebrow at her cousin. "It might help you, too, Randy. You look as if you could use some calming."

"What I need isn't going to be found in your liquor cabinet. Unfortunately."

Quinn glanced down at his wife, a second eyebrow climbing to join the first.

"Randy is having a little . . . crisis of couplelessness,"

Cassidy explained, shrugging the bulging diaper bag onto her shoulder and leveling a pointed gaze at her cousin.

Randy felt herself squirming on the inside, but on the outside she restrained herself to crossing her arms over her chest and glaring. "Shut up," she muttered.

Quinn grinned. "It's nearly five, love," he said, turning back to Cassidy. "The car will be waiting for us downstairs, and we want to leave plenty of time to run through the mess at security."

"Right. Why don't you give me Molly? No sense in you trying to keep them both." She reached out and took her daughter, balancing the little girl on her hip. "Are the bags downstairs?"

"All but what you're carrying. I had the doorman arrange for someone to take them down."

"Good. Then we're all set."

Randy watched, sulking, as Cassidy and her husband linked their free hands, each with a baby on one hip and a glow of marital contentment on their faces. She wasn't sure if it was a lack of sleep or the stirring of jealousy in her belly that made Randy feel vaguely ill.

"Have fun," she managed grudgingly. "I'll make sure the plants stay watered and the mail gets forwarded, and I promise to clean up from any keggers before you get back."

"We'd appreciate that." Cassidy leaned forward to press a kiss to her cousin's cheek. "And if you can manage to look in on Gran once or twice, we'd appreciate that, too. She had a party last night, but we couldn't go because of the twins."

Randy rolled her eyes, but she didn't forget to give Cassidy a hug that encompassed both her and Molly. "Oh, yeah, because you know how thrilled Dame Adele always is to see me. It's going to make her day if I start hanging around and trying to take care of her. She'll probably smack me upside the head with her cane. You're gonna owe me for that one."

"Your sacrifice there is duly noted. But seriously, she's been upset lately with all this stuff with the Council. The fact that her suggestions are constantly being preempted by members of the Witches' Council is really getting her down."

"Whatever." Randy took no interest in the politics of the Council of Others in which her grandmother and cousin were so involved. "You're still going to have to make this up to me, which means you should give me the name of someone with a talent for love potions."

Cassie shook her head and headed for the door with a laugh. "The last thing you need is a love potion, Rand. You've always had men lining up at your door. All you really need to do is to make up your mind."

Before he moved to follow his wife, Quinn took Randy's hand with his customary Irish gallantry and drew her forward to drop a kiss on the top of her head. "And I think the last thing you should fear is spinsterhood, Miranda darling," he murmured, "but if you truly wish to find yourself a mate, I think you know what you ought to do about it."

Randy stroked a hand over baby Declan's fuzzy head while she frowned up at his father. "And what exactly is that?"

Quinn winked at her. "Make it happen. Remember, cousin, all's fair in love and war. And personally, I've never quite been able to tell the difference."

Chapter 2

The apartment had gone way too quiet now that everyone had left. That had been great while she'd been unpacking her bag in the guest room and helping herself to her cousin's bubble bath, but now it was eleven P.M., there was piss-all worth watching on television, and Marc, the jerk who'd stood her up last night, still hadn't managed to locate her cell phone number and grovel like the unworthy, slime-sucking bastard he was. And she had gotten no closer to figuring out what Quinn had meant with that last remark of his than she'd been when he'd first made it.

Flipping past four channels' worth of eleven o'clock news programs, Randy stared at the flat-screen TV and brooded. Cassidy had been right. This mood wasn't like her. Miranda Berry tended to be the sort of woman who figured there would be plenty of time to worry about the future when it got to *be* the future. She'd always been much too busy enjoying her life, and the men who moved in and out of it, to worry about settling down. As she liked to say to her friends and family, she'd been brought up never to settle, and she didn't intend to introduce the word to her vocabulary at this late date.

The problem was that she'd come up with that particular witticism when she'd been eighteen. Now she was pushing thirty-three, and being footloose and fancy free was starting to feel more like just being alone. It didn't help matters that almost all of her friends had gotten married by now—some of them more than once, it was true—but all the same, she was starting to feel left out of the marriage game. Looking at Cassidy and Quinn had gone from making her roll her eyes at their palpable enthrallment with each other to making her wince with envy. And she didn't even want to get started on the way her ovaries had started wailing and gnashing their teeth every time she saw Molly and Declan.

Gah. It was almost like she was finally growing up.

Randy sighed and tucked the chenille throw closer around her legs. Her tank top and sleep shorts might be comfortable, but they didn't do much in the warmth department. She wasn't so far gone into despair, though, that she planned to trade in her customary pajamas for a flannel granny gown. That would mean giving up entirely, which was something Randy Berry was constitutionally unable to do.

If you truly wish to find a mate . . . make it happen.

Quinn's words returned to haunt her. He made it sound like it was easy. Like all Randy had to do to find the man of her dreams was to click her heels together three times or wave her magic wand, and . . .

She froze.

Magic.

Bolting to the edge of the sofa, Randy let the blanket in her lap slither unnoticed to the floor.

That was it! Magic!

When she'd asked Cassidy for a love potion, Randy had been kidding—mostly—but that didn't make the idea worthless. Randy knew very well that magic existed, that it could do things most people never would have thought of before the Others Unveiled themselves to the mortal world, but Randy had grown up in a half-Other family. She'd seen magic happen since before she'd understood that not everyone had a grandmother who could turn into a fox whenever the situation warranted. Randy knew magic could do amazing things, so why couldn't magic find her a man?

"By George," she muttered, "it just might work!"

Springing into action, Randy jumped up from the sofa and ran down the hall to the study. The built-in shelves that lined the walls held Quinn's books on mythology and folklore alongside Cassidy's anthropology texts and obscure academic treatises, but unless she was very much mistaken, Randy would be willing to swear that those same shelves sported a small collection of books on magic and spell casting.

They had been part of her cousin's doctoral dissertation on the use of magic in native populations around the world. At the time, Randy had been unable to imagine anything more boring—especially given the dense, technical language Cassidy tended to use when talking shop—but now her heart beat faster at the idea that one of those books might hold the key to her future.

Shoving open the door, she flicked on the light switch and rushed into the room. Bless her organized little heart, Dewey and his decimals had nothing on Cassidy Quinn. Her shelves were sorted into subject areas, the titles alphabetized by author's last name. Randy didn't give a shit about authors, but at the moment, subject matter had become her utmost concern.

She scanned the shelves. "Languages . . . Latin American tribes . . . local history . . . Maa? . . . magic!"

And was this Fate speaking to her, or what? Displayed prominently in the middle of the shelf with an eye-catching red dust jacket sat a book entitled *Love Spells*.

Score!

Randy snatched it up and flipped to the table of contents. "To mend a broken heart? I think not." She dragged a finger down the page. "To attract a woman? Not really my thing . . . Ah ha! To attract a man! Page ninety-two."

Paper rustled.

" 'As I said in the beginning of the book, to cast a spell that forces one person to fall in love with another would be both immoral and contrary to the creed by which all witches must live. To bend another being's will is unforgivable, but that doesn't mean there's no such thing as a love spell. The spell described here is one that does not compel one person to love another, but instead allows the spell caster to guide her future love into her life.' "

Excitement made Randy wriggle. This was perfect!

" 'Of course, the same cautions apply to this spell, as to all the others in this book. Magic is not something to be used by those uneducated in its power. Casting a spell without truly understanding it can cause it to backfire in a way that could result not in true love, but in—' "

"Oh, whatever." Randy broke off and turned her attention to the actual steps of the spell listed on the next page. "Some lawyer probably made the author put a disclaimer in there." It didn't apply to her. She had magic in her blood. Almost. She scanned the instructions briefly and felt a rush of adrenaline that had her grinning for the first time in more than twenty-four hours.

"I can totally do this," she muttered to herself. "After all, how hard could it be?"

Chapter 3

I'm disappointed there's no eye of newt," Randy announced from her seat on the floor in the living room to no one in particular. The apartment was still empty, and the man of her dreams nowhere in sight. She optimistically chalked that up to the fact that she hadn't gotten around to casting the spell yet.

The instructions had been surprisingly complicated, and the list of necessary ingredients, minus any newt eyes, had proven a momentary setback. It named several items Randy had never heard of and more than one whose existence she frankly doubted. Still, no one had ever said the road to Prince Charming didn't contain some potholes— just look at what Cinderella had gone through!—but she knew that when she got there, it would absolutely be worth it. *He* would absolutely be worth it.

For once in her life, Randy had gone into something fully prepared. She'd actually read through the entire spell twice and made a mental list of what she would need to cast it, and she'd gathered her ingredients ahead of time, something she never did when cooking or, you know,

packing. Normally she was a fly-by-the-seat-of-her-pants
kind of girl, but she wanted to do this right. Otherwise,
there'd be no point in doing it at all.

The book's instructions were elaborate, but Randy had
determination and a certain level of adrenaline on her side.
She'd cleared off her cousin's coffee table, a low, round
expanse of mahogany that shone dark red in the light of
the dozen flickering candles she'd placed on its surface.
She'd turned all the lights off, per the spell, even though
that meant squinting to read the text in the uneven illumination of the candle flames.

On the plus side, the heat the candles threw out certainly kept the chill away.

Fidgeting in anticipation, she bent to the book and read
aloud.

" 'In a shallow silver bowl full of moon-bright river water . . .' Check." She pulled the stainless steel mixing bowl
she'd brought from the kitchen a little closer and poured
water almost up to the brim. Cassidy would never miss
those bottles of Evian, and seriously, where in Manhattan
was someone supposed to get "moon-bright river water"?
The Hudson? Get real. The candle cast a nice little glow
over the surface. That would do.

" 'Place seven scarlet petals from a fully bloomed red
rose.' Check." That one was easy. Quinn, bless his besot-
ted heart, brought his wife flowers so often, his florist had
named the latest baby after him. In fact, there were so
many of the things around the apartment that Randy threw
in an extra handful. Might as well do things right.

" 'Add half of what you need and of what you want a
quarter, for love is never lasting that on whims of fancy
grows.' "

She glanced down at the two lists the spellbook had instructed her to make: one contained two columns of the
things she thought she needed in a man; the other outlined

in four corners of a second piece of paper all the things she *wanted* in a man. And she was just supposed to throw out most of these?

Yeah, right. No way was she giving up "sexy." Especially not since she'd put it on both lists.

She tossed the two complete lists into the bowl and watched the paper slowly darken and sink into the water, dragging rose petals down with it. Her heartbeat quickened.

" 'To the mix add heartsease and a single tear of Venus . . . ' "

Okay, those had been challenging, since Randy wasn't sure what the hell either of them was supposed to be. She'd had to improvise. Venus, she knew, had been the goddess of love, the Roman equivalent of Aphrodite. She remembered vague stories from a unit on classical mythology in her high school English class, something about seduction and sensuality. After a moment of thought, she'd settled on a drop of the very expensive perfume Cassidy kept on the top of her armoire. That had to be close, right? It made a certain amount of poetic sense to Randy, at least. Carefully, she tilted the bottle until one drop rippled the surface of the water.

Her substitute for heartsease was more prosaic. She threw in an antacid. It eased heartburn, didn't it?

" 'A tablespoon of honey and a pinch of bitter tea . . . ' " Easy-peasy, thanks again to Quinn in all his tea-swilling Irish glory. The two ingredients turned the water an interesting shade of gold, but maybe it was supposed to look that way?

" 'A dash of salt to savor . . .' " Randy picked up the ceramic Tweety Bird salt shaker and bounced it vigorously over the bowl. " 'And a bit of rue for patience . . . ' "

At this, she scowled. " 'Rue' what? McClanahan?"

Wait, didn't to rue something mean to regret it? How the hell was she supposed to add regret to a bowl of soggy stationery? Clearly some witch had not thought this spell out thoroughly.

"Eh, I'll just skip it," she scowled at the flickering candle. Suddenly the warmth it gave off felt more like an inferno than a tiny flame. "It's only one ingredient. And I think by this point the idea of me being patient for this whole thing is ridiculous anyway. What's the worst that could happen?"

The candle sputtered, and Randy glared at it before reading the final instruction. " 'And stir three times with willow for to bring thy love to thee.' "

Okay, this was it. Taking a deep breath, Randy lay aside the book and picked up the wooden spoon she'd found in the kitchen drawer. She couldn't swear it was made of willow—how the heck could a person tell?—but it was a wooden implement specifically designed for stirring. What could be more appropriate?

Ignoring the disconcerting heat of the candles and the unexplained buzzing in her ears, she bit her lip and slowly lowered the spoon into the disintegrating mess in Cassidy's mixing bowl. With her heart in her throat, she stirred three times and repeated the phrase the book had instructed to seal the spell.

" 'As I will, so mote it be.' "

That's when the room exploded.

*C*hapter 4

"Well, well. What have we here? A late arrival?"

Randy frowned into the blackness and tried to remember where she was. She couldn't see anything, but she could feel a distinct chill in the air and something hard and rough under her legs. She could also hear. Oh boy, could she hear, because those questions had been asked in a voice as dark and smooth as cocoa.

But why didn't she recognize it? She really ought to recognize a voice that made her want to purr, shouldn't she?

Her frown deepened.

"Miranda Louisa Berry! What exactly is the meaning of this?"

Okay, that voice, she recognized.

Stifling a groan, Randy forced her eyelids open. That took care of the blackness, but no matter how many times she blinked, she couldn't manage to brush away the pinched, disapproving face of her grandmother that currently hovered over her.

"Oh, shit."

"Miranda, I will thank you to watch your language in my home."

In "her" home? She was at her grandmother's house? How the hell had she managed that? The last thing she remembered was sitting cross-legged on Quinn and Cassidy's floor casting that silly love spell. "Shit in a shitstorm!"

"Miranda!"

Randy struggled to prop herself up on her elbows and glanced around her. Not only was she in her grandmother's house, she was in the harridan's formal entry hall lying smack dab in the middle of the hideously expensive oriental carpet that covered the marble floor. Being stared at by at least two dozen people in formal wear. And she still had on her pajamas. No wonder she was freezing.

"Young lady, pick yourself up off the floor this instant. You are causing me a great deal of embarrassment in front of my guests."

"So what else is new?" Randy muttered, but she found herself pushing to her knees anyway. That was how things always went with Adele Berry. No matter how much Randy wanted to thumb her nose at the old biddy, she inevitably found herself obeying the woman's orders as if Randy hadn't managed to come of age more than fourteen years ago. Adele's power of arrogance both awed and mystified mere mortals.

"Allow me to assist you."

The cocoa voice slid over her skin again, raising goosebumps that had nothing to do with the temperature in the room. In fact, that seemed to rise every time it spoke, and this time the speech came accompanied by a lean, tanned, masculine hand that extended into her line of vision from somewhere above her.

High above her.

Craning her neck, Randy followed the sleeve of a dark, severely tailored tuxedo jacket up to a chest of impressive breadth before finally resting her gaze on a face that made the word "breathtaking" sound insipid.

The man had the features of a fallen angel, all dark and

chiseled and so perfect they verged on beautiful. Only the somewhat heavy and sharply arched brows and the wicked twist decorating his mouth saved him from any taint of the feminine. His eyes helped, too, all deep and blue and twinkling with naughty humor.

"Take my hand, Miss Miranda."

Worrying that she might have drool dripping off her chin, Randy resolutely dragged herself back to reality and clasped that strong, warm hand in hers. Then she had to worry if anyone else had noticed the way she'd shivered the instant her hand had touched the stranger's. The jolt of electricity that coursed through her at the contact could have lit up the Empire State Building for a week.

Judging by the widening of his wicked grin, the man at the other end of that handclasp had definitely noticed.

She allowed herself to be lifted to her feet, the pile of the carpet under her bare soles somehow helping her to regain her composure. "Randy," she said, using her free hand to brush back a tangle of her strawberry blonde hair. "No one who knows me actually calls me Miranda."

"Randy, then. My name is Michael. And I must say it is entirely my pleasure to meet you."

The hand clasping hers squeezed briefly before retreating with a gentle slide of fingertips across her palm. It made her thighs clench together.

Dear Lord.

"I thought this evening's invitation list was quite exclusive, Adele." A man of average height and above-average conceit stepped away from the crowd and raked Randy's figure with an insulting gaze. "We have serious business to discuss, after all. Business that will affect the Council. This is hardly the time for . . . uninvited guests."

The insult dispelled the energy between Randy and Michael and had her turning narrowed eyes on the source of the interruption. "And I thought you had to have balls to affect the Council. After all, my grandmother is so very good at it, and if that's not evidence, I don't know what is."

The man puffed out his chest and took a threatening step forward, but Adele stepped in front of him and raised a quelling hand. "Please, Harold, excuse my granddaughter. I can assure you I will deal with this interruption with all possible speed." Her bejeweled hands gestured to a set of double doors that had been thrown open in welcome farther down the hall. "Friends, let us continue our migration into the sitting room to relax after the excellent dinner my chef prepared. I have a very fine bottle of brandy I would be pleased to share with all of you. If you will."

Of course, her guests fell in like obedient little soldiers and filed into the other room. Not that several of them didn't cast curious glances in Randy's direction, and Harold continued to stare daggers at her. Adele, though, pretended not to notice as she herded everyone before her. Then she shut the doors behind the last of them and rounded on her granddaughter like a prizefighter swinging his way off the ropes.

"I demand an explanation for this behavior!" she hissed, stalking forward at a march that conclusively proved she had no need of the cane she never went anywhere without. "You have pulled some outrageous stunts in your day, my girl, but I do believe that tonight you may have outdone yourself. Do you have any idea who those people were in the group you so obscenely burst in upon?"

Out of the corner of her eye, Randy noticed that Michael hadn't joined the others in the sitting room but propped himself against the wall near the doors, arms folded over his chest and a very interested expression on his face. Adele, though, was too worked up to realize that she and her granddaughter were not completely alone.

Randy had been down this road too many times to mention it. You never knew when the presence of a witness might be the only thing preventing a murder. Might as well take advantage of it. "I dunno, Adele. They looked like the same old bunch of stiffs you usually invite to dinner. Was the president of the Weird Fuckers Society here tonight?"

"I told you to watch your mouth. Your father might not have raised you to behave like a civilized person, but I'll thank you to pretend to the title while you are under my roof."

While she might be one of the women in her family who didn't have fur, Randy could feel something rising on the back of her neck that felt remarkably like hackles. "My father raised me perfectly well," she growled, clenching her hands into fists. "He was at least willing to love his kid no matter what she turned out to be, which is a damned sight more than I can say for you!"

"Ladies." Michael stepped forward, an easy smile on his face, and a hard, glittering expression in his eyes. "I'm certain no one needs to work themselves up over this."

Adele turned on him, her expression going predictably regal and discouraging. "This is a family matter, Mr. Devon. It is none of your concern. If you would step into the sitting room, someone will help you to a glass of the excellent brandy I have already mentioned."

As a grand dame of Manhattan's Other Society and a long-time member of the Council of Others governing that society, Adele's tone of voice made it clear she was not a woman used be being gainsaid.

Michael Devon's response made it clear he didn't give a damn what she was used to. "Ah, but it's such a lovely family, ma'am. You can hardly be surprised that a man like me might take an interest in it."

"And neither of you should be surprised when I leave to let you duke this out," Randy said, giving the two of them a tight smile. She appreciated the sexy Mr. Devon's help, but she could take care of herself. And her grandmother's disdain had stopped hurting her feelings a long time ago. Turning on her heel, she stalked toward the front door.

"Where do you think you're going?" Adele demanded. "I haven't finished with you yet."

"You finished with me the second I was conceived, because you knew I wasn't going to fulfill the family legacy, so let's not kid ourselves."

"Whatever I may or may not have done, young lady, I'd much prefer that you refrained from airing family grievances in front of my guests. Though I suppose that must be too much to ask of you."

Randy snorted and reached for the doorknob. "You can take your martyr complex and shove it up your—"

A large hand covered hers. "Though I hesitate to appear as if I don't believe you can take care of yourself, Randy, you may want to delay leaving for the moment. It's nearly freezing outside, and . . . ah, I believe you may have neglected to bring your coat."

Against her will, Randy found herself glancing down at her clothing, the white tank top with the slogan "How 'bout these apples?" emblazoned over two pieces of bright red fruit that had been printed in strategic and eye-catching locations. Her silk shorts of the same color barely qualified as more than tap pants, and her legs were bare down to the tips of her cherry-red toenails. Not exactly the clothes for schlepping back across town to Cassidy and Quinn's apartment.

Although she'd probably get a few offers to help her work off her cab fare.

Still, never let it be said that she failed to out-stubborn the very woman who had passed the trait on to her. "I'd rather freeze to death than stay here," she scowled. "I know exactly how welcome I'm not, so I'd rather go back to my cousin's apartment where I know I *am* welcome. Even if I get hypothermia along the way."

Adele made a sound of disgust. "For heaven's sake, Miranda, can't you leave Cassidy and Sullivan alone for one night? They leave for Ireland tomorrow and will have more than enough to do preparing themselves and the twins for the trip without having you drop in unexpectedly. Have a little consideration for once."

Too pissed off even to point out Adele's mistake about the travel plans of the granddaughter the old woman actually approved of, Randy shook her head and twisted the doorknob. "Screw you, Adele."

She tugged, but the door never budged.

"Please." Michael laid a free hand on her shoulder. "It's much too cold to go outside like that. I'm sure we can find something else for you to wear before you leave."

"What? Wear something of my grandmother's?" Randy glared. "I'm certain she'd tell you the fabric would burst into flames the moment it touched my skin. If I didn't break out in hives at the same instant."

His mouth quirked. "Your grandmother does not strike me as the kind of woman to be caught unprepared. I feel certain she would have something set aside in case one of her guests was to meet with emergency. And failing that, I understand she has a live-in housekeeper. I'm sure she would be willing to lend you a pair of sweatpants, at the very least."

Trish would be happy to do so, Randy knew. But damn it, he was ruining her dramatic exit.

He must have seen the hesitation in her face and decided to press his advantage. "I'll even do the asking for you. Please. It would be silly to leave like this."

Looking up into those dark blue eyes, Randy found herself relaxing enough for a ghost of a smile to quirk her lips. "Right, because everyone loves a Mexican standoff."

"I hear ammo makers are nuts about them."

His smile made her stomach give a funny little flip. Actually, everything about him made something in her flip. She hadn't felt this on edge, this instantly attracted to a man since . . . ever.

"Michael, I beg you will forgive my granddaughter's

appalling manners and let her go to the devil in her own way," Adele announced, punctuating her statement with a thump of her cane. "I can assure you that is what she will do regardless."

Randy opened her mouth to reply in language that probably would have sent her straight where her grandmother had just predicted, but Michael stopped her with a gentle pressure from the hand on her shoulder. Her mostly bare shoulder.

She shivered.

"Mrs. Berry, I can assure you that you have no reason to apologize," he said, his voice all smooth and elegant, two things Randy had never much gone for in men. Before. "I take no offense at your granddaughter's behavior. I find her charming."

Adele's snort might not have been ladylike, but it was expressive.

Randy ignored it. "You're not so bad yourself," she said, wishing she'd met this man in a bar or a club or a prison. Anywhere but in her grandmother's house. "But really, I think we'll all be a lot happier if I just leave."

"I won't be," he murmured, his voice and his glance turning intimate while the hand on her shoulder tightened. "In fact, I would be very unhappy indeed."

That time, her stomach flipped, her thighs clenched, and her vision blurred, but Randy Berry was made of stern stuff. She pulled herself together through sheer force of will. "I appreciate that, and trust me, if you think I'm not going to slip you my phone number before I leave, you're kind of an idiot, but I do have to leave. I'll be fine. It's not like I'm going to walk home. I'll call a cab."

"You appear to have left your purse somewhere alongside your coat."

She scowled. "Shit."

"Isn't that just like you?" Adele said, her tone disapproving. Not that she ever spoke to Miranda in any other way. "I suppose you would have the driver take you to Cassidy's home and then expect her or Sullivan to pay your fare as well? Your lack of consideration is truly astounding, Miranda. I don't know why your cousin puts up with you, but I can assure you that if she and her husband were too busy to attend my dinner this evening, they would certainly not have time to deal with one of your escapades."

Okay, that was it. Randy turned on her grandmother, her eyes sparking in fury. "And I can assure you," she bit off, "that you are full of shit, *Grandmother*. You might value people based on what they can do for you, but Cassidy loves people for who they are, not who she wants them to be. And clearly that means a hell of a lot more, since *you* can't even keep the day of their departure straight. Cassidy and Quinn's plane took off more than four hours ago. They're not at home packing right now; they're somewhere about thirty thousand feet over Greenland!"

In the back of her mind, Randy hoped that seeing smoke billow from her ears and nostrils wouldn't turn Michael off, but at the moment, there wasn't much she could do about it. And it was probably better that he know what she was like before he asked her out. That way she would just be able to relax and be herself until she tripped him and beat him to the floor. Her attention, though, remained on Adele. No sense in turning her back to the cobra.

The old woman drew herself up like a queen, wrapping herself in a cloak of dignity and wounded innocence. "I am sorry to hear you think so little of me, Miranda, but I'm certain you will find yourself mistaken. I know very well when Cassidy and Sullivan are traveling, and I know their flight leaves on Saturday evening, not on Friday."

"It *is* Saturday."

Behind her, Michael shifted and cleared his throat. "Um, actually, Randy, your grandmother is right. Today is Friday."

She half-turned to stare at him as if he were demented.

She really hoped he wasn't, because that could put a damper on their potential relationship. "Uh, no, it's not. If it were, I would have been at work today, and I wasn't. I was at home brooding about the inevitable idiocy of men."

"No matter how highly you think of yourself, Miranda," Adele snapped, "even you cannot change the calendar to suit yourself. Today is Friday, March the seventh. If you don't believe me, turn on a television set or open up a newspaper."

That odd ringing Randy had heard in her ears as she'd cast the spell earlier suddenly reappeared, twice as loud. Her head spun drunkenly. "Friday?"

Michael responded to her hoarse whisper. "Yes, Friday. Randy, is something wrong?"

"Oh, no," she laughed, the sound tinged with hysteria. "Nothing at all. I'm fine. Just fine. So what if I went back in time? That happens all the time. Right?"

Michael stepped in front of her, but Randy's vision had gone all cloudy. "Actually," he said, his expression concerned and frowning. "It doesn't. It almost never happens. At all."

Chapter 5

For a second, Michael thought Randy was going to keel over right in front of him. His hands shot up instinctively to catch her as she began to sway, but she remained on her feet. Barely. Her huge, velvety brown eyes went unfocused, and she turned the color of schoolroom paste, but she didn't faint. He almost thought it might have been better if she had.

Better for him, anyway. Then he could have gotten his hands on those sleek curves.

Swearing, Michael pushed away the thought and carefully grasped her upper arm. Her skin had gone icy. "Randy? Are you okay? Do you need to sit down?"

She gave another one of those disconcerting, high-pitched laughs. "No, no. I'm fine. I may very well have lost my mind, but other than that, everything's perfect."

Adele shot him a look of confusion and something else. Concern. "What on earth is she talking about? Miranda, what is going on here?"

"I have no friggin' clue, Gran. You're the Other; you tell me. How is it that I could have woken up on Saturday, spent Saturday doing things I distinctly remember, seen my cousin and her husband off for a flight that left on Saturday night, and then blacked out for a second and woken up on Friday, a day I also distinctly remember having already lived through? Got any ideas?"

Michael felt his curiosity stirring. "Only one," he said. "Magic."

Adele blinked. "That is impossible."

"Completely impossible," Randy agreed.

Michael found himself thinking this may have been the first time ever. He pushed past it. "I disagree. Look at the evidence. You say Randy wasn't on tonight's guest list, Mrs. Berry?"

"No. Miranda has no place in Council business, nor has she ever expressed any interest in it."

"Then how do you explain her appearing on your carpet just as your guests were leaving the dining room?"

Adele cast him a chilly glance. "I believe most visitors tend to use the front doors, Michael."

He shook his head. "That would explain how someone got inside, not how they appeared in the middle of the carpet seemingly out of thin air. And that is exactly what happened with your niece. If you'll recall, I left the dining room ahead of everyone else to take a phone call. I was here in the hall—the *empty* hall—when Randy appeared."

"Out of the question. It cannot have happened like that."

Michael felt his mouth tighten. "I was here to see it, Mrs. Berry, and I can assure you that I'm not lying. I have no reason to." He turned to the younger woman. "Randy, you say that the last thing you remember is it being Saturday night?"

She nodded, still looking a little dazed. "A little before midnight. I was at Cassidy and Quinn's apartment. They asked me to spend time there while they're away and keep up with things for them."

He had met Cassidy Quinn and her husband on several occasions when Adele invited members of the Witches' Council along with the Council of Others into her home.

Neither of the Quinns held positions on the Council of Others, but both had consulted when their expertise had been called for, and Adele seemed to value their opinions. It was a bit like the arrangement he had with his uncle Harold. While Harold held the family seat on the Witches' Council, Michael couldn't take part in their activities, but he did offer his advice when he felt it was called for, and often when it wasn't. Harold tended to rely on his cunning above his intellect, something that often led to trouble.

"Do you recall anything unusual happening while you were there?" he asked.

"No, I was just—" Randy broke off and shifted her feet. Her lips pursed and she looked down at her polished red toenails.

"Just what?"

"Miranda Louisa, what on earth have you done this time?" Adele glared at her.

She crossed her arms over her chest, pushing those apples together until Michael's mouth watered with the urge to take a bite.

"I didn't do anything," Randy snapped, her entire posture radiating defensiveness. "It was just a lark. I didn't think it would *do* anything. Especially not right away."

Adele thumped her cane on the floor. "Young lady, *what* did you *do*?"

"I cast a spell," Randy mumbled, "but it was just a little one."

If anything, Adele's skin turned paler than her granddaughter's. "That's . . . not possible."

"What? You think just because I'm not a Foxwoman, I can't do anything special? I'm not an idiot, Adele. I can follow the directions in a spell book just as well as the next person."

Michael felt his eyebrows shoot toward the ceiling. "You attempted to work magic?" He frowned at Adele. "Your granddaughter is a witch?"

"Of course not! She's a Berry. There are no witches in our family tree."

"From the look of things, you may have missed a branch." Michael turned back to Randy. "I admit I'm surprised. Witches tend to be human, not Other. You may be the only Other witch I've ever met."

Randy shook her head. "I am human."

Michael tried to conceal his surprise, but he had the feeling he hadn't completely succeeded. "Not a Foxwoman?"

"No. As much as she might hate to admit it, Adele is my paternal grandmother, so my father put a cork in the inheritance of those particular genes. The Foxwoman thing only passes from mother to daughter, not from mother to son, or from son to daughter."

The explanation made sense, given what he knew of Foxwomen, but it didn't answer all of Michael's questions. "So your mother was human, too?"

She nodded. When she spoke again, she was talking to him, but her eyes were on her grandmother. "Adele had a hard enough time accepting the fact that she'd given birth to a human. Can you imagine how she would have reacted if my father had tried to 'pollute the bloodline' by marrying some other sort of Other? She'd have blown like Vesuvius. They'd still be digging the city out from under the ashes."

"That is untrue!" Adele protested.

Michael held up a hand. "I don't think there's time right now to settle this particular family quarrel. Let's go back to the issue at hand. Randy, you are human, with no experience with magic, and you decided to cast a time travel spell? Were you under the influence of a mind-altering substance? Do you have any idea how dangerous that was?"

"Hey, buddy, I don't need anyone else on the 'Randy is a screw-up' bandwagon," she said, glaring at him. "And for your information, I didn't cast a time travel spell. Why the hell would I do that? As far as I'm concerned, Friday sucked rocks. The last thing I wanted was to relive it."

"Then what kind of spell did you cast?"

She suddenly looked uncomfortable, and a rush of hot color stained her cheeks. When she spoke, her chin was tucked down to her chest and it came out in a rushed mumble. "Uhluphsplakay."

"Excuse me?"

"A love spell, okay?" She shot him a killing glance, then swiftly looked back at the floor and scuffed her bare feet against the carpet. "But it wasn't supposed to mess with the time space continuum. It was just supposed to issue a kind of magical cosmic personal ad."

Michael had a hard time believing this woman needed to resort to personal ads. She had the sort of blatantly feminine figure that made a man's palms itch and a face that captured attention the minute it caught the eye. She also had the sort of personality that drew attention instantly. Not the sort of woman who faded into the woodwork.

Now, he could definitely see pinning her up against some woodwork and—

He cut himself off and cleared his throat. If only he could clear his libido so easily. "Are you sure that's what the spell was? Could you have misread something?"

"Like I said, I'm not an idiot. It came out of a book of love spells and it was titled 'A Woman's Spell to Attract True Love.' What's there to misunderstand in that?"

"I think I should take a look at that spell."

Randy threw her hands out to her sides and shot him an exasperated look. "Well, it's not like I'm carrying it around in my pocket, is it? Besides, how would you looking at it help?"

He smiled. "I know a thing or two about magic. I am a witch, after all."

A click from the sitting room doors drew everyone's attention. Uncle Harold stuck his head out of the door and glared at them. "Is there a problem out here, Adele? We're getting a bit restless. There's a great deal of business to discuss tonight, and it's getting late. If you aren't prepared to give tonight's meeting the attention it deserves, maybe it would be better if we—"

Adele stepped forward, her cane clicking in time with her obvious annoyance. "You know very well that the Council's business is always my first priority, Harold. Simply give me a few more minutes to—"

"That won't be necessary," Michael said. He wanted a few minutes alone with Randy anyway. For a number of reasons. "Mrs. Berry, I'm more than capable of sorting things out and giving your granddaughter any assistance she needs. You go ahead and attend to your guests. Uncle Harold, I'm sure you can handle things without me for the evening?"

"Of course I can." Harold's scowl deepened and turned from Adele to his nephew. Michael ignored it. Harold's disapproval wasn't something he worried about. "But I don't see what you have to do with the girl. Let one of Adele's servants see to it and let's move on."

"Take me. Take me now," Randy snarked, looking disgusted. "You must be a real ladies' man there, Harold. I know I'm all a-quiver."

Michael stifled a chuckle and took Randy by the arm to turn her toward the stairs. "If you'll excuse us, I'm sure we'll have this all taken care of in no time."

Before anyone could argue, especially the scantily clad woman beside him, he turned his back on the sitting room and propelled Randy toward the stairs. He definitely had some things to clear up with her. And one or two of them even involved magic.

Chapter 6

Randy couldn't decide if she'd fallen and hit her head while casting the spell and was having an extremely vivid nightmare, or if she was being punished by God for one of her more significant transgressions. Maybe more than one.

As she climbed the stairs beside Michael Devon, she tried to sort out just what the hell was going on. If they were telling her the truth and it really was Friday again—God forbid, because that meant she was supposed to be being stood up again even as she thought about it—then something in that spell had not gone as expected. She wasn't supposed to go back in time. She wasn't supposed to go anywhere. She was just supposed to stir that damned mess, blow out the candles, and then meet the man of her dreams when she ran out for bagels in the morning.

Instead, she'd landed in her grandmother's house twenty-four hours before the idea of casting the spell had so much as occurred to her, being led around by a man who exhibited several of the qualities that had topped her wants and needs lists, outrageously sexy being chief among them. He also seemed intelligent, fairly mellow, and overflowing with charisma, but he lacked the one thing she'd underlined three times on her needs list—he wasn't human.

Or at least not completely human. He was a witch, and while she knew the difference between those and the Others, when she'd written down *human*, she'd been envisioning someone . . . normal. Not someone who could perform magic by waving his wand in the air.

The vision that popped into her head with that thought was *not* helpful.

She squeezed her eyes shut, then had to pop them open again to keep from tripping on the stair treads. "Where exactly are we going?"

He didn't glance at her. "Upstairs."

"Well, duh. Can you be a little more specific?"

"Somewhere we're not going to be interrupted."

Randy wasn't sure if she should be wary or enthusiastic. "What are we going to be doing that can't be interrupted?"

That time he did look at her, and his grin was positively predatory. He didn't answer. Instead, he ushered her down the hall with a warm hand at the small of her back and leaned around her to push open a door. "Please, ladies first."

She stepped inside reflexively. By the time she'd registered that he'd led them to a bedroom, the door had already clicked shut behind him. Randy spun around and fixed her gaze on his face. She didn't feel nervous, exactly, but neither was she perfectly comfortable under the circumstances. She didn't think the love spell had really brought her to Michael, but what if it made him *think* they were meant to be together?

"Okay, it's not like I have anything against sex," she said, fighting the urge to take a step backward. "In fact, I'm a huge fan. I love sex. It's fabulous. But I don't usually have it with men I've only known for twenty minutes."

He glanced at his watch and then grinned at her. "I'll keep that in mind."

"I heard what you said to Adele, but I can take care of

myself perfectly well. I don't need you to 'sort things out' for me. All I need is to go home."

He shook his head, not budging from his position between her and the door. "I don't think that's a very good idea."

"Why not?"

"That spell you cast that brought you here. I want to talk about that for a few minutes."

She sighed. "What about it? Is this where you lecture me about the dangers of silly little humans playing with dark powers they can't possibly comprehend?"

He raised an eyebrow. "I hadn't planned on it. Do you think I should?"

"Of course not. Trust me, the world is in no danger of my summoning the apocalypse. I don't even plan to pull a rabbit out of a hat after this." She made a face. "I think it's pretty clear that this whole magic thing didn't work out well for me."

He took a step toward her. "It didn't?"

"Hell, no. I thought I was going to meet a nice guy and instead I ended up half naked at one of my stuck-up grandmother's swanky dinner parties. I'd rather have a root canal with chamomile tea as the anesthesia than go through this again."

"You and your grandmother do seem to have an . . . interesting relationship."

"Absolutely. In the Chinese sense of the word."

" 'May you live in interesting times'?"

"Exactly." Randy shrugged. "It's no big secret that I'm a huge disappointment to my grandmother. Adele likes to pretend her bloodlines have never been tainted by anything as plebian as a human, let alone that she herself gave birth to one. She's spent most of her life ignoring the men in the family because of their species. The fact that one of them had the nerve to procreate and spawn a female of that same inferior species drives her crazy."

"So you do your best to make yourself impossible for her to ignore."

"Oh, Adele does a fine job with the ignoring routine. Every time I turn up for family dinners, she gets that sour look on her face, like someone let a mongrel into the kennel with her purebreds." She paused and gave a short laugh. "Though now that I think about it, that's a bad analogy. If I could turn into a dog, she'd probably respect me more. Not as much as a real Foxwoman, of course, but more than a human."

Michael tilted his head to the side, a gesture Randy tried not to find adorable. "I'm not sure a lack of respect is how I'd describe Adele's view of you."

"Trust me, it's accurate. Cassidy she respects, but me? Not in this incarnation."

"What makes you so sure?"

"The evidence." She scowled. "Not once in my life has she tried to involve me in her life, not the life that's important to her. Cassidy is the one she calls on to help her out. I'm just an embarrassment. She obviously invited Cassidy and Quinn to this evening's festivities. Do you think for one second it occurred to her to invite me? Of course not. I'm human, therefore I'm of no use to her."

"Hm, interesting. But maybe we shouldn't talk anymore about your grandmother."

"Fine with me."

He took another step, which brought him close enough that Randy could smell him. Not that he wore some kind of an overpowering cologne or anything, but he had a smell that made her want to suck him in, all spice and musk and warm, clean man. "Why don't you tell me some more about this spell?"

It wasn't a question.

"What do you want to know? I already told you I'm not likely to give it a second try."

"Oh, I'm sure you won't. But I'm curious." He smiled,

and a shiver rushed through Randy. Just from him *smiling*. "Humor me."

She shrugged. "I didn't memorize it or anything. I read it out of the book while I did it, so it's not like I remember all the words."

"The basics will be fine."

Damn, he was persistent. "Fine. It said to get a bowl of water, add a bunch of herbs, some honey, salt, a couple of other things. Rose petals, mainly. Then you add some paper. That's pretty much it."

"Was there anything on the paper?"

Randy glared up at him. "Yes." He just waited, looking at her, until she caved. "It was two lists of qualities you were looking for in a guy. It said to write them out and then add part of each of them to the bowl."

"Only part?" he looked curious.

"Yeah, I didn't get that. Why write everything out if you weren't supposed to use it? I threw them both in."

His lips quirked. "Ah. I see."

"That's pretty much it. It was kind of disappointing actually. I was expecting bat wings and thirteen drops of blood or something."

"No blood called for, I take it?"

"No, unless blood is euphemistically known as a 'tear of Venus.' And then, it only required a single one. I couldn't figure that one out, so I had to improvise."

He shook his head. "No, I believe it may be some sort of exotic flower."

"Damn. Oh, well. Maybe that's why the spell didn't work."

His brows shot up but he didn't comment. "Hm. And were there any special instructions about how things were to be added?"

"I put them into the bowl in the order they were listed, if that's what you mean, but it didn't say to wave them through a haze of incense first or anything."

"I was thinking more along the lines of mixing, actually."

"No." She paused. "Well, the last instruction was to stir everything three times, but that's it."

That seemed to catch his interest. "And did you?"

"Sure. I was trying to do it right."

"How did you do it?"

She looked at him for a second. Was this really that interesting to him? And to think when they'd first gotten upstairs, she'd been worried he might be planning to jump her bones. At the moment, he looked more inclined to pull out a set of tarot cards and chant something in Sanskrit. "With a spoon," she finally said, slowly.

"No," he said. "Show me how you stirred it."

"Fine, but I think you need to get a new hobby." Biting back her disappointment and feeling like a big idiot, Randy pantomimed stirring the spell mixture three times.

When she looked up, Michael was nodding, apparently satisfied.

"That explains it," he said.

"Explains what?"

"How the spell misfired and sent you back in time. Someone familiar with magic would have known to stir the spell clockwise. Deosil, it's called. If you did what you just showed me, you were stirring widdershins. Counterclockwise. It completely changed the energy of the spell and sent you here."

Randy stared at him. "That's it? I got sent back in time because I *stirred* in the wrong direction?"

He grinned. "Well, that was part of it. The other part may have had something to do with your 'improvisation.' Spells are tricky. You need to be exact to get them to work right."

"Great," she threw up her hands. "Good to know that's the reason why the thing had about as much effect as making a wish while blowing out my birthday cake."

Michael took another step forward until all of a sudden,

Randy could feel his breath stirring her hair when he spoke. "What makes you think the spell had no effect?"

Her stomach began a gymnastics routine. "Okay, I know it had an effect, because it landed me here, but it had absolutely no effect on my love life."

"Oh, I wouldn't say that," Michael purred just before he sealed his lips to hers and sent her stomach flying off the uneven bars in a triple somersault dismount.

And damn if she didn't nail that landing.

Chapter 7

Michael felt the surprise on her lips, tasted it on her tongue, and smiled. Beneath its sharp tang, she tasted even better than he had imagined, like whiskey and honey and a bright burst of citrus. The flavor was beguiling, addictive, and he stroked his tongue over her lips to gather it like nectar.

One hand rose to cup the back of her neck while the other arm snuck around her waist to draw her against him. He felt her shiver at the touch of his chest against her breasts, felt her stiffen, then melt against him, running hot and rich like butter.

She might have decided that her love spell had been a dud, but Michael knew better. It had brought the two of them together, all right, and whether she recognized it or not, he was her dream man. Now all he needed to do was to convince her.

Hard work, but he was willing to make the sacrifice.

Pressing his advantage, he parted her lips with his and dipped inside, exploring and claiming in the same moment. The hand at her nape tangled in the bright red-gold of her hair while the other swept over the curve of her waist, the flare of her hips, and snaked around to cup her bottom and settle her hips more definitely against him.

Her moan tasted like heaven and went to his head like moonshine. He had to have her.

Changing the angle of the kiss, he drew her even closer and began to walk her backward toward the foot of the bed. He wanted her beneath him, naked and open and eager. The sooner the better.

The back of her knees struck the mattress, and she tumbled down to the soft surface. Michael followed, stretching out beside her, one leg pinning hers down, holding her, but not overwhelming her, no matter how much he wanted to.

And holy hell, did he want to.

He kissed her more urgently, lips pressing harder, tongue stroking deeper, and she met him, welcomed him, returned his kiss with a heat and sensuality that threatened to make his eyes cross. Oh, yeah. If she thought they weren't going to be together, she had another think coming.

She was the one who pulled him over her, who parted her legs to wrap them around his waist, who settled his hips in the cradle of hers and rocked suggestively against him. None of that was his fault, but it was his fault when he broke their kiss long enough to shove her stretchy tank top up off her breasts and leave it bunched in a tangle somewhere under her chin. That was all him, and he had no intention of apologizing. Especially not after he got his first look at her breasts, all white and pink and pouting eagerly up at him.

With a groan, he bent his head and fastened his mouth around one firm peak, sucking strongly, pressing the warm little bud against the roof of his mouth while his hand stroked over its twin with something akin to reverence.

Randy moaned, a strangled, desperate little sound that felt almost like a hand stroking his cock. Her hips twisted, rubbing against him like a cat and just as eager for stroking. Dragging a hand up the outside of her leg, he drew his head back and rasped the edge of his teeth across her swollen nipple in the same instant that his fingers slipped beneath the hem of her shorts to find her slick heat.

They both froze.

Randy's eyes flew open, the brown velvet looking even softer through a haze of arousal. Her lips were parted, curved into a silent 'o' of surprise and pleasure. He watched her while his fingers stroked, teased, explored. He saw every ripple of pleasure in her eyes, felt every shiver, heard her breathless cry when he circled her entrance with one finger before sliding in deep.

"Oh, my God."

Her head fell back, her eyes drifted shut. She clenched around him, her body struggling to keep him close, and her hips arched to take even more of him. Michael bit back a curse of his own. He practically shook with the need to take her. Desire rode him brutally, and he wanted nothing more than to strip off the rest of her clothes, unzip his trousers, and sink into her until they both forgot their names.

The need surprised him, confused him, but he couldn't deny it. He'd never wanted this badly in his life, never knew with such gut-deep certainty that this was right, that this woman was meant to be his. After hearing about her miscast spell, he knew it wasn't magic that made him feel this way; it was something even more powerful. It was fate.

Starving, shaking, Michael forced himself to focus on her face, to watch as her eyes drifted open and locked on his. Her breath came in shallow pants, and her tongue darted out to wet her lips as she spoke.

"I told you . . . I don't have sex with men I've only known twenty minutes."

Without even bothering to look at his watch, Michael leaned down and caught her lower lip between his teeth. Tugging gently, he twisted the hand between her thighs deeper and listened to her gasp. Then he soothed the sting of his bite with a stroke of his tongue and stared intently down at her. "It's been at least forty-five."

Her eyes glittered and her lips curved as she lifted a hand to his neck, tugging him down to her. "Well, in that case . . ." She pressed her lips to his, kissed him so deeply, so hotly, he swore he could feel his eyebrows burst into flames. "Do carry on."

Chapter 8

I'm pleased to see you taking so seriously the values your parents and I worked to instill in you, Miranda."

If anything in the world existed that had the power to kill Randy's libido faster and more thoroughly than having her grandmother walk in on her during what promised to be some really amazing sex, Randy would put a bounty on its head and display the preserved carcass on her living room wall.

Uttering a tortured groan, she broke away from Michael's über-hot kiss and let her arms, legs, and head bounce backward onto the mattress. "Just kill me," she muttered to the ceiling. "Kill me now."

"For heaven's sake, girl, put some clothes on," Adele ordered as she closed the bedroom door with herself on the wrong side of it. "I should hardly need to tell you this behavior is completely unacceptable."

"Feel free not to."

"But we have more important things to discuss at the moment," her grandmother continued as if Randy had never spoken.

Randy's teeth clenched tight and she yanked down her

top with unnecessary force. "Fine." She pushed herself away from Michael and rolled off the end of the bed to stand on legs that hadn't caught back on to the whole muscle-control thing yet. She locked her knees to stop the quivering. "I'll just leave you two kids to chat and see myself out. No, no. Don't anyone bother themselves about me. I'll be fine. I'll call. Really, I will. Toodles."

Michael caught her wrist before she'd taken so much as a step. "That's not necessary." His tone stayed mild, but his eyes glittered a warning. "You should hear this."

"Oh, trust me, sweetie, I've heard it all before."

Adele drew herself up and gave him her Queen of the Universe stare. "I am sure that's not necessary, Michael."

"Yeah, Michael." Randy tugged at her wrist. "Not necessary at all."

"Oh, but I beg to differ." Rising himself, Michael tugged Randy to the small sitting area near the fireplace and urged her onto the love seat. When that didn't work, he gave her a little push. Her butt hit the cushions and bounced twice, but at least she had the satisfaction of landing with her eyes on a level with his crotch and seeing that he was no happier with Adele's interruption than she'd been.

He turned away from her and waved Adele to the armchair opposite while he settled down beside Randy. "Adele, I think it's time you told your family what's been going on. That is why you invited them, after all."

"Mine must have gotten lost in the mail."

Adele scowled at her granddaughter's comment. "I invited Cassidy and Sullivan."

"See, that's just one of my many talents," Randy said, moving to rise. "Not only do I always know when I'm not wanted, but I also know when I want to be somewhere— anywhere—else. So, if you'll excuse me?"

Michael pressed her down with a hand on her shoulder, but his words were directed at Adele. "True, but Cassidy and her husband were unable to join you, while Randy is sitting right here."

"Under duress," she muttered.

"I may be old," Adele snapped, "but I am neither a fool nor blind. I can see my granddaughter clearly. What I do not see is how you think she can assist in a problem among the Others. Perhaps you have forgotten, but she is only human."

And she's got a mean right hook, Randy thought, but she kept that to herself. Both the thought and the hook. You'd think that after all these years, she'd be used to hearing her grandmother condemn her with words to that effect.

You'd think.

"Human, maybe," Michael said and laid his hand on Randy's knee. She suppressed a shiver. "Ordinary, I think not."

Adele looked skeptical. "Isn't that what being human means?"

"Seriously," Randy rounded on Michael with a roll of her eyes. "Do I need to sit here and listen to this?"

"I think you both need to sit and listen." Exasperation finally broke through his façade of calm. "For two incredibly capable, intelligent women, I have to say you're acting like idiots."

Adele opened her mouth to protest, but Michael cut her off. "You," he said, jabbing a finger at her, "are holding so tightly to your preconceived notions and your old-school prejudices that you refuse to acknowledge what's right in front of you. You keep calling Randy 'human' like it's a fatal weakness. Did you happen to miss the fact that no matter what you call her, she not only managed to perform magic, but actually put a wrinkle in the fabric of time? I know ninety-year-old elders on the Witches' Council who have never managed to pull that off! Say what you like about her parents or her species, but your granddaughter has talent."

Randy blinked. "I do?"

"And you," Michael continued, turning that finger on Randy, "you've erected a wall against your grandmother that's so high, just looking at it would give a Tibetan Sherpa altitude sickness! You refuse to even give her a chance to approve of you. You're so busy being rebellious and demonstrating that you don't need your grandmother's approval that you make it impossible for her to give it even if she wanted to. I don't know how you two got to this point, but I think it's time to declare a cease-fire. Even an idiot could see that the main reason you keep sniping at each other is that you're each too stubborn to be the first one to try something different!"

Adele shifted. "It is?"

Michael glared at her. "Don't start with me."

Unsure whether to offer him a cigarette or throw him out the nearest window, Randy settled for a short laugh. "Okay, then. Feel good to get that off your chest, tiger?"

His expression told her he was not amused. "Peachy."

"Much as I appreciate your attempt to break up this cat-fight," she said, ignoring the roaring in her ears and pushing to her feet, "I think this situation is a little more complex than you're giving it credit for."

"What's complicating it?" he demanded, standing with her so he could maintain his advantage of height. "Your godawful stubbornness? Your inability to give up so much as an inch of your wounded pride and offer your family an olive branch?"

Shaking with fury, she stood toe to toe with him and shouted right back into his face. "How about the fact that my family seems to be allergic to olive branches and it's none of your goddamned business that my grandmother wouldn't even ask for my help washing the dishes, let alone give me credit for actually being capable of making a valuable contribution to anything! If Adele wanted my help, she'd ask for it, but since I'm human, and therefore worthless, your little kiss-and-make-up scene isn't going to change anything! So *BACK the HELL OFF*!"

"Miranda!" Adele's cane thumped against the carpet. "Michael is merely trying to help. There's no reason to act so abusively toward him. I expect better of you."

"Yeah?" Randy had more than enough fury to go around by this point. "Since when?"

The old woman's lips tightened, but she remained silent.

Randy just shook her head. "Perfect. Everything is so much better now, Michael. How can I ever thank you?"

"By parking your ass back on the love seat and hearing me out."

That wasn't so hard to do, especially now that Randy seemed to have yelled herself out. She didn't so much park as collapse and bury her face in her hands. "Fine. Whatever. Just get it over with so I can go home, okay?"

Michael settled back down beside her, but he didn't try to make her look at him, which was a relief. She'd probably have bitten his hand off if he tried.

"I'm not going to defend your grandmother's decision not to involve her *whole* family in the current situation, but I will admit that these events are somewhat sensitive."

Randy snorted into her hands. "Is that why I saw at least thirty people coming out of the dining room? You guys certainly have a different idea of confidentiality than I do."

"I had sixteen guests," Adele said, sounding almost sulky, which Randy supposed represented a slight improvement over disdainful. "Not thirty. Four witches, four shifters, four vampires, and four of the minor Others. And all of them have a vested interest in what's going on."

At that, Randy raised her head and looked across the short space at Adele. "And what is the situation? A thousand-ton asteroid is hurtling through space toward us and the Others are going to blast it out of the sky with their amazing powers of laser-vision and hubris?"

"Sarcasm isn't going to be helpful, Randy." Michael's

tone carried a warning. "It's nothing quite so movie-of-the-week, but your grandmother does have quite a situation on her hands. She didn't just invite us all over for the pleasure of our scintillating company."

"I have no trouble believing that." Randy let herself fall back against the cushions of the love seat and adopted a world-weary expression. "So what vast conspiracy against your rightful claim to the throne is afoot now, Adele?"

Michael shot her a killing glance and raised an eyebrow. "Maybe you would care to rephrase that?"

Randy debated saying no, but something in Michael's face told her she might end up eating her words. She sighed. "Fine. What seems to be the problem, then?"

Adele inclined her head to acknowledge the wording. Randy thought she'd never looked more like a queen. "The bottom line is that someone is trying to undermine my position on the Council of Others."

"Someone seems to be intercepting the plans Adele prepares to present before the Council and rushing to put them to the membership before Adele has the chance to do so," Michael clarified. "Then when the ideas are approved, the liar gets the credit and your grandmother is forced to grin and bear it or else look like a sore loser who can't resist saying, 'I said it first!'"

Randy frowned. She had to admit this wasn't what she'd been expecting to hear. From the way her grandmother told it, Adele's family had built the Council from bare stone, and it would collapse the minute she or one of her heirs stopped holding it together through force of will. From what little her father had told Randy about the Berry family, a Foxwoman of their bloodline had always served on the Council, rarely as the head of it, but often as a power behind the throne.

"How is that even possible?" she asked, truly puzzled. "You've been on the Council for nearly forty years. From what Cassidy says, every single person presently on it knows how significant your part is in it. How could anyone think they could undermine you at this point?"

"Quite easily," Adele said, her bearing almost painfully regal. "Power is a strong motivator. Someone who could convince the Council that their advice would serve them better than mine would find himself with an awful lot of it in a very short period of time."

"But who on earth could possibly accomplish that?"

Michael took Randy's hand and laced their fingers together, squeezing gently as he held her gaze squarely with his. "We think it may be my uncle."

Chapter 9

At first, Randy laughed, but when Michael and Adele didn't join in, just sat there watching her with intense expressions, she fell silent. When she finally spoke, her voice sounded slow and uncertain, even to her. "You're serious. That pompous twit?"

"Absolutely." He nodded. "It's why I came to this meeting tonight."

Damn it, Randy thought, this sucked. It was one thing for her to plot the old woman's humiliation, but she'd be damned if she'd put up with anyone else doing it. This wave of protectiveness she felt toward her grandmother was unprecedented and unsettling. She wasn't at all sure she liked it, or liked Michael for setting it in motion.

"I asked Michael to help me," Adele said, "just as I planned to ask your cousin and her husband. We may think we know who is causing all of this trouble, but we can hardly stop him without evidence."

Randy looked at Michael. "And what's your plan? What do you get out of this? The guy you suspect of being behind this is your uncle. Are you going to try to intervene before anyone else finds out so that you can hush everything up and spare your family from the rest of the community knowing your uncle is a power-hungry sleazeball?"

"Miranda, that was uncalled for!"

Michael shook his head. "No. You might find this hard to believe, Randy, but I *like* your grandmother, and I have a lot of respect for her. I don't think she deserves what Harold has been doing to her."

" '*Has been doing*' to her? This has been going on for a while?"

"Nearly six months, we think. It was a while before anyone recognized the pattern of what was happening, and another two months before we were able to narrow it down to a manageable list of suspects. So we've only had three weeks or so to figure out what's been going on."

When Michael stopped and just looked at her with those killer blue eyes gone all patient and expectant, Randy sighed. Damn it, he was going to try to make her be the bigger person here, wasn't he? "Fine," she broke down, "I don't suppose you'd care to explain it all to me?"

At least he had the grace not to allow his expression of satisfaction to linger. "As you said before, Adele takes her position on the Council of Others very seriously. It's something that's quite important to her."

No one needed to tell Randy that. From what she could tell, the Council had always been more important to Adele than most of her own family.

"I feel very strongly that I have a responsibility not only to uphold the legacy of our family, of all the other Fox-women in our lineage who have served the same role, but also to make a contribution to the way the Others are adjusting to their new place in society," Adele said. She sounded more plausible than most presidents Randy had ever heard. "I'm sure you know what a pivotal point in history we're currently going through."

Of course she did. Randy wasn't an idiot. She might be human, but she was related to people who weren't, and she'd be damned if she'd stand at the door and wave when the species police came to take them away. She'd followed the Unveiling and the subsequent treaties negotiated between the human and Other delegations more closely than she'd ever followed anything in her life. Except for the year when Missy Rubino had been running against her for Homecoming Queen, and there had been extenuating circumstances back then. No way had she been willing to let the slut who stole her boyfriend get that crown, not if she had to rip it off Missy's skanky blond head.

"Yeah, I get that," Randy nodded. "I might not pay a whole lot of attention to the everyday crap the Council fixates on, but I do own a TV and I have read a newspaper once or twice. I've heard all the scare tactics. I know about leash ordinances and Jim WereCrow laws."

"Then it won't surprise you that some of us are very concerned about ensuring that the Others don't become the next great victims of discrimination. It also should not surprise you that there are quite a few people in the Other community who see the current situation as a way to gain power, potentially by discrediting those of us who already possess it."

"And Harold is one of those people?"

He nodded, his expression grim. "We believe he planted some sort of surveillance system here in your grandmother's house. At this point, we're reasonably sure it's confined to the first floor."

"A surveillance system?" she repeated, nonplussed. "As in bugs in the telephone receivers? What, is my grandmother the new Godfather all of a sudden? Is your uncle gathering evidence for a racketeering charge?"

"Of course not. Don't be ridiculous," Adele said. "This isn't some silly human crime investigation. Harold Devon is a witch, just like Michael is. We believe he's set up some kind of spell in this house that lets him listen in on my private meetings."

Michael stepped in before Randy could react to the 'silly human crime investigation' remark. "Adele is a very important woman in the Other community, and at the moment, that makes her an important woman in politics in general. The leaders of our communities are spending their time these days with international heads of state, negotiating treaties and making laws that affect every sentient being in this world. Your grandmother has the power to call the President of the United States, the Chancellor of Germany, and the Prime Minister of Japan, and make them take her calls. That's the kind of power some people would be willing to do anything to get for themselves."

Randy's head spun. She got what he was saying. For the first time in her life, she really got it. For a split second, Adele ceased to be just her grandmother, and Randy's mind allowed her to see that having Adele as a mostly estranged grandmother was a little like having Queen Elizabeth as a great aunt—Randy was far enough removed from royalty to not be interesting to anybody, but close enough to resent how much everybody wanted a piece of her relative.

The realization tilted her whole world on its axis, made Randy feel almost petty. She didn't like it at all.

"This is serious business, Randy," Michael prompted when her silence stretched on.

She dragged her gaze back to his face and glared at him. "I got that part, Michael. What I'm trying to figure out is how spying on Adele going on about her daily life gets your uncle any closer to landing a spot on the Prime Minister of Japan's bowling team."

"It's not that much of a stretch, Miranda," Adele said, sounding almost non-condescending. "All someone has to do is find out what strategic suggestions I'm planning to make to the Council of Others—who in turn will make them to the Commission on Equal Rights—and preempt them. Then the eavesdropper gets the credit for the suggestions, and I and the Others I've been working with are cut out of the process. Not only that, but if we try to protest, we either look like sore losers, or like leaders who can't manage their own security well enough to prevent our ideas from leaking out before we're ready. Either way, we lose and Harold wins."

"But wouldn't the Council get a little suspicious?" Randy asked. "I mean, if Harold is a non-entity for years and then all of a sudden he becomes one of the great political minds of the century, wouldn't that raise a few flags?"

Michael shook his head. "Harold is not a member of the Council of Others. He's on the Witches' Council, which has only been working with the Others for about five years now. And not only that, Harold's term just started nine months ago. Our council representatives are elected every five years. This was our election year."

When he fell silent, Randy took a very deep breath and let it out slowly. "Well, shit," she said mildly, shaking her head. "What are you guys planning to do about all this?"

Chapter 10

When, oh when, would Randy learn to keep her damned mouth shut? Whenever it was, it would be too late to keep her from skulking around her grandmother's house in the middle of the night like an inept cat burglar. At least cat burglars knew what they were looking for. All Randy had to go on was Michael's vague description of what to look for that might be serving as an anchor for the spying spell and his and Adele's insistence that it must be found tonight.

You'll know it when you see it, he had assured her. *Remember what you felt when you performed the last part of that love spell you cast, that weird, shaky, light-headed feeling? That was from the magical energy. If you felt it then, that means you're sensitive to it, so you should feel the same thing if you come into contact with the anchor. Then just let me know, and I'll take care of it.*

When she'd asked what "you guys" were going to do about this situation, she had not been using the term euphemistically. She'd really meant what *they* were going to do about it, not what she was going to do to help. Randy had always thought of herself as more of a moral support kind of girl.

She thought that even more when she stubbed her toe on one of the legs of an Edwardian settee.

"Shit!"

She hadn't been in this room in years, and now she was paying for her unfamiliarity with the layout.

"Shh," Michael hissed. "What's the matter?"

"I stubbed my toe because someone wouldn't let me turn on the friggin' lights," she snapped, which wasn't nearly as satisfying when she had to do it in a whisper. "What was the reason we couldn't do that again?"

"The meeting is still going on right down the hall and the rest of the house is supposed to be empty." That time his voice came from right beside her ear, and Randy jumped. She hadn't heard him approach. "We don't want anyone to know we're searching in here, especially since Adele went back and told them we already left with me escorting you home."

"And the reason we had to do this tonight instead of waiting until tomorrow when everyone is gone and we can, you know, see what we're looking for?"

She felt him sigh impatiently against her ear. "Because once we find the evidence, we'll need to act fast. The only way to put an end to his ambitions is to publicly discredit him. If we find his spell tonight and confront him with it in front of all of the people he's been lying to, his dreams of political power will go up in flames."

Randy grumbled something and went back to squinting into the darkness and keeping a weather eye out for that buzzing sound in her head she'd heard at Cassidy's.

"Besides," Michael murmured as he slipped past her, his hand finding her bottom unerringly in the darkness and giving it an affectionate squeeze, "the faster we get this out of the way, the faster we can get on with what we were doing upstairs before your grandmother interrupted us."

The man could have a second career as a motivational speaker.

After a few more minutes of enthusiastic but futile searching, Randy was beginning to feel grumpy. "You know, it would help out a lot if you could give me *some* kind of a physical description here. I mean, is it bigger than a breadbox?"

She could almost see that look of his, the one that said he wasn't amused. "It's magic, Randy. It doesn't have a physical description. It's like electricity that way, all right?"

"You don't have to get all grumpy."

"Well, pardon me, but—"

Whatever he'd been planning to say, he stopped and went suddenly silent. Randy turned toward the direction from where he'd last spoken and opened her mouth to issue another quip when she felt it. The sudden thickening of the air in the room, the weight of something heavy abruptly making its presence known. And then she heard the buzzing.

"You found it."

"Here. On the desk. It's attached to a small sculpture or something."

If he said more, she couldn't hear it. For a few seconds, she couldn't hear anything, but at least her eyes had begun adjusting to the dark. She could just make out a dark silhouette near the bookcase on the inner rear wall of the study. She moved cautiously toward it, giving the settee a wide berth.

She didn't notice until she got five or six feet from it that it was the wrong shape to be Michael, too squat and too wide, but by then it was too late. She was already within reach.

The buzzing in her ears ceased abruptly the second the man laid hands on her. In its place, she heard nothing, or an eerie sort of silence that should have sounded like nothing, but was too noisy for that. She knew even in the darkness that this was Harold, not because she remembered his face, but because the anger and hatred rolled off him in clouds of poison gas.

If Randy could have held her breath, she would have, but she was much too busy shouting for that. "*Michael!*"

"Shut up, you little bitch." Harold shifted and the back of his hand made violent contact with Randy's mouth. She cried out involuntarily this time and tasted the sweet coppery tang of blood.

It wasn't just the unexpected blow that made Randy's head spin, it was the thick, oily stench of magic that surrounded him. The magic she'd felt in casting her love spell had been dense, but not . . . icky. Harold's power had a definite ick factor. It made her feel dirty where his skin had touched hers. Damn, but she wanted a shower.

First though, she wanted to demonstrate to this jerk what happened to men who hit Randy Berry.

Everything seemed to happen simultaneously. Even before the blow registered, she heard Michael's roar of fury and sensed him launching himself at her attacker through the darkness. As impressive a speed as he clocked, though, he wasn't nearly as fast as Randy's knee. It came up with the swiftness of reflex and the power of righteous anger, and it made solid, vengeful contact with Harold's gonads.

He uttered a strangled screech, but instead of releasing her, the hand that had grabbed her upper arm clenched tight, the fingers digging into her skin like vice grips.

"God, you *suck*!" She tried to ram her elbow into his solar plexus, but since he'd bent double from the force of her knee, that target was nowhere in sight. Instead, she threw herself off balance and nearly toppled ass-over-elbows across his back.

"Randy! Move!"

Michael issued the order in a barely intelligible growl, but it didn't matter. "I *can't*! He's got my arm!"

She heard Michael swear and felt the impact when he charged into Harold from seemingly out of nowhere.

The darkness was driving her crazy. She hated the vulnerability of not knowing exactly where everyone was, of not being able to plan effectively for each person's movements so she could either get out of the way or give some assistance. All she could see were vague shapes and shadows, mostly just differing shades of black. She would have given her eyeteeth for a Maglite.

She heard a thud and a grunt and felt herself yanked abruptly to the left.

"Damn it, Randy, stay still!" Michael barked.

She decided to ignore that, since it was an idiotic order, given the fact that she wasn't precisely moving under her own steam here. Instead, she decided the best she could do was to upset Harold's balance. In one swift motion, she stopped struggling to pull herself away and leaned hard into his grip while at the same time letting her knees buckle under her to send her to the floor.

She heard curses—some from Harold and some from Michael—and felt her attacker's hold momentarily loosen. Desperately, she yanked again at her arm and felt his hand slide away.

"Damn you!" Harold roared.

Randy could have given a rat's ass. "I'm loose!" she shouted. Crawling to safety seemed ridiculously slow, so she dropped to her stomach and rolled several feet away across the carpet. The front panel of Adele's desk brought her to an abrupt stop when it made solid contact with the side of her head.

Damn it, at the rate this was going, she could spend a week in an Epsom salt bath and she was still going to look and feel like the loser in a ten-round heavyweight title match.

Michael didn't bother to answer her, but she could forgive him for that. It sounded like he had his hands full.

From the other side of the room, she could hear grunts and curses and the solid thud of fists of flesh. It sounded like a schoolyard rumble. Weren't witches supposed to duke it out in a more civilized manner? Magic wands at twenty paces?

Deciding she'd had more than enough of this bastardized game of Marco Polo, Randy reached out and grasped the edge of the desk. She hauled herself up carefully and traced the smooth surface of the wood toward the corner until she felt the cool metal of her grandmother's banker's lamp.

"Yes," she muttered, and being very careful not to tip it over, she traced the curve of the neck up to the base of the lightbulb and found the switch with trembling fingers.

She flicked it on.

For an instant, even the dim, shaded light of the desk lamp blinded her, and Randy blinked against the reflexive tears that welled in her eyes. More curses echoed behind her and she spun around just in time to see Harold yank himself out of Michael's weakened grip.

The older man stumbled into the bookshelves lining the wall behind him and struggled to catch his breath. His previously immaculate navy suit looked like he'd just stripped it off the body of a bum, wrinkled and askew with buttons missing and hems torn. His tie had disappeared completely, one shoe lay in the center of the floor where he and Michael had recently struggled, and his hair resembled that of Albert Einstein after a close encounter with an electric socket. His sneering face looked flushed, and Randy could see where he'd be sporting a hell of a black eye in a few more hours.

Michael looked a bit disheveled himself, Randy decided, but on him, it was sexy.

"I always knew better than to trust you, Michael," Harold panted, his lip curled into an expression that made him look like a disgruntled jackass, which Randy supposed was pretty much what he was. "You're so much like your self-righteous father. Neither of you ever understood what it takes to get ahead in this world."

"That's a hell of a statement from someone who's spent most of his life trying to take what his own brother built through work, talent, and integrity. Even after he died, he was still a better man than you," Michael said. Randy could see his hands clenching into fists at his sides, but he kept his cool no matter how much it was costing him. "What you should have realized was that I'd never let you get away with cheating your way to the top any more than he would have."

Harold laughed, the kind of braying, slightly manic laugh the villain always gave just before he made his last, desperate bid for freedom. Randy couldn't decide whether or not that counted as a good sign.

"You're a good deal too late," he crowed, sneering at his nephew. "I've had months to advance my plan. The votes have already swung my way. All I need is one more triumph over that Berry bitch, and I'll have both Councils eating out of my hand."

"But you're not going to get one more triumph, Uncle Harold. It's over."

The older man's face clouded with rage. "It will be over when I've left you both dead!"

Some instinct made Randy drop behind the apron of sturdy old oak in the same instant that Harold raised his hands and shouted a word she didn't understand. She had no trouble, though, understanding the impact of something powerful hitting the wall above her head, just about where she would have been if she'd remained standing. She also understood the acrid tang of the smoke that told her anything standing where she had been would now be raining down on her like ashes from Mount St. Helens.

The disadvantage of having good reflexes, though, meant that the desk now effectively blocked Randy's view of the rest of the room. She couldn't see what Michael was doing or whether he needed her help. All she could do was listen and pray that he had ducked as quickly as she had.

"Randy!" His voice made her scramble to her knees and peer cautiously around the side of her barricade. The coffee table and a couple of armchairs obscured her view, but she could still make out that Michael remained in one piece and that Harold appeared to be gearing up for another attempt to change that. "Smash the bug!"

The bug? She was afraid for his life, and he wanted her to swat flies? Had he sustained some kind of a head wound?

"No!"

It was Harold's cry of protest that jogged her memory. In a rush of motion, she stood and lunged for the small, abstract glass sculpture beside Adele's phone. Even before she touched it, she felt the energy that pulsed off of it, and out of the corner of her eye, she saw Harold turn abruptly and throw himself at her with a screech of protest.

Her hands closed over the cool glass and lifted high above her head. Later, she would think it would have been much more satisfying if she'd planned it this way, but what happened was frankly a total accident.

She intended to hurl the sculpture to the bare wooden floor beside the desk and let it shatter into a million pieces, but Harold's thick skull just got in the way. Instead of throwing the sculpture to the floor, she bashed it hard against the man's skull and felt it come apart in her hand. Harold's cry died in mid-utterance, and he collapsed into a heap at the side of the desk.

Michael actually stepped on him in his haste to get to Randy.

"Are you all right?" he demanded.

"I think—" She looked down at her hand and broke off. "Oh, shit."

Her hand looked like it had gone through a paper shredder. She had blood and bits of glass everywhere and even as she looked at it, the hand began to tremble.

Michael's curse was much pithier.

The door flew open and banged into the wall behind it. A crowd of onlookers gathered in the entryway.

"What's going on in here?" Adele demanded, pretending to be shocked at the sight in front of her. "What's happened to Harold?"

At least, Randy assumed she had started off pretending, but when her gaze fixed on her granddaughter's bloody hand, the shock turned genuine.

"To hell with Harold," Michael growled, not bothering to look in Adele's direction. He'd already begun stripping off his shirt, and he used the cloth to wrap around Randy's hand in a makeshift bandage. "He's not hurt, just unconscious. But Randy is bleeding. We need to get her to the emergency room. She should have stitches."

"I don't need stitches," Randy protested, knowing it was probably a lie, but she also knew from the quivering sound of her voice that she was probably going into mild shock.

"Let me look at that," a woman said, pushing forward and striding briskly to Michael's side. She had curly, sand-colored hair that had been cut short, a decided air of competence, and freckles on what looked like every inch of her skin.

Randy didn't think she'd ever seen the woman before, but when Michael glanced at her, his expression shifted into distinct relief.

"Betsey," he practically sighed. "Thank god you're here. Do you think you can do something with this?"

Randy frowned as he passed her hand over to the stranger. "Do something? Like what? Finger painting?"

Betsey chuckled. "I'm sure you could do that yourself, hon, but Michael here was asking if I could fix it." She unwrapped the shirt from Randy's hand with great care. "I'm a witch, too. Healing work is my specialty."

Randy tried not to look skeptical. "Abraca-Bacitracin?"

"Not quite, but I like that one. Mind if I use it in the future?"

"Knock yourself out."

Michael hovered over her the entire time Betsey worked. He winced every time the witch hummed and actually whimpered when he saw the tiny shards of glass lift from Randy's flesh and dissolve into thin air. Randy had to admit the entire experience may have been more traumatic for him than it was for her. By the time her hand looked as if it had run into nothing worse than a kitten with a bad temper, Michael looked as white as a sheet and had little drops of sweat glistening on his forehead.

"All set," Betsey announced cheerfully. "Just keep it clean and slap a bandage over the really bad spots for a couple of days and you'll be good as new."

"Thanks." Randy rubbed her thumb over a long, pink scratch and grinned. I have to admit, I'm impressed."

The witch wrinkled her nose. "Thanks, but it's just parlor tricks. Luckily, there wasn't any nerve or tendon damage, or I would have had to send you to the hospital. I'm great with first-aid, but not so much with the major wounds." She sighed. "Power is a fickle mistress."

Adele appeared at Betsey's side and squeezed the other woman's hand. "Be that as it may, we're all grateful," she said. "I wish there were something I could give you in return."

Betsey's expression took on a hint of speculation. "That's not necessary, but if you wanted to explain to me why Harold Devon is lying unconscious on the floor with a minor scalp wound while we all ignore that fact, I wouldn't tell you to shut up."

Adele smiled a bit grimly. "That's a bit of a long story, Betsey, my dear. One that I think calls for more of my best brandy."

Michael had seized Randy's hand almost the minute that Betsey released it, and he wasn't satisfied until he'd examined every inch of it to make sure she hadn't missed a single wound. Once he was satisfied, he lifted it to his lips and pressed a tender kiss into her palm.

Randy felt it all the way down to her toes.

"If you don't mind, Adele, I think Randy has had enough excitement for one night. She needs some rest." Michael laid a hand against the small of Randy's back and urged her toward the door. "I'm sure you can explain all this without us. If you'll excuse us?"

For the second time that night, Michael began to shepherd Randy away from a crowd of her grandmother's curious guests. She had no reason to protest, but this time her grandmother stopped her before she'd taken three steps.

"Miranda."

Adele placed her hand on Randy's arm and hesitated. Looking down, Randy noticed for the first time how that hand had grown older. It bore wrinkles and age spots on the pale, delicate skin, but its grip remained sure and unexpectedly tender.

"Randy." Now Adele's voice softened, and Randy raised her head in surprise. "I want to . . . to thank you. For your help tonight. You did me a great favor."

Her grandmother's voice sounded rough and awkward, but none of that mattered. Randy could feel her heart fluttering almost nervously, and she realized that what mattered wasn't the ease with which Adele was saying this; it was that she was saying it at all.

"You're welcome," she managed, and her own voice was rough. She cleared her throat.

Tentatively, Adele leaned forward, paused, then closed the distance and pressed her lips to her granddaughter's cheek. Randy's heart stopped for a split second, then resumed beating with even greater strength.

When Adele pulled back, her eyes almost looked misty. "I would very much like it if you would come for dinner on Sunday." She glanced at Michael. "Both of you, if you'd like. But you especially, Mir— . . . Randy. It would make me very happy."

For the first time in her life, Randy couldn't quite manage to speak. She nodded instead.

"Good." Adele took a deep breath and stepped back, resettling her commanding air like a cloak onto her shoulders. "You go up to bed. I'll handle everything else down here."

"Good," Michael muttered, resuming their trip to the door at a greatly increased pace. He walked slightly behind her, masking the way his hand slipped from the small of her back to caress her bottom through the red silk of her shorts. "Because there are a few things *I* intend to handle upstairs."

Chapter 11

Sheesh. All the man had to do was touch her, and Randy was ready to trip him and beat him to the floor. It amazed her. It baffled her.

It made her want to weep with joy.

By the time they reached the stairs, her skin tingled and her heartbeat had reached the speed of sound. On the landing, she had to press her thighs together to ease the ache between them. And when her back hit the same mattress he'd pinned her to earlier, she had already decided that if he didn't come inside her in the next fifteen seconds, she was going to die of a brain aneurysm. Her circulatory system had not been designed to take this kind of pressure.

Her head spun, her senses swam, her ears rang, and she didn't give a damn about any of it. All she cared about was the man above her, touching her, loving her, the fact that it was absolutely vital to the continuation of life itself that he never stop.

It was like they were picking up exactly where they'd left off before. The hand between her legs shifted, one finger withdrawing only to be replaced by two. She moaned and arched into the penetration, dazedly acknowledging that nothing in her life had ever felt so good. So right. God, if she could find this without a stupid love spell, maybe it was a good thing it had backfired. If sex with her dream man would be better than this, she wouldn't be able to live through it.

She wouldn't even be able to live through this if he didn't hurry it up.

Tearing her mouth from his, she sucked in a desperate gulp of air and slipped her hand between them until she cupped the ridge of his erection. Then she squeezed, half a caress, half a warning. "Seriously, you need to hurry up and get inside me. Like, now."

He shuddered above her and blew out a tortured breath. "Right. God, you're right."

His hand withdrew from her to strip her shorts off and toss them carelessly aside. Before her hips hit the mattress again, he had his own trousers down and was kicking them off with equal haste. Randy fumbled with the buttons on his shirt, getting enough of them open that the rest popped off when she shoved the halves aside and set her palms against the smooth ridges of his muscular chest.

He was too far gone to let her continue for long. Impatiently, he brushed her hands away and slid his own between her thighs, hooking them in his elbows and pushing her knees high as he settled himself against her.

Randy's breath froze in her chest at the first press of bare flesh to bare flesh. Her eyes widened and her heart stuttered and time spun away more crazily than it had when she'd cast that spell. It seemed to slow and stop all around them as he shifted and pressed within her. His gaze locked with hers, blue eyes burning into brown, as he sank deep and deeper still until he came to rest hilt-deep inside her.

She pressed her hands against the tops of his shoulders, not to push him away but to brace herself against something solid as the world spun crazily about her. When he moved against her, beginning a slow, lazy rhythm specifically designed to drive her out of her mind, she realized the grip was futile. Her nails dug into his skin and her hips rose and she gave herself up to the amazing, glorious sensations of fullness, of rightness, of completion, that having him inside her created.

Every movement lifted her higher, pushed her further into a cloud of desire. The arousal shocked her with its strength, but it was nothing compared to the astonishing realization that she could no longer imagine being with anyone else. It was as if by coming inside her, he had pushed away every other memory, every other desire and set himself up in their place. He filled every corner of her, not just of her body, but her mind. And her heart.

Restlessly, she shifted, bringing her knees even higher, tightening her body around his, trying to absorb his very essence into her skin, into her *self*.

She heard him gasp and bite off something that may have been a curse, felt him stroke deeper, move faster. The tension between them coiled like a spring ready to snap. Randy felt it sweep over her, carry her along like a cresting tide toward shore.

Arching beneath him, she struggled to match his pace, then to urge him faster. Hands clutching him to her, she lifted herself into him, wrapped herself around him and threw herself into her climax, knowing even as her mind went blank that he followed her into the sunburst.

Miranda Berry had fascinated him from the first moment he'd laid eyes on her, and Michael knew that wasn't going to change anytime soon. And he wasn't just saying that because she currently lay damp and spent and panting beneath him. Really. There were a lot of other things he admired about her, and he was sure he'd be able to list them all just as soon as he remembered his name and how to control his muscle and skeletal systems.

He had to admit that when he'd come to Adele Berry's

dinner and meeting, he hadn't expected to end the evening buried in his hostess's granddaughter, but he couldn't regret it either. He'd never been half so content in his life.

The end of the scene downstairs provided the icing on his personal piece of cake. It made him ridiculously happy to see the wounds between Adele and Randy beginning to mend, and he intended to be there to witness each and every one of them heal over. At least half of their previous problems, he suspected, had to do with how much the two women had in common, though he still wouldn't say as much to either of them under threat of torture. Hell, he wouldn't mention it under real torture. The one who heard it would probably disembowel him, and then she'd get angry.

In the short time he'd known Randy—all of about five hours now—he'd seen how much of her grandmother she had in her, and he suspected it was an awful lot more than either of those women would be prepared to acknowledge. They both possessed sharp tongues, iron wills, and the kind of innate dignity that made weak men quiver and strong men wary. In Adele, those qualities aroused his respect.

In Randy, they aroused something entirely different. And if he didn't stop thinking about it, neither of them would be able to walk in the morning.

Shifting carefully, Michael pressed up on his palms and eased their bodies apart, coming to rest at her side. He draped one arm across her to keep her close and forced his eyes open just enough to look at her.

She was adorable. Her hair was tangled, her cheeks flushed, and her mouth open as she fought to calm her breathing. She looked like she'd been thoroughly laid, which of course pleased Michael to no end. If he had his way, she was going to spend an awful lot of time looking just like this until they were both too old to remember how it worked.

Randy cleared her throat. "That, ah . . . that was . . ." she paused to lick her lips, ". . . uh . . . fun."

Michael grinned into the bedspread and squeezed her in a one-armed hug. "I kinda thought so."

She didn't open her eyes, just lay beside him and breathed deeply and evenly. She didn't feel as relaxed as Michael would have liked. His brows drew together.

"Are you okay?"

She snorted. "Fine. You didn't hurt me, He-Man. I'm made of stronger stuff than that."

He slid his hand up to her chin and turned her to face him. "That wasn't what I meant."

Her eyes opened and locked on his. "What did you mean, then?"

He raised an eyebrow. "I'm not claiming to be Casanova, but women don't usually end up more tense after I make love to them than they were when I first got started."

"You'd rather I started snoring?"

"I'd rather you tell me what's on your mind."

"You don't really want to know."

He waited.

Randy laughed. "I was thinking about Adele."

He pursed his lips. "Well, that's a new one. I've also never had a woman tell me that my technique in bed reminds her of her grandmother."

"It had nothing to do with your technique, which I'm sure you already know." She looked back up at the ceiling and grinned. "I was just thinking about what Adele would normally have said if she'd caught me in this sort of situation. Something about living down to her expectations, I'm sure."

"Because we made love?"

"It's not about the sex. It's about having the sex on the first date. Hell, we haven't even been on a date." She grinned. "So technically, I jumped into bed with you *before* the first date. This is not the kind of ladylike, decorous behavior Dame Adele expects from the members of her family."

Michael tucked a piece of hair back behind her ear, unable to resist the urge to rub a thumb over the delicate arch of her cheekbone. The light dusting of freckles there looked like cinnamon sugar. "Oh, well. She'll live. In fact, I think she'd better get used to it. Quick."

Randy turned her head to look at him and quirked an eyebrow. "Does that mean you have something more in mind than a one-night stand?"

Smiling, he leaned forward and captured her lips with his. When he raised his head, they both had to struggle to catch their breath. "I have quite a lot in mind. After all, it's not every day that fate and magic conspire to bring me together with the woman of my destiny."

"Is that what I am?" Randy grinned and wriggled closer.

"Among other things." Another heated kiss made his voice even darker, even rougher. When she slipped her hand between their bodies and squeezed him affectionately, he nearly lost the power of speech completely. "You little witch," he growled.

"Am I?" she asked, her voice genuinely curious. "I didn't think casting one spell qualified me."

Michael trailed a line of kisses down her throat and up the slope of her breast. "It doesn't. That was a figure of speech."

"Oh." Randy registered a vague sense of disappointment, but really, who wanted magic powers? If she had those, she might have to develop some sort of a sense of responsibility. Perish the thought.

Michael heard her quiet "Oh," and lifted his head. "Are you upset?"

She shook her head. "Nah, I'm pretty cool with who I am. In my family, if I had special powers, that would actually make me more ordinary." She wrapped her arms and legs around Michael and shimmied her entire body. When his eyes rolled back in his head, she laughed and pressed her lips to his ear.

"But since you've got the magic in this relationship, I think it's only fair to warn you that you'll have to fix my parking tickets for me. After all, there ought to be some benefits to dating a witch . . ."

"Oh, I'll show you benefits," Michael chuckled, his grin going sharp and wicked. Slipping his hand beneath her, he raised her hips high and speared deep within her body.

Randy shrieked and let her head fall back against the pillows. Every molecule in her body was suddenly focused on the intense, erotic heat of him, the utter completeness she felt with this man buried inside her.

"Oh, yeah," Randy sighed and curled her hand around his neck to tug him to her. "That works."

Epilogue

And he left me some kind of message about me standing him up. Can you believe that?"

"No."

"Like I'd ever have agreed to go out with him anyway, even if it was weeks ago." Randy scoffed, pushing off with her foot to set the enormous nursery rocker in motion.

"Of course you wouldn't have."

Randy Berry raised an eyebrow. "I'm detecting a certain lack of attention to my conversation in your voice, Cass."

Cassidy Poe Quinn rolled her eyes and continued to shove onesies into a voluminous diaper bag. "Miranda, it's four forty-five in the afternoon. I had two hours of sleep last night because the twins were up with colic starting at midnight, and Sullivan and I have a plane to catch in just over three hours. I'm sympathetic, but I'm also half-comatose. Take what you can get."

Randy felt a distinct stirring of déjà vu and grinned like a madwoman. She was getting a huge kick out of reliving this conversation without the angst that had tormented her last time. "Bitter, party of one, your table is ready."

"Miranda Louisa, you could try the patience of a saint—"

"Which is something I'm very pleased to report you're a far cry from, Cassie love."

"Must be a family trait, because Randy wouldn't qualify for the title either."

Both women turned to the door of the nursery at the sound of those deep, masculine voices, but this time, Randy barely spared a glance for Sullivan Quinn and his twin babies. Her eyes went right to Michael Devon and locked on like a homing beacon.

"And that's exactly why you guys are crazy about us. Or at least, one of the reasons," she said, wriggling her eyebrows suggestively.

"Here I was thinking it was just because we guys are crazy," Quinn grinned.

Cassidy rushed forward immediately. "I'm sorry, honey. I was just finishing up their bag while they were napping. Have they started fussing again?"

"They're fine. I told you a drop of whiskey would settle them down." Quinn dropped a kiss on his wife's forehead. "Are you all set then? The car will be waiting for us downstairs."

"I'm ready. Why don't you give me Molly? No sense in you trying to keep them both." She reached out and took her daughter, balancing the little girl on her hip, then looked at where her cousin had taken up a position at Michael Devon's side and shook her head. "I wish we didn't have to rush off, so you could tell us exactly how this happened. It nearly bowled me over when the two of you showed up on our doorstep. I didn't even realize you knew each other, let alone that you were involved."

Randy glanced sideways at Michael and grinned. "Oh, it kind of took us by surprise, too."

"Well, I'll call when we get settled in and pry it out of you then."

Michael grinned down at Randy and took her hand in his. Together, they walked Cassidy, Quinn, and the babies to the door and waved them off.

"Have a safe trip," Randy said, giving Cassidy and Molly their good-bye kisses. "We'll make sure the plants stay watered and the mail gets forwarded, and we promise to clean up from any keggers before you get back."

Quinn laughed and leaned forward to kiss her on the cheek. "Never mind that. Just make sure the bedsheets are changed."

"Quinn!" Cassidy used her free hand to smack her husband on the chest while he and Michael laughed like lunatics.

Randy just rolled her eyes to the ceiling and shook her head. "Men are such pigs. Makes you wonder why we put up with them."

"Ah, but I think the last thing you're fearing at the moment is how to put up with us, cousin," Quinn murmured. "You seem to have found exactly what you've been looking for."

Randy stroked a hand over baby Declan's fuzzy head and grinned up at his father. "I did, didn't I?"

Michael extended his free hand and shook Quinn's. "I'd say we both did."

They watched the little family load themselves into the elevator, then shut the apartment door and turned back toward each other. For a long minute, Randy just looked up at this man she'd magicked into her life and said a heartfelt prayer of thanks.

"You know what?" she murmured, as she stretched up to kiss him through her cat-in-the-cream smile. "I'd say you were absolutely right."

Read on for a sneak peek at

Swimming Without a Net

by

MARYJANICE DAVIDSON

Coming December 2007 from Jove

Fred saw the lights on in her apartment and stomped up the stairs. This time she'd give Jonas a piece of her mind, as well as Dr. Barb, and never mind that the woman was her boss. Enough was enough! Clam globs in her face, garlic breath, sexual harassment. And it wasn't even Wednesday!

She unlocked her door and shoved it open, and was momentarily startled to see the happy couple sitting stiffly on her couch as opposed to grooming each other or, worse, getting to third base.

Standing just inside her doorway were two strangers. One was a young man—early twenties?—with startling orange hair (Jack O'Lantern–orange) and matching eyes. Beside him was a petite young woman of about the same age, with dark blue hair and eyes that were even darker, the way small sapphires almost looked black in the right light.

She knew at once they were Undersea Folk, and mentally groaned. Apparently the high point of her day was going to be dislocating Number Four's thumbs.

Before either stranger could speak, Jonas leapt up from the couch, said (too heartily), "Good, great, you're here, we told your friends we'd wait with them, but now you're here so we'll be going, see you, good-bye."

"Good-bye," Dr. Barb managed as Jonas dragged her out the door. "Young lady, whoever does your hair is doing a magnificent—"

Jonas slammed the door.

Fred surveyed the mermaid and merman. "Hit me," she said at last.

The two exchanged puzzled glances. "Those are not our instructions," the man said. "I am Kertan. This is Tennian. We were sent by the High King."

"Well, I didn't think you were here to take a survey. Something to drink? Some chips?"

"No, thank you," the woman—Tennian—said in a soft, lovely alto. "You are Fredrika Bimm, of Kortrim's line."

"If Kortrim is my bio-dad, you're right. But I prefer to think of myself as being of Moon Bimm's line. That's my mother," she added helpfully.

"Yes, His Highness has told us of your lady mother," Kertan said. He towered over her and had the ropey muscles of a long-distance swimmer. Which, of course, he was. She was having a terrible time not staring at him. Both of them. Their coloring was so extraordinary! It was odd to be in a room and not feel like she had the freakiest hair there. "We were instructed to try you at your home if we did not find you at the Aquarium."

"You went to where I *work*?"

"Yes."

"Oh my God," Fred said, and collapsed on her couch.

"We asked of you, and spoke of you to your friends. They brought us to your—" Kertan looked around the tiny apartment with an unreadable expression on his face—"home."

"You didn't say who you were, did you?"

"Our business is with you, not them."

"I'm going to take that as a no." She rolled over and

stared at the ceiling. "Thank God. My boss doesn't know I'm a mermaid and I'd like to keep it that way."

Again, the two strangers exchanged glances, and again, it was Kertan who spoke. "We are charged by the High King to summon you to the Pelagic."

"The Pelagic?" Fred could almost feel her mind buckle under the strain, and she giggled until she lost her breath. "I don't know what you guys think it is, but here, a Pelagic is an open zone in the ocean that's not near a coast or even a sea floor. How can you bring me to *a* Pelagic? And will you sit down? You look like a couple of Army recruiters. Unclench."

Neither of them moved. "A Pelagic is a meeting that can only be called by a majority of the Undersea Folk."

"I thought you guys were a monarchy."

"Our good king has acceded to the request of his people," Tennian almost whispered.

"Can you speak up, please? It's hard to hear you over the roaring in my ears."

"Will you come?" Tennian asked, slightly louder.

"To this Pelagic thing? Sorry, I'll need a little more info before I go gallivanting off with you two. Like, what exactly is it? Where is it? And why am I invited? And will you two *sit down*? I'm freaked out enough."

The two Undersea Folk gingerly sat in her kitchen chairs. Fred's apartment was an open design . . . the kitchen, the dining room, and the living room were all one big space. The small bedroom was off to the left, the bathroom off to the right.

Fred had fooled the eye into thinking the place was large and airy by painting all the walls white. The place was stark enough to belong to a monk, which suited her fine. She hated clutter.

She spotted the brand-new Aveda bag beside the kitchen chair, and nudged it beneath the table with a toe. "So. You were saying?"

"As you know, Fredrika, the royal family makes their home in the Black Sea. It is also the seat of our government."

"Right, the king and Artur. Got it."

"And His Highness Rankon, and Her Highness Jeredna."

"He's got sibs? He never said. And would it kill you guys to have a Jenny or a Peter?"

"It is not for us to know the workings of the royal mind," Tennian murmured.

"Ha! I know all about the workings of Artur's mind, and he's only got one thing on it. That's—never mind. You were saying?"

"May I have a glass of water?" Kertan asked.

"Sure." Fred jumped up, glad to have something to do. She guessed what Kertan's problem was—simple dehydration—and filled two glasses, one for each of them, to the top. As Artur had told her last year, Undersea Folk could walk around on land, but not for long, and they weakened quickly.

Tiny Tennian drained hers in three gulps and politely asked for a refill. And another. Thus, it was a good five minutes before either of them got back to the subject at hand.

"I assume you guys hang out in the Black Sea because it's enclosed? Easier to stay hidden? I mean, up here, you're—we're—myths. No one's been able to prove the Undersea Folk exist."

"You are correct, Fredrika," Kertan said, setting his empty glass down on the kitchen table. "Your studies of the sea have served you well."

"Yes, I have my name on all sorts of pretty papers."

"Many centuries ago the royal family chose the Black Sea for precisely that reason. That is not to say we all live there; the Undersea Folk are scattered all over the world."

"I live in Chesapeake Bay," Tennian whispered.

"But the seat of power has always been in the Black Sea. However, there are many of us, and it can be a difficult place to get to in a short time without rousing suspicion. So the Pelagic will be held in the waters of the Cayman Islands."

"Ah, the glorious Caymans. What are you, repping the Chamber of Commerce?"

"No," Kertal the humorless replied. "We will wait while you collect your things."

"Hold up, hold up. So this Pelagic, the purpose of which neither of you have bothered to explain, won't be where the royal family hangs out, and we won't be going to Turkey. But we'll have a fine time hanging out in the Caymans."

"I do not know how fine a time it will be," Kertal said soberly.

"Oh, here we go."

"Many of our people do not wish to remain myths."

"Oh ho."

"This goes directly against the wishes of the royal family."

"Fascinating."

"Thus, the Pelagic: a meeting of all Folk, to decide a common action. They are quite rare; the last one was held—ah—" he glanced at Tennian and the small woman shook her head "—was a while ago. Decades."

Fred smelled a rat. Or a fish. But there was time to get to the bottom of that later. "So you guys are getting together to figure out whether to go public or not?"

"Not 'you guys.' All of us. You, too, Fredrika."

She raised an eyebrow. "Is that a fact?"

"The High King insists."

"So? I'm not a subject."

"Excuse me," Tennian murmured, "but you are."

"Want to arm-wrestle for it?"

"The king requires your presence," Kertal droned on. "As does His Highness, Prince Artur."

"And I'm *definitely* not at *his* beck and call. Sorry you came all this way for nothing, help yourself to more water, good-bye."

"The prince suspected you would be . . . intractable."

She folded her arms across her chest. "Try un-budge-able."

"He asked us to remind you that he saved your life."

"He didn't stop me from getting shot!" And why was the thought of seeing the red-headed bum again so thrilling? Not to mention meeting other Undersea Folk. Of course, if they were all as stodgy as these two, it'd be a long time in the Caymans. Which reminded her . . . "How long is this Pelagic supposed to last?"

"Until the majority comes to an agreement, approved by His Majesty."

"But that could take—I have no idea how long that could take. How many mer-dudes will show up?"

"Thousands."

"Thousands?"

"Perhaps. There is no way to tell."

"Is there anything you *can* commit to?"

"We cannot leave without your agreement and attendance."

"Oh, friggin' swell." Fred rested her chin on her fist and thought. The other two watched her do it, and said nothing. Finally she said, "Is Artur sending duos of Undersea Folk to *all* the Undersea Folk?"

Again, they exchanged a look. But this time Tennian spoke up. Barely. "No. You are considered a special case, and essential to this gathering."

"According to whom?"

"The entire royal family."

Fred gave thanks she was sitting down, because otherwise she was fairly certain she would have fallen on her ass.

Read on for a sneak peek at

Thunder
Moon

by

LORI HANDELAND

Coming January 2008 from
St. Martin's Paperbacks

B y the time I drew my Glock, the animal had melted into the trees on the north side of the clearing and disappeared. I ran after it anyway, even though I didn't have any silver bullets.

In this gun.

"What's the matter?" Cal followed; he had his weapon out, too.

"You didn't see the—?" I stopped. Had I really seen a wolf?

Yes.

Did I want to tell Cal?

No.

"Never mind." I put away the Glock. "A shadow. Maybe a bear."

Not a wolf in these mountains, but bears we had.

Cal narrowed his blue-gray eyes on the trees. "They don't usually come this close to people."

"Which might be why it took off so fast."

"Mmm." Cal holstered his weapon, too, but he kept his hand on his belt just in case.

I was kind of surprised he hadn't seen the wolf. The animal had been right in front of him; he should have at least detected a movement, even if he had been focused on the mysterious gaping hole in the earth.

I checked the ground but found no tracks. Though the rain still fell in a steady stream, a bear would have left some kind of indentation. A wolf should have, too.

"We may as well head back," I said. "I'm sure Jordan has a list of problems the length of my arm for us to deal with."

"Probably," Cal agreed. "What do you think that orange glow was?"

"A reflection?"

"Off a UFO?"

"Okay." Hell, stranger things had happened—right here in Lake Bluff.

Cal laughed at my easy agreement. "Anyone else live out here we could talk to? Maybe they saw something."

"My great-grandmother had a friend who lived—" I waved in a vague northerly direction. "Although I'm not sure how much she can see or hear anymore."

I hadn't been to visit Quatie in a long time. My great-grandmother had asked me to check on her whenever I was in the area, but I'd had a helluva year, considering the werewolves, and I'd forgotten. I needed to remedy that ASAP.

"Probably not worth going over there," Cal said.

"No," I agreed, but made a mental note to stop by another day.

We got into our cars and reached the highway without getting stuck. Then Cal went one way and I went the other.

I decided to drive straight to the mayor's house. Claire Kennedy was not only in charge of this town, but werewolves had nearly killed her, and her husband, Malachi Cartwright, knew more about them than anyone.

Myself, I'd been skeptical about the supernatural. Even though my great-grandmother had been a medicine woman of incredible power and she'd believed in magic, I'd been tugged in two directions. I'd wanted to be like her; I'd wanted to believe. But I'd also wanted to please my father—hadn't learned until much later that such a thing was impossible—and he'd been a cop, filled with skepticism, requiring facts. I'd been confused, torn—until last summer when I'd had no choice but to accept the unacceptable.

I turned the squad car toward Claire's place, uncaring that it was nearly midnight and she had a new baby. Claire would want to hear about this.

Before my tires completed twenty revolutions, headlights wavered on the other side of a rise. I was just reaching for the siren when a car came over the hill, took the curve too fast, and skidded across the yellow line. Out of control, it headed right for me.

I yanked the wheel to the right, hoping to avoid both a head-on collision and being hit in the driver's side door. The oncoming car glanced off my bumper, but the combination of speed and slick pavement sent me spinning. I was unable to gain control of the squad before I slammed into the nearest tree.

My air bag imploded, smacking me in the face so hard my head snapped back; then everything went black.

Read on for a sneak peek at

Wicked Magic

by

CHEYENNE McCRAY

Available now from St. Martin's Paperbacks

R hiannon sat on a couch in the common room, her legs tucked up beside her, Spirit at her side. The cocoa-colored cat had stayed closer to her ever since she had been kidnapped just a few short months ago by the Fomorii. She'd been saved by Silver, Hawk, and Jake and a few of his officers, but so many witches hadn't made it.

At this moment the room was filled with D'Danann, PSF officers, and witches, discussing how to get to Ceithlenn and the demons. They had come to the agreement that the goddess must be near the location where they had battled the Fomorii and the Basilisk.

The chattering around Rhiannon became nothing more than a low drone as she petted Spirit and pushed all thoughts from her mind. Especially of a certain D'Danann warrior whom she'd almost had sex with in the basement.

Bless it! She didn't even know the man.

As she reached deep inside her for some semblance of calm, she began to feel light-headed. Her vision blurred and her ears felt as if they were stuffed with cotton. Her hand stilled in Spirit's hair.

Everything went hazy and she felt as if she were being transported out of her body, traveling, traveling. And then she stopped.

Rhiannon found herself in a large and sumptuous penthouse room. She looked at her hands then ran them down her skirt and felt the soft brush of her palms against the material. Her sandals sank into plush carpeting and she felt her chest rise and fall with every breath.

It smelled strange. Like burnt sugar and jasmine.

When Rhiannon raised her head, she saw the vivid image of a woman pacing before a window. Unfortunately, the wooden blinds were drawn so no view could be seen.

The woman turned and Rhiannon gasped.

Sara.

But not. Sara had been a white witch in the D'Anu coven who defected to serve Darkwolf, a Balorite warlock who practiced black magic. Copper had told Rhiannon how Sara had absorbed Ceithlenn's essence when the door opened to Underworld.

Sara was even more beautiful with red hair. It wasn't a natural shade, but it suited her. She now had the most interesting eyes—they seemed to shift colors like a wavering mirage. A revealing leather catsuit barely covered her nipples or her crotch.

Just like the flame-haired being.

Rhiannon's heart beat faster.

She felt as if she were drifting, dreaming, yet still there, whole, in the room.

Ceithlenn. The name rolled through Rhiannon's mind and her heart moved into her throat. Sara was the goddess's human form.

Something stirred in the corner of Rhiannon's vision and she gave a soft gasp of surprise. Darkwolf. She ground her teeth from thoughts of what the evil bastard had done. If it wasn't for him summoning the Fomorii, *none* of this would be happening.

Not far from him was Junga in her Elizabeth form. The sight of her made Rhiannon want to throw up. That bitch had given Rhiannon the scars on her cheek.

She looked back to Darkwolf, who was staring at Ceithlenn. His handsome features were blank. The stone eye Rhiannon remembered seeing when she'd been captured by the Fomorii was still resting on Darkwolf's chest. But it was cold and lifeless, not the throbbing red that it had often become.

Tension suddenly crackled in the air and Rhiannon's attention snapped back to Sara . . . *Ceithlenn.* She was sniffing the air, her gaze slowly sweeping the room.

Then her eyes focused directly on Rhiannon.

As if Ceithlenn could see Rhiannon there, in the room.

Suddenly a sensation like invisible fingers digging into her brain caused Rhiannon to cry out and drop to her knees.

Ceithlenn's power grasped at the Shadows deep inside Rhiannon, driving into the places no one should have been able to touch.

Rhiannon screamed from the pain and clasped her hands to her chest as she fell from her knees to her side.

Ceithlenn growled and extended her hand, palm first.

Rhiannon's heart felt lodged in her throat as she writhed on the floor.

The room seemed to billow. Expand.

A tremendous *boom* shattered her ears.

A great force slammed into her chest.

Excruciating pain filled her mind, her body.

She screamed again before everything went dark.

R hiannon blinked, then had to clench her eyes tight against the light coming in through her curtains. Dear Anu, her head ached and she thought she might puke.

Despite that, she felt somewhat comfortable, which was a strange contrast. The cool sheets hugged her, the mattress soft beneath. Spirit was curled up against her side and rubbed his head on her arm, acknowledging that she was finally awake. Scents of sandalwood and cypress hung in the air and she felt as if oil had been rubbed on her chest, belly, arms, and legs.

Something had happened . . . but what? She couldn't quite grasp it . . . Whatever it was perched on the edge of her thoughts and stayed just out of reach.

She finally managed to get her eyes open and squinted to try to ground her vision. Her whitewashed vanity table and purple dresser drawers came into view, although they seemed to swim a bit. The yellow wall behind them was almost too bright. She blinked again and saw that her bedroom was much cleaner than normal. She wasn't exactly the world's neatest person.

How had she ended up in bed?

And jeez, where did this headache come from? She was a witch, for Anu's sake.

Her skull hurt as she turned her head to see the rest of the room. The open doorway came into view next and then she lowered her brows.

Keir sat in one of her chairs beside the door. His arms were folded and he was looking directly at her.

She blinked. Instead of a leather tunic and pants, he wore a black T-shirt that hugged his muscled chest and a pair of snug jeans that looked so good on him her mouth watered.

Okay, there had to be something *seriously* wrong with her.

"What are you doing in here?" she asked in a voice that came out rough and dry. Goddess, she needed a drink of water.

Keir leaned forward as he uncrossed his legs and bent his knees. He rested his forearms on his thighs as his gaze held hers. "Are you all right?" he asked. He didn't sound as gruff as normal and it threw Rhiannon off balance.

She pushed herself to a sitting position and dizziness caused her eyesight to blur again. The sheet fell away and she looked down to discover she was in one of her robes. A royal blue satin one that gaped at her breasts. She hurried to tighten it while she avoided Keir's eyes.

When she looked back at him, she took a deep breath. "I'm fine."

"What happened?" His look intensified and his manner returned closer to what she was used to. Commanding. Authoritative.

This Keir she could deal with.

She scowled. "What are you doing in my room?"

"What happened?" he repeated, his voice growing in strength and his dark eyes narrowing.

Truth was, she didn't know. But she wasn't about to let him badger her. "Take a hike."

He frowned for a moment, then realized what she'd just told him. "I am not leaving until you are well."

"Oh, yes, you are." She pushed back the covers, and swung her feet over the edge of the bed. The moment she got to her feet she knew she'd made a big mistake.

Her head spun and her knees gave out. Just as she started to drop, Keir was there. He caught her to him, holding her tight and keeping her from falling. For a moment she allowed herself to sink against him, her cheek against his chest. She felt boneless, like she didn't quite have a grasp on reality.

He smelled so good. Woodsy and male, and the scent of the clean cotton T-shirt. With his hard body pressed to her softer one, that burning, spellfire sensation in her belly traveled between her thighs and up to her nipples. The roughness of his jeans and his hard chest rubbed against her through the satin of her robe.

"Let me go," she finally managed to get out. She didn't

dare look up at him in case he took that as an invitation to kiss her like he had last time.

But he clasped her chin with his callused fingers and tilted her head back. Instead of a hard, possessive kiss, he just brushed his lips over hers in a touch so light it surprised her. His breath was warm against her lips and she almost moaned. She ached for more. Wanted more.

While she was still looking up at him in surprise, he eased her onto the bed so she was flat on her back. He tucked her in like she was a child. At that moment she didn't have the strength to argue or spar with him.

"Why are you wearing jeans and a T-shirt?" she asked instead. "What happened to your leather gear?"

Keir scowled. "Your law-enforcement officer, Jake Macgregor, insisted we look more like the people of your world to 'blend in.'"

Rhiannon couldn't help a small smile. "What about your weapons?"

Keir gestured to a chest draped with his long black coat. "My weapons are inside. I wear the coat over this new clothing."

"You look good," Rhiannon found herself saying. But then he looked good in leather, too. And most likely he would look good in nothing at all.

That line of thought had her *gently* shaking her aching head.

Keir sat in the chair, leaned forward, and rested his forearms on his thighs again. This time he spoke gently, "Tell me what happened, *a stór*."

Rhiannon wasn't sure what to think of this different Keir. She paused, then decided to answer his question. "I remember sitting in the common room and I was petting Spirit." She concentrated hard, her head aching with the effort. "But nothing else until I woke up." She studied him. "How did I get here?"

"I carried you," he said.

Heat crept up her neck to her cheeks. "Who changed my clothing?"

"Silver and the healing witch, Cassia," he said.

"You didn't watch, did you?"

He shrugged and her cheeks grew hotter. She pushed herself to a sitting position again, this time crossing her legs Indian-style. At once her vision swam. She placed her head in her hands until the dizziness passed. It was as if something was in her mind, taunting her, making her feel as if she were being watched—and not just by Keir.

And the darkness in her mind and her body—it wanted to come forward and she had to fight it back.

The bed dipped and springs creaked as Keir sat next to her. His hand enveloped one of hers and she raised her head. "I should get the healing witch now," he said. He was so close to her she noticed the purple marks on his neck from the fight with the Fomorii.

Rhiannon took a deep breath and let her hands fall to her lap, but he still kept a tight grip on one of them. "I told you, I'm fine."

She just couldn't remember a blessed thing and that was ticking her off. So were the dizziness and the weakness. Had she come down with some kind of virus? Since she was a witch it was unusual for her to catch anything a normal human would.

"So, how long have I been asleep?" Rhiannon glanced at the curtains. It looked like it had to be late afternoon.

He squeezed her hand. "Two days."

Shock flooded Rhiannon, causing her skin to tingle. Her jaw dropped as she stared at him. "You're screwing with me."

Keir maintained his steady gaze. "You were in the common room. You screamed and fainted. That was two days ago."

For a long moment she looked at him, his words not quite sinking in. "This doesn't make sense."

"Silver thought she saw you in a trance, as if you were having a vision."

Flashes came to Rhiannon at his words. Punk red hair. Catsuit. Darkwolf.

Stabbing pain.

Nothing.

"Bless it." Rhiannon took her hand from Keir's and pressed all her fingertips to her forehead as she lowered her head. "It's there. Not quite, but I can *feel* it at the edges of my mind."

Memories of pain accompanied by a fresh bout of real pain made her stomach churn. She grasped her hands to her belly and looked up at Keir. "Were you sitting in that chair very long?"

"Most of the time." He reached up and brushed her hair from her face. "I could not leave you."

"Why?" Her heart beat a little faster at his touch and the sincerity in his expression. "I don't get it."

Keir trailed his fingers from her hair to her cheek in a featherlight brush that made her shiver. "I was concerned for you, *a stór.*"

Rhiannon swallowed and drew away from his touch, which was doing crazy things to her body. "You keep calling me that. What does it mean?"

He looked almost embarrassed as he said, "My treasure."

Heat rushed through Rhiannon and she barely kept from putting her hands to her burning cheeks. She felt like she'd just landed on another planet.

Keir, looking embarrassed and saying sweet things to her?

Who is this guy? What happened to the real Keir?

"Has it honestly been two days?" she asked as she forced herself to think of other things than the way this man was working his way under her skin. Her voice rose as it occurred to her that she hadn't asked the important questions.

"What's been going on with tagging the demons? Any sign of that goddess?"

"It has been quiet since the day you took ill." Keir leaned closer and stroked the back of her hand with his thumb, causing her to shiver. "After the last battle, we felt it best to wait a short time before tracking the next Fomorii as they are sure to be more aware of us now. We have still kept to the skies in search of signs, but have found nothing."

She shifted from sitting Indian-style so she could draw her knees up against her chest. "How do the Fomorii and C-Ceithlenn—" She stumbled over the name and a brilliant white bolt of pain shot through her head. She ground her teeth before she spoke again. "How do they even know what happened to the demons and Basilisk?"

His thumb stopped moving across her knuckles. "Silver used her cauldron to scry. From what she was able to see, one demon witnessed our attack and escaped to tell the goddess. That is all we know."

"We can't sit around and wait." Rhiannon's heart beat a little faster. "How could I have slept for so long? This is too important."

Keir growled and her gaze shot to his. "You *will not* involve yourself again."

"What are you talking about?" Despite the pain in her head, Rhiannon jerked her hand away from his and almost shoved him right off the bed. "I certainly *will* be a part of this. Down to fighting the last demon."

His expression turned even more fearsome. "No, not if it could kill you—"

"What do you care?" She gripped her sheets in her fists and glared at him. "You don't even know me."

"Damnation." Keir thrust his hand through his thick black hair. "I—Rhiannon—*Damn!*" He looked flustered and angry all at once. "Ceithlenn is beyond dangerous. I will not have you in the middle of a war."

At the mention of the evil goddess's name, Rhiannon

shuddered and pain shot through her head again. Something . . . Something about Ceithlenn remained just out of reach . . .

When she tried to grab at the memory, the pain only grew worse.

She held one of her hands to her forehead as she clenched her teeth. The pain was like a white-hot rod through her skull.

"You are ill." Keir's voice softened and he stood. The bedsprings creaked as they released his weight. "I will get the healing witch."

Rhiannon couldn't begin to pretend it was nothing. Her head hurt so freaking bad. "Can you tell Cassia that I have the mother of all headaches?" She scooted down and her head was on her pillow again, as she tried to get some reprieve from the pain by relaxing. Wasn't working.

He gave her a sharp nod, picked up his long coat, and turned away.

"Keir," Rhiannon called out to him before he was through her doorway. She swallowed hard. "Thank you."

He looked at her for a long moment then bowed from his shoulders and walked out of her room.

Read on for a sneak peek at

Howl
at the
Moon

by

CHRISTINE WARREN

Coming November 2007 from
St. Martin's Paperbacks

S am let her eyes narrow. "And what would that be?"

"I'm going to need you to do me a favor," Graham said.

Sam shrugged and dropped her teasing glare. "Sure, no problem. I'll put it on your tab. What's going on?"

"The pack is going to start setting an example of interspecies cooperation."

Sam quirked an eyebrow. "You mean we don't already?"

The question was only half-humorous. The Silverback Clan had a long history of interspecies cooperation, dating back to the time before their Alpha had actually mated with another species. The fact that Graham's family had operated Vircolac for centuries and always opened its doors as neutral ground for all Others played a part in that, as did the pack's long association with the Council of Others. In fact, compared to a lot of the Others out there, the Silverback Clan looked a lot like a supernatural version of the United Nations. Only functional and quite a bit more effective.

"This time we're doing it specifically with the humans, and with the government in particular," Graham said. "I discussed it with Rafe and the rest of the Council last night. I think the consensus labeled it as a 'gesture of good faith.'"

"Which really means that Rafe wanted it and the rest of the Council decided they'd rather watch the pack do the real work of it than dirty their own hands taking it on."

"Exactly."

Sam just shook her head. "Okay, so what are we on the hook for this time? More surveillance duty? Security for a contingent of humans from Trinidad and Tobago who want to consult with the Council on treaty negotiations with their local population of were–Gila monsters? I can round up volunteers. I'll ask for the ones who like palm trees and sunbathing. You know, to put the visitors at ease." Her words were joking, but she had already reached for the phone. Her job around here was to make things happen, and Sam was good at her job.

"Actually," Graham pursed his lips and developed a sudden fascination for his fingernails, "it's that word 'volunteer' that I wanted to talk to you about. You in particular."

Sam's head started shaking before he even finished speaking. "Oh no. You know what happened the last time you sent me on some other kind of assignment. It took me months before I could find where you'd filed the bar receipts."

"I handled the office just fine."

"You put them under 'M,' Graham, and when I asked why, you called them medical expenses."

The Alpha shrugged. "Don't worry. This time, you won't be going anywhere. This is a desk job."

Sam eyed him with growing suspicion. He wore his most charming smile, the one that said he was about to convince you to invest your last dollar in a housing development in the middle of the Okefenokee Swamp. Missy called it his Conner smile. Conner was the name of their second son.

"Lay it on me. I'm a big girl. I can take it."

"We need to clear off some desk space in here," Graham said. "We're going to be having a visitor for a little while."

"Oh, my goddess! We're being *audited*?"

Graham shuddered. "Bite your tongue. No, nothing like that. I've agreed to let a select branch of the U.S. military have the opportunity to recruit pack members. Strictly as volunteers, of course. An army officer is going to be setting up a minioffice space with us for a few weeks."

Sam's glimmer of suspicion exploded in a siren-blaring and red flag–waving supernova of alarm. "Who?"

"Noah Baker."

Yeah, that's what she'd been afraid he would say.

On the surface, there was nothing wrong with Noah Baker. For a human, in fact, he'd made quite a few friends in the Other community since his sister had gotten mixed up with, and subsequently married to, a sun demon. Everybody seemed to like the man, from his demonic new brother-in-law, Rule, to Graham, to Rafe De Santos himself. Even Rafe's wife, Tess, liked Noah, and she wasn't one to suffer fools lightly, or even at all. But then, Noah Baker had proved to be no one's fool. A major in the army's highly selective and newly developed supernatural squadron, he had grit, training, and a cool head under pressure. Not to mention a talent for making large objects make even larger booms.

The only person Sam knew who *didn't* see the human as an all-around swell guy was Sam herself.

Something about Noah just made Sam's hackles rise every time he got within twenty feet of her, and it didn't seem to matter what form she was in at the time. Human, wolf, or were, Sam's teeth went on edge when Noah walked into a room and her hormones went haywire. She'd gotten to be friends with his sister, Abby, but with Noah, the best Sam could manage felt more like a tense cease-fire. And now Graham expected her to share office space with Noah?

Too much a Lupine to directly challenge her Alpha's word, Sam took a more subtle approach.

She forced a smile of her own. "Well, you're the boss. When can we expect the troops to land?"

"How about now?"

Noah caught the flash of surprise and annoyance on Samantha's face and stifled a grin. He knew he made the Lupine tense just by walking into the room, but then, she did the same to him. Unlike him, though, he suspected Sam had no idea why they disturbed each other so badly. She probably wrote it off as lousy chemistry.

Oh, it was chemistry, all right, but Noah couldn't describe it as lousy. Not by a long shot.

Samantha Carstairs made Noah Baker feel about as predatory as her closest friends and relatives actually were. He might not get furry on full moons, but looking at the luscious female Lupine made him want to howl at one. It had been that way from the first time he'd set eyes on her, while he still thought she was a kidnapper holding his little sister captive. He'd taken one look at Samantha and felt his entire body go on alert. A few parts had even gone on *high* alert.

She had the body of an athlete, not as sinewy as a runner or as fine as a gymnast but covered in sleek, firm muscle and decorated with curves just generous enough to make a sane man look twice. Noah had looked more than that, taking stock from the top of her mane of wavy, richly brown hair to the tips of her feminine feet. Of course, by the end of their first meeting those feet had turned into paws and tried to pin him to the ground in the middle of the small park down the block, but even that hadn't put him off. He'd dated women with bigger vices than occasionally shifting into timber wolves.

After a second of silence, Samantha started to squirm and Noah deliberately shifted his gaze to the other werewolf in the room. Stepping inside, Noah set a cardboard file box down on the chair beside the office door. "Thanks for agreeing to put me up, Graham. I appreciate it."

The Silverback Alpha shook his hand, relieving the last of Noah's worries that the Lupine might still hold a grudge over the way his sister had briefly set the pack's Luna in harm's way a few months back when she'd been pursued by demons. Apparently, Graham didn't like having demons surrounding his wife.

"It's no problem," Graham said. "In fact, I was just telling Sam I think it might be good for some of our young males. Give them a place to channel their aggression other than in a dominance challenge."

Noah smiled. "I'll do my best."

He looked around the spacious room, taking note of the territory Sam had already marked. The huge cherry desk stationed in front of the door to Graham's private inner office had the look of a sentry's gatehouse, and Noah had no trouble picturing her fending off intruders and interlopers. Her area only took up one end of the grand old sitting room, though. There would be plenty of space for him. And he'd be near enough to give the electricity between them time to spar.

This grin he didn't bother to suppress. "Where would you like me to set up?"

Graham shrugged. "That's up to Sam. She's the one who keeps everything in its place around here."

It didn't take a mind reader to see that Sam wanted to put Noah outside with the trash. Or maybe to banish him to another continent. But that wasn't her decision.

Sam forced a pleasant expression onto her face. "I'll have one of the staff bring in a desk and some chairs. If we set them up near the fireplace on the far side of the room, it should give you some privacy for your sales pitch."

And get Noah as far from her as possible without banishing him from the room. Still. He'd save his fighting for other battles. "That works for me. Why don't you just tell me who on the staff I need to talk to, and I'll take care of my own supplies. I'm sure you have plenty of work to do without worrying about me."

"Great." Graham clapped Noah on the back. "I'll leave you to it, then. If you think of anything you need, just let Sam know. I'm putting her entirely at your disposal."

Noah saw Sam's eyes widen and her lips part to protest, but Graham had already retreated to his inner sanctum and closed the door behind him. Patiently Noah waited for Sam to turn her wary gaze back to him before he let the satisfaction bloom across his features.

"That," he said, his voice low and purring, "suits me perfectly. I can hardly wait to get started."